TEXAS RECLAIMED

LONE STAR REDEMPTION

BOOK THREE

SHERRY SHINDELAR

The steadfast love of the LORD never ceases;
His mercies never come to an end;
they are new every morning;
great is Your faithfulness.

— LAMENTATIONS 3: 22-23 (ESV)

CHAPTER 1

March 1866
Philadelphia, PA

Ben McKenzie gripped the edges of the oak bureau and stared at himself in the beveled mirror. A bead of sweat glistened on his brow. Perpetual dark circles underscored his eyes.

Piano music drifted up from the parlor he'd vacated minutes before. Dressed in yellow silk like the first flower of spring, Olivia Edmondson would likely be surrounded by admirers as her nimble fingers slid across the keys. But surely, she'd notice his absence all the same. After all, they'd agreed their fathers would announce their engagement this evening.

He shouldn't have allowed himself to be nudged into a proposal. Not yet. He had no business making a promise when he had another promise long overdue.

Ben loosened his royal-blue cravat from its tight bind on his throat. His head throbbed. Stupid of him to think today would be the time to cut back on his medicine. Medicine? That's what the doctor called it, and so did Olivia and his family. He knew better.

His bones seemed to grate against one another like nails on a chalkboard. Twenty-two hours since his last dose. Maybe if he only had a few drops, half a teaspoon full of laudanum, it would be enough to make it through the evening.

His hand shook as he picked up the small bottle from the lace doily.

Every pore in his body stretched forth in anticipation of the sweet taste of the brown liquid on his tongue. No. He flung the bottle to the floor. The glass clunked on the tightly woven carpet and rolled against the desk leg. His breath caught as he waited to see if the stopper would hold or if the liquid would ooze out. When it held, the crest of his tension eased back a notch.

Curse the doctor who'd ever given him the first dose of the tincture of alcohol and opium.

Lying there exhausted beyond endurance in that hospital cot in Wilmington, with his legs knotted with scurvy and curled beneath him and his stomach as useless as a shriveled prune, Ben had been willing to swallow any concoction the nurses offered. He'd been deaf to the hiss of the serpent which slithered its way into his veins.

Ben's fingers curled into a fist atop the bureau. A whole year he'd been home. Regaining his health. Working for his father. Courting Olivia. But falling short of everything he'd vowed to do when he'd hobbled out of the hell on earth that had been Andersonville.

How could he expect to get a grip on his need for laudanum and bring an end to the war in his soul if he didn't show himself a man by keeping his promises?

His chest squeezed as if someone had tightened a vise around it. He strode over to the window and threw up the sash, desperate for fresh air. Beyond the barren maples and winter-dead lawn, the western sky glowed orange above the tree-topped ridges. Maybe freedom lay somewhere out there. He had to get out of the house and away from Philadelphia. He couldn't marry. Not yet. Not until he set things right.

He stared down at the bottle still lying on the carpet. Surely, half a teaspoon wouldn't hurt. Just enough to abate his symptoms until after he went downstairs and set matters straight with Olivia.

With leaden feet, he walked over to the desk, bent down, and picked up the bottle. His palm tingled against the cool glass. He could almost hear the hiss of the serpent eating away at everything he had been. This is how it'd been last time he'd abstained. Except he'd made it for a whole week. Then he'd given in for one sip, followed by another, and another...until the fetter was fully fastened again. *Dear God, no. Don't let it be so.*

He marched back to the window, opened the bottle stopper, and drained the contents onto the bushes below. *Lord, help me to be the man You've called me to be.* He slung the bottle as hard as he could.

~

"I've got to talk to you." Ben pressed his hand to Olivia's arm and guided her away from a circle of ladies clothed in a colorful array of silk, satin, and taffeta.

Olivia's tiered silk skirt swished against the floor as she moved beside him. "I thought you'd gotten lost, my love," she whispered from behind her fan. A web of lace daisies confined her carefully coiffured hair. "I played Chopin, and you missed it."

"I heard every note." He nodded to her mother as they passed.

"You two hurry back, now." Cheeks rosy, Mrs. Myrtle Edmondson beamed at them. Scattered streaks of gray highlighted her curls. A woman willing to feed any stranger at her door, but likely to throw anyone who disappointed her daughter into a social dungeon. "Mr. Edmonson is warming up for his speech."

His sister, Evelyn, walked up to her with a tray of hors d'oeuvres and shot Ben a puzzled frown. Just like Evie to discern his mood.

Across the room, Ben's father glanced up from his high-back leather chair where he sat amongst a cluster of business associates. The war had aged him—gray at his temples, deeper creases at the corners of his eyes, and a paunch above his trouser waist—yet still he poured himself into his newspaper company, from dawn to dusk, determined to leave a legacy to the only son he still claimed and the grandchildren to come. An unlit cigar wiggled beneath his heavy mustache as he tapped his silver pocket watch and shot Ben a knowing look. To him, the engagement was another step toward installing Ben as a full partner in his *Philadelphia Sentinel*.

"Can't this wait until after dinner?" Olivia followed Ben through the French doors. "I was ready to tell Mrs. Palmer about my plans for my wedding dress. Hers last year looked like a hand-me-down."

"It can't wait."

Cool evening air drifted in as he led her onto the white-columned side porch. The sunset was now a rosy pink capping the stunted peaks of the Alleghenies. From the yard, crickets and katydids chirped their melodies, while someone's fiddle rendition of "Lorena" floated out from the parlor above the hum of chatter.

Romantic. Only, that was the opposite of what he was looking for.

Carrying herself with perfect poise, Olivia inhaled and curled her gloved hand around his bicep. "You impatient boy. If you wanted a moment alone with me, all you had to do was ask.

No need to make it sound so serious." She pivoted in front of him. Her lips parted in expectation.

He stuttered to a halt. Four years ago on this very porch, he'd kissed her for the first time. A young officer home on furlough from war, under the spell of spring and the most charming belle he'd ever met. He didn't even know that man anymore. "It's not that." He took a step back. There was no easy way to say it. "I...I need to postpone the engagement."

"You *what*?" She gaped at him. Her face paled. "My father's getting ready to make the announcement."

"I know." A sigh rattled through him. "That's why I had to speak with you." Sweat dampened his linen shirt sleeves. He didn't want to hurt her.

Her hazel eyes flashed at him. She jabbed a hand to her hip. "You spoke to me the other night when you proposed. You asked, and I said yes."

More like, he'd asked after a thousand hints. With her curled up beside him on the horsehair sofa, practically in his lap. "I'm not reneging on the proposal, but I need to delay the official betrothal."

The mournful notes of "Lorena" carried on the breeze.

"Why?" She lifted her chin. "Not ready to give up bachelorhood?" A slippery smile wove its way across her lips. "Well, I can fix that." She slid her hands inside his black wool frock coat and smoothed them over the gray silk of his waistcoat, scattering his heartbeat. "Just like I did the other night."

Thank goodness, he'd cut their sofa time short, or she'd be here telling him he was obligated to marry her. "I have to go to Texas."

Her hands fell away. "You've got to be joking."

He stepped back. Best stay clear of her skirt folds and every other part of her. "No. I've told you many times—"

"Have you had your medicine?" Her brow deepened into a ridge above her slender nose.

She might as well have slapped him.

"What is that supposed to mean?"

"Just that you're sometimes a bit disagreeable when you've been too long between doses." She shrugged her bare shoulders.

If only he could throw that despicable bottle on the floor at her feet and shatter it with his boot. "My medicine has nothing to do with this. I have unfulfilled obligations. I promised Jeb—"

She snorted. Her pearl earrings jiggled. "Not Jeb Scott again. We've been over this. I'm sorry your friend didn't survive the prison camp, and I'm thankful he helped you come back to us alive. But I'm not going to let a dead man hold up my wedding. The war is over. You did everything you could—"

"All I've done is post a few flimsy pieces of paper."

"Two letters. And never a word back from that man's kin. Even after you offered to send a bank draft. It's not your fault if they're dead, illiterate, or too rebellious to communicate with a Yankee."

"Lieutenant Scott saved my life." He stuffed his hands in his trouser pockets. "And I'm going to honor my word to him. I'm going to make sure his mother and sister are taken care of."

"Hire a Pinkerton man, for goodness' sakes. Your father has the money. Send a couple hundred with the man in case he finds the family in great need, and tell him to convey to them it's all they'll get. You don't want them trying to weasel more out of you a year down the road."

He glared at her.

"What?" She arched her eyebrows and tugged her white cotton gloves on tighter. "It's taken a year for you to regain your health. I won't have you throwing it away on some foolhardy trip you can hire someone else to make. Personally, in my humble opinion, you've done more than enough."

Humble? Not hardly. She could be kind, going to visit the soldiers' hospital with baskets as part of her weekly routine.

She could be spontaneous and unpredictable, ready to go for a ride in the country or a row on the Delaware River at a moment's notice, then spend the next day dragging him on a day-long shopping trip to find just the right hat. She was many things, but humble was not one of them. "It's not your call, Olivia. And I'm not an invalid. I'm perfectly capable of fulfilling my commitments."

Her gaze hardened to a glare. "Doesn't sound like it to me. You're talking about postponing our engagement. Our wedding..." She sputtered. "I've waited for you. Three years. Don't you think I had other fine officers home on furlough chomping at the bit to court me?" She thudded her fingers against his chest. "You've got another thought coming, Ben McKenzie, if you think I'm going to allow you to wiggle out of your promise to me. Everyone in that room is expecting the announcement tonight. And you're not going to disappoint them."

That defiant set of her chin drove into him like a needle. His voice hardened. "I'm going to Texas. I'm not taking back my proposal. Just delaying the announcement. Three months. Six months at the most."

Fiery hazel eyes glared into his. "My father makes the announcement tonight, or there is no engagement. Period."

He scrubbed his hand over his jaw.

"And in case you've forgotten what you'd be missing..." She grabbed his lapels and jerked him close, her bosom pressed against his chest. "Let me remind you." She wrapped her hands around the back of his neck and drew his head down to hers.

A heavy floral scent, some fine French perfume he couldn't name, overwhelmed his senses as their lips met in a hot, angry kiss. Desire sparked and entwined with the gnawing need for his medicine. His arms tightened around her as a groan escaped his throat. But love? He could barely remember what that felt like. Maybe the laudanum had dulled his heart, or was it Andersonville that had done the trick?

His silk waistcoat wadded in her fingers, she broke the kiss. "See?" Her eyes glistened with victory. "You're not going anywhere."

He pushed free and swallowed hard. It'd be so easy to stay. Walk in there. Please her family and his. Send another letter or a Pinkerton man. The path of least resistance. There were no guarantees anyone in Texas needed his help. How many weeks of travel was that, anyway? Train, stagecoach, and horseback to reach western Texas. Maybe even hostile Indians.

Olivia grabbed his sleeve. "You ready to come back inside? We'll finish our discussion later after the guests leave. Go on a stroll beneath the full moon." She practically purred.

He touched his finger to his thumb, where a trace of stickiness from the brown bottle lingered.

If he stayed, the liquid serpent would engulf him. "I'm sorry."

CHAPTER 2

MARCH 1866

NEAR WEATHERFORD, PARKER COUNTY, TX

ora Scott snatched the jug from the dark corner of the near-empty smokehouse and threw it out the door as hard as she could. It cracked against the water trough and rolled across the gravel. Not good enough. Fists at her sides, she stomped over, yanked it up, and smashed it against the metal trough. Pottery shards flew.

Four months, and she was still finding traces of the habit which had taken her father's life. Taken him from her long before he drew his last breath.

Her father had started drinking with a vengeance seven years ago when her younger sister, Amy, died of diphtheria. Grief and drink had hollowed out the man she once knew. Then, when her brother Mitchell died raiding the Yankees near Vicksburg in the summer of 1863, her father had crawled farther into the jug and never came out. If only her mother could have outlasted him, the relief and freedom would have probably added twenty years onto her life. If and when Cora married, it would be to a man who was nothing like her father.

Cora stared at the empty prairie that stretched toward the canyons. Grasses that should be filled with cattle. Her mother had loved this land. So had her father once, and her brothers too. She would not abandon it.

A red-tailed hawk circled in the distance.

A tug on her sleeve. She turned.

Not quite as tall as her shoulder, Charlie stared up at her, his light-copper skin belying the fact that her father's gray eyes stared out from his face. "I saddled Sandy."

"Thank you." She handed the boy the small sack of chittlins she'd retrieved from the smokehouse. "You can add these to the pot of beans cooking over the hearth. I'll be back before sunset."

"I should come too." He puffed out his chest.

"Not today. You finish making furrows in the garden so we can get the planting started." She ruffled his smooth, dark hair.

"I want to go with you." He stuffed his hands into the pockets of his patched trousers and trudged along beside her as she headed for the well-chinked log stable. "It's too far for you to go on your own."

She quirked her mouth to the side and smiled down at him. Already acting like the little man. "I'll tell you what. You run and grab Pa's rifle. I'll take it with me, and I promise to be home before dark, but going to see Mr. Coffin is something I've got to do on my own."

Charlie spit on the brown dirt at their feet. "That's what I think of him."

"Me too." Her smile faded. She could don her best dress, smile, and bat her eyes at the man. She'd rather go hungry than stoop to flirting with vermin. But it wasn't hungry they were talking about. It was losing their land. "You'd best fetch the rifle while I fill my canteen from the well. I want to be home in plenty of time to finish fixing supper."

He hurried to the porch while she filled her canteen and turned to her sorrel Quarter Horse, Sandy, tied to the corral gate. The mare had been a gift from Jeb. Was he still among the land of the living? It'd been almost a year since the war had ended. Surely, he'd be home by now if he'd made it through. Home? She scoffed. This had stopped being his home a year before the war. Jeb had no idea Pa was dead. Didn't even know about Charlie.

She loosed the lead rope from the weathered pole. Sandy nickered, and Cora rubbed the mare's neck, her fingers trailing through the blond mane.

If Jeb were here, he'd find a way to keep Mr. Coffin's grubby fingers off their home. Pa probably wasn't sober when he'd put the deed up as surety for his gambling debt, a debt he'd never spoken a word about. She had no idea of it until Mr. Coffin rode out here in his fancy suit and fringed buggy to deliver the news shortly after she and Charlie moved back from town.

Charlie stepped alongside her as she stuck her left foot into the stirrup and heaved herself into the side saddle.

"Here you go." Charlie handed the Enfield rifle up to her. "Is it for the Comanche or Mr. Coffin?"

"I hope it's not for anybody." Seven miles to town, and she wouldn't draw an easy breath until she made it to the outskirts of Weatherford. But she'd not let fear hold her hostage, not after being in town for almost four years, listening to her father say, "Someday we'll move back to the ranch, someday we'll fix the place up, someday this and that…" Well, someday had come a month after he passed.

*B*en smoothed his hand over his sweat-dampened hair and donned his felt slouch hat, with its dented crown. Weatherford at last. Five days by railway from Philadelphia to Cairo, Illinois, and then another five on a steamboat down the Mississippi to New Orleans, followed by a steamer across the Gulf to Galveston, train to Houston, and a stage beyond Dallas to Weatherford. It felt as if he ought to be all the way to California by now, instead of the Texas frontier.

"Good day, Mr. McKenzie. See you around town." Dressed in plaid, the drummer who'd spilled one story after another for the last two days scurried out of the stage with his case of tonics for sale. "Stop by the saloon, and I'll buy you a drink."

Last place Ben needed to go. "Good day, to you, sir." Ben edged down the step and braced himself against the stagecoach door. His stomach twisted worse than a shirt having every last drop wrung out of it by a skilled washerwoman. Twenty-one days and twelve hours without his medicine. If he had any sense, he would have holed up in a hotel in Cairo or New Orleans until the worst had passed. But he had a promise to keep.

The stagecoach driver with his rumpled hat and rawhide vest dumped a trunk at Ben's feet. Flakes of dried mud crumbled beneath the weight. "Where'd you like this carried, Mr. McKenzie? You see that two-story fancy building down the street there with its columns and wrap-around porch? That's the Carson and Lewis House, finest hotel in Weatherford." He chewed on a cigar stub. "But if you're looking for something a little less pricey, there's Mammie Sykes's place at the end of town. Mighty good cookin', and she rents rooms besides."

All he needed was a simple room. Provided the proprietor could keep her nose to herself. "If you could have one of your boys take the trunk to Mammie Sykes's, I'd be much obliged." Ben straightened and dusted off his blue linen sack coat.

The driver waved to a boy at a shoeshine stand in front of Miller's Dry Goods. The boy sped his cloth into action polishing his elderly customer's boot at bullet speed and then hurried over.

A mule-drawn wagon rumbled past them. A fellow on horseback and wearing a wide-brimmed hat and chaps followed.

After listening to the driver, the blond, freckled boy, all of ten or eleven years, lifted one end of the trunk and slid it onto his back. "I'll show you the way, sir."

"Much obliged." Ben squinted in the sunlight. He'd worked on tuning out the incessant throb across his temples, but the piercing pain behind his eyeballs was another matter. The sooner he got himself a cool pitcher of water and a decent bed, the better off he'd be. His money belt pressed against his waist. "Could you tell me where the bank is?" He picked up his pace alongside the young man.

"Don't got one."

A couple of thousand people in the county and no bank? There'd be no easy solution for what to do with his money.

Livestock mooed from a corral down the street past the livery stable. A harness and blacksmith shop stood across the way. A weathered building with the word *Hides* painted on a shingle stretched along the corner. The odor wafted on the breeze.

But the boy turned at the intersection past a clothiers, and…

Ben halted. A druggist. The slender green building called to him. He needed a herbal remedy for his headache, didn't he? But that wasn't all he needed. His hand trembled in anticipation. Would it really be the end of the world if he bought a small bottle of laudanum? What if he only took half a dose? Just enough to slack off the worst of the pain and the severe cramps. A half dose every other day, and then he'd work down to a quarter every third day until the tincture was gone. One last bottle. It'd been insane to quit so abruptly. Who knew if his stomach could even function without it?

"Need something, sir?" The boy gazed up at him.

Yes. No. Ben curled his fingers inward and dug his nails into his palms. "I'm wondering if you have heard of the Scott family. Mr. and Mrs. Harold Scott. I believe they have a ranch—"

"Dead." The boy lowered the trunk to the ground.

The word reverberated through Ben. "Dead? Both the man and wife?" He gripped a hitching post. Had he come too late?

"Yup. But I just saw Miss Scott a little bit ago."

"Miss Cora Scott? Where?"

"Down by the land office, and she was fit to be tied." He wrinkled his nose and pointed at the other end of the main street.

Ben dug in his pocket for a dime. "Take my trunk on to Mammie Sykes's, and I'll give you a nickel more next time I see you."

"Yes, sir." The boy tipped his cap and hunched over to tug the weight onto his back once more.

Ben's chest tightened as he strode past a log cabin with a doctor's shingle and a clapboard attorney-at-law's office. When had Jeb's mother died? Would Ben's coming here last fall have made a difference? According to Jeb, the father had been a difficult man. Jeb's lack of confidence in the man's ability to take care of his family was the reason he'd made Ben promise to look after them.

He reached the town square. A two-story brick courthouse loomed solid amongst the scattering log and frame structures. Two ladies—one dressed in drab brown and the other in mourning purple and black—strode by him with polite nods. They'd probably flee to the other side of the street if they heard his Pennsylvania accent.

He halted at the whitewashed building with the large black

letters that spelled out *Land Locator*. Adjusting his hat, he exhaled and ascended the steps.

A middle-aged couple sat by the window, their clothing and faces careworn. The man's dusty boots beat a steady rhythm against the oak plank floor. The lady fumbled with a small drawstring sack on her lap. A make-shift reticule?

Behind a desk, a young man wearing spectacles and a tweed sack coat looked up from his paperwork. "Can I help you, sir?"

"He can get in line after us." The middle-aged man shifted a chaw in his cheek.

A female voice echoed down the hallway. "—offering you half of my land. That's more than fair."

A male voice replied, the words indiscernible.

"Sir?" The desk clerk peered at Ben over his spectacles.

Ben chewed his lip. "Would that happen to be Miss Scott?"

"I'm afraid so." The clerk quirked his mouth to the side.

Her voice resonated. "I don't care what my father signed. You took advantage of him. You—"

The man's low rumble interrupted her.

A door banged against the wall. "You have about as much sympathy as a tin can."

"You have a week to come up with the funds, Miss Scott."

The door slammed, and hard-soled shoes struck the plank floor like the rat-a-tat-tat of repeated gunfire.

Ben stepped into the hallway.

Cora Scott bounded toward him, wide-brimmed straw hat and strands of silky chestnut hair hanging loose around her slightly tanned face. She bunched a fold of her purple linen skirt in her hands on either side. Sharp blue eyes sliced into him. Her scowl could cook raw meat without a flame.

He jumped aside to avoid a collision. His breath caught in his throat as the door slammed.

Jeb had mentioned a quiet, thoughtful sister who liked to

race across the prairie, climb trees, and laugh. Obviously, a lot had changed since he'd left home.

The middle-aged couple murmured. Down the hall, a red-haired man with whiskered jowls and a silk-covered barrel chest strode out of the office. A smirk contorted his lips. "Carter, send in the next one."

Ben turned and reached for the door handle.

Already half a block away, Cora Scott marched down the mud-caked street, close enough to the middle that a man on horseback had to swerve out of her way. Her loose braid bounced against her back with each step. A fighter, no doubt, like her brother, except Jeb had been soft-spoken and even-tempered.

Ben followed at a distance but hung back beneath the awning of Miller's Dry Goods as Miss Scott mounted a sorrel mare and rode off toward the edge of town. Head held high, shoulders thrown back, and gripping those reins like she was ready to whip somebody with them. But she had started her horse with a gentle click. The animal would not feel the brunt of her anger.

No use trying to introduce himself until she settled down. He scrubbed his hand over his jaw and headed for the livery stable. He'd rent a horse and ask directions. Somehow he'd help her. He'd keep his promise.

CHAPTER 3

The late-afternoon sun beat down on Ben as he neared the gate of the eight-foot-high cedar pickets that encompassed the Scott homestead, a half mile in from their land boundary marker. A double-log cabin sat atop a small rise. The thickest walled stable he'd ever laid eyes on and a few smaller scattered outbuildings populated the rest of the yard. No sign of anyone, not even a horse. He nudged his mount through the open lopsided gate with its bottom corner scraping the ground.

The roof of the log home had seen better days. Weeds grew up alongside the covered porch which stretched the entire length of the cabin. A limestone chimney rose out of each end, and a wide door barred the entryway between the two cabins. Jeb had talked of this place. Mr. Scott and his brother-in-law had built their home to be like a small fort in order to protect against Comanche and Kiowa raiding parties.

Someone had to be home. A trickle of smoke rose out of the chimney on the right, and the heavy shutters were open, welcoming the breeze into the house.

Crunch. Crunch. The sound drifted from beyond the side of the house. He nudged his horse left. Beyond the stables and what appeared to be a smokehouse, with its blackened, windowless sides, Cora Scott stood in a plowed field striking the dirt with a hoe. A wide-brimmed straw hat shielded her face, but it was her, all right, same purple plaid skirt and blouse.

He directed his mare to the hitching post in front of the weathered porch and dismounted. A steady stream of breath leaked through his teeth. Had she received his letters? Was she still waiting for her brother to ride through that gate someday? Ben scrubbed his hand down his face and stepped toward the garden.

Thump. Thump. Miss Scott swung the hoe against the clumps of dirt. Alone and determined, working the land that she appeared to be in danger of losing. She stopped and swiped her forearm across her brow, her gaze landing on him.

Without taking her eyes off him, she unscrewed her canteen and took a drink. Her hoe rested against her shoulder, ready for use, as if he might turn out to be some creature in need of whacking. "There's a water bucket back by the well, if it's a drink for your horse you're after."

Pain crept up his left leg as he walked toward her. Over a year since the prison camps, his strength still lagged like a puny colt's. "I'm looking for Miss Cora Scott."

Her eyes narrowed. "You some Yankee, or one of Mr. Coffin's agents? I saw you staring at me back there at the land office." Her chin lifted. "You might as well head back to your horse. My brother's around here with his rifle. I already had my say with Mr. Coffin." A slight drawl flavored her rebuke. She positioned the hoe between them.

He halted a few feet away.

A murder of crows landed at the far end of the field and

pecked at the loose soil, as greedily as the prison gangs at Andersonville snatched up everything of value in sight.

Words scraped his throat. "I was a friend of Jeb's."

Cornflower-blue eyes locked on to him. Beautiful eyes that tugged at him like an ocean current. "'Was'?"

The crux of his message summarized in one simple word. *Was.* He nodded.

The fight faded from her expression. She wrapped her fingers around the hoe as if it were an anchor. "I've been expecting you."

"You have?"

The brisk breeze lifted her hat brim, and a wisp of loose chestnut hair rippled across the bridge of her slightly freckled nose. "Not you, exactly. Someone like you. Someone with words I don't want to hear."

"You didn't get my letters?"

"Two or three arrived from Pennsylvania. But my pa wasn't about to open any mail from Yankeedom. Threw them right in the fire."

"Then...you still don't know?" His swallow ate its way to his gut. How was he going to make it through the telling?

"No." Her voice dipped to a whisper. "But I figure if it was good news, Jeb would have written or showed up here himself."

Ben's tongue felt like sandpaper. His mouth watered for a drop of laudanum. Anything to brace himself against the pain he was about to deliver. "I reckon maybe we should go sit in the shade of the porch?" *God help her. And me.*

Leading the way, Cora tromped across the field with leaden feet, her shoes sinking into the mixture of clay and questionable loam. How could the girl expect to get anything out of this soil?

Touching her hand to his horse's muzzle, she mounted the porch and plopped down in a cane rocking chair. Her hat slipped down her back, and she tossed it over to the thick oak door that barred the way between the cabins. Sweat dampened a strand or two of hair above her slightly tanned brow. She motioned for him to pull up the other rocker.

Slouch hat in hand, he perched on the edge of the seat with its half-dozen broken reeds.

Back ramrod straight, she clasped her hands in her lap. "Tell me how my brother died. Did you serve with him?"

A bitter taste rose into his mouth. "We were in Andersonville together."

She shuddered. Word of the horror must have traveled all the way to the stretches of the Texas frontier in the year since the war's end.

"We were close friends..." Brothers. Closer than any family member Ben had ever had, digging each other out of a quagmire of misery deep enough to smother any trace of humanity or hope from a man's being.

"Tell me—"

The oak door swung open. Ben stood.

An Indian boy, dressed in settler clothes, stepped out onto the porch, an Enfield rifle in hand. He wasn't pointing it, but he gripped the barrel just above the trigger guard, aiming the barrel above Ben's head. His scowl said he knew a thing or two about shooting, and he wouldn't be above trying it.

She'd talked about a brother with a rifle. But how could this Indian boy be her brother? Jeb had mentioned an older brother, Robert. Where was he?

"Charlie." Miss Scott rose and reached for the weapon. "This is...a friend of Jeb's."

"Not Mr. Coffin's man?" He handed her the rifle, but the set of his mouth said he wasn't quite sure if he should.

"I'm Captain Benjamin McKenzie." He extended his hand.

The boy stared at it. "You a Yankee?"

"Yes. Jeb and I both served in the Northern Army. Cavalry, to be exact." He sat back down, and so did Cora.

She laid the Enfield on the ground at the side of the chair, and Charlie came to stand beside her, placing his hand on her arm. "Where's Jeb?"

"He's…not coming home." She blinked hard and turned her gaze toward the pickets and the prairie beyond. Her voice faltered. "Continue with your story, Captain McKenzie."

Ben swallowed. "Do you want me to speak in front of the boy?"

"He can handle it. Besides, it's only him and me here. Your saying will save me from having to repeat what happened."

Just him and her. The loneliness in that statement thudded like a rock to the bottom of Ben's heart. The boy and her. No one else? And three hundred acres of ranch, according to Jeb. How could she think of tackling such a horrendous challenge all on her own?

"Captain McKenzie?"

He shook himself and leaned forward, elbows on knees. "Jeb was the bravest, truest friend I ever had. I first met him in Belle Isle Prison Camp in Virginia." More of a cold, windswept anthill than a prison. Crowded. Miserable. Never enough to eat. "Jeb and I became messmates. Fended for each other." Ben closed his eyes to the memories and shuddered.

"Jeb was captured at Chickamauga, and from what I heard from his comrades, he stood strong with General Thomas in the face of horrendous firepower. Inspired his fellow soldiers and helped hold the line. He and a few others were captured as part of the rear guard after the battle. Your brother was a man of honor willing to put himself at risk for others."

"That sounds like him." Miss Scott's voice shrank. She pressed her lips together and clutched Charlie's hand. "But you said something about Andersonville."

Ben blew out his cheeks. "We were transferred there. Belle Isle was too crowded. Andersonville, with its open air and available wood, was a welcome reprieve at first..." He rubbed his right hand over his left thumb, back and forth. "Things got a little rough as more prisoners were added. Jeb and I befriended another group of fellows, several from my old regiment. Ten of us in all." An acid taste arose in his mouth. The guards had treated them like dogs.

Miss Scott hunched her shoulders as if bracing for the worst. He would not give it to her.

"I was mighty sick for a while with scurvy, but Jeb made sure I had food through it all. Just as my health began to improve, his began to falter...." His voice broke off. His head rang as if someone had clashed two cymbals by his ear. He needed water...and laudanum. But he would not disturb their grief with his needs. "Jeb asked me to find you. He was concerned about you and your mother. It grieved him to know he might not see you again on this earth."

Cora winced.

Ben planted his palms on his knees. "He wanted me to tell you how much he loved you and missed you. Missed climbing trees with you, sitting around the fireplace with the family, your smile." Ben could see how a man could miss such things about Miss Cora Scott, and not just in a brotherly way either.

Her chest heaved. A sob broke from her throat, but she coughed it back.

Ben's arms twitched, instinct tugging at him, but he gripped his knees instead. Olivia would have been in a heap of hysterics by now if someone were delivering her this news.

Tears brimmed in Cora's bloodshot eyes. "If only I could have told him how much I loved him and missed him."

"He knew."

She swiped her nose. "He and Pa...they had a falling out... that's why he left, went north to learn printing from my uncle, my mother's brother in Illinois. But he'd do anything for the rest of us. He promised...he'd come ba..." She squeezed her eyes and gulped. "How bad was Andersonville?"

"There's only so much that needs to be said, Miss Scott."

A robin landed on a rail. Spring. But winter settled deep on the porch.

The boy stared at him wide-eyed. Did his lip tremble? "What are we going to do, Cora?"

She swiped her nose with a handkerchief. "We're going to finish our visit with Mr. McKenzie. Offer him some of the beans cooking in the kitchen, then send him on his way."

Send him on his way and lose her land to a greedy swindler in a week? That wasn't happening. Not if Ben could help it.

"I can't stay for supper, Miss Scott." The way his stomach felt, he'd be doing good to get on his horse and get out of there with any dignity.

"But you can't leave yet. You...your words are all I've had from my brother since the war started." She strangled the handkerchief in her hold, her sea-blue eyes drawing him from the safety of his shore into the unknown. "I'm sorry. I don't mean to impose."

"No imposition. I traveled all the way to Texas from Pennsylvania to see you...your family."

"You did?" Her eyes startled wide. "My brother must have meant a lot to you."

"I owe him my life."

She sucked in a breath and bit her lip as if the floodgates of emotion threatened to break open.

He stood. "I'll come back tomorrow."

"Please do." She blinked up at him, her face a couple of shades paler than when he'd first arrived.

He tapped his hat to his head. "You can count on it."

And the insidious whisper crept through his mind as he descended the steps. *How can they count on anything from you?*

You'll be lucky to make it out of bed tomorrow if you don't hurry to town before the druggist closes and get yourself a dose of medicine. If you care about helping Miss Scott, you'll do what you have to to bolster yourself up. Just a couple of doses.

He mounted the mare and headed out the gate. He hadn't come to Texas to listen to whispers. *Dear God, help me.*

CHAPTER 4

From the parlor, the mantel clock chimed five. Cora grabbed a rag and opened the oven door on the side of the fireplace. The smell of hot cornbread wafted her direction as she pulled the pan out and set it on the oak work table.

Almost the whole day gone and no sign of Mr. McKenzie. She'd baked the cornbread and brought in a butter pat from the springhouse in anticipation of his visit. A small, inadequate thank you for him traveling all the way from Philadelphia to deliver the news of Jeb's passing. Her swallow stuck in her throat. Jeb...

She smacked the back of her hand against her cheekbone, swiping away an errant tear. Hadn't she done enough of that last night? Crying off and on all evening, then after Charlie had fallen asleep, she'd buried her face in her pillow to release the full brunt of her grief. Such foolishness. She'd suspected the truth for months now, had known it was a possibility for years, but somehow the spoken words made it real.

Earlier today, she and Charlie had finished planting the peppers, beans, and sweet potatoes. She prayed it wasn't futile.

A week from now, this might not be her land. Mr. Coffin had given her that long to pay up or clear out. One day gone. Six left. The number throbbed in her head. She didn't have time to mourn.

She'd honor Jeb by figuring out a way to hold on to the ranch. Mr. Coffin had refused her offer of half the property when the amount owed was worth less than that, but maybe someone else would welcome the opportunity, and somehow...

Who'd have that much money on short notice? And who'd settle for half a ranch?

Even from his grave, her father was still ruining her dreams.

Footsteps charged through the back door and into the kitchen.

"He's here." Charlie huffed and snagged a dried apple from a ring. His straight black hair hung across his forehead. "I'll help him with his horse." He scurried toward the front entrance.

She wiped her hands on her apron and tugged it off. Today she wouldn't ask about all of the horrors. Mr. McKenzie probably had no desire to live through such things again. Instead, she'd ask him to share a good memory of her brother for her to treasure. She smoothed her blue cotton skirt and touched her braid, half tempted to loosen it. Foolishness. What did it matter what she looked like? It wasn't as if she was expecting a gentleman caller.

She strode into the wide hallway with its log walls running down the middle of the house. A breeze filtered in through the half-open back door. Once, this had been their dining room and informal visiting area, but she'd sold the cherry table and chairs, along with the fancy china her mother had brought with them from Nashville. Better to do without such niceties than have no money for seeds and supplies to get them through the spring.

Tucking a stray strand of hair behind her ear, she opened

the front door. Wisps of white clouds lined the western horizon beyond the pickets and rolling hills.

Ben McKenzie stepped onto the porch. In place of yesterday's crumpled, travel-dusted clothes, he sported a black sack coat over a blue waistcoat and a white shirt.

He removed his slouch hat. "Afternoon, Miss Scott."

Dark circles underscored his hazel gaze, and a sallow hue tinted his tanned face. Was he still worn out from his long travels, or was it something deeper? He carried himself with a firmness of chin and posture that evoked the image of a leader, but there was a haggardness about his features that bespoke a man weary of battle.

She tugged her gaze from him and stepped aside. "Afternoon, Captain McKenzie. Won't you please come in? The boy will take good care of your horse."

The edges of his lips lifted as he glanced toward Charlie, leading a mare to the stables. "Big change from yesterday. No rifle."

"Yesterday he thought you were one of Mr. Coffin's associates. Today he knows you were a friend of Jeb's."

"Seems like he wants to take good care of his sister." He blinked in the hall's dim lighting.

"Well on his way to being a little man." She propped the door open with a rock-filled tin can. "I leave the doors open when it's warm. Helps bring in fresh air and light."

"Jeb mentioned how you used to have to lock things up around here after dark due to Indian raids."

"Used to?" If only that were the case. She led him past the parlor and bedrooms to the kitchen. "We pretty much stay inside at night. Even let our chickens roost in the trees. Padlock the shutters and the outside doors too. Do the same for the stables."

"Do or did?" He paused at the entrance to the stone-floor kitchen, his gaze scanning her face.

"Do. There hasn't been a raid in this county for eight months, but I'm not taking chances." She motioned for him to have a seat at the small kitchen table with its two chairs. "The fall of 1860 was a terrible year. Unspeakable. One hundred families abandoned their farms and ranches. Pa was determined to stay. But when the Indians figured out almost all of the men in the county had left for war..." She shuddered and retrieved two cups from the cupboard. "Pa moved us to town right after the harvest in '61. Charlie and I didn't return until three months ago. That's why the place is a bit unkempt."

Mr. McKenzie's brow furrowed as he sat down in the chair with a loose spindle in its back. "Sounds dangerous. Yet you chose to come back instead of staying in town?"

She halted. "This is our home, much better than some little room in a boardinghouse where a body has to tiptoe around the other guests and feel as if they're a charity case."

Mr. McKenzie's eyes lit, as if someone had struck a match to a wick. "Your determination is admirable."

What was that supposed to mean? She pressed her lips together. What was she doing spouting off to a guest, anyway? "I apologize. It's just that you're not the first person to scold me about my choice."

He folded his hands on the table. "I didn't intend to scold, Miss Scott. I was merely concerned."

She set her two best cups, porcelain imprinted with a swirl of painted ferns, on the table. "Charlie and I can take care of ourselves."

He cocked his eyebrows, as if to say he doubted it. "Surely, you have other relatives."

Her nose twitched with the effort to not glare at the man. Instead, she turned to the hearth for the coffeepot. "All of our kin are back in Tennessee and Indiana. Besides, we have a three-hundred acre ranch." Her stupid voice wavered. She glanced at the yellow-print tablecloth and matching curtains.

Her mother had turned this place into a home. She and Cora had spoken of the day Jeb and Michael would return to it. Now no one was coming home, not even her mother. And how had this conversation gone so wrong? "You... you were going to tell me more about Jeb."

"I will." He mopped his forehead with a handkerchief. "But before I do, I have other matters to discuss while the boy is at the stables."

"What kind of matters?" She poured brew into his cup.

"Maybe you'd best sit."

She filled her own cup and eased down across from him. "Is it about Jeb?"

"Your land."

"What about it?" She stiffened. "Were you...listening yesterday to my meeting with Mr. Coffin?"

He nodded and cupped his hands around the steaming cup.

Her shoulders tensed. Her father's shame seemed to bleed into every relationship. "My business with Mr. Coffin isn't any of your concern."

"I gave Jeb my word I'd look after you and see that you were well situated."

"I appreciate the thought, but I don't need looking after." She squirmed up from the table and grabbed the pan of corn-bread. "As I said before, Charlie and I will be all right." She sliced through the soft, warm treat. This man needed to mind his own business. Thank goodness, Charlie wasn't in here. He wouldn't understand her refusal—

Ben McKenzie cleared his throat. "I paid the debt."

The knife clunked against the work table. "You did what?" She pivoted to face him.

A lock of dark-brown hair clung to his damp forehead. "I settled the debt." He slipped a paper from his inner coat pocket.

Her legs wobbled as she took the paper. Mr. Coffin's signa-ture and *paid in full* were scrawled across her father's promissory note. Paid. Coffin no longer had a hold over her. She should drown Ben McKenzie with thank-you's and make him a beefsteak dinner if only she owned a cow, but her chest tightened. She dropped the paper onto the table as if it had scorched her hand. "I can't accept this. We're not able to repay you. It might be years before we—"

"It's a gift. For Jeb. If it wasn't for him, I'd be buried in a shallow grave in Andersonville."

Jeb *was* buried in a shallow grave at Andersonville. "I can't accept such a gift from someone I don't know." A thought pricked her. What if this was some trick? Was it possible he was somehow in league with her enemy? "Why were you in Mr. Coffin's office yesterday?"

"Someone told me I could find you there." His voice tightened. "I'm not after your land, if that's what you think."

She searched his eyes. The sheen of fever, not deceit, seemed to hover there. Was he ill? She touched her collarbone. What was she doing accusing Jeb's friend?

He leaned forward, elbows on the table. "Today was the first time I met Mr. Coffin. A rather unpleasant experience. He was reluctant to let go of his opportunity to nab the property, but he accepted the money in the end." He puffed out the last words as if he were having trouble breathing.

Three hundred dollars. This man had paid three hundred dollars to help her and Charlie. She sank onto her chair. "I'm sorry. I didn't mean to insinuate anything. It's just that we can't pay you back—"

"A gift, I said."

What if this was the Lord's answer to her prayer? Better to sell the land to Jeb's friend than Coffin. "I know what. Monday morning, I'll meet you in town at the courthouse and sign over half of the ranch to you. It'll be yours as an investment."

His shoulders sagged. "I'm not after your land, Miss Scott."

"But you surely can't intend to just hand over three hundred dollars and walk away."

His voice firmed. "I'm not leaving Texas until I know your finances and means of provision are secure."

"But don't you have a life to get back to across the Mississippi?"

"I have a promise to fulfill first."

She stared at him. If she met this dark-haired, hazel-eyed stranger at a barn-raising, she'd more than fancy a dance, but she didn't need anyone feeling sorry for her, no matter how fine-looking he was. "I appreciate your concern. But I can look after Charlie and me. I was doing that long before Pa passed away." Days when her pa couldn't even get off the floor to make it into bed. Months when her wages as a clerk in the mercantile barely paid their room and board.

Ben McKenzie pinched the bridge of his nose and looked at her as if she was some school child who kept writing on her chalkboard that two plus two equals five. "I beg your pardon Miss Scott, but I respectfully disagree. You might have managed while you were in Weatherford—"

"What do you know about how we did in town?"

"I asked a couple of folks."

She crossed her arms. Folks who would have pitied her. Or looked down their noses on Charlie for him being half Comanche, and illegitimate. "You've been busy."

"Jeb wouldn't have expected anything less of me." He scrubbed his hand over his smoothly shaved jaw. "I'm no expert at ranching, but I know you and Charlie...that it'll take more than two people to get this place up and going and keep it running."

She glared at him. Friend or not, who was this man to tell her what she could and couldn't do? She'd spent the entire war listening to *could nots*. "If I need help, I'll hire it when the time comes." As if she could afford to do any such thing. She pushed up from the table and headed to the sink.

Footsteps pattered down the hall. Charlie burst into the kitchen, wobbling beneath the weight of two overloaded saddlebags. "Where should I put these, Captain?" He heaved the leather pouches onto the stone floor.

Cora gaped at him. "'Put these'?" She jabbed her hand to her hip as she pivoted toward Ben McKenzie. "What did you say to Charlie?"

"Mr. McKenzie said I could take the saddle and the rest of the tack off." Charlie looked from one of them to the other. "I figured he might stay a while."

A sigh rattled through her guest. "I wouldn't make any plans without asking you, Miss Scott. I didn't mean for him to bring the bags inside." He dug in his trouser pocket and motioned Charlie over. "But I'm hoping that perhaps I could board in the stables—"

Her jaw dropped.

"Just until I finish helping fix things up. The fence needs patching and the corral, not to mention the roof..." He pressed a nickel into Charlie's eager palm.

"Thank you, Mr. McKenzie." Charlie grinned.

The nerve of the man. She marched over, half tempted to snatch the money from the boy's hand. "You can't just invite yourself..." She bit her lip. He practically owned half the place as of today. But she wasn't going to have some man she hardly knew taking over her life. She wasn't a damsel in distress. "Charlie and I can take care of the fixing up."

Charlie gaped at her.

Ben McKenzie shot her that look again, as if she were an ignorant child. "I don't mean to impose." He swallowed hard. "Staying in town at Mammie Syke's place will suit me fine. I can ride out..."

He lifted his gaze to hers. Troubled eyes, tired, too shiny, feverish. His skin had paled further beneath his shimmering of a tan since his arrival. Sweat glistened on his forehead. "I just need to rest a bit."

Her temper dissipated. "Are you all right?"

He massaged his fingers over his mouth and chin. "Just tired. It was a long trip. And I haven't taken time to rest since I arrived in town."

Hadn't taken the time because he'd been busy rescuing her. She winced. His look was too much like her mother's before they carried her to bed...for the last time. Cora's heart stuttered. "You don't look well." She turned to the sink and grabbed the pitcher and a clean cup. What kind of sister was she? Berating the man her brother had sent in his stead.

⁓

*B*en swallowed the water, savoring its cooling effect as it flowed past his parched lips and down his throat.

Charlie frowned. The untucked left side of his flannel shirt flapped over the top of his patched trousers as he wiggled. "Did you travel on a boat? Maybe you're seasick."

Ben tried to smile at the gray-eyed boy, but his mouth wouldn't cooperate. "Two boats, a train, and a stagecoach." If only the cymbals between his temples would stop clashing. Elbows on the table, he slid his fingers and palms over his face, blocking out the light. Had he answered Miss Scott's question about him not feeling well? "It's nothing I won't get over. I was... feeling poorly before I left Pennsylvania." Feeling poorly ever since he'd set foot in a prison camp. His innards and soul shackled still. "I felt it best to continue my journey and rest up when I got here." He swallowed back acid. If he didn't find him a spot to lie down and soon, he'd likely empty the contents of his stomach all over Miss Scott's floor.

"Come on, Cora. You've got to let him stay." Charlie shifted from one foot to the other. The paper crinkled. "What's this?"

"Never you mind." She confiscated the note. "I want you to fetch Captain McKenzie a mattress from the loft."

Ben massaged his eyes, shutting out the howl for laudanum that crept up his spine and into his skull. "I don't need anything fancy, just a bit of straw to lie on in a stable. I don't want to put you to any trouble."

"We'll fix you up a bed in the room over the stables. Our ranch hands used to sleep there." Her voice had softened from the rumble of thunder to the quiet pitter-patter of a spring rain. "Do you need a doctor? I could ride to town."

"No." The last thing he needed was a doctor. He opened his eyes to blue irises as soothing to his fevered being as the water had been to his throat. "Thank you for offering. Just a place to sleep and a little water would suit me fine. I can pay you for the room and boa—"

"You'll do no such thing." She swatted at his hand. "Now, you sit here until we get the room ready." She bent down to pick up the saddlebags.

"I'll carry those." The chair scraped against the stone as he stood with effort. His head spun.

"I don't mind." She lifted the swollen leather pouches off the floor.

"No." He puffed out his chest. "I'll not have you waiting on me, Miss Scott. Fixing up a room is more than generous. I'll meet you at the stables."

She shot him a frown. "If you insist."

Clomp. Clomp. Charlie's footsteps thudded overhead.

Ben snagged the bags from Miss Scott's hands. His breath caught as his thumb brushed against her callused palm. Was it the sudden weight of the bags combined with his fevered state…or her unexpected touch that almost buckled his knees?

CHAPTER 5

hump, thump, thump. The door rattled, sounding more like gunfire in Ben's head than a knock. "Hold on." His parched tongue stuck to the roof of his mouth. He blinked at the unfamiliar rafters overhead. A loft, not the boardinghouse. Gathering his bearings, he rolled out of the bunk with its straw-stuffed mattress, his ankle bumping against the chamber pot. "Just a minute."

Sunlight filtered in through the boards of the steepled roof and the wide-open window. The brightness assaulted his eyes as he opened the door. His head spun, and he braced himself against the doorjamb. Surely, his body would return to normal sooner or later without the laudanum.

Miss Scott stood there, a covered plate in her hands. Her eyes widened, and the small crease between her eyebrows deepened as her gaze perused him from head to toe.

He glanced down at his untucked shirt. Didn't he have any sense at all? He shoved his shirt into the waist of his trousers and ran a hand over his tousled hair. A chill shivered through him. Fever or the results of his sweat-dampened clothes? "Morning, Miss Scott." Didn't feel like morning.

She pressed her lips together, stood upon tiptoes, and peered over his shoulder into the room.

He frowned. "Can I help you?"

"I came to see how you're feeling and if you're ready for breakfast." The breeze, coming in through the open windows, tugged a few wisps of her chestnut hair loose and dallied them across the bridge of her nose.

The sweet scent of hay heaped on the other side of the loft mixed with the aroma of bacon and fried potatoes. Fancier fare than she could likely afford to be handing out to a guest or anyone else. His health had to improve. He had to turn this place into a real ranch. For her.

She shifted the plate closer.

"Thank you." His stomach rumbled, but would he be able to keep it down if he ate? Whether or not he could make it down the stairs to the well and outhouse was debatable. "Perhaps you could set a little aside for me for later."

"This is all yours." She pushed the plate with its checkered cloth covering farther toward him. "On second thought"—she clutched it back against her apron—"I'll set it on the table inside your room. I've got linens down below. I'll fix the place up while you go to the well and get cleaned up for the morning."

He straightened. "I don't want you to have to look after me. I'd be obliged if you could place the plate on the table, and the linens on the chair, and then don't worry about the rest and go about your day."

She blew out a breath. "Isn't that exactly what I said to you yesterday, Mr. McKenzie, that I didn't need looking after?" She waved a finger his direction. "You'd better expect I'm going to listen as well as you did."

He blinked at her, his cracked lips fighting their way into a slight smile despite the discomfort.

She peeked over his shoulder once more. "The only question is whether you need any help carrying your chamber pot down to the necessary."

His cheeks flamed. "I'd have to be half dead before I need help with my pot, Miss Scott."

She flinched. "Well, you make sure that doesn't happen, then." She flipped a strand of hair from her eyes. "And I've had another thought, too, Mr. McKenzie."

"That you're going to call the sheriff on me if I don't clear out by sundown?" He attempted humor beyond the misery of his head and stomach.

"No." She rolled her eyes. "I apologize for my less-than-welcoming behavior yesterday."

"No apology required." He shifted his weight. He needed to get down the stairs to the well and beyond.

She fidgeted. "Seeing as you're going to be here a while, and since you're a partial owner—"

"I'm not an own—"

"At the very least, whether or not you put your name on the deed, you've got a place to stay until we can start making payments to you." She pressed her lips together. "And that being the case, and since you're here in Jeb's stead, I deem it only proper that I consider you...as a brother."

He gaped at her. A brother? What a change from yesterday. He scrubbed a hand over his jaw. She was welcoming him into her family. She would accept his help. He would have a chance to repay Jeb...as much as he possibly could. Warmth seeped into his chest.

She blushed. "Well, you are here in Jeb's place, and otherwise, it wouldn't be quite proper you staying on the ranch." She rushed through the words as if she might change her mind if she took the time to think better of it.

Cora Scott was beautiful when she blushed. Forget that.

She was just plain beautiful. Not what he should be thinking about, considering he had a girl back in Philadelphia anxiously awaiting his permission to announce their betrothal.

"It's a fine idea." An invitation with boundaries, opening some doors while closing off others. As sick as he was, maybe his brain would actually listen. "And in light of that, you can call me Ben, and I'll call you Cora."

Cora moved aside and frowned as Ben made his way down the loft steps, leaning heavily on the rail. If he got any worse, he might not be able to handle the stairs on his own. She gnawed her lip. He'd get better, wouldn't he? Now that he had a chance to rest? If he had any thought of working today, she'd send him right back upstairs to his room. As if he would listen.

Had she really told him she wanted him to be her brother? Her neck heated. The man probably thought she was tossed about as a wave. Jumping down his throat and practically tarring and feathering him over his generosity one afternoon, and then the next morning, asking to be his sister... But she was only trying to make right what she'd bungled yesterday. If Jeb trusted this man, she could too.

She stepped inside the open door and set Ben's breakfast tray on the wobbly table. The room wasn't anything fancy. Before the war, Jackson and Burke, her father's two hired ranch hands, had lived up here. Now there wasn't much, except for a bunk, a rough-hewn table and chairs, a washstand, and a few hooks for clothes. Ben's bulging saddlebags lay against the wall. An undershirt poked out of the top of one. His watch, made of shiny silver, lay next to the washbasin.

A breath shuddered through her as she pulled back the blanket that covered the bare straw tick. The upper part was damp, and so was the pillow, almost soaked. Sweat. Fever. Plus his coloring, and the smell.

His ailment went far beyond being tired. What if he had cholera? No telling what he could have picked up in his weeks of travel. She hugged herself, pressing her arms against her apron. He'd come all of this way out of friendship with her beloved Jeb, who had thought of her even when his own life was at an end. Ben was as close as she'd ever get to her brother again, this side of heaven.

Swiping her nose, she turned his pillow over. She'd fetch the linens and make his bed up properly. Fix the room up a bit. After what he'd done yesterday, maybe he didn't have money to pay room and board in town. Maybe he didn't have enough money to travel back to Philadelphia. What if his future as well as theirs depended upon making a go of this ranch?

The possibility gripped her as she climbed down the worn stairs. A splinter from the railing poked her index finger. A board creaked beneath her step.

Sandy nickered from her stall, and either Comet or Ben McKenzie's rented mare responded.

Charlie scraped a shovel across the hard-packed dirt in the back of the stables, mucking out Comet's stall. The boy loved Pa's old gelding.

Sandy swung her head, turning her long-lashed dark eyes toward Cora.

"Good morning, girl." Cora meandered over and rubbed her hand over the sorrel's nose.

The shovel ceased, and Charlie's head bobbed over the side of the stall. "I saw Mr. McKenzie. Only, he didn't say much. Just hurried off to the privy."

Cora picked up the sheets from where she'd laid them across the railing. "Mr. McKenzie's not feeling the best. I'm going to tell him we don't need any help today."

"But he's staying?" Charlie skipped over.

"Yes." A smile flittered across her lips. She'd stayed up more than half the night wrestling with the decision, but for the first time since her mama became ill, she awoke with a heart eager for the sunrise. "For a while, I reckon." Just as long as Ben could keep it straight about who was in charge here. She needed help, not a boss. She'd had enough of listening to men like her father and waiting, waiting, waiting.

"Oh boy." Charlie hopped up and down. "Maybe he can take me hunting. I could show him the best spots."

She ruffled the boy's hair. "One step at a time, little man. We need to get him well first, and then we've got some work to do."

"Hunting is work. It puts meat on the table. Maybe we'd bring back an antelope or a buffalo."

The boy needed a man in his life. A man who'd teach him things. Not someone who'd vacillated between ignoring him and treating him like a servant, as Pa had. "A deer would suit me just fine, or even a rabbit. But no asking today. Not until he's better. You hear me?"

He scuffed his shoe. "I hear you. But tonight I'm going to clean my gun."

A mouse scurried out of the way as Charlie hurried back to his shoveling. At the stall door, he turned. "Mr. McKenzie's going to be all right, isn't he?" A frown clouded his features. "I mean, not like ma and pa."

Her chest tightened. "Of course." But what if he wasn't? "But we should pray for him. And after you finish your chores here, bring me the small hen. We'll have chicken tonight, and I'll make Mr. McKenzie some broth."

The Lord had sent Ben McKenzie here, hadn't He? Six days before Coffin would have kicked her and Charlie off the place with nothing more than their two horses and buckboard wagon could carry. God had come to her rescue. Surely, He wouldn't allow Ben to die.

~

*B*en trudged through the mud. Skeleton-like hands grabbed at him. Filthy men dressed in rags crawled toward him. He dodged their grip and ran for the palisade walls.

Andersonville. How did he get back here? He had to get out. The dead line lay ahead. He couldn't breathe. He was choking. They'd shoot him if he crossed it. A barrel-chested Reb jumped in front of him, bayonet aimed at Ben's midsection. Ben shoved him out of the way and lunged.

A piercing pain ripped through his gut, the steel tearing his insides. Still, Ben dove, landing on his side, his hand outstretched toward his prize. His fingers closed around the grime-covered laudanum bottle.

No! His cry echoed through his soul.

Thump. Thump. Thump. Ben jerked awake. His heart pounded in his ears. He rolled to his back. A dream. It'd only been a dream. But he could taste the brown liquid. His mouth watered. An ache akin to homesickness washed over him. No. He clenched his hand. He hadn't survived three-and-a-half weeks of torture to give in now.

God, you've got to help me. I can't do this. God, please—

Thump. "Mr. McKenzie, you all right?" Charlie called through the rickety pine door.

Charlie. Ben swung his legs over the side and sat up. The room spun. He ran a shaky hand over his hair and pushed off the bed. "Coming. Just a minute."

Ben leaned against the doorjamb to steady himself as he opened the door.

Charlie blinked up at him. "Cora sent me to see if you're feeling up to coming to supper."

"Tell her I thank her kindly." The words scraped his

parched throat. "But I won't be able to make it this evening." It'd taken him all day to struggle through breakfast.

"She cooked a chicken for you."

For him. What had happened to the woman ready to shoo him out of her house yesterday for helping her out? "I'm honored, but tell her not to trouble herself on my account." His head throbbed to the point of nausea.

"I got to wring its neck. It was a chubby little Dominique hen, and it tried to waddle…"

Ben couldn't handle another minute on his feet. He drifted back to his bed as the boy finished his story.

He sank onto the straw tick. "I hope you and Cora have a fine meal. Save me a little for later."

"She won't let you get away with not eating." Charlie meandered into the room, pivoting a full three-sixty on his heels as he surveyed the place. "She's worried about you."

Cora Scott worried about him? Almost enough to make him smile. But he'd come here to help, not add another burden on her shoulders. "Tell me, Charlie, how are you set for supplies? For instance, does your sister have enough flour and coffee?" He laid his arm over his forehead, peering beneath it.

Charlie ambled to the saddlebag on the table and fingered the leather flap. "She's always saying how we have to be very careful and only use a little at a time. So our food will last until harvest."

When Ben got better, he'd ride into town and buy them a month's worth of supplies. What if he didn't get better?

Charlie threw back his shoulders. "Now that you've whipped Mr. Coffin, we could go hunting." He turned to Ben and grabbed the stool from beside the washstand. "Kill a big deer for her. Then she wouldn't have to worry." Eyes bright, he carried the stool to the bedside and plopped down on it. "Even better if we could find us a buffalo. Cora doesn't think we can do that, but we could show her."

The edges of Ben's mouth tugged upward. "We'll work on that."

"I could show you the best hunting places. I have Comanche uncles. I don't remember much about them, but I'm sure they showed me how to hunt buffalo. Maybe if I dream about it, I'll remember more..."

Comanche uncles? The boy looked Indian, but with gray eyes. And Cora called him a brother. A half brother by blood? Or merely adoption? Ben settled back on his pillow as the boy talked. The throb in his head lessened. But his tongue felt like gauze. "Charlie." He interrupted during a pause. "Could you fetch me a glass of water?"

"Sure." Charlie hopped up. "You need to get well. So I can show you how to hunt with a bow and arrow. I bet you don't know how to do that." He poured a glass from the pitcher on the washstand.

"I've never tried archery."

"Well, I'm good at it. I know how to shoot a gun, too. Maybe some time, you could show me your carbine. I see it over in the corner." Charlie handed him the glass.

"Sometime. Leave it be for now." Ben rolled up onto an elbow and gulped down a few sips. Too much too fast. Air burned his throat. "I'll tell you what." He lay back down after a couple more swallows. "We can work out a bargain. You do a few chores for me, like fetching water from the well. And I could pay you as I did yesterday for my saddlebags."

Elbows on his knees, Charlie settled his chin on his fists. "Cora says I'm not to take more money from you."

Hmmm. "All right. This is what we'll do. You do a few chores for me, and I'll take you hunting and show you my carbine when the time comes."

"That's a deal." Charlie sat up straight. "And maybe your Colt revolver too?"

"Only if you find me a buffalo." He teased.

"I'll do it. You just watch and see…"

Ben lowered his forearm over his eyes as the boy talked about the adventures they'd have.

A mockingbird trilled through the open window. Ben shuddered. Olivia's pet mockingbird, Delilah, could imitate more than two dozen bird songs. Olivia loved to have Delilah by the piano while she played… A world of silver and crystal, scrolled trim, imported furnishing, and fancy gatherings. A world away from here.

In his haste to pack and come to Texas, he'd forgotten to include a picture of his almost-betrothed. Now as he tried to summon her image in his mind's eye, her facial features and form came readily enough, but his heart was as unmoved as a wooden block. Once it had not been so. During his time at Belle Isle and the early days of Andersonville, he'd pined for Olivia. But his dreams of her had faded as everything within him shriveled up. The man who loved Olivia had not returned from prison. Would he ever?

Charlie's voice ceased. Footsteps clicked against the floorboards. Ben shot up to a sit, sending his head reeling. He closed his eyes a moment before refocusing on Cora standing there, staring at him. Her hair was coiled in a loose braid at the base of her neck.

She frowned. A not-quite-white apron covered her green dress. She'd rolled her undersleeves to her elbows, more forearm than he was used to seeing on any female other than a child or servant. But then, this was the frontier, not Philadelphia. "I came to see what happened to Charlie."

Ben braced himself to stand. "Sorry about that. I should have sent him—"

"Stay put." She touched his shoulder. "I'll fetch you some broth."

Warmth pooled in the spot of their connection. "I don't want to put you to any trouble."

She jutted a hand on her hip. "The only trouble you're putting me to is making me wonder if I need to ride to town and fetch a doctor to make sure you listen and take care of yourself."

He settled back against the wall and gazed up at her. Who was he to say no to Cora looking after him for a few days? He would make it up to her. "I'm at your command, Miss Scott."

She blinked at him, flustered as a bird fluffing her wings. A slight blush colored her cheeks. "If only that were true, I'm sure the ranch would run smoother."

He cocked his eyebrows. "We'll see about that when I'm up and around." His cracked lips hurt with his extended attempt at pleasantries. "But for clarification, the duration of your queenship is only until I'm feeling better."

"I imagined as much, Mr. McKenzie. I'll be surprised if it lasts that long." She turned toward the door. "Come along, Charlie. You don't want to wear our guest out."

"He's no trouble." Ben's eyelids drifted closed. "I don't mind occasional company. But it's Ben, not Mr. McKenzie."

"Ben?" Charlie perked up.

"Mr. McKenzie to you," Cora corrected. "Come fetch your supper."

The notes of the mockingbird scratched against the cymbals in his head. Maybe a shot of whiskey would dull the pain. Or would that stir up a new craving? His thoughts drifted...

Cool fingers touched Ben's forehead. He jerked awake.

"I didn't mean to startle you." Cora's voice smoothed over him. "I brought you some broth." She stepped back, her brow furrowed.

Had it only been a few minutes? He sat up from the wall and drew the quilt around him. Quilt? He'd only had a blanket before, but now the colorful star-patterned quilt lay across his lap. "I'd appreciate a bit of broth. If you could, leave it—"

"I'll do no such thing." She scooted the stool next to the bed and sat, holding a large cup in her hands. A copper kettle rested on the table across the room. "I figured you could drink it from a cup. Do you need me to hold it?"

The din in his head settled as his gaze dropped into hers. "I can manage." He reached out, and she slipped the container of steaming broth into his cold hands.

The delicious aroma wafted toward his nose. He blew the golden surface, sending ripples across to the other side.

"I brought you a slice of bread too." Cora tucked a strand of chestnut hair behind her ear. "Charlie and I ate our dinner, and I put the rest of the chicken in the springhouse. You can have some of the meat tomorrow."

"I'm much obliged." He sipped. "Delicious." Fit for a king. He slowly polished off half the cup, savoring every sip.

Cora leaned forward. "So are you going to tell me what you believe is wrong with you?"

He half choked, coughing the soup back up from his windpipe.

She reached out as if she might pat him on the back. "You all right?"

He nodded and wiped his mouth. Best deflect. "I'm sure there's a number of things wrong with me, Miss Scott. I have more than my share of faults." The corners of his mouth edged upward.

She waved her hand at him. "You know I'm talking about your illness. I'm worried about you." Her voice wobbled, going straight to his heart.

He lowered the cup to his lap. "A stomach ailment. Started at Andersonville." That much was true. The doctor had given him the laudanum for his stomach. What if his digestive system couldn't function any other way? "Traveling must have aggravated it." Not a complete lie. But not the truth either.

She bit her lip. "I could fetch the doctor tomorrow."

"No." His voice came out harsher than he'd intended. "No, thank you. Rest, and broth, and plenty of water should set me on the right course." Provided he could keep it down.

Her brow furrowed. "We'll see." She fidgeted with her hands in her lap. "I'll be praying for your quick recovery."

He needed all the prayers he could get. He curled his fingers around the cup and drew it to his lips once more. "If you need to hire a ranch hand to help out until I'm up and around—"

"We'll wait for you. Charlie and I can manage until then."

Wait on him? He closed his eyes and savored the thought. She'd decided to accept his help.

"Benjamin?"

His full-given name on her lips leached the tension from his shoulders. "Yes?"

"Did Jeb…I've got to ask…did he pass away due to a stomach ailment?"

He sucked in a breath. Was she being kind to him because she was afraid he'd die like her brother? His lungs deflated. "This isn't Andersonville. In that place, with the green corn mixed with husks they fed us, when they fed us at all, and making us sleep in the open"—*unless one dug a hole to crawl into*—"one could pass away from a sore throat and cough. But your brother was strong. He made it almost to the end."

Jeb could have escaped if it hadn't been for him. What would Cora think if she knew the whole story?

She stood up. Was there moisture in her eyes? "Well, just so you know…I've already lost more family than I can count on one hand. So don't you go dying on me, Ben McKenzie. You're all I have left of Jeb."

So that was it.

She reached for his cup. "I'll fill it up once more, and then you can tuck yourself in and get some sleep." The hem of her green plaid skirt swished against the floorboards as she strode over to the copper kettle. "If you need Charlie or me to sit with you tonight, or sleep down below just in case you have need—"

"I'll be fine on my own, Miss Scott."

It made sense that she was doing all of this for Jeb. Better that than just out of obligation for the land. She hardly knew Ben, after all.

So why did it bother him?

CHAPTER 6

ora settled onto the cane-bottom chair a couple of feet from the bunk and opened her leather-covered Bible. As she read about the prophet Samuel traveling to Bethlehem in search of God's newly chosen king, the honks of migrating geese carried in through the window. Last night after supper, she'd moved her reading time with Charlie to the stable loft, figuring company would offer Ben a welcome distraction. This evening, they'd eaten supper there, as well. No use sitting in her kitchen worrying about the man when she could be here doing something.

Charlie sat on the stool, elbows on his knees, eager to hear the account of the boy David once again.

Ben stretched out on the bunk, his forearm over his eyes and her mother's quilt tucked beneath his armpits. She'd finally convinced him it wasn't a crime for him to lie down in her presence. He could play the gentleman after he gained his strength. Four days of rest, yet his coloring had not returned. If anything, the dark circles under his eyes had deepened, and his face appeared thinner.

Charlie wiggled. "Cora, you got to keep reading. What

happened when Samuel looked at all of the brothers, and God said no to each one? Maybe David was out killing a lion."

Ben peeked from beneath his arm. His hazel gaze studied her, sending flutters into her belly that had no business being there. "I want to hear about the lion."

She smiled. "Well, I think he was just out watching the sheep. His father and brothers didn't think he was important enough to bring in from the fields to see the prophet."

Charlie perked up. "David killed a lion and a bear. You told me so."

"Yes, he did to protect his sheep. But that was a different day."

"Protecting sheep is mighty important work." Ben pushed the quilt down to his waist.

He was doing it again. Throwing the covers off and then tugging them back on an hour later. His fever came and went. Yet the man kept his suspenders tight on his shoulders and his shirt tucked despite its array of wrinkles. Trying to maintain a proper appearance because of her?

Charlie tilted his head. "How about buffalo? Did any of them try to hurt the baby sheep?"

"No buffalo in the Promised Land." She turned the page.

"Why not?"

Ben rolled up onto his side and reached for his cup. "Because it's way across the ocean, and buffalo can't swim. Besides, there probably wouldn't be enough grass there for them to eat." He swallowed a long sip. A drop dribbled onto the stubble covering his jaw and glistened in the lamplight. A handsome man, and the four days' worth of beard made him look even finer. If only the life would come back into his cheeks and eyes.

Charlie rubbed his nose. "Have you ever been across the ocean, Ben?"

"Mr. McKenzie," Cora corrected.

"But if he's my brother, can't I call him Ben?"

"I'll leave it up to your sister." Ben eased back down on the bed. "But as for the ocean...I traveled across the Gulf of Mexico in a steamer from New Orleans to Galveston on my way to Texas. And believe me, the way the ship rocked, I felt as though I was in the middle of the ocean."

"Did you see any whales?" Charlie picked up a crumb of cornbread from his empty plate.

"No, but I saw dolphins."

"What's a dolphin?"

"That's a story for another day. We've got to finish listening to your sister read to us about David. I can't wait until we get to the part about Goliath." A cough racked through him.

Cora bit her lip.

Ben winced and returned his forearm to his eyes. Was he in pain? He wouldn't say so if he was. Tomorrow she'd go to town to see the druggist. She couldn't sit around and do nothing. Ben had said no doctor, but surely, there had to be some remedy that would help.

Charlie frowned. "You need more water?"

"I'm fine for now." Ben cleared his throat.

"We'll make sure you have plenty before we go back to the house for the night." Cora smoothed her finger over the Bible's cracked cover. "But Mr. McKenzie's right. I've got to finish our reading. We're at the good part where Samuel asks if there are any more sons, and the Lord reminds him that He looks on the heart of a person."

In the stables below, a horse whinnied. She glanced out the small window. The sunset glowed pink on the horizon. Twilight. In the distance, a faint whisper of a coyote howl trailed on the breeze. What if it was something other than a coyote? A shiver ran up her spine.

Ridiculous. Her family's land hadn't been attacked by Indians in almost five years, had it? But still, she was half tempted to grab hers and Charlie's bedding along with the rifle and bunk down in the stables tonight. Regardless of his being sick, Ben was a man who knew how to fight.

She moved her finger along the page to find her place. How had she ever thought Charlie and she could make it on their own on this ranch without any help? With Ben, they stood a chance. With Ben? Where had that thought come from? She hardly knew the man, yet he'd rescued them from Mr. Coffin. He'd done it for Jeb, and he'd stay here and help them for Jeb's sake.

The rope-tight tension in her shoulders and back that had almost solidified into bone in the years since her mother's death loosened in his presence. It was foolish of her to let anyone matter besides Charlie. Her years on the frontier had taught her that.

Crossing her ankles beneath her skirt, she read through the verses, all the way to where David declared he could defeat the giant who'd defied the armies of the Living God. She paused. The same God who'd enabled David to slay the bear and the lion was with her. If only she could move that knowledge from her head to her heart. She gnawed her lip as she closed the book.

"Thank you." Ben tugged the covers back up to his chest. The murmur of his voice resonated within her.

Her gaze flittered to the shadowed eyes of the man drinking in her every move. Forget what the frontier had taught her. Her heart wasn't listening.

~

*B*en's eyes fluttered open. A sweet, sickly smell filled his nostrils. So familiar... His senses heightened in alert. He rolled away from the wall, blinking in the brilliance of the midafternoon sun that streamed in through the half-open window. He startled.

Cora was back. Dressed in a dark-blue linen dress, she sat on the chair by the bed, her hair loosely drawn back in a black snood. Pretty as an angel.

He pushed up on his elbow. "Charlie said you went to town."

"I did. I just returned a little while ago. I wanted to come see how you're feeling."

The aromatic smell tickled his nose again. His mouth watered. Could one hallucinate odors? He swung his legs over the side of the bunk. Best not do it too fast, or he'd be seeing black spots. "I wish you would have told me you were going. I have some money I wanted to give you for supplies."

"You've done more than enough." Her voice softened. "I wanted to do something for you."

"I'm not here to take charity. I've been staying here and eating your food. I plan on doing my share."

Her hand shifted within the fold of her skirt. A spoon. The fingers of her other hand curled around something—a small bottle.

He stiffened. The hairs on his arms jumped to attention. "What..." He pointed. Words failed him.

"I've been worried about you. Today's the fourth of you being in bed, and you're not looking any better. I know you said no doctor. So I went to the druggist." She held up the container of brown liquid.

Laudanum.

He gripped the edge of the mattress as if it was a cliff edge. His fingers itched to snatch the bottle from her hand and pour the elixir down his throat.

She tipped the bottle toward the waiting spoon. "He said this helps all manner of stomach ailments. I don't have to see every time you head toward the privy or empty a bedpan to know you're ill."

His hand shook as the liquid slithered onto the silver surface. There was no condemnation. It was medicine. She'd brought it to him. He didn't have to ask. All he had to do was open his mouth, and relief would be delivered to his tongue. He'd be able to keep his commitment. Just a few spoonfuls— surely, not more than one bottle. It wouldn't take much to get him on his feet again. He could be a real help to her, instead of being an invalid. He could repair the corral, work on figuring out what happened to her cattle, and turn this place into a successful ranch.

She lifted the spoon toward him. "Here you go."

His lips parted. The clank of shackles rattled through his mind... *Dear Lord, help me.*

No!

The word reverberated through every cell of his being. Without thought, he slammed the spoon from her hand, sending the silver utensil and its poison across the room. Brown liquid splattered on the rough oak floorboards, and the spoon struck the table leg before rattling to a halt. The bottle tumbled from her lap, spilling its contents onto her skirt and the rag rug at the bedside.

She jumped to her feet, upsetting the chair in the process. "What...? Why...?" A deep furrow knotted her brow.

"I'm so sorry. I didn't mean to strike your hand." Laudanum on the floor, on her skirt, the bottle. The odor filled his nostrils and made his skin crawl, calling to him a song as sweet as Odysseus's sirens. "Get it out of sight. Now. Please." He doubled over, elbows on his knees, and drove his fingers through his hair. He had to get it out of his head, out of his nose, before he gave in. "All of it. Every last drop. Even the smell of it."

She stumbled toward the washstand, but she didn't move fast enough.

Head reeling, he snatched the rug and the bottle from the floor and pushed past her to the open window. Shoving the sash up, he threw them out with all of the force he could muster. A sticky residue clung to his fingers. He could lick them. Just a taste... No.

Washcloth in one hand and the pitcher in the other, she gaped at him as if he were a madman.

At the moment, it didn't matter. He grabbed the pitcher from her, held his hand above where the liquid from the spoon had splattered and doused hand and floor with the water as though putting out a fire. "All of it. Every trace of it. Now."

A strand of hair falling against her cheek, Cora lowered herself to her knees and scrubbed. The dark-blue linen folds of her garment mingled with the dirty surface.

Nausea clenched his stomach. He would not, could not be sick right now. He hadn't meant to yell at her or order her about. He snatched the towel from the washstand and roughed the material over his fingers. The smell invaded his head and leached at his self-control as he poured water from the basin onto the spot on the floor by the bed and scoured the oak boards.

Finished, he dropped to his elbows and knees, exhausted. Cora's steps sounded on the stairs, departing. Would she ever be back? Would she ever forgive him or respect him again?

CHAPTER 7

Cora's whole body shook as she stumbled into the kitchen. Ben was like her father. The realization roared through her. That same hungry, haunted look that had contorted her father's face every time he'd tried to stop drinking. Why had she not recognized it in Ben? She slammed her fists against her thighs. She should have seen it. And he'd already started to worm his way into her affections. Coming here in Jeb's stead, paying off the debt, and practically inviting himself to take up residence under their roof.

Her stomach reeled. Brow damp with sweat, she rushed out to the side of the house and emptied the contents of her stomach onto the ground. Swiping her hand across her mouth, she kicked dirt over the spot. She glanced toward the stables. Ben McKenzie would have to go.

She wasn't about to have a man who'd allowed himself to be enslaved to drink, laudanum, or any other concoction living on her property. Somehow, some way...she'd repay him for the loan. But he couldn't stay.

She'd lived too many years with her father. Drinking all evening. Passed out on the floor, too drunk to make it into bed.

His hands shaking when he reached for the bottle. Ben's hand had shaken when she'd brought out the laudanum. That was his poison—not whiskey, not brandy. Laudanum. And she'd waved it right in front of him. She cringed.

It didn't matter that he'd slammed it from her hand. He'd give in sooner or later, just like her father. Why, there'd almost been fear in his eyes. Fear that he'd take the so-called medicine.

That's why he was laid up, too ill to work. He was trying to do without it. Her heart wobbled.

"It doesn't matter." She said the words out loud. How many years had her mother waited and hoped Pa would put the bottle aside for good? And before the bottle, it'd been gambling. There'd been good months, even good years, until her sister, Amy, had died almost eight years ago. No more good years after that. Not even good months. Then, when Mitchell was killed at Sharpsburg, not even good weeks. Her father probably didn't see a sober day after that until his own death. And her poor mother...

Cora would never tie herself to a man like that. She stomped back to the house. And what were all these thoughts about being tied to anyone? Ben was practically a stranger. She hardly knew him. How had she ever come up with the idea of welcoming him into the family as a substitute brother? She marched into the kitchen where the meager supplies she'd bought in town still sat. The small sack of sugar on the table brought her to a halt. A luxury she could ill afford, but somewhere in her foolishness, she'd planned to make Ben a pie.

She shoved the sack into the cupboard and grabbed a bar of soap and a couple more rags from the dry sink. Best get back to the stables, before Ben got desperate enough to start yanking the floorboards up.

Outside at the well, she cranked the handle, drawing the bucket up from the cool dark below.

Charlie jogged over, his hat brim flopping with the beat of

his feet. "I finished three rows of beans. Can I go visit Ben?" Dirt caked around his fingernails. A smear covered his jaw.

"No." She stiffened. "Mr. McKenzie isn't feeling well."

"Talking to me might make him feel better." He hopped on one foot. "He says he likes it when I visit."

Cora let out a huff and heaved the full bucket off the hook and onto the stone wall of the well. A granddaddy long legs scurried out of the way. "Not today. I want you to find some long sticks from the woodpile and whittle them into poles for the beans."

"But, Cora, them beans ain't going to need poles for weeks." He dug his toe into the dirt. "And Ben promised me I—"

"I don't care what he promised you." She pointed toward the furrowed garden. "Do as you're told."

Charlie's whole demeanor drooped.

She clasped his shoulders and lowered her forehead to his. "I'm sorry. It's not your fault. Ben's too sick for visitors."

Slowly, his stiff body relaxed beneath her hold.

"What's wrong with him?" The boy backed up a step when she released him. "He ain't going....to ...?" His lip trembled.

"No, he's not going to die." She swiped a lock of hair from Charlie's forehead.

He pushed her hand away. "You said you were going to get him medicine."

"I did, but it was the wrong kind. I'll go to town again tomorrow and see if the doctor's around. Ask his advice."

"I want to see Ben."

A sigh rattled through her. "Later. You can take him his supper." She waved at him. "If you make good progress on the bean poles."

He shot out a breath that vibrated both lips. "If you say so." He pivoted on his heels, hands in his pockets, casting a furtive glance at the stables. "There might be some poles in one of the stalls."

"No." She pointed to the woodpile and picked up the bucket as Charlie meandered his way to his chores.

A flock of robins dotted the patch of bluebonnets down toward the creek. But Cora's glower held tight as she hurried her steps to the stables.

She jolted to a halt as she crossed the threshold. Ben had come downstairs. He sat on the bench, his blanket wrapped around him and his head against the stall wall. Bits of straw clung to his stockinged feet. She would have guessed he was asleep if it wasn't for his right leg jigging up and down as if he were running a race. Her swallow caught in her throat. He wasn't well… He looked…vulnerable…someone in need of—

A board creaked beneath her foot. His eyes flew open. That same haggard look.

"I'm sorry, Cora." He pushed himself up on unsteady legs.

She pressed her lips together and picked up her pace. Water sloshed from the bucket onto her skirt as she headed for the stairs. "I'm cleaning. Don't come up."

"Thank you." His voice sank. "I'll repay you. I know you probably don't understand—"

"I understand plenty. And I don't want your money." She spit out the words. How dare he come here with this kind of secret and get her and Charlie used to his company, get her to care?

~

Heart weary, Ben sat on his bunk, cupping his soup bowl in his hands. He'd paced for two hours after Cora cleaned his room, every fiber in his being stirred by the close encounter with what his body craved more than food or even water.

Charlie sat a few feet away in Cora's usual spot, the cane-bottom chair. He rolled a canvas ball from one hand to the other. Too quiet. Did he know what had transpired?

"Aren't you going to eat?" The boy tossed the ball and caught it.

Wrapped in a blanket, Ben settled back against the wall and stirred the spoon in his broth. "Did Cora say anything to you about me today?"

Charlie shrugged. "Just that you were sick and didn't feel like visiting."

At least she'd spared him from losing the boy's respect. "Do you suppose she'll come up this evening?" Foolish question. Of course she wouldn't. How would he rest tonight without a glimpse of her smile or lake-blue eyes or without hearing the soothing sound of her voice as she read? Her presence eased the grating of his bones and the gnawing turmoil in his gut.

"Nope." Charlie wiggled his knees toward each other and then away, in and out. "Says she has too much work to do." He knitted his brow. "Did you make her mad?"

Ben exhaled. How in the world should he answer that? "Not mad." She was probably furious. "Just...disappointed, I'd guess." She probably thought he was weak, insane, lower than the bottom dregs of society, a man she didn't want to be near. Thank God, she'd allowed the boy to come up, at least. "We had a disagreement. Grownup stuff."

Charlie shrugged. "Maybe you'd better say sorry."

He gulped. "I did. But sometimes sorry isn't enough."

"You can do extra chores, or give her a gift. Or smile and say something nice."

If only it was that simple, but the way she'd looked at him as she'd come down the stairs with her used rags and bucket, it was as if she'd like nothing better than to rid herself of him along with the dirty water. "I plan to do more chores than you can count when I get to feeling better." Yes, that's what he'd do.

God willing. He'd show her his worth. He'd earn back her respect.

"How many chores is that?" The boy rocked forward.

"I don't know." Ben sipped his lukewarm soup. "I'll let you keep the tally because you're going to help me."

"I am?" He beamed. "How about hunting and fishing?"

"We'll start with the front gate. Then the corral." Ben discarded the spoon and lifted the bowl to his lips. "We'll surprise your sister." No use giving Cora something to say no to, as she had his money this afternoon. When he got better, he'd ride to town himself and buy supplies for them.

"Can we read?" Charlie hopped up and meandered toward the saddlebags.

"Bring them over here. I'll dig out the Dickens book, and you can read me a few pages."

"It'd sound better if you did it. Quicker too." The boy heaved the leather satchels and wobbled over to the bed.

Ben's throat burned from too many weeks of stomach upset. "You need the practice. I need to rest." He set the empty bowl on the bedside table. *Great Expectations* probably wasn't the best story for Charlie to read, but it was the only book, other than *Last of the Mohicans* and his personal Bible, he'd brought with him. "The story's about an orphan, taken care of by his sister, but Pip's sister is nothing like yours. He wasn't blessed with a sister like Cora who loves you dearly and would do anything to protect you."

"Cora's the best sister ever." Charlie took the book. "But I miss Mama Scott. She was a real momma to me." Charlie plopped down in the chair and fingered the embossed leaf design on the book cover.

Ben stretched out on the bunk and tugged the wool blanket up to his shoulders. "I imagine Cora is a lot like her."

"In some ways. Not as quiet, though." He brightened. "I bet Cora would be brave enough to fight a mountain lion."

Ben smiled as he rolled onto his side and wedged his arm under the pillow. "I don't doubt it. How about you read some?"

Charlie opened the cover as if it were a treasure and read the first page, tripping over the words *Pirrip* and *blacksmith*. He looked up. "The boy in the story never saw his mama. But I remember my Comanche mother."

"You do?"

"She was a good mother too. Left me because she had to. Figured my pa's home was the best place for me. Safer. And she was sick. That's what Mama Scott told me."

So that's how he'd come to be part of the family. Mrs. Scott had taken in the child of her husband's unfaithfulness. "I'm sure Mama Scott was right. You're a lucky boy to have had two mamas that loved you."

"Pa didn't." The words dropped like rocks.

Ben frowned. "Maybe he just didn't like to say so."

The boy shrugged and returned to reading about the orphan Pip. After a couple of pages, he looked up. "Ben?"

"Yes?"

"You're going to get well, aren't you? And stay with us?"

Ben swallowed hard as he gazed into the boy's big gray eyes. How should he answer? "I'll get well sooner or later." He'd get better a whole lot sooner if he'd taken that spoonful of medicine today instead of scaring the devil out of Cora and making her think...making her think what?

"But you gotta stay. Cora said you're like a brother to us now." Charlie closed the book and leaned forward, waiting.

From the way Cora looked this afternoon, the brother invitation had been canceled. But Charlie had lost too many people already, been hurt too much.

A slow stream of air leaked from Ben's lungs. He had a life in Philadelphia, his commitment to his father that he'd eventually take over management of the newspaper, and an almost-fiancée chomping at the bit for him to hurry back and make good on his proposal. "I'm not leaving anytime soon. You and I have a heap of work to do. I may even have to go find us some cattle."

"I'll come too. I know how to tie a calf..."

Ben closed his eyes as the boy talked on. The need to make a dangerous promise or break a heart had been averted. For now. The cymbals started in his head again. Every bone in his body ached. He'd been stupid to say no to the medicine. But Cora and Charlie needed a whole man, not one shackled to a bottle.

CHAPTER 8

Cora smoothed her hands over her violet linen skirt, swiping away dust from the ten-mile ride. Two days in town in a row. She'd never get her garden finished at this rate. But Ben needed a doctor despite his insistence otherwise. The sooner he got well, the better.

Charlie was already too attached. What in the world was she going to do? It didn't matter that Ben had been best friends with Jeb. She'd not subject Charlie or herself to the long-term pain of caring about someone who didn't have the fortitude to break free of their self-imposed chains. Her mother would have saved herself decades of pain and heartache if she'd kept walking the first time a young Ambrose Scott had tipped his hat to her.

Swiping at a fly, Cora frowned at the narrow green building down the block that housed the druggist. A lot of good that visit had done her. As she pivoted away and tapped a finger to a loose hairpin, a gig rattled past driven by an elderly man. The lady beside him hid behind her wide-open parasol as if the sun might cause her to melt. Three cowboys wearing chaps, thick boots, and wide-brimmed hats rode past on the other side, exuding clouds of dust. One nodded. She quickly averted her gaze and turned toward the plain gray building with two shingles. *Harrison, Attorney-at-Law*, and *Dr. Tucker*.

She shuddered as she knocked. The last time she'd stepped foot in this building, it was to watch her father draw his last breath.

The housekeeper, Mrs. Ruddy, answered the door. Her rosy cheeks outshone her dull red hair which hung in a loose chignon. "Why, good morning, Miss Scott. What brings you into town? I heard you and the boy moved back out to the ranch."

"Yes, we did." Cora winced. Hopefully, she wouldn't be subjected to a lecture on the foolhardiness of that venture. "I'm wondering if Dr. Tucker returned from San Antonio."

"Afraid not. Do you know what he did?" Mrs. Ruddy beamed and stepped wide for her to enter the small waiting room with its rag rug and spindle-backed chairs.

"I have no idea." But she was about to hear every detail, no doubt. Mrs. Ruddy kept tabs on everyone and wasn't prone to keep too quiet about them either. Unfortunately, she probably hadn't spared any details about Cora's father. The lady's mouth outran her good heart on a regular basis. Cora entered and removed her straw hat with its royal-blue ribbon tied around the band.

Mrs. Ruddy laid a hand across her bosom. "Dr. Tucker up and got himself married. Found some pretty little plantation princess half his age. Her pa's going to set them both up fine somewhere over by the coast. We won't see the likes of Doc Tucker again. Already sent for his medical books."

Cora frowned. "Yesterday, when I was in town, the druggist said the doc was around."

"Mr. Gregory must have been referring to Dr. LeBeau." She winked. "He graciously offered to continue coming here one week a month until the town finds another doctor. Much better-looking than Dr. Tucker and still a bachelor. Of course, you already know that."

"The doctor who attended to my father." Mrs. Ruddy sounded like an advertisement for a mail-order groom. But Dr. Arthur LeBeau did leave an impression.

The man's calm, matter-of-fact bedside manner had been a solace when he sat beside her delivering the news about her father. He'd fallen from his horse in a drunken stupor and was in a deep coma, unlikely to wake up. Dr. LeBeau had taken her hand in his to comfort her. Only, she'd sat there like a stone wall, feeling little but relief. Was it wrong to not feel grief?

"Yes, you poor girl. I'd forgotten Dr. Tucker had already left on his trip by then. If Dr. LeBeau couldn't save your father, no one could."

Her father had been beyond saving for years. "May I see the doctor?"

"Is something ailing you, dear?" Mrs. Ruddy patted her arm. Freckles dotted her cheeks beneath the crinkles which lined her eyes. "Have a seat. You look a little pale. You couldn't be in better hands. "

"It's not me—"

The office door clicked open. "Miss Scott." Dr. LeBeau stepped into the hallway. Over six feet tall, he resembled Ben McKenzie in height, but that was where the similarities ended. He held his long, slender fingers toward her. Instead of briefly clasping her hand, he bent at the waist and brushed his lips across her gloved knuckles.

She squirmed and drew her hand free as soon as it was polite.

A smile played across his thin lips. "To what do I owe this pleasure?" His murky blue eyes studied her. Dark, slicked-back hair, and an even darker mustache and goatee, outlined his light-complexioned face with its angular features.

The man made her feel as if they were at a cotillion. "Perhaps we might speak in your office?" She wouldn't shame Ben by giving Mrs. Ruddy fodder for gossip.

"Certainly." He waved her toward a short-back chair in front of a worn oak desk. He closed the door behind them as she gathered her skirts into the seat.

Sunlight filtered in through sheer green curtains and cast rays onto three books encased by bronze bookends on the far corner of the desk. A lion and man wrestling?

"I figured if I was going to be in Weatherford one week a month, I might as well bring a few of my own furnishings." Dr. LeBeau settled in behind the desk. "It's a scene from the Coliseum in Rome. A gladiator fighting a lion. The question is, 'Who will win?'"

She shook her head. "The lion looks mighty ferocious." Teeth bared and aimed at the bare gladiator's armored forearm.

"I vote for the man." LeBeau steepled his fingers. "He has intellect and strength."

"Doesn't the lion have that too?"

LeBeau cocked his eyebrows. "The man's mind is superior, and I prefer to imagine he discovers a way to overcome the lion's powerful might." His lips curved upward into a smile that left little doubt he conceived himself equal to the challenge of the battle on his desk. "But you didn't travel all the way to town to discuss bookends." He leaned forward. "What can I do for you today, Miss Scott? I've been concerned about your well-being since I heard you moved back to your ranch."

"Charlie and I are fine." She lifted her chin as she gave the standard walled answer. On the way here, she'd practiced half a dozen times how she would present the issue, but she'd prepared the speech for Dr. Tucker, not Dr. LeBeau. She pressed her palms to her skirt folds. "It's my brother Jeb. Well, not really him. A friend of his came to let us know Jeb passed away in Andersonville."

"I'm terribly sorry to hear that, Miss Scott. I offer my condolences. I remember you'd held out hope." He whipped a handkerchief from his coat pocket and offered it.

She shook her head. "I'm all right."

He laid it carefully on the desk more on her side than his and rested his forearms atop a ledger. "I reckon it might be years before all the losses from the war trickle in. But you said Andersonville? Was he a guard?"

She should have left the Andersonville part out of it. "My father and Jeb had a falling out a couple years before the war. Jeb went to live with relatives in Indiana. He enlisted with a regiment there."

"A Yankee?" His eyebrows shot up.

She squirmed in her chair. "Yes, but a beloved brother all the same."

"Of course, Miss Scott. I meant no disrespect." He cleared his throat. "And this other Yankee traveled all the way to Texas instead of sending a letter?"

"My pa threw away the letters without reading them." She fiddled with the lace on her sleeve cuff.

"I see. But I don't understand. If your brother is deceased, why are my services required? Has the grief been too much? I could prescribe—"

"That's not it. Jeb's friend, Mr....Captain McKenzie is ill."

He folded his hands. "What type of illness? Is he able to come see me?"

"Captain McKenzie is a bit stubborn about seeing a doctor. Doesn't even know I'm here. But I'm concerned."

LeBeau fingered his watch fob. "I'd be happy to drive out, Miss Scott. As a matter of fact, I'd be pleased to give you a ride in my buggy, and you could tie your horse up behind."

"Would you? I'd much appreciate it."

"Be happy to." He smiled. "But could you describe his symptoms so I'll have an idea of what to bring with me?"

She blew out a breath. Ben would likely see this as a violation of his privacy, but so be it. The doctor wouldn't have any hope of helping if he wasn't aware of the root cause of the symptoms. "He's been sick in bed for the last five days. A stomach ailment, but more. Feverish, headache. I...I offered him some laudanum."

"That often relieves digestive ailments. Did it not alleviate the symptoms?"

Her mouth felt like sandpaper. "It turned out to be the problem."

"Excuse me?"

"I could tell from his adverse reaction at the very sight of the medicine that the laudanum was the problem. That he needed it...too much, and hadn't had it for a while." Just like her father.

"I see." Dr. LeBeau exhaled and settled back in his chair, smoothing his fingers down his mustache and bearded chin. "That happens to some folks. They take it as medicine, and before they know it, they're dependent upon it. The physical ailment for which they took the medicine in the beginning goes away, yet their need for the relief doesn't. I don't know if I can do anything for the mental ailment, but I can examine the man and prescribe something for his stomach and his headache. It'll be up to him to work through the rest."

"I'd be much obliged if there's anything you could do to help."

"I'll do all I can." He rose and walked around the desk.

She stood.

Chin firm, he held out his hand.

She glanced at his for a moment before responding and offering her own.

He gently encased her hand in both of his. "I'm sorry you've had to deal with so much, Miss Scott. The loss of family, and now this man showing up at your house."

She swallowed hard. "I owe him a great debt. I'm sure he

traveled here at significant personal expense and effort." Not to mention saving her land by emptying his purse. And here she was betraying him. Not betraying...helping. If anyone could do something to alleviate Ben's illness, Dr. LeBeau could. "It's just that I can't have someone..." She slipped her hand from Dr. LeBeau's skilled fingers.

"I'm sure he has good intentions, Miss Scott." The murky blue pools held onto her gaze. "But such men when without their medicine can be like caged lions, and with their medicine? The opium eventually dulls their minds and their souls."

Like her father. Why had Jeb sent Ben McKenzie to her?

CHAPTER 9

A buggy's *clickety-clack* rumbled through the open window. Ben rolled out of bed and wrapped a red wool blanket around his shoulders to ward off the cool breeze as he crossed the room. Cora had left on horseback, not in a buggy. He'd waited all afternoon for her return. The only clue he'd been able to get from Charlie was that Cora had ordered him to keep quiet about where she'd gone.

The cymbals in his head had softened their tone since the incident with the spoon and the laudanum yesterday, and the ache in his bones had slackened. Perhaps the burst of energy and anger had jarred his constitution onto a new path.

Ben ran a hand over his hair and shoved the thin curtain aside. A tall gentleman in a frock coat and top hat climbed out of the gig and offered his hand to Cora. Did she blush as she accepted his assistance? The man's fingers lingered on hers a moment or two after her feet had safely reached the ground. Ben's jaw tightened.

Cora glanced up toward his window, her brow furrowing. The man turned. A goatee and slim mustache defined his face, along with his narrow nose. His skin looked as if it'd escaped the erosion of sun and wind. He'd probably lived a pampered life, one of those plantation owners who'd avoided serving in the war due to their large number of slaves.

The man lifted his gaze to Ben's. Ben had never been close enough to clearly see the eyes of an opponent across a battlefield before the shooting started, but it felt like he just had. He drummed his fingers on the sill.

At least Cora hadn't fetched the sheriff to run him off her land. But who was this? A beau? It'd never occurred to him she might have one, but if she did, why hadn't the fellow been out here saving her from financial doom? Not that it was any of Ben's concern. He had his own lady waiting for him in Philadelphia. A lady who'd welcome him. All he had to do was heal the minor rift created by his delay in making their betrothal official.

The man retrieved a black satchel from the buggy floor and stepped toward the stables. A doctor?

Withdrawing from view, Ben threw off the blanket and tugged his suspenders over his shoulders. He smoothed his hand down his wrinkled shirt and donned his sack coat. His stomach cramped, almost doubling him over. But he gritted his teeth and straightened as steps sounded on the stairs. Pitcher in hand, he swigged down a couple of gulps of water. He opened the door before the second knock.

Mr. Dandy stood there, matter-of-fact, a black leather bag in his hand. Definitely a doctor. Not a beau. But still a man who didn't know when to let go of a lady's hand.

The man looked him over head to toe. "Mr. McKenzie, I presume?"

"Captain McKenzie." Ben leaned his shoulder against the jamb.

"Dr. Arthur LeBeau. Miss Scott asked me to stop by and see you."

Stop by? More like ride miles out of town to see him. A couple of hours in a buggy with Cora. "I appreciate her concern. But I don't need a doctor."

"She's worried about you." LeBeau scoured him with a gaze. "And a quick glance at the pallor of your skin, your sunken cheeks, and the dark circles under your eyes leads me to agree with her assessment of your health."

Ben glowered at the man.

LeBeau lifted his chin toward the house. "Miss Scott rode all the way into Weatherford to ask me to examine you. She told me about your problem."

The last word stung. He crossed his arms. "Exactly what did she say my problem was?"

LeBeau blew out a breath as if he were dealing with an obstinate child. "She warned me you aren't partial to doctors. It's your choice. But out of respect for Miss Scott, I ask that you at least allow me to take a look at you. Or would you prefer I leave and have her ride in again when you're flat on your back and can't get out of bed?"

If only he could kick the door shut in this pompous dandy's face. It'd been a doctor who had enslaved him to the drug to begin with. Instead, Ben stepped back and walked over to the chair. "Out of courtesy to Miss Scott." He sat, sorry he hadn't taken the time to make the rumpled bed. "My problem is my stomach. I've had it ever since my stay in Andersonville."

A shadow of a smirk played at the corners of LeBeau's lips.

Ben ground his teeth. Cora had told him about the laudanum. How dare she?

LeBeau set his bag on the bed, all trace of the smirk gone. "Open your shirt."

He'd rather eat dirt, but he complied. He'd give this man no further fodder for his amusement.

LeBeau drew a stethoscope from his bag and pressed the hard metal tube to Ben's sternum. The doctor moved it over a couple of inches. "Breathe in. Hold it. Breathe out." He repeated the process several times front and back. Then the man poked and prodded with his fingers along Ben's neck and under his jaws, followed by peering into his mouth and eyes. Finally, LeBeau ordered him to lie down. More prodding around his stomach and abdomen.

Ben stared at the ceiling. A bitter taste arose in the back of his mouth.

"I'll give you something for your stomach." The doctor drew back.

Ben swung his legs off the bed, pulled his shirt down, and tugged his suspenders over his shoulders. "The druggist already tried that."

"The druggist didn't know you had the habit."

"What habit is that?" Ben stood, hands clenched.

LeBeau rolled his eyes. "I recognize opium withdrawal when I see it."

"I bet you never spent a day in a prison camp."

"It doesn't take a prison camp to get hooked on laudanum. Fine ladies in the wealthiest plantations in Texas and Louisiana manage it without ever entering the army." LeBeau pulled a bottle from his bag. "I served as a regimental doctor in the Fifth Texas Infantry, part of Hood's Brigade. I put our men back together the best I could after Northern factory boys tore them up."

"I never spent a day in a factory in my life."

LeBeau's lips twitched as if he would respond. Instead, he held up the bottle. "Quinine."

"I don't have malaria."

"Recent practice has shown that it can assist with inflammation and ailments of the intestines, as well." He picked up another bottle and shook it. "Or you could try an antimony pill. Metallic. Guaranteed to purge."

Ben reached for the quinine, ready for this conversation to be finished. His joints throbbed and so did his head. "How much do I owe you?"

"I'm doing this as a favor for Miss Scott."

"Don't do her any favors on my account."

"Pay me when you've recovered enough to head back to Yankeedom."

Ben pressed his lips together. He wasn't about to spell out his intentions to this interloper. "Will do."

LeBeau snapped his bag shut. "I'll have to return to Dallas in a couple of days. I'm only in Weatherford one week a month." He pivoted and scanned Ben with a measuring gaze. "Should I leave a bottle of laudanum with Miss Scott in case you have need?"

If he had need? He had a roaring need as ferocious as a half-starved lion. "Don't leave anything like that on this property."

LeBeau shrugged. "Admirable. I wanted to make the offer. Many men would like to be free of the habit, but in the long run, most find themselves so deeply entrenched, they relinquish the attempt and content themselves with keeping their doses to a minimum."

The man had no clue to the ravages of the demon medicine if he believed there could ever be contentment. "I'm not one of those men, Dr. LeBeau." Ben leaned heavily against the bunk post. If he didn't sit soon, his legs were going to collapse. "Thank you for the quinine. I assume you know how to find your way back to your horse."

LeBeau shook his head and smothered a quick quirk of a smile as his eyes crinkled. Amused. "Have it your way. I wish you the best of luck. If you have further need of me, have Miss Scott send a message."

How amused would he be if Ben shoved a fist in his face?

"I'll have no further need." He'd let his stomach turn inside out before he called for this man.

He would show Dr. Arthur LeBeau and Miss Cora Scott that they didn't know anything about him.

~

An orange glow lit the eastern horizon above the tree line as Cora lugged the full bucket from the well. She'd left the chickens and the pig to Charlie this morning. Sooner or later, she'd have to speak with Ben. For a whole week, she'd allowed Charlie to be the go-between, carrying Ben's meals up to him and visiting. And she'd sat alone in the kitchen picking over her food, miserable and missing Jeb while shutting the door on her only living connection to him.

How had Jeb come to be best friends with a man who was like Pa? Jeb had tolerated Pa's weaknesses about as well as he would swallowing saltwater. Would Jeb have come back a different person if he'd lived to return home from war?

A few times, she'd glimpsed Ben on the way to or from the well or outhouse. At the height of his illness, he'd hobbled or dragged along so much that she'd worried the day would come when he couldn't get down the stairs, but he'd been walking straighter, surer, the last couple of days. But how much strength did a man need before he was ready to get on a stagecoach to begin a two- or three-week journey?

A chickadee fluttered to a landing on the corral gate and lifted its beak for a staccato note. Thrilled to greet the morning or lonesome for its fellow feathered companion?

Water sloshed on Cora's hem as she set the bucket down by the stable door and inserted a key into the padlock. The main door was padlocked on the outside, and the side door on the inside—a precaution started by her father and uncle years ago and followed by many of the outlying neighbors in order to protect their horses from Indian raids. Who knew if it was still necessary? But she wasn't taking any chances.

The lock clicked. She stuffed the key back into her pocket and reached for the latch—

The door swung open. Ben.

Her knees wobbled. He wore a clean shirt and trousers. Though still a tad on the pale side, his face had lost its yellow pallor. For the first time since he'd sat at her table and told her he'd rescued her from Mr. Coffin, his dark-brown hair was combed, and his beard was neatly trimmed to a light covering.

"Y-you're up?" Why did she stutter?

"A man can't stay in bed forever." His lips edged upward into a not-so-warm smile.

He was probably still displeased she'd sent a doctor to examine him. "You're feeling better?"

"Yes." He grabbed the bucket handle before she could. "Allow me. I've already fed the horses and given them the left-over water from the night." A whisper of a grunt rumbled in his throat as he lifted.

The man was still recovering his strength. "Charlie and I can take care of the horses. I don't want to put you to any trouble."

"A good cavalryman cares for his horse before himself." He carried the bucket to his rented bay mare, who munched on the contents of a feed sack near the grooming area. "Charlie does a great job, but I figure it's time I pitched in."

His shirt hung looser on him than it had thirteen days ago when he'd ridden into the ranch. But he was still a man who'd hook her gaze across a room and hold it.

The horse nickered and dipped its mouth to the cool drink fresh from the well.

Cora fumbled with her hands. "I'm thankful your health has improved, Mr. McKenzie."

"The name is Ben." He shot her a glare and grabbed an

empty bucket. Sweat beaded on his forehead as he poured half the water into the second container. "When I'm up to it, I'm going to ride the bay into town and return her to the livery stable. I didn't intend to rent her so long."

"I hadn't thought of the expense. Charlie and I could ride in tomorrow and do it for you. Then, when you're well enough to leave, I can give you a ride in the wagon to the stagecoach."

"What do you mean, 'leave'?" His voice turned sharp as he set the second bucket in front of Charlie's horse and pivoted toward her.

"When you're ready to head back to Philadelphia. I figure it might be another couple of weeks. But when the time comes, I'll give you a rid—"

"I have no intention of leaving Miss Scott until I've helped securely establish this ranch." He planted his feet wide and folded his arms. "That's a matter of months. Maybe even through winter."

She gaped at him. "That's out of the question. I've decided to go with my original idea of how to repay you. I'll advertise the land and sell up to half the ranch. I'll send you the money. I give my word on my brother's grave, I'll repay you every penny."

He snorted. "I'm not going anywhere. I made a commitment to Jeb, and I plan to keep it."

"You've kept it." Her voice wavered. She could not have this man hanging around for months weaving himself into their lives. What if he became like some grafted branch it'd tear the tree apart to remove? "You saved us from Mr. Coffin. And I am eternally grateful."

"Are you, now?" Eyes flashing, he stepped toward her. "By my recollection, eternity ended about eight days ago, when you offered me the medicine, and my sickness momentarily got the better of me."

Sickness? Not exactly her word for it. "You have been very kind to us."

"But that doesn't matter, does it?"

"I don't want to offend you, Mr. McKenzie."

"You already have. By avoiding me every day since then. You can't even look me in the eye."

She glared into those hazel globes now and bit back a sluice worth of words that threatened to burst forth. "I'll pay you back for the land."

"I don't want to be paid back."

"I'll find a buyer. I'm thinking that Dr. Arthur LeBeau might be interested—"

"I'm sure he's interested." His lip curled.

"What is that supposed to mean?"

"Nothing." He laid his forearm across the bay's back. "Has the good doctor expressed interest in the land?"

"Not specifically. But he has means, and he already has some land in the northwestern part of the county. I believe he'd—"

"I've changed my mind." He smacked his hands together. "You offered to sign over half of the land to me, and I accept."

"That was before, and you said no."

"Before what?"

She pressed her lips together. The man was begging her to come out and say it. "I offered, and you said no. I've determined to find a different solution."

"I thought you were a woman of your word, Miss Scott. I mean, that's what your brother told me."

Jeb or Charlie? "I am. I made the offer, and you declined it."

"I was a sick man. I didn't know what I was saying. If there's any eternity in your gratitude, you'll do me the courtesy of extending your offer."

She crossed her arms. She couldn't have this man living on her land or anywhere near.

He closed the distance between them. "You owe it to Jeb."

"Owe what to him?"

"To give me another chance. To prove to you that the man who needed...the medicine so badly that he had to knock the spoon from your hand to stop himself from taking it...that he isn't who I truly am." The muscles in his throat strained, the cords rigid along either side of his neck. His gaze bore into her, asking, demanding...

How could she with any decency say no? And goodness knows she couldn't handle the ranch on her own. But maybe it'd be better to give up on her dream and move back to town than allow him to become—

The door creaked.

She pivoted toward the sound.

Charlie stood there, hands in his pockets, face glum. A cowlick stood up on the crown of his head.

Cora pressed a hand to her chest. "How long have you been standing there?"

A chicken clucked behind him.

Charlie shrugged. "What medicine? Why did Ben knock a spoon away from you?"

Ben flinched. "That's a discussion for grownups."

"You can't listen in on other people's conversations, Charlie." Cora swatted at a gnat.

"Why don't you like Ben?"

How much had the boy overheard? Cora's tongue stuck to the roof of her mouth. "It's not that I don't like Ben. It's just that he has a life and responsibilities back in Pennsylvania—"

"You can't make him go. We need him. He said sorry." His brow furrowed.

Her stomach knotted. "You don't understand, Charlie."

"If you make him leave..." He threw back his shoulders. "I'll go to."

What? Where had that come from? Her hands dropped to her sides.

Ben stepped beside her. "Young man, I don't want to ever

hear you talk about running off. You hear me? Your sister has her reasons for being displeased with me."

The boy dug his toe in the dirt. "Yes, sir."

Ben rubbed his neck. "Now, go do your chores and stay out of your sister's way until breakfast."

He lifted his chin. "What was wrong with the medicine?"

"Chores. Enough questions for now." Ben waved him toward the door.

Cora sniffled. Charlie's mutiny stung like a hornet. In less than two weeks, Ben already had as much sway with the boy as she did.

"Cora..." Ben spoke beside her.

"I have work to do." She wasn't about to stand around and let this man witness her hurt. She marched out the door. Charlie was her brother, not Ben's. She could order Ben off her land right now, and lock Charlie in his room for the next week. But that wouldn't fix anything.

The chickens clucked as she stomped past. Too bad it wasn't time to wring one of their necks.

If only Ben was the kind of man she'd want Charlie to tag along after. The kind of man she could care about without her stomach churning as if she were being tossed about at sea.

Her father had been nice-looking in his youth, or so her mother had said. A persistent charmer, who'd pursued her mother as if she were the light of his world. He'd burrowed his vices deep.

Her family had left Nashville and moved to Texas for a new start due to his gambling. He'd disgraced the family name by cheating in a horse race. At that point, he drank and over-imbibed on occasion, but eventually, alcohol took over, and he crawled deeper and deeper into the bottle. He'd never struck her mother, but seeing the man she loved wallowing in a stupor had broken her heart.

Cora would rather cut off her right hand than entangle herself with such a man.

Across the yard and down the hill, the palisade gate creaked. Ben's words echoed in her head...*give me another chance.* And the way his eyes had...pleaded. The bottom dropped out of her stomach. How could she say no?

How could she possibly say yes?

CHAPTER 10

*B*en scuffed his boot against the straw-covered dirt as the door flapped shut behind Cora. How had he gotten into such an argument? Demanding she sell half her land to him. Forcing his presence upon her. Refusing to leave. He was here to help, not set up an enemy camp.

He drove his fingers through his hair. Maybe he could have held his tongue a little more if Cora hadn't suggested she could sell the land to LeBeau. Did she fancy the fellow? How well did she know this arrogant slacker, anyway?

And what was it to him? The medicine must have completely dulled his head for him to beg her to allow him to stay. If he had any brains left, he'd rest up for a few more days and ride out of here. He'd done his duty.

The bay lifted her head and studied him with dark oval eyes and long lashes.

Puffing out his cheeks, Ben grabbed a pitchfork and began mucking out the mare's stall, digging the long prongs into the soiled straw and tossing it over his shoulder.

Cora didn't have a right to condemn him. He'd abstained from his medicine for over a month now, the longest he'd ever gone. And it'd cost him. Torture every bit as ravaging as the hunger pains at Andersonville.

Maybe that doctor back in South Carolina knew what he was talking about. Knew Ben's stomach had been ruined and couldn't function without the medicine. Ben slapped his hand against the wall. Dust flew. Two harnesses clinked together.

In the back stall, Cora's horse whinnied. He'd forgotten to give the sorrel water.

He picked up the bucket and glanced out the window at the empty corral. A sigh rattled through him. It didn't matter what Cora thought of him. He'd blown Jeb's opportunity to escape from Andersonville, ruined his friend's best chance of returning home. It was his fault Cora didn't have her brother here. She needed help to survive on this ranch, and he wasn't about to abandon his commitment to some weaseling doctor to pick up the slack.

An hour later, he walked onto Cora's back porch. A weathered board creaked beneath his weight. A warm south wind rippled the back of his sack coat and hair.

Hat in hand, he knocked.

The latch rattled, and she stepped into the entrance, nose red and eyes puffy.

He winced. He'd never intended to make her cry. His prepared speech fell away.

She folded her arms. "If you've come for breakfast, I was about to send Charlie to the stables with your plate."

A strand of chestnut hair slipped onto her forehead from the loose braid dangling over her shoulder. His finger twitched in response.

The scent of bacon and eggs crept through the doorway. His stomach rumbled.

"I came to apologize. I said some things I didn't mean back there." He cleared his throat. "I have no intention of forcing you to sell your land to me. The payment to Coffin was a gift, on behalf of Jeb."

Her gaze drifted over him. "So if I stop trying to pay you back, will you go home when you get to feeling all the way better?"

He glanced down at his boots. "I'll stay in town if I need to. Rent a room again from Mamie Sykes. Ride out in the mornings. But I'm staying in the area until we get your ranch fixed up and get you some cattle." Then what?

She rubbed her hands over her arms. "It'd be a waste of time and money for you to stay in town."

Exactly what he was thinking. He glanced into her puffy eyes. "But I'd do it if it would help alleviate some of your concerns about me."

A trace of a smothered squeal squeaked through her teeth. "I know you think I'm a terrible person." She swung her arms wide, almost clipping him with her fingers. "But I'm not. It's... it's my father."

"Your father?" Ben jerked to full attention.

"Never mind." She sniffled.

"What does my medicine and helping you with the ranch have to do with your father?"

Her face reddened. "It's not medicine." She practically spat out the words.

He reared back. "What is it, then? The doctor in South Caroline prescribed it for me in the hospital when I was in such bad shape I couldn't even get out of bed. They didn't know if I was going to live or die. The druggist gave it to you. And your Dr. LeBeau was eager to offer me more." Why the devil did his voice shake?

"I didn't know the previous doctor prescribed it. I only know the way you looked at it... The way you reacted to the sight of it... It's more than medicine to you."

Heat rose up his neck and flooded his cheeks. "What does your father have to do with me or my medicine?"

"I'd rather not say."

"I'd rather you did." He flexed his hands at his sides. A muscle in his jaw twitched.

She lifted her gaze to his. "My father's need for his whiskey took over his life. Just a different type of bottle."

He stumbled back a step. She might as well have slapped him. It was as if she'd bored a hole right through him.

"I'm sorry." She mumbled. "It's none of my business."

"You're right about that." His words cut sharp as he donned his hat and stomped down the steps.

He was nothing like her father, the man who'd cheated on his wife, the man who hadn't shown Charlie love, the man who'd left his children with a skeleton of a ranch and no means to maintain it. Jeb had sent him here for a reason because Jeb hadn't trusted their father to take care of the family. Ben was going to show Cora a thing or two. He muttered under his breath, "In case your memory fails you, Miss Scott, I didn't grab the bottle and drink it. I threw it across the room."

His hands clenched as he marched across the yard to the stables. He'd skip breakfast. He had a palisade gate to repair.

∾

Cora swiped her arm over her forehead as she stirred the beans around a ham hock. At the end of the crane, rice simmered in a kettle. The wood beneath crackled as muted flames licked the bark. She'd warned Ben to be home before dark. Hopefully, the man would listen. Ben hadn't lived on the frontier long enough to have the dangers ingrained in his brain, as they had been in hers, leaking all the way to her heart.

In the ten days since the confrontation with Ben, he'd fixed the palisade gate, porch, and corral, working himself to exhaustion. Yet every morning, he'd be up with the rooster's crow ready to help with the animals and work on the outbuildings and structures. He only paused when she sent Charlie to bring him his noon meal. The boy ate with her, but as soon as he finished, he rushed out the door to work at Ben's side. For his part, Ben had managed to speak less than a couple dozen words to her, measuring them out in spats of two or three as if they were coins to be hoarded.

A rumble. She stood and listened. A wagon. They were back. She set the spoon down and hurried into the hall and out the front door.

Charlie hopped down from the wagon, grinning from ear to ear. A black-and-white collie puppy squirmed in his arms. "Cora, look what Ben bought me. Ain't he cute? His name is Jack."

Was there no end to the decisions this man made without bothering to ask her? First, the trip to town and now this.

The corner of Ben's mouth twitched upward. "I figured he'd be a good yard dog when he's grown. Warn us...about intruders and help herd the cattle."

Us. The word unleased a wave of qualms through her midsection.

Charlie skipped toward her. "He'll be tough like a bear when he grows up." He shoved the bundle of fur and wiggles into her arms before she could open her mouth to protest.

Two dark eyes gazed up at her from a black mask. One ear dipped downward, and a pink tongue lolled to the side as the puppy grinned at her. How could she say no?

Charlie patted Jack's forehead. "Can he sleep in my room? I've got an old blanket I could put on the floor."

"You don't want to make him too comfy." Black hat tipped back on his head, Ben lifted a crate from the rear of the wagon. "He's got to be tough to do his duty."

"I'm sure a little comfort and companionship won't hurt him." Cora gently handed the puppy back to Charlie.

Ben snorted. "That's been my thoughts on the matter all along." He stepped past her and stomped his boots on the reed rug before he entered the house.

All along? She didn't need a lightning bolt to strike her to know his comment had nothing to do with the puppy.

"Ewww." Charlie laughed and held Jack at arm's length. A wet circle stained his not-quite-white shirt.

"Set him down." Cora dusted her hands on her apron and headed for the back of the wagon. "You can wash out your shirt after you carry in a load."

"I'll have to train him when to go potty." Charlie set Jack on a patch of leaves and rubbed his hands on the grass.

The puppy bounded around chasing his tail, then smacked at the ground with his oversized paws to send the leaves flying in the air.

Cora gawked at the wagon bed. A sack of flour, a keg of nails, a bundle of rope, and another crate. A sack of sugar bulged out the top, next to a bag of coffee beans. Coffee. She hadn't had real coffee since 1862. She'd swallowed boiled water flavored with sassafras leaves, barley, or worse in the years since, but real coffee? A rare commodity in Texas since the war. How much had Ben spent?

She reached for the crate.

"I'll handle that." Ben's rich, deep tone jarred her, igniting warmth in her chest. His flannel sleeve brushed close to her arm.

"I can do it." She stumbled over her words as she gazed into hazel orbs with gold speckles. Her cheeks heated, and she glanced away but returned her gaze to his. If he'd used laudanum in town, would it show in his eyes?

His eyebrows quirked upward. "You have a question?"

"No." She grabbed the nail keg.

"Here. This one is for you." He switched the keg out for the coffee beans and handed the nails to Charlie. "I'd love a cup."

She trailed behind him as he carried the crate in. "Coffee's expensive, you know."

"I noticed. And not easy to find." He settled the crate on the kitchen table. "So we'd best limit ourselves to a cup a day, or water down the beans a bit." He planted both hands on the oak surface, palms down, waiting.

She cradled the sack to her chest and struggled to bite back her objections. He shouldn't spend so much on them. She'd never be able to pay him back. Obviously, he had no intention of listening. "I...we...shouldn't—"

"Shouldn't stand around when there's a wagon to unload and coffee to brew?" He cocked his eyebrows and headed out the door before she could manage a rebuttal.

She shuddered. The coffee, the puppy, all the repair work... Ben was weaving his way into their lives. What did he get out of this? How much had Jeb's friendship meant to him that he'd go to so much trouble to help his kin?

It wasn't as if Ben was an expert craftsman or rancher. His first attempt at fixing the palisade gate hadn't gone well. The latch struck the plate too high. Undeterred, he'd taken the gate off and repositioned it a second time. The fact that the work didn't come easy to him but that he was honing the skills for their sakes sent her stomach into a worse tumble.

Blowing out a breath, she unloaded sugar, baking soda, salt, a couple jars of peaches—

Charlie lumbered in, both arms wrapped around the sack of flour. "Where should I put this?"

"In the corner by the cupboard." She smiled.

Charlie eased the sack down on the spot. "When I finish unloading, I'm going to find Jack a blanket. There's one in the barn—"

"Stick with finding something in my scrap basket. Jack doesn't need a full blanket. He's got plenty of fur."

"But, Cora, he's only a puppy." Charlie reached into the crate for the string of dried apple slices.

"Ben's right about not babying him." She'd sunk low, using Ben's approval as support.

"Then he might need to come into my bed to keep warm."

She pointed her finger at him. "No. But in a couple of days, after we get all the use out of the ham hock, I'll let you give it to Jack."

"Thank you." He jumped up and down. "That'll make his tail wag. And speaking of dinner, can Ben eat with us? I bet he's like Jack. I don't think he likes to eat alone."

She jabbed a hand to her hip. "Did Ben give you that idea?"

Doe-eyed Charlie gazed up at her. "No, he didn't say a word. But I know what it's like to not be at the table with everyone else."

She flinched. Years ago, her father had tried to make Charlie eat separately from them after the boy had first arrived. Her mother hadn't stood for it. Figurative coals burned atop her head. "Ben can join us for dinner if he wants."

"He'll want to." Charlie grinned, gave her a quick hug, and bounded toward the hallway.

"Wait." She waved him back.

He pivoted. "Yes?"

She shouldn't ask, but she did, voice lowered. "Did Ben stop at any other stores other than the mercantile and the livery stable today? Like the druggist?"

"No. Just the blacksmith's. Only, he paced back and forth a couple of times in the block across from the druggist."

"But he didn't go in?"

"No. Was he supposed to? He finally said he had to go to the post office to mail a couple of letters, and I went with him."

A quick *ruff-ruff* sounded in the front yard.

Charlie fidgeted. "I've got to go check on Jack."

"Go ahead." She touched his shoulder and turned back to the kitchen.

Ben had been tempted but hadn't given in. At least not this time. She hugged herself. What was she doing allowing him to come to dinner? Was she insane? Why had the Lord allowed this man to come into their lives?

What if she and Charlie could make a difference in Ben's life?

Foolish thought. How many times had her mother clung to that same hope?

CHAPTER 11

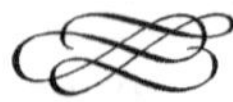

Seated in the Scott kitchen, Ben savored a sip of coffee and soaked in the warmth of the fire crackling in the hearth. Even if Cora adamantly refused to meet his gaze, she'd at least invited him to share a meal with them, an unexpected blessing. Maybe tonight, he'd actually be able to sleep instead of the restless tossing and turning half wakefulness which had plagued him for weeks.

This rustic kitchen was a world away from the chandelier, polished cherry table, silver serving set, and imported carpet of his family's dining room, with Olivia a short carriage ride away. Was she still angry with him? She'd come to the train station to see him off with pouty lips and had given him no more than a peck on the cheek. She was probably accepting gentleman callers in his absence to spite him. And if she wasn't, she would be after she received his letter explaining that Jeb's family was destitute and the situation would take months to remedy. A letter in which he hadn't been able to cough up the word *love*, but had barely managed *my dearest* and *soon to be betrothed*. A letter in which he neglected to mention that Jeb's mother had passed and left his twenty-four-year-old sister in charge.

He glanced Cora's way and ventured into uncharted territory. "Finest coffee I ever tasted."

She arched an eyebrow and set a plate of food in front of him. "A luxury."

"True." Getting this woman to accept anything from him, even a small compliment, was as challenging as marching uphill in mud. "At Andersonville, I dreamed of having a sip of coffee. The only thing better were my dreams of a chunk of freshly baked bread, hard on the outside and soft inside." His mouth watered at the memory.

"You dreamed about bread?" Charlie quirked his mouth to the side, his bangs falling across his forehead.

"Even the thought of it made my stomach feel a little fuller." Ben inhaled the aroma of beans busting their seams interspersed with ham. "We used to spend hours planning the first meal we'd have after we were freed."

"I'd like to hear more about Andersonville." Cora sat down across from him with a direct glance.

First time he had her earnest attention since the bottle incident, and his words dried up. His gaze fell on the cornbread in the middle of the table. "I'll tell you one thing. Your cornbread may be the best in the county as far as I know, but I don't know if I can eat it. They fed us green corn at the prison camp. Didn't bother taking the husks out. Just ground it up, baked it, and gave it to us and little else."

Charlie scrunched up his nose. "Didn't that taste terrible?"

He shouldn't say it, but he did. "There were men willing to eat shoe leather and worse." Hunger that gnawed a man's stomach inside out and then started on his soul.

Cora sucked in a breath.

Charlie gaped at him. "Wouldn't that hurt their teeth? I've heard that my mother's people drink buffalo blood, or if they're really thirsty, they might drink their own—"

"Charlie." Cora shot the boy a deep frown.

"I just want to know what the prisoners ate." Charlie stuffed a spoonful of rice in his mouth.

Ben lowered his gaze and stirred his beans. "That's all I'm going to say on the matter." His voice cut sharper than he intended. "Should we say grace?"

A whimper and a flurry of scratching and scraping, like tiny twigs brushing against wood, sounded against the outside door down the hall.

"Jack." Charlie jumped from his seat.

One look from Cora sat him back down again. She bowed her head, her voice not quite steady. "Let's say the Lord's Prayer."

Stupid of him to give Cora such details about the camp. She didn't need to know her brother had suffered so.

He mouthed the words of the prayer along with Cora and Charlie. "Our Father who art in Heaven, hallowed be thy name. Thy kingdom come, thy will be done on earth as it is in Heaven. Forgive us our trespasses as we forgive those who trespass against us..."

Did Cora believe in such forgiveness, or were they just words to her? Goodness knew he had committed more than his share of trespasses. His need for laudanum was a cardinal sin in Cora's judgment. But that would be nothing compared to what would happen if she discovered he'd failed Jeb.

Prayer finished, Charlie hopped up and opened the door.

Jack scampered in, ran to Charlie's chair, and then bounded back to paw Charlie's legs. The boy laughed and scooped the puppy up.

"Not at the table. He stays on the floor."

"Ahhh," Charlie mumbled, set the puppy down, and hurried to plop into his seat. "You could tell us about one of your battles, Ben. Did you ride a horse and have a saber?" He palmed a small piece of ham, eyeing his sister to see if she'd noticed.

"Charlie, we're done bothering Ben with our questions." She tapped her fork on her tin plate. Wisps of chestnut hair fluttered about the sides of her face. A crinkle extended from the outside corner of each eye. Had the sun or worry etched the first lines on her smooth, youthful face?

Ben stabbed a chunk of ham. "I was in the cavalry and had a fine-looking horse and saber, but your sister's right. Enough war talk tonight." He shot Cora a glance and cleared his throat. "I have some questions about the ranch, but if you prefer, they can wait until after dinner."

She gnawed her lip. "What about the ranch?"

He finished chewing his ham. "I'm wondering what happened to your family's cattle. Jeb used to talk about the herd, and the round-ups, and accompanying his father to sell cattle in Louisiana."

"The war is what happened. No men around to do the ranching. Not enough help to take care of the cattle. Ranchers all along the frontier lost their herds."

He pressed his palms together and touched his fingers to his lips. Her father had been around. Best not to mention it.

"The raids got so bad, family after family moved into Weatherford or farther east to Dallas. The folks north of here in Elm Creek built themselves a fort. Texas formed the Frontier Regiment, but the men were spread so thin, it wasn't anything a body could count on."

"So the beeves died or were stolen?"

"Some of them. The rest wandered across the grasslands and woods living wild. Ranchers from the larger spreads have been scouring the prairie for their brands and rounding them up."

"At least they branded their animals."

"Sure. The ones that wandered off during the war, but not the calves. There's three- and four-year-old mavericks out there with no brand. Who's to say who sired them? There have been disputes."

"I bet. The kind that could leave a man dead."

She lifted her chin. "I'm not asking you to get involved in any of that."

He exhaled and laid his forearms on the table. "And if I don't, who will round up your cattle?" Never mind that his knowledge of the animals didn't extend much beyond barns and stockades. But the war had taught him plenty about riding hard, living rough, and rounding up men. Could cattle be that much different?

Cora's shoulders rose toward her ears. "I hadn't planned that far ahead yet. I figured the garden combined with hunting would be enough since we owned our land free and clear, or at least I thought we did until Mr. Coffin showed up with the promissory note."

This girl needed all the help she could get. "Your courage is admirable. Most women would have clung to the safety of town."

She waved her hand at him like some plantation mistress dismissing a servant. "I had enough of town life and working all day for a pittance. I was done waiting. The war was over. It was time for action."

Cora lifted her chin. Her gaze fell into his. Unguarded for once. Full of spirit. Lamplight glistened in her blue irises.

His pulse quickened. She was quite a woman. A smile erupted across his lips.

The corners of her mouth twitched upward, but then she seemed to catch herself and glanced away.

Charlie slipped Jack a bite of cornbread. "We like adventure."

Ben swallowed a spoonful of beans. "I can see that." He sipped his coffee. "I'd like to hear more about why your sister wants to be a rancher."

Cora dragged her fork through her rice. "Not much left to tell. Other than the fact that I have no intention of giving up land that too many of my family members worked and died for." She sat tall, chin lifted.

He'd work together with her on that if she'd let him.

Charlie chimed in. "I bet if the Comanche knew Ben was our friend, he wouldn't have to worry about them attacking him."

Ben blinked at the abrupt change in topic.

"That's not so." Cora's voice cut sharp. "And don't you count on them showing us any special favor. None of us should risk our lives on it."

The boy's shoulders drooped.

"Count on what?" Ben quirked his eyebrows upward. "Do they consider you as a friend because of Charl—"

"There's no 'they' about it." Cora straightened. "The Comanche have dozens of different bands. And then there's the Kiowa."

"But you've got to tell Ben what happened—"

"That's a story for a different day." Cora stood. The blade of her voice softened. "Come put your plate in the wash pan and take Jack with you to check on the horses."

"All right." Charlie scuffed his toe, got his plate, and whistled for Jack to follow.

Wagging his white-tipped tail, the puppy padded behind him into the hall.

Ben swallowed the last of his coffee. Maybe he'd best leave, too, and wait a day or so before pushing for an agreement regarding the livestock. Only, he didn't. "I'm serious about my offer to help round up the cattle."

She set down the empty plate she'd picked up. "I appreciate—"

"You've mentioned that." The word grated on his nerves. He'd seen the extent of her appreciation. "Although since I don't know the area well, I could hire a ranch hand. Someone familiar with the frontier. It's been a year since the war ended. No telling how many beeves you've lost already to thirst, wolves, or greedy ranchers taking more than their share. There's no time to waste."

Cora dusted her hands on her apron. "I thank you for your offer." Her frown settled deep.

Here came the objection.

"I've been mulling over a different idea." She scooped up her plate and his, carrying them to the sink. "In the next county, Mr. Charles Goodnight has amassed a large herd, and so has Mr. Oliver Loving. From what I've heard, they're fair men. I could contact them and propose a deal. They could have a percentage of my family's cattle for rounding them up and driving them to market with their own."

Ben's foot beat a rhythm against his chair leg. Not a bad plan if the men could be trusted. He should encourage it. He could volunteer to contact the men and negotiate the deal. Maybe he could fulfill his commitment earlier than expected. Stay on a little longer to further strengthen the outbuildings... Then leave Cora and Charlie on their own? Not hardly. "Goodnight and Loving might be good men, but their own cattle would be their top priority. If you want to make a real go of the ranch—"

"If they're not interested, I could ask Dr. LeBeau for advice. He knows a bit about ranch—"

"I'm sure the good doctor knows a little bit about everything."

"What's that supposed to mean?"

"It means he ought to stick with doctoring. He barely knows anything about that."

She mumbled something beneath her breath.

"What did you say?" His pulse throbbed in his temple,

amplifying the dull ache behind his eyes that started about noon every day. Why was he letting all of this get to him?

She clasped her hands in front of her. A dishrag dangled against her apron. Her face colored. "Nothing."

"I'd like to know."

She swiped a strand of hair from her eyes and crossed her arms. "I was wondering if you were displeased with the doctor because he wasn't able to help you."

His chair scraped the floor as he stood. "LeBeau gave me quinine for my stomach. What other help do I need?" Once upon a time, he'd known how to hold his tongue and his temper. Before the war. Before Andersonville. After his return home, the laudanum settled him down to a bland numbness as long as he had his regular dose. Turned him into a rabid lion when he didn't. *God, help me conquer the lion.*

Cora pressed her lips together and glanced away.

She didn't need to speak what he already knew. He reminded her of her father. The man she had zero respect for. A man who couldn't be trusted.

He tossed his napkin on the table. "For your information, Cora, I have a family back in Philadelphia. One that respects me. My sister, Evelyn, misses me dearly. And my father is eager for me to finish my business here and return home so I can become the managing editor of his partnership's newspaper. Imagine. And on top of that, though I know it may be difficult for you to believe, I have a girl waiting for me in Philadelphia. One who isn't pleased about my side trip to Texas. She's anxious for me to make good on our delayed betrothal announcement."

Cora's head jerked.

He snorted. "I didn't come to Texas to fight with you for the privilege of helping you. I'm done."

Jaw clenched, he marched out the kitchen door before he said something he'd regret.

~

*B*en slammed the stable door behind him. He had half a mind to grab his horse. If he had a horse. Ride out of here and be done with Cora and the ranch for good. She didn't deserve or even want his help. He'd had enough of her ingratitude. She looked down her nose at her father—the man who seemed to have enough faults to pave the way from here to Dallas—but she'd likely inherited a double portion of the man's stubbornness.

If it wasn't for Charlie, he'd leave tonight and move into the boardinghouse in town. Let Cora find out how well she could do on her own without his help. Sooner or later, reality would knock that uppitiness right out of her.

And what about that look Cora gave him when he'd mentioned Olivia? She was probably shocked that a woman wanted to marry him. Well, he had news for her. There'd been a number of young ladies who'd shown marked interest in him the spring of 1863 when he'd come home on furlough. Olivia stood out amongst them all. He'd eagerly courted her and written to her in the months between his return to the field and his capture at Chickamauga. After Andersonville, he hardly knew who that young man was. That spring seemed like another lifetime.

And here he was in Texas dealing with the most contrary woman he'd ever laid eyes on. Jeb probably had no idea what his sister was really like after their years apart. Ben scuffed his boot against the ground. Bits of straw and dust flew as he slugged over to the post, dug a Lucifer stick out of his pocket, and lit the lantern to dispel the almost dark. The metal lid clanked down as he blew out the match. The sorrel snorted, probably as ornery as its owner.

He grabbed a curry comb, then tossed it aside. He wasn't

about to look after Cora's mare for her. He'd feed the animal and water it. The same for Charlie's quarter horse. Not that he'd mind helping the boy with his animal, but Charlie enjoyed the task, had a real bond with his mount.

Ben stomped to the well and back, sloshing water as he returned, glaring at the lamplight which poured from the kitchen window of the double cabin. A light flickered to life in a different room. For the frontier, it was a good-sized home, with four rooms, a wide hall in between, and a loft. A home built for a family. His step slowed. Cora had lost so much. And Charlie had barely found his place in this world.

A waning moon just shy of full hovered above the horizon in the shadowy dusk.

Eyes glowed at Ben from the corner of the smokehouse and scurried toward a patch of sage. A possum. It'd probably found a hole under the fence or swung down from a tree branch.

An image flashed. A different palisade, fifteen feet tall beneath the scorching heat of South Georgia. Henry Dawson, out of his mind with fever and dressed in filthy, shredded rags, stumbling across the dead line. Ben yelled and hobbled toward him. Too late. A bullet from a Rebel guard sliced through Henry's chest.

A stench filled Ben's nose. He blinked away the past. Cora's yard returned. Still, bile rose in his throat. The wretched odor of twenty thousand unwashed bodies, many of them more dead than alive, mixed with the rot of the already deceased, engulfed him. A cold sweat broke out on the back of his neck and beaded on his forehead. He dropped the buckets and raced to a patch of sage, losing his supper.

Hands shaking, he swiped his mouth and made his way to the stables with the horses' water.

In his bunk after midnight, sweat soaked his shirt. Another dream of camp. He clamped his watch shut and swung his legs over the side of the bed. Tonight, the need for laudanum pulsed like a hot coal in the center of his mind. He got to his feet. He needed air.

CHAPTER 12

Cora threw off her quilts. Three hours of tossing and turning were more than enough. She swung her feet to the rough-hewn floor. Her stomach twinged, as unsettled as her thoughts.

When would she learn to hold her tongue? There'd been no need to confront Ben about his struggle with laudanum. Not after all the generosity he'd shown them. Careful not to bump into the cedar chest at the end of her bed, she crossed to the shuttered window and pressed her forehead against the sash. How could she be so stupid?

It was her father. Anything related to him made her feel like smashing another whiskey jug. But Ben was not her father. He could not be blamed for her father's sins. She didn't deserve to have Jeb as a brother. With his dying breaths, Jeb had worked to secure her provision and protection. And what was she doing? Everything short of pointing a shotgun at the man he'd sent.

Her fingers brushed against the cool, smooth wallpaper that covered the planed logs. A bit of civilization and frivolity, a gift from her father to her mother when this room had been theirs, and he had yet to succumb to the bottle.

The wooden sash pricked her forehead. What did Ben mean when he said he was done? Done fighting or done helping? What if he actually left and didn't come back?

All he had keeping him here was his promise to Jeb. Ben had a girl waiting for him back in Pennsylvania. Cora swallowed hard. She hadn't imagined him being in love. And here she'd been worrying he might have his sights on pursuing her. Foolish thought. Why couldn't she have just taken him up on his offer to oversee the cattle?

She needed air. This house was like a prison at night, stuffy and too warm, with its locked shutters. She stumbled through the dark to fetch the key from the top of her bureau and returned to the window to shove it upward. The padlock rattled as she twisted it off and thrust the shutters open.

Cool night air smacked her in the face. She inhaled the scents of grass and pine. Cicadas buzzed in the distant trees. Footsteps.

Her muscles snapped taut. Indians? Surely not. Her heart thundering, she leaned over the sill and grabbed a shutter. Something moved by the corral. Not an animal. She stiffened. Not an Indian either. She exhaled. Ben.

Hands in his pockets and shirt sleeves rolled to his elbows, he pivoted at the corral gate and strode halfway to the stable door before turning and retracing his steps. Pacing back and forth. Agitated.

Her swallow stuck in her throat. What if he was thinking about riding into town for laudanum? It'd be her fault, or at least she'd share the blame with his own weakness. Weakness? Was that what it was? What if Jeb had returned home the same way?

She wouldn't blame Ben if he rode out of here and never returned.

A coyote howl echoed through the dark. The hair on the

back of her neck stood up. What if it wasn't a coyote, but a signal instead? She'd told Ben to stay inside at night.

She grabbed her shawl and hurried outside.

The dew-kissed grass dampened her stocking feet as she strode across the yard, glancing at the cedar picket palisade. The Comanche had only breached it once. With the cabin and the stable barricaded and secure, the only casualties had been a pig, a dog, and a horse. With much care, the horse had survived. Over her mother's objections, she'd slept in the stable with Charlie watching over it for days while her father rode with a posse to pursue the raiders. It was the last time her father had gotten his blood up about anything, except retreating to town.

Pebbles crunched beneath her feet.

Ben turned toward her and halted by the corral gate. No smile, but his gaze scoured her from head to toe.

Breathless, she hugged her long red shawl, a gift from Jeb before he left home, tight across her chest. The long fringes hung down to her knees.

Ben's brow furrowed. "What's wrong?" A shadow of stubble darkened his face. It must have been there at dinner. She'd hardly noticed then, but now, it gave him an air of roughness that caused her knees to wobble.

"You shouldn't—" *Be out here. It's not safe.* She bit back the words. After the way she'd treated him, he'd probably scoff at her concern.

"Shouldn't what?" He folded his arms and leaned back against the post, but he was a long while tugging his gaze back to her face.

Heat rose up her neck. Why hadn't she had the sense to put on her dress before she marched out the door? "I heard you out here, and I was worried."

He snorted. "Afraid I might ride off with one of your horses?"

She gnawed her lip. "Afraid there could be a Comanche raiding party somewhere out there." She fingered the fringe. "Afraid you might decide to leave."

He stuffed his hands in his pockets. "Other than the part about the raiding party, it seems like my leaving would suit you just fine."

Breath leaked out of her lungs. "I'm sorry."

He cocked his eyebrows. "For what?" The breeze rippled a lock of his hair.

"For everything." She latched onto the top rail of the corral, new and firm beneath her hands, part of Ben's repair work. "I deserve to have my mouth washed out with soap."

He snorted. "I could find a bar in my room with a little extra lye."

She quirked her mouth to the side. "I was wrong about what I said at dinner. I need your help. So does Charlie."

He stared at her. "Do you mean it, or is this your way of feeling sorry for me? I'm not standing on a street corner begging for alms, you know."

"It's painfully obvious that Charlie and I could use all the assistance we can get. It's just that my father—"

"I am not that man." His voice rang loud enough to bounce off a canyon if there'd been one nearby.

A coyote howled.

Cora shuddered. What if there were raiders within hearing distance? "It isn't safe for you to be out here at night. Not safe for either of us."

He frowned. Didn't he believe her? Didn't he care?

What would it take to make this man listen to her? "The Comanche killed my uncle." The words scratched her throat.

His eyes widened. "Jeb never said anything about that."

"There's probably a lot of things Jeb never told you." She rubbed her hands over her arms.

His voice softened. "What happened with your uncle?"

She fingered the groove atop the pine railing. "My uncle migrated here with us. Helped my pa build the cabin and the palisade. We were the only neighbors within twenty-five miles with such fortifications." Once upon a time, her father had been a hard worker when he put his mind to it. "We'd been here five years. I was fifteen. I'd gone to town with Uncle Rick, and we'd been delayed. It was nearly evening. A Comanche raiding party swooped down on us about five miles from here. We couldn't outrun them with the wagon." Her heart pounded now, all of these years later. "My uncle drove up to a scattering of boulders and ordered me to hide. He died fighting the warriors." Her eyes burned.

A stream of air leaked from Ben's lungs. "I'm sorry." His brow furrowed. "How did you escape? Didn't the Indians realize you were there?"

A shiver rolled through her. Her uncle had lain sprawled on the ground, bloodied, scalped. "I...crawled to another patch of rocks. Scared to death. Shaking. I heard a warrior ride up. I rolled to face him, praying with all of my heart for God's mercy. I was certain I'd die that day... But he just stared at me. Face and chest painted red and black. A scar marred his cheek. He raised his spear, ready to release it."

"And?" Ben's voice scraped across the quiet.

"He said something in Comanche, then turned his horse and rode away. He said something to the others too. A couple of them glanced in my direction. But in the end, they rode off too." Her voice broke. Tears clung to her lashes. She would not cry. Not here in front of this man. God had spared her. Why? So she could help her mother, or raise Charlie? Or was there another purpose she had yet to decipher? She pressed her fingertips to her eyes, ready to bolt if Ben took a step toward her.

"That's amazing." He drove his fingers through his hair. "Is that why Charlie figures the Comanche won't hurt you? Do you have any idea why the warrior left you unharmed?"

She blew out a slow breath. "I have an idea. But I know at the deeper root of it is that the Lord protected me."

"Hmmm." He scrubbed his hand over his jaw. "What a blessing to have such certainty."

Did Ben not have that? Their gazes connected beneath the moonlight, his eyes dark, mysterious in the shadows, drawing her like magnets. An unexpected twinge stirred in her belly.

Where in the world did that come from? But hadn't she sensed it all along? The attraction? All the more reason why she must push him away. But now the threat had been removed, hadn't it? He belonged to someone else. She'd best remember that. After all, it was good news. He could be a friend or an adopted brother like she'd thought of before. She could encourage him and be a good influence.

A tree frog trilled nearby, answered by its mate.

Cora cleared her throat. "There was something that happened the year before the attack, too, that my family figured was the reason the warrior spared me."

"What was it?"

She reached for her pocket handkerchief. No pockets. She must be daft marching out here like this. But when she'd heard the howl... She sniffled. "It's a story for another day. We'd best get inside."

An owl hooted.

Ben scanned the horizon. "You know if there were raiders out there, they'd have to get over the palisade or through it to get to us. Besides, you already put the story off once at supper."

"At supper, I said another day." She tightened her shawl. "And this is still the same day."

"Are you sure about that?" His rich voice worked its way inside of her. "I reckon it's past midnight. New day."

"Still, I'd prefer not to stand in the open in middle of the night."

"I'll walk you to your door." He motioned toward the cabin.

She fell into step alongside him. Her cheeks warmed at his nearness. What was wrong with her?

"Thank you." The porch creaked beneath their footfalls. She reached for the door latch. "You'd best get back to the stable and stay put until sunrise."

"I'm waiting for the story." He leaned a shoulder against the doorjamb as if they had all the time in the world.

She crossed her arms. Did he have no sense of the night? But he'd settled down since she'd come outside, no longer pacing, and the sinew-tight grip of his jaw and lower face had eased. She'd helped with whatever had been troubling him. Helped? It was likely her fault to begin with. But she'd managed to make it better. "I saved a Comanche girl."

"You did what?" He straightened. "How?"

"A year before the attack on my uncle. I was out riding and came across an injured girl in some bushes on the outskirts of the ranch. She was about nine or ten years old. She didn't speak any English, just Comanche. I could understand enough to figure out that her horse had come across a rattler and bucked her off. Her leg was broken. I made a splint, got her onto my horse, and walked them back to our house. My mother and I cared for her for weeks. Even taught her some English. She got stronger. One day, she was gone. There were multiple horse tracks outside the palisade the next day. Her kin must have come for her."

Ben's gaze lingered on her face. "The warrior who spared you could have been one of her kin."

"That's what we figured." She leaned against the door. "But as I told Charlie, there are hundreds of Comanche who live within raiding distance of here, and only a few of them might have reason to be kind to us."

"Duly noted." He hooked his thumbs around the bottom of his suspenders. "All the more reason why you need protection."

Provided by him or from him? That was the question. But

tonight, the air contained too many howls, too many unknowns. She glanced down at Ben's boots. "I'd appreciate it if you could negotiate with Mr. Goodnight for me."

"If that's what you wish."

Her gaze drifted up to his, the contact so palpable that it made her head swim. Too personal, especially here after midnight, and her dressed in her nightgown. "And if that doesn't work out, we'll talk about what to do next. Only, don't go telling them you're a Yankee. That won't help the negotiating."

"All I have to do is open my mouth, and they'll know I'm not from Texas." He smiled, a warm smile that worked its way inside her. "But I'll tell them I'm there on behalf of a Texas belle."

"I've never been a belle."

He shrugged. "Not all belles sit in parlors or ride carriages. Especially in Texas." His rich voice carried on the breeze as he ambled off the porch.

She called after him, "Lock the stable door behind you. Don't take chances."

Already in the yard, he pivoted on his heel. "If I didn't believe in taking chances, I'd be back in Philadelphia already." He stuck his hands in his pockets. "But I'll lock the door. Good night, Cora."

Her pulse quickened. Why did he have to do that? Make things sound like they were about her, when, of course, they weren't. He'd be here insisting on helping out even if she was a ninety-year-old grandma and wrinkly, as long as she was Jeb's kin. But still, it seemed as if there had almost been a trace of flirtation in his voice. Silly imagining on her part.

She pushed her way in the door and locked it behind her. Ben was practically betrothed. That was the only thing that made him safe. But how safe was a man who could send her heart to pattering?

CHAPTER 13

$\mathscr{B}$en aligned the log across the two sawhorses. Five inches in diameter should be about right. He'd sacrificed a young pecan tree in order to find a suitable replacement for one of the posts supporting the cabin's porch. A deep crack a foot long threatened to split the existing one in two. "Hold her steady now."

Charlie patted Jack on the head and stood. "Jack wants to help too."

"This is man's work. Jack will have to wait." He rocked the log. "You've got to put all your muscles into it."

Sleeves rolled up to his elbows, Charlie gripped the wood. "You'll see how strong I am."

Ben smiled and picked up the draw knife from the ground.

Dew glistened on the grass beneath the early-morning sun. A bluebird's wavering call fluttered from a nearby tree.

Post end against his right hip, Ben gripped both knife handles and leaned forward as far as he could down the seven-foot log. Good, solid work is what he needed to keep his mind off Cora. The way her loose hair had fallen like folds of silk across her shoulders and down her back last night, lapping against the red shawl… He connected the blade with the wood at an angle and drew the knife back toward him, shaving a ribbon of bark and lichen along the way.

"It's like lifting up a cover." Charlie held his end steady. "I wonder if there's any bugs in there." He stared at the newly revealed smooth cream-colored streak.

"Hold her steady," Ben commanded as he drew the blade to the end. He ripped the last threads holding the bark in place and tossed the ribbon to the ground.

"Can I have it?" Charlie reached down to pet Jack, who pawed at his shins.

"We'll see." Ben winked. "You show me a good morning of work, and you'll earn all the shavings."

"Maybe I'll make a fort with them."

Ben rolled the log a couple of inches and nodded to the end. Charlie grabbed it and nudged Jack away with his foot. Draw and peel, draw and peel. They finished off the bottom half in a short while. Time to switch ends.

The back door banged, and Cora came around the side of the house, her hair in a loose knot at the back of her head, tiny wisps flying about her face. She carried a wide reed basket by one handle, allowing the open mouth to whap against her skirts.

Ben removed his slouch hat and ran a hand over his hair. "Morning." It was the first time he'd seen her since last night. She'd sent breakfast out to him with word he was welcome to come to supper.

A rosy pink colored her cheeks. "I came to see if you had any laundry for me to do. I've had mine and Charlie's soaking since last night. Forgot to ask for yours."

He rested his hand on the log. It wobbled, almost throwing him off balance. His neck heated. Last thing he needed was to look like he couldn't even stand up straight. "I wouldn't want to put you to any trouble."

"I haven't seen a stitch of your clothing in two-and-a-half weeks." She jabbed a hand to her hip. "You do believe in bathing, don't you?" A smirk tugged at her lips.

"I've been washing my clothes out in the washbasin."

"You probably slosh water all over the floor and only get your clothes half clean." She rolled her eyes. "If you'll fetch me your clothes, I'll do them."

"Yes, ma'am." With a chuckle, he saluted and hurried off for the stable. Her very presence added an extra layer of sunshine to his day.

By the time he returned with the basket half full, she'd already headed to the back yard. Charlie lugged a bucket of water toward her washstand, an old cart with one end propped up on a low stone wall and one side of the railing removed. Two wooden tubs sat on its bed. A rusty iron kettle swung over a fire pit. Cora knelt beside it, arranging kindling atop logs.

Ben set the basket by the cart and quickstepped to the kettle before the boy had a chance to accidentally douse the wood. "Let me help."

"It's heavy." Charlie heaved the bucket handle upward, elbows close to his chest.

Cora scooted out of the way as Ben poured the water into the kettle. "Charlie tells me you two are thinking about riding the land today."

Ben handed the bucket to the boy. "I figure the cattle situation has to be the top priority. I'll finish stripping the log this morning and then let it set a couple days." He rubbed the back of his neck. "I need a good understanding of the layout of the land before I bring cattle here." Good understanding? What he needed was to find an old-timer with a thorough knowledge of ranching and soak in every word the man had to say.

"I suppose so." She tucked a strand of hair behind her ear. "Charlie will be a big help. He can show you the land boundaries."

"That's the plan." Ben's Adam's apple dipped as Cora trailed her fingers from her cheekbone to her collarbone.

"I think Cora should come too." Charlie swung the bucket like a pendulum. "I might not know all the boundaries." Suddenly, the boy who knew everything, didn't? A smile snickered at the corners of his mouth. "I'll bring my rifle in case I see a deer."

"You ought to bring your rifle in case you see a raiding party, but don't go shooting unless Ben tells you so." Cora dusted her hands against each other. "I'll have supper waiting."

Ben flexed his fingers. His gaze fell into her murky blue irises. "We could all go and bring food, have a pic—" He bit his tongue.

A frown clouded Cora's expression.

Stupid of him to get anywhere near the word *picnic*. Best to stay away from anything that smacked of more than business, or he'd be banished to the stable loft for his meals again. "You're the expert on the boundaries, Cora."

"Charlie can show you well enough for now. I've got laundry to do."

"We could wait for tomorrow?" My goodness. What had gotten into him? He was worse than some schoolboy.

"Tomorrow, I'll have the gardening." She headed toward an overturned washtub by the stone wall. "Besides, knowing the exact boundary markers isn't essential until we find the cattle."

He beat her to the tub and snatched it from her grasp.

She huffed. "I can carry that."

"Just being a gentleman." He dodged her reach and clunked the thick oak tub with its iron bands onto the cart.

She jabbed a hand to her hip, but there was a flicker of light in her gaze. "You have your own work to do. If I can't handle the laundry on my own, I have no reason to be out here on this ranch."

"Don't worry, you'll have the whole afternoon to yourself, and then tomorrow, I plan to ride into town."

She blinked at him. "You just went to town yesterday."

"But that was before you commissioned me to locate Goodnight and Loving."

"I'm sorry. I should have spoken up earlier." She blew out a breath. "But I can point you in the right direction. You don't have to go into Weatherford. Goodnight's ranch is in Palo Pinto County, west of here. And from what I hear, Mr. Loving owns a large stead in Keetchi Creek Valley, same county."

Ben tipped his hat back and swiped his arm over his forehead. "If they're rounding up cattle, they could be anywhere riding the range." He hooked his thumbs around his suspenders. "From what I can tell, most everyone west of here travels to Weatherford for supplies, so I'm betting someone there should have an idea about their current whereabouts. Besides, going into town will give me another opportunity to look for a horse for myself. I can't keep using yours."

A furrow dipped between her eyebrows. "I didn't know you were planning to buy a horse."

There it was again. That concern that maybe he'd take up roots and not skedaddle as soon as his task was complete. "I can't head off to search for cattle a week or two at a time on your horse. I want you to have Sandy here in case you need her."

"I suppose you're right. It's just that I'd hate to see you go to the expense of purchasing a horse and then not be able to take the animal with you when you catch the stagecoach home."

That day could take its time coming as far as he was concerned. "I'll sell her when the time comes." He picked up the bucket and headed for the well.

Passing Charlie on the way, he switched his empty bucket for the boy's full one and took charge of filling the kettle, catching glimpses of Cora scrubbing away on the washboard.

His shirt, his trousers... Taking care of his things like—he cut the thought off before it had a chance to sprout.

Six more trips, and not only was the kettle well on its way to boiling, the rinse water brimmed near the top of the oak tub.

"Charlie and I will head off soon." He cleared his throat and stepped clear of a bee buzzing on a clover blossom.

"Good idea." She straightened. His soaking-wet shirt dangled from her hand. "I'll fix you some bread and cheese to take. And be careful. Keep a look out for rattlers and raiders."

"We'll keep our guns handy." He exhaled. Did he dare venture his question? "I've been thinking..." He flexed his hands at his sides. "Although I'm willing to negotiate with Goodnight or Loving and work on a deal, maybe you'd prefer to be there too. In case there's anything we need to discuss before finalizing an agreement. I'm fine acting on your behalf, but I figure you might want a say so."

What was he doing handing her half of the reins, when he'd had them firmly in his hands? He ought to have his head examined for inviting Cora. He should meet with the men on his own. Quicker trip, more decisive with fewer potential objections—not to mention the impropriety of traveling overnight with a woman who wasn't his wife. He didn't know how they did things out here in Texas, but back East, that'd be a marrying offense, regardless of the nine-year-old chaperone. He stuffed his hands in his pockets.

Cora tossed his shirt into the kettle of boiling water and wiped her hands on her canvas apron. "I'll think on it."

He shrugged. "Suits me fine either way." Right. That's why his pulse strummed in his wrists. He pivoted toward the corral without another word, his only tell the tapping of his fingers to his leg.

"Ben?"

He turned. Their gazes met, her irises the shade of bluebonnets, a field of spring in one look.

"You find out where one or both of the men are"—her voice wavered—"and I'll go with you and Charlie to negotiate with them. No use sending you all the way across the county and have you come back to consult with me before taking care of business."

He sucked in his cheeks, squashing the smile which threatened to erupt. "Makes good sense. Don't want to waste time." He tipped his hat and walked off.

Around the corner, he smacked his gloves against his trousers as he strode back to the corral, trampling grass and a pile of ants in his wake. She had said yes. It was about time she got away from this place and thought of something other than chores. A song buzzed through him—

Whoa. His feet stopped moving, almost toppling him on his face. Realization struck. He was falling for Cora Scott.

He scrubbed a hand over his jaw. Mercy. Couldn't be. He started forward, drifting toward the well. Once there, he leaned his hands on the cool stone wall, beneath the shade of the small roof. For a whole year, after he'd returned from the war, he'd delayed proposing to Olivia, his feelings mired in mud. And here he was…a whistle on his lips and a spring in his step.

It had to be the laudanum, or the lack thereof. The brown liquid had dulled his heart and his head. Now that he was free of its talons, any bit of sunshine felt like the Fourth of July.

He cranked the bucket up, lifted the dipper from its hook on the side post, and poured the water over his face and down his shirt. That should bring him to his senses. He didn't have to worry. This infatuation—if it was even that—was just his first breath of freedom from the dungeon which had enclosed him ever since Andersonville, or even before that in Belle Isle. Besides, Cora Scott wanted nothing to do with him. No danger there. It'd be a tall order just to earn her respect and friendship. That was his goal. Best not forget it.

<h1 style="text-align:center">CHAPTER 14</h1>

The next day, Ben squinted in the midday sunlight as he stepped out of the livery stable. A carriage clicked past headed for the main part of town. The stink of manure from the livestock yards a block away stung his nose. Carried on the breeze, the bawling of a calf rang out above the moos.

Charlie plodded up. "They won't kill the poor calf, will they?"

"Why would they do that?" Ben shifted his gun belt for the holster to strike farther back on his hip—not that he needed to be armed in town, but the road between Weatherford and the ranch was a different story.

Charlie's brow furrowed. "I've heard that the ranchers sometimes kill the calves on the trail because they slow the herd down. It doesn't seem fair."

Ben ruffled the boy's dark hair. "Good thing his mama birthed him here before they started out on the drive. The owner will probably take him back to the ranch and give him a chance to grow up."

"Maybe he belongs to Mr. Goodnight."

"I don't think so." Ben placed his hand on Charlie's

shoulder and steered the boy toward the saddle and harness shop.

Mr. Dawkins at the livery stable had been helpful. Goodnight had been in town a couple of weeks back, outfitting for a cattle drive. Last Dawkins heard, the rancher had headed north by way of Elk Creek to round up more cattle. Rumor had it Loving had amassed a couple thousand head but seemed content to sit tight.

Charlie hurried to keep up as they stepped into the rutted street. Dust flew as a mule-drawn wagon rumbled by.

"Can we go to Hammer's today?" Charlie coughed. "The place with all of the hides. We didn't get to go last time."

"Maybe. If we have time before we head home." Ben led him onto the boardwalk in front of the blacksmith's.

"Cora sure liked the deer we brought her yesterday."

"Yes, she did." She'd smiled and given a clap as they'd ridden up from their tour of the ranch. Ben's chest had swelled. A yearling buck, already gutted, lay across the back of the sorrel. Ben strung it up in the shed, then stripped the animal of its hide after carving a thick slice of fresh venison for Cora to fry. "She'll be busy brining the meat today."

"I helped you spot it." Charlie puffed out his chest." Maybe next time, I can take the shot."

"We'll see." Ben blinked as they stepped into the dimly lit store. The sweet smell of leather filled his nostrils. Harnesses, horse collars, bridles, and their various parts hung on pegs along the barn-like walls. Saddles straddled narrow benches, and strips of leather, both wide and narrow, lay haphazardly on a long table with a draw knife on the end.

A balding man with spectacles sat on a stool on the other side of the counter. A smudged leather apron covered his chest. "Can I help you?"

Charlie halted inside the door and knelt by a long-eared bloodhound stretched out on the worn plank floor.

Ben tipped his slouch hat back and strode over to the counter. "My name's Benjamin McKenzie. I'm helping manage the Scott place. Mr. Dawson over at the livery thought you might be able to point me in the direction of Mr. Charles Goodnight."

"I thought I recognized the boy." He lifted his chin toward Charlie. "Isn't he the one the Scotts kept at their place?"

Kept? As if he were a discarded pup? "That's Charlie Scott." Was that really his last name? The father probably hadn't even given him that.

"Scott? Is that so?" The man cocked his eyebrows at Ben and picked up an awl. "You wouldn't be one of those Yankee carpetbaggers would you, trying to take Miss Scott's land?"

"Just the opposite. Mister...?"

"Mr. Stein."

"Well, sir, I was a good friend of Mr. Jeb Scott. Came here to help Miss Scott manage her ranch, but what I need to know is if you have any idea where I might find Goodnight."

The man looked him over. "What business you got with him?" Stein tacked a leather strip to the wooden counter and stretched it taut.

Ben discharged a grunted breath. "That's between me and Mr. Goodnight. It'll be a profitable meeting for him if I find him, but if you don't have any information, I won't waste any more of your time." He rolled his shoulders beneath his suspenders and turned to go. "Good day, Mr. Stein."

"Hold up there, Mckenzie. Didn't say I didn't know." Awl in hand, Stein bored a hole in the leather. "Just thought there might be something in it for me."

Ben hooked his thumbs around his gun belt. "You give me good information, and next time I pass through Weatherford, I'll bring you a smoked venison roast. The boy and I got ourselves a deer yesterday."

"Did you, now?" The man looked up over his spectacles. "If I was that Scott girl. I'd send the boy back to his kind."

Ben narrowed his eyes. "His sister isn't going to send him anywhere."

"Sister? Yeah, I heard that. That pa of hers..." He leaned over and aimed a spew of tobacco toward the spittoon.

Ben's fingers curled inward. "Charlie, let's get out of here." He pivoted toward the door.

"What about my venison?" Stein called after him. "Goodnight rode off to find horses. I could tell you where—"

Ben slammed the door behind him as he pushed Charlie into the street.

The boy looked up at him. "I don't like that man."

"Never mind him. We'll head over to the dry goods store. Dawson said Mr. Miller might know." Ben ground his molars and steered toward the main street. With folks around like Dawson, no wonder Cora had felt less than welcome in town.

Past the town square with its two-story brick courthouse, then the doctor's office and the attorney's, he kept his eyes straight ahead, not daring to venture a look down the lane that led to the druggist. After a couple more blocks, Ben slowed his step to a steady pace better suited for Charlie's shorter legs. A smattering of folks filtered by.

A carriage spurred ahead of a heavily laden ox cart loaded with barrels. At the end of the street, three prairie schooners, filled to the rim beneath their canvas bonnets, sat lined up in front of the Carson and Lewis House. Pioneers spending one last comfortable night at the fanciest hotel in town before heading off into the frontier?

"Howdy." A gray-haired man with his beard down to the top of his trousers sat smoking a pipe in front of Millers'. The rocker creaked back and forth.

"Good day." Ben tipped his hat and moved aside as two ladies stepped out of the store.

The dark-haired one wore a beautiful tapestry of a shawl over a blue cotton dress. She beamed down at Charlie. The honey-blond one, who hung on the other's arm, smiled and dug a peppermint stick out of a small sack. "May I give it to the boy?"

Ben nodded. "Certainly, ma'am. I'm sure he'd appreciate it."

Charlie grinned. "Thank you." His fingers wrapped around the treat.

A pheasant feather dangled from the blonde's felt hat as the two strode down the walkway, their skirts swishing together as they chatted.

Ben pushed the door open. A cacophony of aromas greeted his nose. Wood, coffee, oil, and cigars. Barrels of brooms and ax handles stood next to the woodstove, along with kegs of nails. Scattered offerings of potatoes, carrots, and onions lingered in other barrels. Tin plates and cups, iron pots, and oil lamps filled the shelves alongside more feminine wares.

Mustache wiggling, Mr. Miller bustled from around the glass-fronted counter with a sack of coffee in hand. His thin layer of sandy hair clung to his forehead. "Afternoon, Mr. McKenzie. Busy day, busy day. Settlers coming through." He added the sack to a wooden box, already half filled with pickled edibles, everything from eggs to beets. "Good thing you bought your supplies the other day. I just sold the last of my coffee and sugar."

"Not shopping today." Ben ambled over. "Just looking for information."

"Glad to do what I can." Miller swiped a neckerchief across his sweated brow.

Charlie tugged at Ben's sleeve. "Can I go outside? I want to watch the wagons." His red-tinged lips closed around the candy.

"Go ahead." Ben ruffled the boy's straight black hair. "Stay out of trouble."

As the door jingled shut, Miller sighed. "I was sorry to see Miss Scott move back to the ranch. No place for a young woman on her own. Mrs. Miller told her more than once that she needed to get herself a husband."

Ben's eyebrows shot up to his hairline. That probably went over as well as a bag of rocks. But why wasn't a fine-looking woman like Cora, with all her spirit, not married yet? "Was there a...?"

"Beau? There was more than one that showed interest over the years, from what I heard and saw. Frank Taylor was a fine candidate. Courted her before the war, but rumor had it that she turned him down in the end. Didn't want to leave her ma alone with that father of hers. Then that little Indian boy showed up. Offspring of a Comanche Mr. Scott had tucked away at some trading post. After Cora's mother took sick, God rest her soul, Cora all but became a mother to the boy. Taylor and most of the other young men were away at war." His voice wobbled. "Some never returned."

Had Miller lost someone in the war as well? Ben wouldn't pry. Another question loomed more imminent. "Did Taylor come back?"

"Came back a lieutenant. Fine soldier. Only, he met him a belle over in Mississippi from his time there, one who didn't have family she was bound to look after. They live in Dallas." Miller tossed a bundle of tapers into the box, their wicks joined. "After Mrs. Scott took ill, Cora didn't have time for socializing. Her whole household depended upon her. After her mother passed, Cora was the only one with any backbone in that family."

Cora working, carrying the load of her whole family, watching her mother die... Had she loved the Taylor fellow? Did she long to have a beau, or had she given up? He swallowed hard. His gaze drifted to a roll of violet ribbon on the counter. Wouldn't that look fine in her ha— No. He shook himself. *Don't even think it. You have a girl. Besides, Cora Scott wants nothing to do with you. And the way LeBeau looked at her that day? She doesn't need help finding a beau.*

Miller settled a bag of sugar next to the coffee. "I would have kept her on at the store with a few hours, but finances being what they are, I couldn't offer more. Northern folks like you and those settlers who came in today are mostly the only ones who can afford to stock their larders. Some of those ranchers, though, like Mr. Goodnight—"

"That's exactly who I wanted to talk to you about." Ben stepped closer. "I have business to discuss with him on Miss Scott's behalf. I hear he's putting an outfit together, planning a cattle drive."

"You'd better believe it. He was in here a couple weeks ago —another reason my shelves are emptying out. He's rounded up over a thousand head and hired him a crew of men. Even bought himself an old army wagon and had a woodworker north of here reinforce it with bois d'arc wood. Strongest wood around. Had him build some high-falutin' contraption on the end, like a miniature cupboard all set up for meal fixing. So proud of it, he brought me outside to show it off."

Ben rubbed his hands together. "But where is he now?"

"Headed east toward Fort Worth. He needs more horses before he starts for Colorado. I'd try the Circle R or Gary's Ranch. Either one's a good bet."

A few minutes later, Ben strode out of the store, directions in mind, and a can of peaches in hand. Maybe he couldn't buy Cora the ribbon, but they could all enjoy the fruit as a treat tonight as he shared the good news. Venison, peaches, and a trip to plan.

Where was Charlie?

Blinking in the sunlight, Ben glanced down the street and stiffened. Charlie stood a couple of blocks away, kitty-corner to the Carson and Lewis House, surrounded by three boys. Ben headed toward them.

One boy might be Charlie's age, but the other two had to be at least two or three years older. One of them had the chest and arms of a junior blacksmith. Their tense postures and hands on hips didn't bespeak a friendly conversation. The tallest one swaggered up to within a foot of Charlie. Ben picked up his pace.

"Why don't you go back to the reservation?" The tall one's voice carried half a block away, his scraggly hair falling across his forehead.

The junior blacksmith muscled closer. "My pa says Injuns are worse than dogs."

Charlie stood, ramrod straight, fists clenched at his sides.

Ben charged toward the huddle. "You boys—"

"Leave him alone." A little girl sprung onto the walkway from the street, coming out of nowhere. Her black hair hung down her back in braids. She couldn't be more than six or seven, but she plowed into the mix like a mama bear ready to protect her cub.

"Why, you're an Injun' just like him." The junior blacksmith curled his lip.

"Enough." Ben pushed in front of Charlie and the girl. "You boys shut your trashy mouths and get out of here." He jutted his finger toward the alley.

"My pa says—"

Ben narrowed his gaze at the tall upstart. "Did your pa tell you to bully little girls and boys years younger than you? Go pick on someone your own size before I take my gun belt off and use it like a whip on your backsides."

The three slunk away.

Charlie crossed his arms. "I don't need no girl protecting me. I was getting ready to punch them."

"They called me a name too." The little girl bounced up and down. The ruffles on her red linen dress with black trim jiggled all the way down to the hem just below her knees. Big brown eyes shown out of an olive-complexioned face. She did appear to be Indian and full of spunk. "I just wanted to help."

"I don't need no help." Charlie threw back his shoulders.

"Charlie." Ben's voice snapped. He turned to the girl. "Thank you. We appreciate your assistance."

She wiggled and blushed. "You're welcome."

Charlie scuffed his boot against the dirt.

Ben smiled at the girl. He'd have to encourage the ego-wounded boy later. "Where's your ma or pa, little miss?"

"Pa's coming." She tipped her head toward the street. A braid swung across her shoulder.

A well-built man with a black slouch hat and frock coat hastened across the street, a slight limp slowing his pace.

The little girl ran up to him and slipped her hand into his.

"Thank you for rescuing my daughter." The stranger

extended his free hand as he drew near. "I'm Major Garret Ramsey."

"Benjamin McKenzie at your service, sir. And if I'm not mistaken, your accent tells me you're of the Northern persuasion."

"Yes, Mr. McKenzie, Second U.S. Cavalry."

Ben inhaled. A fellow soldier. "Sixth Pennsylvania Cavalry Volunteers. A captain."

Garret grinned. "Well, what do you know? Another Pennsylvania man down here in Texas. I'm from Pittsburgh."

"Philadelphia." Ben shook Garret's hand again heartily.

"What brings you to Weatherford, Texas, if you don't mind me asking?"

"A promise to a fellow officer, and friend." Ben placed his hand on Charlie's shoulder. "To see that his family's provided for. What about you?"

"My wife and her sister count Texas as their true home. I was stationed about a hundred miles west of here at Camp Cooper before the war. Now that the fighting's over, we've decided to move back, try our hand at ranching. My brother-in-law, Lieutenant Devon Reynolds, First Texas Cavalry, USA, is with us. Three of my men from the Second Cavalry are coming along for the adventure, as well. They'll be arriving later this week with our lumber." Garret swiped his hand across his chin. "We know horses, but Lieutenant Reynolds is the only one amongst us who has any experience with cattle. And his knowledge of them is very limited."

"I'm in the same boat. I'm a newspaperman by trade and was a cavalryman during the war, but I'm green when it comes to cattle."

Garret chuckled. "We'll have to confer and share our vast knowledge, Mr. McKenzie. Or should I say 'Captain'?"

"Ben. And I'd be happy to. Save each other from ignorance."

"Garret." He touched the head of the suddenly shy child

who hid her face against his hip. "This here is Little Star. My daughter." A twinge of a hitch caught his voice on the last word. There was a story there.

"Glad to meet you, Little Star." Ben leaned down and extended his hand. "You're quite the brave young lady."

She peeked out from the fold in her father's coat, scooting her body farther behind his leg, and touched her fingers to Ben's.

"She alternates between being shy and treating the world as if it's her oyster. But as soon as you get to know her, the shy completely disappears."

Little Star poked her head from around her papa's leg. "What's the boy's name?" A smile dimpled her cheeks.

"The boy can talk," Charlie mumbled and turned sideways away from her, closed-lipped.

Ben arched his eyebrows. Still sore? "This is Charlie. I'm helping his sister, Miss Cora Scott, and him with their ranch about ten miles southwest of town. Thankfully, they know much more about ranching than I do."

"Just the three of you?" Garret's smile dimmed. "That's a lot of work."

"I'm up for the challenge."

"Well, as I said, we'll have to confer. We may not be cattle experts, but my family and I know the frontier. In addition to my service at Camp Cooper, Lieutenant Reynolds was a frontier scout and served in the army at Fort Belknap before the war. My wife and her sister spent their youth beyond the borders of what we call civilization." The crow's feet at the corners of his eyes deepened. "Once we build a couple cabins and get settled, we'll have all of you over to our place. We bought a few hundred acres west of here in Palo Pinto County. I've never seen it, but I estimate it's around thirty miles from Weatherford. From what I hear, this town is still the last major supply stop between here and the frontier."

"I'd be honored to pay you a visit, and even before that"—dare he be so bold as to speak on Cora's behalf?—"you're welcome to stop by our—the Scott ranch if you need anything at all." *Our*? Cora would have his tongue. And for his own sake and for the sake of Philadelphia, Olivia, and all they entailed, he'd best wash that word right out of his brain.

"We'll be sure to do that." Garret tugged on his coat lapels. "Meanwhile, you must meet my wife and the rest of my family before we depart." He nodded toward three prairie schooners. "We're off to a late start today. I anticipate seeing our new home tomorrow. There's a valley and a canyon. I scouted near the area years ago, and my brother-in-law rode through there on more than one occasion during his scout years. We're all eager to see what we can make of the place."

"I bet." Ben fell in step beside him. "I'd very much like to meet your family."

Still attached to her father's coat by a hand, Little Star skipped along between him and Ben, peaking back at Charlie who trudged behind. "You and I are going to be friends."

Charlie glowered.

"I have my own horse," she said. "I'm a good rider."

"I'm a better rider." Charlie jutted his chin.

"We'll see."

"I'm going to shoot a buffalo someday."

"Why would you want to hurt a buffalo?"

Charlie rolled his eyes. "Girls. Don't know nothing."

"Charlie." Ben nudged his arm.

"I know a lot." Little Star stuck out her lip.

"I'm Comanche." Charlie puffed out his chest. "Comanche hunt buffalo."

"I'm Comanche too." She stretched as tall as her three-and-a-half feet could take her.

Ben exchanged a look with Garret. A couple stories there, and nothing that would win either of them favor with the rest of the community. The bullies on the corner would likely not be the last of it.

Trying to hold on to her father's coat and look at Charlie at the same time, Little Star almost tripped. "My mother has a buffalo robe."

"Someone had to kill it, then." Charlie's voice had firmed with finality.

She rolled her lips in. "Hmmm. You're right. Maybe you'll give me a buffalo robe."

"I'm not giving you anything."

"We'll see." The dimples returned. And so did the skip in her step.

Ben chuckled. Charlie was going to have his hands full.

Little Star was a bold little thing. As strong-willed and determined as Cora. Only, Cora seemed to have lost her skip long ago, buried beneath an avalanche of hardship that a shovel couldn't penetrate.

But what if he could find a crack in her wall?

CHAPTER 16

$\mathcal{C}$ora dipped a sprig of dried rosemary into a bowl of marinade and brushed it across the venison roast on the spit. The roast, driven by the mechanical spit jack, slowly turned beneath the needle-like leaves. As she stood, she cast a side glance at Ben's scuffed boots, crossed at his ankles.

He leaned against the cupboard, grinding peppercorns with a mortar and pestle. Too comfortable, too familiar in the close confines of the kitchen.

She dusted her hands on her canvas apron. "If you have work to do, I could call you when it's ready."

"I'm going to work on the buck hide after supper, but first, I want to finish telling you about the settlers." A smile lit his face. "Running into Major Ramsey today was a godsend. I believe he and his family could become good friends."

"Friends with you." She wasn't exactly the most social person in the county. When was the last time she had a close friend? Jeb, in addition to being her brother, had been her best friend ever. And Frank Taylor? A beau. Smiles, horse rides, dances, and moonlit walks. A flurry of stomach tumbles, but had there ever really been any depth of feeling?

"With us," Ben corrected her and handed her the pepper.

Us again. "It would only be temporary."

"Temporary?" A frown swiped the sunshine from his face.

"I...I mean, you'd only be friends for a little while until you have to head back East."

His countenance stiffened as hard as the pestle he set down on the table next to the cupboard.

She squinched her eyes shut for a moment. She should have kept the comment to herself. But the reminder was good for both of them. In a few weeks, a few months, he would leave. That's what she wanted, wasn't it? Then what? She'd be safe. Or would his departure leave a gaping hole in her life?

Pepper granules tumbled onto the hearth as Cora overshot her mark in seasoning the roast.

Ben exhaled. "I hope they'll be your friends even when I *do* return to Philadelphia. It'd comfort me to know you have good-hearted, dependable people like them to turn to in times of need." He crossed his arms. "Besides, when I make a good friend, there's nothing temporary about it." His stare bored into her.

A huge part of her prayed that was so. That Ben McKenzie would be her friend no matter what. Her stupid heart ached for it. She dropped her gaze to the kettle where sliced carrots and turnips jumped about in simmering water, and reaching up, she grabbed a stirring spoon from a hook. "You can invite them here sometime. Though thirty miles is a huge distance. Most people wouldn't travel that far unless it's for cattle or a barn raising."

"I believe you could count on the Ramseys whenever you have need." His tone lost its hard edge, but the crevice between his eyebrows remained. "The Reynolds, too, for that matter." He slipped a stem of dried parsley from the bundle hanging from the string overhead. "I didn't tell you the most interesting part. Mrs. Ramsey and her sister were captives of the Comanche."

Cora stopped stirring and gaped up at him. "What?"

"Mr. Ramsey didn't share all of the details. Just pulled me aside after I'd met the whole family and said I'd probably hear it elsewhere sooner or later, but the two women were captured in their youth and lived with the Comanche for years. After a while, it was of their own free choice. The little girl I told you about is the daughter of Mrs. Ramsey and her late Comanche husband. Mr. Ramsey adopted the girl as a baby."

Cora stepped away from the hearth. "There was a family... well, there have been many families who've lost loved ones to the Comanche. But this family was attacked north of here in '53, the year we immigrated to Texas. Shook my parents up. My father and uncle insisted that my mother and us children stay in Dallas while they traveled ahead and built a log cabin. They wanted us to be safe." Back when her father was a provider and a protector.

She tucked a stray strand of hair behind her ear. Her mother had wanted to turn back. It'd been evident in her eyes and in the tremble in her hand, but she hadn't said a word. Her loyalty was to her husband and his dream. Going back to the past he'd lost for them in Tennessee wasn't an option.

"I'd always wondered what had happened to the two girls. The men in the area gathered a posse, but nothing came of it. Then, seven years later, shortly before the war, the cavalry found one of the girls, all grown up. She had a baby with her. The story was in all the papers. Some said she was the wife of a war chief, and he'd died in the battle trying to help her escape. This might be her."

"Very well could be." Ben rubbed the back of his neck. "Major Ramsey served in the cavalry before the war and was stationed at Camp Cooper."

Cora shivered. If her family had arrived on the frontier before Mrs. Ramsey's family all those years ago, Mrs. Ramsey's fate could have been hers. Only a matter of a few days had separated Cora's family from heading down the same trail. She could only imagine the pain and suffering the woman had gone through as a girl. "I'm thankful to learn she's all right. That she has her own family now, and a husband who loves her." Would she ever have that?

"Yes, the two look very happy together." Ben sighed.

She turned her focus to the venison roast, spreading out the pepper with the rosemary sprig.

Silence engulfed them. The heavy air filled with nothing but the crackling of the fire and the low rumble of the boiling water.

In the yard, Jack barked a playful yelp, but in here, there was just the two of them. What would it be like to have Ben as a close friend, the kind of friendship he'd had with Jeb? Loyal, standing by each other no matter what. What would it be like to be more than friends, to have him court her? To be his wife?

Cora's stomach waffled. Where had that last thought come from? Time to slap some distance between her and Ben. "You mentioned that you have a...that you have a sweetheart back in Philadelphia. Did you say you were betrothed?"

A muscle in his jaw twitched, and he crossed his arms. "I reckon that depends on how you define *betrothed*." He straightened and walked over to the dry sink, emptying the bucket of water he'd hauled in here fifteen minutes before.

"What's that mean?"

He dangled the bucket against his leg. "It means I put my future with Olivia on hold because I wanted to come here and fulfill my promise to Jeb before I entangle myself in an even deeper commitment."

"Entangle?" The word fluttered across her lips before she could stop it.

"Excuse me?" He arched his eyebrows.

"Nothing."

"You said something."

"Just that you should go call Charlie to supper. It's time to wash up."

Entangled. That was the word he used. That didn't sound like a man eager to marry. Didn't sound like a man in love. The thought should worry her, but it didn't. Instead, it was like the first strike of dawn to a morning glory's enclosed petals.

~

A scattering of oak, hickory, and hackberry dotted the outskirts of Mr. Gary's yard amongst a swath of brown and green grasses. Hopefully, Goodnight hadn't moved on from here in the couple of days since Ben had ridden into town to inquire of his whereabouts. He glanced at the gathering of cowhands by the corral beyond the barn and held his arm out to Cora. "Why don't you hold on to me for now, show them we're together? Otherwise, they might swoop over to see you like honeybees to a blossom."

"I hardly think so." She lifted her gaze to him, blue eyes deep as a sunset sky today, shaded beneath the brim of a neatly woven straw hat. A red ribbon fluttered down the back against her hair. A small crease formed between her eyebrows.

"You don't know how long they've been out on the range thirsting for a lady's smile." *Or how you outshine them all.*

She rolled her eyes. "Well, to be safe..." She curled her fingers ever so lightly around his elbow.

His heart skipped a beat at her touch. *Steady, McKenzie.* Two-thirds of a day riding at her side had definitely gone to his head, despite the fact the conversation had focused on the business of ranching. The barrage of questions from Charlie about the battles Ben had fought in had been the only verbal detour. Nothing personal on Cora's part, and nothing touching on

Andersonville. Or Philadelphia. A subject to be avoided as much as his days at the prison camp.

Along the railing, men clapped and cheered as one of their number tried his hand at a bronc. A cowhand shot up above the crowd's heads every few seconds as the horse beneath reared and bucked. According to the lady at the main house, Mr. Goodnight was supposed to be amongst the spectators.

Charlie ran ahead, plowing his way through tall grasses reaching almost to his hips rather than detouring to the worn path.

Thud. A collective groan arose from the men, and the horse galloped to the end of the corral beyond the crowd, a stout blue-gray beauty with fire in its eyes and a muscular frame built for strength, unusually large for a quarter horse. No saddle, only a rope rigging and a bridle. The rider must have been insane to try to master such a creature with so little gear.

"Howdy, miss."

"Howdy, ma'am." A couple of fellows made way as Ben led Cora to an empty spot at the railing next to Charlie.

The boy dangled over the second rung halfway to his waist as if he might decide to scurry into the action at any moment.

"Whoa." Cora slipped her hand from Ben's arm and grabbed ahold of the boy's suspenders, tugging him back a foot. "You need to stay put."

At the corral center, a man stumbled to his feet and limped across the hard-packed dirt. Dust and dirt marred his checkered vest and tan trousers.

A fellow hooted from the crowd. "Don't forget your hat, Simmons."

"Why don't you give it a try, Harry?" Simmons huffed and bent down to retrieve his hat, wincing as he stretched back up.

"I've got more brains than that." The short, squat one named Harry chuckled.

The blue roan galloped toward the populated end, and

Simmons quickstepped to the railing. Another laugh erupted amongst the crowd.

"Anyone else care to prove their metal?" A man with gray streaks in his rust-colored beard called from atop an unhitched wagon just outside the arena. Mr. Gary? A wide-brimmed hat protected his eyes from the glistening afternoon sun of mid-May.

The men shuffled and nudged each other.

A few more took notice of Cora, the only lady at the corral, and gave her an appreciative smile or nod.

Ben caught her hand and drew it back to the sweet spot in the crook of his arm. His treasure. If only that were so. Warmth spread through his chest as her fingers fell into place without protest.

The man atop the wagon stood. "No one brave enough?" He hitched his trousers. "How about you, Charlie?"

Charlie shot up from his lookout between the second and third rungs. "Me?" The wood jarred as he bumped his head. "Oww."

"Not you, young'un." A heavy-set man in bad need of a shave and a bath glanced down at the boy. "Mr. Charles Goodnight."

Farther along the railing, near the gate, a tall fellow with short-cropped dark hair, close-set eyes, and a goatee stepped forth. "I've already got all of the horses I need for the day, Gary. That blue looks too chunky for my taste."

"Don't know what you're missing, Goodnight." Gary spat a chaw of tobacco to the ground from his perch.

Goodnight saluted. "I have to leave you one good horse."

One good horse? Hopefully, more than that and not the one in the ring. Ben aimed to place a saddle on an animal of his own today and trail his rented horse behind him on the way home. What if he volunteered to ride the blue? He'd practically lived in the saddle during the summer campaigns in the war.

Dealt with many an ornery horse. But he had never broken a spirited, wild one like this. And all of that was before Andersonville and laudanum had eaten him inside out.

"Jones." Gary jabbed his finger toward a younger fellow with slicked-back hair. "Bring Ginger out."

"Yes, sir." Jones slipped down off the railing. "Should I saddle her?"

"No need. We'll tie the blue up to her tail, nice and tight, not much wiggle room. He'll have another thought coming when he goes to chin the moon. A horse can't buck if he can't lift his head."

Jones jogged toward the stable.

Harry called out, "Maybe now, Charlie will be brave enough to ride her."

"You ought to do it, Harry," another cowpoke suggested.

"I'm not riding that beast." Harry backed up a step.

"Don't get your feathers in a ruffle." Gary jabbed his thick hands to his hips. "My boy will do it."

A sandy-haired boy sprang off a crate. "Pa. Not the blue."

A murmur went up amongst the men.

Eyes wide, Charlie wiggled up from his lookout. "He's going to make the boy do it?"

"We'll see." Ben frowned at the man on the wagon.

Gary puffed out his chest. "My boy's broke a dozen horses with a bronc tied up to Ginger or one of the other mares. Simmons, throw a saddle on the blue."

The blue, as if he could hear every word, galloped to the far end of the corral and returned at a charge. Dust flew beneath his pounding hooves.

Jones returned with a chestnut American Saddlebred mare, and Simmons lugged a saddle, neither of them going farther than a few feet beyond the gate, as if they were afraid the horse might charge like a bull.

Gary hopped down from the wagon. "I can see I'm going to

have to saddle him myself." He waved toward Tyler. "Come on, boy. You got some riding to do. Show these men up."

"But Pa…" Tyler dragged his feet. "Please. I can't." Tears filtered down his cheeks.

The blue snorted and pranced out of reach.

Ben flexed his hands. He could volunteer and save the young'un.

Charlie tugged on Ben's sleeve. "He's scared. I…I think I could do it. His pa shouldn't make him."

"You're a brave boy, but you're staying put." Ben gripped his shoulder and whispered, "I could go."

Cora shot him a wide-eyed glare. "Absolutely not. Neither of you."

Ben narrowed his eyes. "I'll do as I see fit."

Gary grabbed ahold of the blue's halter. "Tyler, get over here—"

"I'll do it." Goodnight stepped forward. "Only leave Ginger out of it. I'll show the blue what he's made for."

Claps, cheers, and relief ensued as Goodnight slapped his own saddle on the horse. Gary held the halter tight while Goodnight tugged on thick leather gloves.

The blue ignited as the man sank onto its back. Gary jumped clear as the stallion pitched and bucked. Pebbles and dirt flew. The saddle skirts flapped as Goodnight dug his boots deep into the stirrups. The blue jerked its chin up and reared, front legs pawing air. Goodnight flopped like a ragdoll atop the bucking, contorting mass of horse flesh. Would the man or the horse win? Up and down the length of the corral, the pair fought.

Men cheered.

"C'mon. C'mon, you can do it." Charlie pumped his fist against the worn wood.

Suddenly, the horse leveled. Was he beaten? The animal snorted, then blew a gust that echoed around the corral.

Quicker than a snap, the horse took off at full gallop, charging for the side of the corral. A communal gasp went up as the blue's four hooves left the ground in a leap that carried both rider and animal over the railing. The animal struck ground and darted across the field away from the trees with Goodnight still in the saddle.

"He's headed for the creek bluff," Harry called out.

This could be serious. Ben started at a jog and picked up speed, Cora and Charlie right behind him. The whole crowd flocked after the runaway.

Horse and rider dove between a couple of hackberry trees. The branches barely missed the man. The blue's hooves sprang into the air, and both rider and animal disappeared over the side of the bluff.

A rumble and a neigh echoed up.

Ben reached the edge first. Four or five men ran up alongside of him. Cora bumped into his back.

"He did it," the cowhand congregation hollered.

Charlie skidded to a stop and whooped. "He's still on."

Mud encased the animal's legs all of the way to the saddle skirts, but Goodnight sat astride, bent over, hands on his thighs and boots scuffing against the brown ooze.

Goodnight swiped his arm across his forehead and waved.

At Ben's side, Cora gaped. "Amazing. Did you see that?" She turned to Ben. "He held on. Through it all. My goodness." Her eyes lit up like fireworks.

Ben snorted. Next thing he knew, she'd be asking for a formal introduction to the man. "It's not that special." He kept his voice low.

"Not special?" She nudged his arm. "He rode him off the cliff—"

"Maybe a smarter man would have let go."

"Maybe you just don't know..."

Her words faltered as his glower deepened.

He smacked his gloves against his trouser legs and stomped away from the crowd. He'd had enough of the scene.

"Where are you going?" Cora trailed after him. "We need to talk to him—"

"I will. After everyone gets done slapping him on the back." He lengthened his stride. Hopefully, she wouldn't catch up.

Across the field and past the outbuildings, he walked. He'd check on their horses they'd tethered next to a fence on the other side of the main house.

At the stone well, he filled a bucket and wiped the back of his neck with his neckerchief. His stomach burned as if someone had prodded him with a branding iron. It acted up every time his temper flared nowadays. The anger, the pain, the continued weakness. All of it indelible scars scratched in him, body and soul, by Andersonville. Or was it from the medicine? Laudanum. The quinine LeBeau had given him helped alleviate the worst of his ailments, but it was nothing compared to laudanum. He could almost taste the brown liquid even now. He shook himself and picked up the bucket, sloshing a bit on his trouser legs as he quickstepped to the horses. As if he could outrun the hunger.

CHAPTER 17

Twenty minutes later, he stood by the gate, half listening to Charlie tell about how they'd dug the blue out of the muddy creek bottom. The boy's words flittered past Ben's ears. Instead, his gaze locked onto Cora sashaying back through the tall grass with a cowhand on either side. At least she clasped her hands in front of her instead of hanging on one of their arms.

Stupid of him to let his temper get the better of him and leave her alone like that.

Surrounded by others and bespeckled with dirt, Goodnight led the blue into the yard, his gaze traveling Cora's way more than once. The man obviously spent too much time on the trail and not in town, where womenfolk could be found.

Ben strode over to Cora, tipped his slouch hat to the men, and placed her hand on the crook of his arm.

She crinkled her brow but complied.

As they reached the gate area, Gary climbed onto his wagon and puffed out his chest. "Anyone else want a go at the blue before I have the boys give him a good brushing?"

Ben halted. A chance to prove himself. He eyed the animal

as Goodnight led it through the gate. The horse shook its head and nickered. Twigs and leaves clung to the animal's blue-gray coat. Spatterings of mud clung to its legs.

"What are you doing?" Cora tightened her grip on his arm.

Ben stood tall and called out to Gary. "The blue's tuckered out. You got any others?"

"Ben," Cora hissed under her breath.

"Well, Mister...?" Gary spit out a chaw.

"McKenzie."

"Pleased to make your acquaintance." Gary nodded from his perch. "I could round up another bronc if you care to have a go."

Cora sputtered. "Mr. McKenzie, may I talk with you for a moment?" She yanked on his sleeve, her eyes sparking.

"Excuse me." Ben clamped his arm to his side and dug his boots into the pebbled ground, forcing Cora to halt.

"Take your time with the little lady." Gary nudged his hat back. "We'll put the blue to stall and see what we can round up for you."

Stiff-backed, Ben followed Cora around the corner of the main house, dragging his heels to temper her giddy-up speed. He stopped in the shade of a pin oak and slipped his arm free of her grip. "You want to talk to me?"

She swung her arms wide. "You can't ride a bronc."

His eyes narrowed. "Says who?"

"I don't want you to get hurt."

"Let me worry about that. I can take care of myself."

"These men have had years of practice."

"I was in the U.S. Cavalry in case it slipped your mind, Cora." He bored his gaze into her. She had some nerve. "I might not be a cattle expert, but I know horses."

"That was before—"

"Before what?" The words struck like a hammer. His pulse throbbed in his temples.

She blinked at him, lips pressed shut. The answer was in her eyes. That same doubt. That same *you're like my father*.

"Before prison camp?" He lowered his voice. "Before laudanum?" He practically spit out the word. Did she think him wounded beyond repair?

She glanced away.

That was her answer, all right. Dousing him with the sins of her father again.

"Couldn't your father even ride a horse?"

"This has nothing to do with my father." She jabbed a hand to her hip.

He blew out a breath. "Who are you to tell me what to do?" He shoved past her and headed for the corral, his hands clenched at his sides.

She caught up to him, her voice low. "You were sick for weeks."

He wasn't back to full strength, not by a long shot. His stomach was a tempest more often than not. But he wasn't going to stand by the wayside like some invalid. "Mind your own business, Cora."

"But you are my business." Each word was emphatic as if she wanted to drill it into him.

"Since when?"

Her gaze shifted to the corner of the house.

Charlie stood there with a deep frown. Had he overheard any of the disagreement?

Digging a hole in the dirt with his toe, the boy glanced between Ben and Cora. "What's wrong?"

"Nothing." Ben bit off the word and stalked toward the corral.

Charlie caught up to him. "You're not feeling well?"

Ben jerked to a halt and ground his molars, fighting the urge to glare at the child.

The boy looked up at him with big, rounded eyes. "I don't want you hurt." He latched onto Ben's hand.

Ben groaned. Not him too. Probably Cora's influence. Well, he'd show them what he was capable of.

He took a step. Charlie stepped with him, holding firm to his hand with a sweaty palm. Ben puffed out his cheeks. How did he end up with a child to look after? One who tagged along like a pup. A pup with a gaping hole in his life. A pup who needed him.

Ben scrubbed a hand over his face. He had no business risking a serious injury without good reason. He had...a family to take care of. Not quite his family. But the boy sure seemed like it. And Cora? What was she? At the moment, more of a pain than anything. But no one he was willing to let go of.

He scuffed his boot against the sand and headed toward the corral, managing to work his hand free of Charlie's along the way.

Gary stood alongside the gate chuckling as Jones struggled to slip a rope harness over the head of a black mustang. Goodnight leaned across his saddle which he'd thrown over the top railing. Several others stood nearby. All eyes turned toward Ben as he approached.

Ben hooked his thumbs around his suspenders. "Don't bother with the saddle. I want to see her run. Turn her loose in the corral. I'm in the market to buy a horse. I'll break her on my own time."

A chuckle came from one of the gathered cowhands. "Talking about the horse or the woman?"

Ben rested his hand on the gate and admired the mustang. "Good question."

The scent of roses filled Cora's nostrils as she waited by the vine-covered trellis at the porch corner. In the distance, the men talked by the corral, but she hung back close to the main house. She'd best stay clear of Ben until he settled down. If only she could have expressed her concern unseen, without having to call him away from the men.

Charlie broke from the group and ran over to her. "Ben decided to not ride the wild horse. He's going to buy her instead."

A slow exhale leaked from her lungs. He was going to listen. Thank goodness. She'd let her worry get the best of her, but less than a month ago, he'd struggled for strength to even get out of bed.

"He said I can help with the horse when we get home." Charlie grinned. "Oh, and Mr. Gary said you're welcome to help the women folk fix food for the men. There's going to be a picnic out behind the house."

So that's where the other women were. That didn't mean she belonged there.

Across the yard, Ben strode over to Mr. Goodnight. Finally, he was going to talk to the man. That's where she should be. "Why don't you go play, Charlie? I need to help Ben."

He hopped on one foot. "I'll see if I can help at the stables. Maybe I'll meet Tyler, the boy who was afraid to ride the blue roan."

"That's fine. Just make sure you come when I call. We can't stay too late." She tapped her straw hat farther down on her head and stepped toward the men. Tonight, they'd camp in the open rather than riding through the night. Just her, Charlie, and Ben... Her pulse quickened.

A chipmunk scurried past, cheeks full.

Cora lifted her skirts and stepped around a pile of dried manure.

Goodnight's voice carried on the breeze, something about horses.

Cora caught up to the two men when they paused in the shade of a post oak tree with wide-reaching branches. Tufts of rich brown hair poked out around Ben's ears and at the back of his collar, beneath his black slouch hat.

Goodnight unscrewed his canteen. "Afternoon, ma'am."

She smiled. "Afternoon, Mr. Goodnight." She touched Ben's sleeve. His muscles flexed beneath the heavy blue cotton.

No smile lit his face as he turned to her. "Excuse me a moment, Mr. Goodnight. I need a word with Miss Scott." Ben tapped his fingers to Cora's elbow and led her away, without bothering to formally introduce her to his companion.

"What's wrong?" As if she couldn't guess. His eyes spat fire. She should have listened to her intuition to stay clear of him for a while, but how could she do that when there was business to discuss?

"Nothing." He hooked his thumbs over his gun belt. "I'm talking with Goodnight like you asked me to. If I have any questions, I'll find you."

She lifted her chin. "I don't need to be told my place."

"You're sure good at telling everyone else what to do."

"I didn't tell you what—"

"Right." He snorted.

She'd only been looking out for his safety. "I'm sorry I asked to speak to you in front of the men at the corral." She crossed her arms. "But I need to be part of your meeting with Goodnight. That's the whole reason I came."

He narrowed his eyes. "The night we stood out by the corral talking, you asked me to negotiate for you."

"But then later, you said I should come too." She jabbed a hand to her hip.

"Travel with me in case there were questions, not stand over my shoulder monitoring every word."

"I'm not about to go beautify the picnic table while you men decide the fate of my cattle."

His voice turned to flint. "You want to negotiate? Go ahead. Leave me out of it." He pivoted toward the stables, opposite direction of Goodnight.

Cora swung her hands wide. What in the world? She wasn't going to stand by and be left out of the decision-making. He'd pushed for her to come—before she'd intervened and caused him to lose face in front of the other men. She huffed out a breath. If she joined his discussion with Goodnight after her having interrupted Ben for a second time today, it'd be as if she were taking charge.

"Ben?" She hurried after him and grabbed him by the arm. Heat poured through his sleeve.

His eyes sliced into her.

Her hand dropped. If she didn't remedy this, he might still go off and hop on some insane stallion. "I..." Pulling the words up through her throat to her tongue was like wrenching up a bucket of lead. "I trust you to negotiate for me."

"Hmmpf." His glare flicked over her from head to toe. "No, you don't."

Her sharp exhale flung a stray strand of hair from her cheek. "I'm trying to." She twisted her hands together. Couldn't the man see trusting him was like extracting shrapnel?

His shoulders eased down. "I believe you are."

The ratcheted tightness in her chest loosened. "You could talk to me before you sign any final papers." Was she really going to let him handle this without her?

"These men don't sign papers. They shake on it. A man's word is his bond."

Like Ben's bond to Jeb. He'd traveled to Texas to honor his word to her brother. Paid Coffin a thousand dollars, endured her ingratitude...and she was worried about trusting him? It was amazing he still talked to her. The way he looked at her, letting him negotiate would just be the beginning of her making amends for not believing in him today.

She dug her nails into her hands and swallowed a stomach full of objections and temper. "All right, but I want a full report."

~

An hour later, she sat on a log, nibbling on bites of pork roast, ignoring the conversations going on around her. Goodnight and Ben talked so long that Mrs. Gary carried their food to where they'd taken up residence on two barrels beneath the oak tree. Charlie sat with Tyler. A few people stared at Charlie, probably due to his skin color, but proceeded to treat him naturally.

She swatted a fly. The shadows lengthened. If those men didn't hurry—

Cora's tin plate clunked as she set it down and jumped to her feet.

Ben strode around the corner, empty plate in hand, head high, shoulders back, no trace of a glare or clenched jaw.

She hurried over. "So what happened?"

He shrugged. A hint of a smile twitched at his lips. "Hadn't you better finish your meal?"

"I want to hear every word." She latched onto his arm and peered into his face.

He glanced at her hand on his sleeve. His eyes lit like coals, a slow, steady burn. The anger was gone. This was deeper, more welcoming, drawing her to him with the force of two magnets.

Heat streamed through her, sending a fit of fidgets and wobbles through her limbs. She dropped her hold. What was she doing touching him? It must be the leftover effects of walking around the yard on his arm. "You'd better tell me, or I'll march up to Mr. Goodnight and ask."

"He probably wouldn't tell you."

She glowered at him.

"I'm just having fun with you, Cora." Ben's smile broadened. "Why don't you get your food, and we'll sit in the front yard beneath the oak? I'll fill you in while you finish eating."

"All right." She started to scurry, then slowed her step. No use acting like a child.

Skirts swishing, she grabbed her food and quickstepped back to Ben.

Charlie rose from his spot on the grass and headed toward them.

Ben pointed at the boy. "Stay there for now."

Good. It'd be their private conversation. She walked up alongside the man, and he slipped her plate into his hands as they strolled away from the crowd. He led her around the side of the house to the front, past the roses, and down the lane. Near the tree, weathered acorn hulls crunched beneath their feet.

She sat down on the wooden barrel where Goodnight had rested earlier. "Tell me what happened."

"It went well. Goodnight's willing to help." Ben handed her the plate and laid his empty one against the scaly ridges of the tree trunk. "He's agreed to include any cattle we can muster on his drive and take them to market. We'd give him a thirty percent cut."

"Thirty percent sounds like a lot."

"You've got to consider that he'll be using his hired men, and they'll ride the horses he purchased and work to feed, water, and safeguard our cattle. But he's leaving the first of June, so we don't have much time."

"That's less than two weeks." Her voice faltered.

Ben took his hat off and ran his hand over his hair. Sweat dampened a couple of strands across his forehead. "I'll make it work. We'll be back to ou—"—he cleared his throat—"*the* ranch tomorrow afternoon. Next morning, I'll hit the trail looking for your mavericks. Goodnight told me about a couple of creeks where he'd noticed gatherings of renegade cattle. He's even agreed to loan me one of his men. A young Mexican, not quite hardened to the trail yet, but he's been around enough to know the county and beyond."

She bit her lip. "The man's generous."

Ben shrugged. "He says folks have to help each other out here on the frontier if they're going to survive. Plus, he stands to make a profit." He fumbled with his hat, knuckling a shallow dent around the circumference of the crown. "All the same, he said it's best not to get our hopes up about the number of your family's cattle we might find."

"Why not?"

A frown crept across his face. "There's been a lot of rustling. Men collecting strays and mavericks, claiming the animals are part of their herd, putting their brand on them. There's been others abusing the tally system."

"What's that?" She swallowed a bit of pork.

"A system set up by carpetbagger courts. His words, not mine. He gave me a dirty look when he mentioned the word." Ben settled the hat on his lap.

"You are a Yankee." Her voice softened the word.

"Yeah, but I reckon he's willing to overlook it since I'm helping a Texas damsel in distress."

She rolled her eyes. "I'm not a damsel or in distress."

"But even a fiery mistress of a ranch can use help from a knight now and then."

Knight. Is that how Ben saw himself? She flickered a glance his way. The description fit. No armor, but his rugged, stubble-covered jaw, his strong hands covered in leather work gloves, the gun on his hip, and his whole demeanor said he'd protect her.

His hazel gaze met hers.

She glanced away. She'd best not forget the wound this man carried, deeper than flesh. "You were telling me about the tally system?"

He tugged off his gloves. "If a cattleman comes across somebody's cattle like yours mixed with his, he's supposed to keep a record of it. He can sell your livestock, but then he's supposed to settle accounts next time he's in the area and give you money or cattle equal to what he took. Only, there's too many scoundrels. Take the cattle, sell them, then never show up in this county again."

She shuddered. "So...am I going to have any cattle left?"

He leaned forward, forearms on his knees. "Goodnight says he's seen several dozen, and I'm sure there's more he hasn't seen. I'm going to work hard to round up every one of them before June first. I bet I can gather at least a hundred for the drive. Rest assured."

Her fork hung in her fingers. It would be hard work. Maybe she should go, too, but she had a garden to look after.

His gaze dropped to the slice of cherry pie on her plate. "You going to eat that?"

"I reckon—"

He reached out and broke off a piece of the top—crunchy brown crust.

"Well." She gaped at him. "Aren't you taking liberties?"

He grinned as he stuffed the bite into his mouth. "A man needs to be fed well if he's going to venture out to round up cattle for you."

For her. "Didn't you already have a piece of pie?" She covered hers with her hand.

"It was about half the size of yours." He wiped the crumbs from his mouth.

"I bet if you go ask Mr. Gary's sixteen-year-old daughter, she'll give you another piece."

"I'm not interested in sixteen-year-olds."

What was he implying here? "You have to be interested in a girl to ask her for pie?"

"No. I just figure it's part of my pay." He slipped two fingers beneath her hand and nabbed another piece of crust.

She swatted at him, almost toppling the remainder onto her lap.

He laughed.

The sound warmed her all over. My goodness. Was he flirting with her? She needed to bring some sanity to both of them. "You're in pretty good humor for having just found out we might not have that many cattle to sell." *We*. He even had her saying *we* now?

The merriment faded from his face. "There's more news."

"Bad?"

"No. It's a good opportunity. But it's a serious undertaking."

She sliced her pie in half with her fork and slid half to the side of the plate nearest him. "What is it?"

His eyes lit at her gesture, and he dug his fork out of his trouser pocket. "There's a widow, southwest of Weatherford, right over the border in Palo Pinto County interested in selling all of her cattle. Goodnight heard about her while he's been here. He doesn't have time to travel down there and round up her scattered herd before he heads out on the trail for New Mexico. He's willing to give me a letter of recommendation, advising her to sell the herd to me. Of course, if he makes a second drive before fall, he'd be willing to take our newly acquired cattle to market for a percentage."

Her throat tightened. "Buy a herd?" Was he serious?

"A small herd." He devoured a bite of pie. "From all indications, your original herd won't be enough to put your ranch and income on solid footing."

She fingered a fold in her skirt. "But how much would that cost? We don't... We can't afford that."

He swallowed another bite. "Don't worry about the cost."

Her stomach dropped. "You're going to spend more money on us, aren't you?"

He blew out his cheeks. His gaze didn't quite meet hers. "It'll be an investment. You and I will split the profits fifty-fifty."

"Do you have sufficient funds with you in Texas to make a purchase like that?"

"I can cover it." But the deepening of trace lines at the corners of his eyes into crevices said differently. It was no light matter.

Her tongue scraped her mouth like sandpaper. "I can't ask you to invest that much."

"You're not." He cocked his head toward her. "I'm volunteering. I'll still have enough to purchase a horse. By the way, I decided to buy a quarter horse instead of the mustang. The black is a beauty, but I need a trail-broken animal that is used to cattle since I'm going to hit the range in a couple of days, not one that's never been ridden before." He finished off his portion of the pie, pressing the plate against her lap as he scooped up the remnants. "And I'm betting Mr. Miller back in Weatherford will allow me to purchase supplies for the trail on credit. Just until Goodnight returns with our share of the money from the cattle sale. I'll put the quarter horse up as collateral. She's a fine-looking animal."

His horse as collateral? Buying supplies on credit? He wouldn't have enough to get home to Philadelphia if this gamble didn't pay off. The thought throbbed in her head. What then? And she had no idea if this was money he'd saved for years, or the profits from a previous business venture, or his inheritance. What part of his life was he risking for her and Charlie?

"Do you know you get this little furrow..." He touched the tip of his finger above the bridge of her nose. Touched her. Actually dared touch her. "Right there. When you're worried."

His hand fell away. But the heat that swept over her didn't.

Her gaze drifted into his, soft, steady hazel irises. Eyes filled with determination. Had she ever witnessed such commitment? Goosebumps spread over her limbs.

She opened her mouth to protest, then shut it. She would honor this man's sacrifice. This man was not like her father. Not yet. Maybe he never had to be. Maybe she could help him not be. Risky thought. Unquenchable.

Quiet words bubbled forth, uttered with her gaze on the horizon. "There's more to being a hero than breaking a horse."

His eyebrows shot up almost to his hairline. "What did you say?" His voice a low rumble of disbelief.

"You heard me." She stood. The corners of her mouth edged upward despite the rock in her throat. "I'm not repeating it."

She struck out at a fast clip as if she could outpace the compliment.

But the deep tone of his voice reached out to her. "I heard you." And she would have to be deaf not to sense the smile that followed.

CHAPTER 18

Ben tossed a tiny leg bone into the waning fire and wiped the rabbit grease from his hands onto the patchy grass. They'd put an hour's distance between them and Mr. Gary's before picking out a campsite.

A faint hue of pink hovered on the western horizon. The rippling chirp of a tree frog sounded from the nearby cedar trees.

Charlie leaned forward, elbows on knees, gnawing on a hindquarter. "I can't believe I shot him right through the heart. I got a squirrel before and a couple of groundhogs, but never a rabbit."

Ben grinned. It'd been worth the gamble of losing the meal and eating dried venison in order to allow Charlie a chance to make the kill.

"You did a mighty fine job, Charlie." Cora dabbed a little water on the corner of her neckerchief and wiped her mouth. Her straw hat lay on the log beside her. The length of the day and the breeze had taken its toll on her now loosely bound braid. Wisps of chestnut hair fluttered about her face with its traces of auburn.

She'd removed the white undersleeves and rolled the sleeves of her blue-green plaid dress halfway to her elbows. Back East, a man rarely caught sight of so much of a woman's arms.

Ben tugged his gaze away from her and fished a biscuit from beneath the folded cloth on the ground between them. He leaned back against the rock, grinding a spider into the sand with his boot toe. His taste buds rejoiced as he bit into the buttermilk biscuit. He flickered a glance at Cora.

She jerked her attention to the horizon. Realization hummed through him. She'd been looking at him.

Had he really referred to himself as a knight today? Sometimes he didn't know what was going to pop out of his mouth. *There's more to being a hero than breaking a horse.* That's what she'd said, with a blush on her cheeks. A complete about-face from her doubt and discouragement a couple hours before. She was gifting him her trust. All he had to do now was make good on the plans he'd laid out before her.

Easier said than done.

He savored another bite.

Rounding up what was left of Cora's cattle in the next two weeks across several hundred square miles was the least of his problems. Goodnight had given him a list of the water holes to check. The real task would be purchasing the widow's herd at a rate he could afford and getting them to market. The money sack he had stuffed in an empty spittoon in his room over the stable wasn't guaranteed to be enough. A wiser plan might be to bring Garrett Ramsey in on the deal for a share. Ben would pay Garrett out of his half later. Cora would have her half just as he promised. But who would drive the cattle? He rubbed the back of his neck.

Charlie finished off his rabbit. "Tyler thought we might stay the night at his house."

Ben swallowed his last bite. "His pa did offer."

Cora's eyebrows edged upward. "What'd you tell him?"

Draping his arm over his knee, Ben tipped his face toward Cora. "I thanked him kindly but told him we'd best head toward home as soon as possible."

She blinked. "We could have stayed and left before sunup."

A smile tugged at his lips. "You should know, Cora, I'm as determined to protect you from wild cowhands as you are to protect me from wild broncs."

She gaped at him. "I don't need protect... I... Good—"

A chuckle rumbled under Ben's breath.

Charlie's brow furrowed. "What would a wild cowhand do?"

"After all those weeks on the trail, they forget what a girl looks like. They might stare at her or talk to her all night long and not let her get any sleep. We couldn't have that. Or they might drag poor Blue or one of the other broncs out to show their riding skills."

"Hmmm." The boy tossed his scraps into the embers.

Ben stirred the fire, avoiding Cora's blatant gaze.

Charlie's head jerked up, eyes bright. "Is that why you wanted to ride the bronc, Ben?"

Heat crept up Ben's neck. "No, I mean..." Had it been so obvious that even a nine-year-old could see it? The boy needed a neckerchief tied over his mouth at times.

Cora squirmed. "Ben has a...someone...a gi..."

Ben shot her a look.

"What do you mean, 'someone'?" Charlie stroked the rabbit fur at his feet.

Cora bit her lip.

"I don't remember if I tethered the horses tight enough." Ben stood. "I don't want them getting spooked if a mountain lion comes by in the night."

"If a mountain lion attacks in the night, I'd better have my shotgun by my side." Charlie jumped up. "I'll help you check on the horses."

Ben stuck his hands in his pockets. Sage and juniper scratched at his trouser legs as he strode to the brush where they'd hidden the horses. Charlie followed a step behind. It was Cora's idea to hide them there in case of Indian raiders. She knew this country. Wise woman. Wise enough to discern the truth in Charlie's comment about the bronc, and unlike Charlie, not liable to forget the conversation in favor of a mountain lion. She'd probably seen it from the moment Ben opened his mouth at the corral, unlike him who'd acted without thought, hot under his collar over the way her eyes lit up over Goodnight. What did it matter to him what Cora thought of anyone? If he'd been thinking straight, he would have introduced her to the rancher.

Right. About as appealing as swallowing cactus needles.

Footfalls silent, Charlie crept along beside him. "I'm glad we didn't stay at that ranch. This is more of an adventure."

Ben held back a scraggly branch for Charlie to enter the grove. "Day after tomorrow, I'll have to head out on the trail to round up those mavericks we talked about earlier."

"I could come too." He held out his palm to Lightfoot, his mare.

The horse nickered and turned its nose at the rabbit smell.

Ben tugged on the rope securing his new quarter horse, Penny. "No. This time, you need to stay at the ranch and help your sister. You'll be the man of the family while I'm gone." He winced. *Family.* Where had that come from?

"I like that we're a family." Charlie dug a carrot stub from his trouser pocket.

Of course, the boy would latch onto that word. "It'll be your duty to look out for Cora." Ben rubbed Penny's neck and moved on to the other horse.

By the time they returned to the campsite, Cora had cleaned up from their meal, except for the tin coffeepot which rested on a flat stone by the embers.

Ben's breath hitched.

Braid unraveled, she sat raking her fingers through her hair which flowed over her shoulders and halfway down her back.

Beautiful silk. What would it feel like to touch the lush tresses?

Snap. Charlie stepped on a twig.

The spell broken, Cora startled. "You're back." She swept her hair over her other shoulder. "I figure it's time we turn in for the night." Her ribbon slipped from her fingers, and she snatched it from the dirt. "I have to comb it out at night, or it gets tangled."

Ben shrugged. "I've seen a woman's hair before." He'd seen hers the other night. Loveliest he'd ever laid eyes on. Maybe if he didn't pay much notice, she'd leave it down. "I'll put the fire out." He kicked sand onto the embers. The fire she kindled within him was a different story.

"I reckon you ought to." Cora stood and turned to the boy. "Charlie, you'll sleep over here next to me."

Bedrolls unfurled, Cora bedded down close to Charlie, with the boy and several yards between her and Ben. In response to Charlie's request for a bedtime story, Ben told about a fishing trip he'd taken with his grandfather. Propped up on her forearm and her head resting on her hand, Cora listened.

Beneath the canopy of stars, her eyes shone like embers in the night, catching him up short in the middle of his story, making him forget whole lines.

"...the cat stole the last fish." His voice trailed off.

Charlie's breathing shifted to the quiet puffs of sleep.

Cora glanced away and whispered across the distance, "Maybe we should take turns keeping watch."

"Why?"

"In case there really are cougars. Or other things that sound like mountain lions. It wouldn't be impossible for Comanche to come this far east."

Ben straightened. He shouldn't have said anything to spook her. Even back in the security of her fortified ranch, a howl was enough to set her on edge. "We should be safe. There's several settlements between us and the Comanche and Kiowa trails." Or so he'd been told. "Besides, I'm a light sleeper, and I have my gun right here." He tapped his hand to the Spencer rifle at his side. "My Colt's even closer." He nudged the bottom of his holster which poked from beneath his folded coat, a makeshift pillow.

"All right." She rubbed the corner of her blanket between her fingers. "I reckon it's just been a while since I camped out." A heaviness settled across her features. "I used to go with Jeb to look after the cattle, days on end. Long time ago." Her words faded.

His chest deflated. "I'm sorry Jeb didn't make it back." His voice wavered. A shiver ran down his spine. The last time he'd slept in the open had been at Andersonville. Bile rose in the back of his throat as he shoved the memory aside.

"Those were good times." Cora laid her head on the crook of her arm. "Having him gone is like a hole in my heart."

What could he say to that? "He was my best friend."

"Mine too."

They fell into silence. The staccato chirp of katydids filled the gap.

"Cora?" He ran his hand over his hair. "I made up the line about mountain lions to distract the boy."

Her voice wafted on the breeze. "I don't mind you protecting me from wild cowhands."

He blinked wide. Goodness. Enough to knock his knees from beneath him if he'd been standing.

She tugged the blanket up to her ears and rolled over.

"Good night, Cora," he whispered. "Looking out for you is my pleasure."

No sound but the katydids and Charlie's breathing, but no doubt she'd heard.

His head spun as he settled into his blankets. Settled? How would he sleep now? He wanted to court Cora. Show up at her door with a bouquet of bluebonnets and Indian paintbrush, hair combed back, dressed in his finest. Sit in a porch swing with her. She didn't have a swing, but he could build her one. Go for a stroll by the creek. Take her into his arms...

He shook himself. Stupid to let a couple of gazes go to his head. Her words were probably nothing but affection for her brother rubbing off on him. Or gratitude for his willingness to invest every penny he possessed into her ranch.

But still, what if he stayed in Texas? No doubt...he was needed.

What would happen if he sent Olivia a letter explaining that he had strong reservations about marriage and he'd understand if she wanted out of their courtship? Only, it'd been more than a courtship. He'd proposed. Olivia had accepted. Could a letter undo all of that?

~

Cora awoke in the middle of the night. Had something scurried across her stockinged foot?

A coyote howled. Or was it? She shivered and sat up.

Buried beneath his covers, Charlie snored beside her.

Something thrashed to their right.

She jumped.

Ben threw his arm out of his blanket. "Get away."

Heart pounding, she sprang to her feet, but there was nothing there.

A deep groan resonated from Ben's throat. He rolled over murmuring. Asleep. Dreaming?

Gathering her shawl, she crept over.

His face contorted. In pain? Fear?

Palms clammy, she knelt at his side, clutching her shawl around her.

Strands of brown hair clung to his brow. A faint shadow of stubble darkened his strong jaw. His shirt, loose at his collar, crumpled across his chest. Should she wake him? Touch the shoulder of this man who had become her protector?

"Ummm." He twitched. His brow crinkled. More murmurs. He licked his lips. "Lau...nenum."

A silent scream ripped through her. No. She jerked back. Her knee hit the rifle, bumping it against Ben's shoulder.

Quicker than a breath, he shot up, eyes wild. He lunged for her. She squealed, falling onto her backside from a squat. He grabbed her arms and pinned her to the hard, pebbled ground. His hands clamped like vise grips. Bristles jabbed her side. His shins pressed against her thighs.

"Ben." She gasped.

He jerked. Squeezed his eyes shut, then opened them again. "C...ora." He panted as if he'd been running. "What?" His hands fell away from her. He rocked back on his heels. He gaped at his surroundings as if he'd never seen them. "I'm so sorry."

Grinding her heels into the pebbles, she scooted out of his reach. A sharp edge of a rock dug into her palm.

Charlie sat up and rubbed his eyes. "What happened?"

Ben scrubbed his hand over his face. His chest heaved. "You can't sneak up on me, Cora. What were you even doing over here?" He dropped to his knees. "I'm sorry. Did I hurt you?" He reached out, then dropped his hand back to his thigh. His face sagged.

Trembling, she rubbed her arms. "No...I'm all right. Just shaken."

"You can't sneak up on me, especially not when I'm sleeping." His brow furrowed. "At the camp...at Andersonville, men would steal things from other prisoners in the middle of the night. If you didn't protect yourself, you wouldn't have a scrap of food to live on. You wouldn't survive."

Charlie stared at him. "You attacked Cora because you dreamed she was one of the bad guys?"

Ben winced. "It was similar to a dream." He fumbled. "I would never intentionally harm a hair on your sister's head."

What if he'd grabbed the Spencer or the revolver? Her throat tightened. She fought to steady her words. "I'm fine, Charlie." She touched the boy's shoulder, nudging him down into his covers. "I accidentally woke Ben up in the middle of a nightmare. Sometimes a person doesn't wake up all the way. He was still dreaming." She kissed the boy's forehead. "Go back to sleep."

He nodded and rolled over, snuggling deep in the blankets.

A breath shuddered out of Ben. He stood, ran his fingers through his hair.

Her gaze to the ground, she edged her way back to her bedroll. Ben was dangerous in more ways than one. But the scariest part of it all was the one word. *Laudanum.* Even after all of these weeks, he wasn't free of its siren's call. Would he ever be? She couldn't take the risk.

Quiet-footed, Ben moved to her side and knelt.

She stiffened and yanked her blanket up to her throat.

His brow furrowed. "I'm not going to hurt you. Not even going to touch you." A well of pain echoed in his whisper. "I just need to know why you came over to me."

Did the man think she'd been making overtures or something? Heat blazed across her cheeks. She glanced at Charlie and kept her voice low. "I heard a coyote."

Ben exhaled. "I see." He scanned the tree line. "I'll keep watch the rest of the night."

"I don't want you to have to do that. It was probably nothing." Maybe she'd even imagined the sound.

"I'll stay awake just the same."

"There's no need." Her words cut sharper than she intended.

He flinched. "I wish I could take back what happened."

She pressed her lips together. *I wish you could too.*

Shoulders sagging, he rose and stalked to his bedroll. Only, he didn't lie down. Instead, he drew a blanket around himself, cradled his rifle across his lap, and leaned against a rock.

She should say something. Forgive him. Be understanding. "I know you didn't mean to hurt me," she whispered. But the words were mere pieces of lint stuck into a gunshot wound. Not nearly enough.

CHAPTER 19

Ben hefted the saddle onto the multi-colored blanket on his mare's back. The early-morning sun streamed through the open stable door. Two stalls down, Cora's horse snorted, eager for attention.

He ground his teeth as he cinched the girth strap beneath his quarter horse's belly. How in the world could he have attacked Cora? He rested his head against the saddle fender. What was wrong with him? If only he could scour every trace of Andersonville from his brain, heart, and soul.

Cora hadn't treated him the same in the day and a half since the incident. Hadn't met his gaze. Even Charlie had seemed a little skittish yesterday but had warmed up to almost his usual self by this morning. Cora would not forgive or forget so easily. He didn't blame her. What if he hadn't come to himself? What if he'd done worse, struck her or choked her? Goodness knows, he'd done as much in Andersonville in the name of protecting his mess's meager supplies.

With a heavy sigh, he secured the saddle to his new mare, Penny, and clunked up the steps to his room. His open saddlebag lay on his newly made bed. Two envelopes poked out of the leather pouch. He'd picked them up at the post office in Weatherford yesterday afternoon on their return from Mr. Gary's ranch. Not eager to read the contents, he'd left them unopened. He didn't need to see the signatures to recognize his father's and Olivia's handwriting. He could only hope there'd be a note from his sister, Evelyn, stuck in with his father's.

He could save them to read until he was by the campfire tonight on the trail. But what if something needed an immediate reply? Slapping his gloves against his thigh, he yanked the mail out of the bag and sat at his small pine table. Bracing his foot against the wobbly table leg, he started with his father's, dated April 22nd, 1866, a response to the first letter Ben had dashed off the day he arrived in Weatherford. His second letter had probably only reached Philadelphia in the last week or so.

Ben scanned the page. Family news. Talk of wrangling at the paper between partners. A wish for Ben's health and a speedy return. ...*Your level-headed editorship would be a welcomed counterbalance to young Thorson's sensationalism*...Level-headed? Did that word apply to him anymore? Besides, the elder Thorson, a full partner with Ben's father, wouldn't likely welcome anyone who interfered with the reign of his son. A section from Evie followed. She'd finished her college term. Her description of a dance made him laugh.

His merriment evaporated as he opened his mother's two pages. Talk of home and the soldier's hospital she visited with Olivia. His mouth dried. *Olivia.* He skimmed the paragraph and slowed down on the next. Encouragement. Concern for his health. They all missed him. The word *all* was underlined. Was he taking his medicine?

Medicine. He almost crumpled the letter. What he wouldn't give to have never tasted it. But how would he have lived through those early weeks in the hospital, skin and bones, gnarled legs, and a wrecked stomach without it? *Lord, give me the strength to never, ever taste it again.*

Shoving his fingers through his hair, he returned to the last paragraph. A reminder to store the Scripture in his heart. Scripture? He had repeated verses day and night on the battlefield, in the camps, and in prison, reading his Testament until the pages blackened with soot and mud after months in Andersonville. They had once meant so much, but by the end, they were as dry as his swollen tongue.

God, forgive me. He squeezed his eyes. *You were there with me in the darkest night. I know.*

He folded the missive and tucked it away. His swallow slunk down his gullet as he opened the second. Perfumed. He sniffed the paper. Lavender. Olivia often wore it in the evenings. During the spring of their early courtship, he'd been charmed by it. Now, it invaded his nostrils, smothering his breath like a too-hot, stuffy room. Was it the scent or the exhumed memories of too many evenings spent on the sofa with Olivia much too close, praying no one would come down the stairs while they immersed themselves in kisses.

He coughed and shoved the letter in its envelope unread. What in the world had he been thinking, spending time like that with her when his heart had been half dead? He stood and strode to the window, shoving the sash upward.

The morning breeze fluttered the curtain. Ben gripped the sill and sucked in air. In truth, he hadn't been thinking, not for months since his return from the war. Instead, he'd drifted, numb, heart and brain embalmed by the brown liquid. Going through the motions of courtship, work, and life.

And now?

The back door of the house banged shut. Cora appeared around the corner, bucket in tow, and headed for the well, her step light but sure. A woman of character and strength, with backbone enough to tackle this ranch on her own with a nine-year-old boy. A woman who breathed spring into his soul and ignited his heart.

He needed to make amends for what had happened the other night. Show her that wasn't really him. But what if it was? No. He scrubbed his hand over his jaw. He'd find her cattle, take them to Goodnight, and show her he was a man to could be counted on.

~

Sweat moistened Cora's brow as she squatted in the garden pulling weeds from beneath the bean tendrils. Tomorrow, she'd run them up on poles. A bee buzzed near her ear. The delicious smell of dampened earth filled her nostrils. An early-morning rain had left the ground pliable. By tomorrow morning, the top covering would be crusted again. Later in the summer, the hardness would go inches deep and leave cracks if left unwatered. She and Charlie would form their own bucket brigade from the well.

Where would Ben be by then? On a cattle drive deep into Colorado Territory with the widow's cattle? Or back in Pennsylvania, having had his fill of ranching? He'd been gone a week now, rounding up the mavericks with Goodnight's young hired hand. How was he fairing? Despite the fact he'd only eaten with them in the kitchen a handful of times, the extra chair at the dinner table felt empty without him.

His shoulders and his gaze had drooped when he'd said goodbye to her, his features clouded with guilt and regret. She didn't blame him for his nightmare-induced roughness. Jeb might very well have reacted the same. But it was the word he'd whispered that had chilled her affection. *Laudanum.*

Clickety-clack. Clickety-clack. A wagon?

She stretched up to a stand. Her rifle leaned against a post at the end of the row. Not that she expected to need it. Glancing down at her bare shins, she loosened the gathered folds of her green skirt from her waistband. The hem of her chemise tumbled toward the top of her worn boots, along with the green.

A horse and gig trotted through the palisade gate. The sole occupant, a tall man in a topper straw hat, snapped the reins and guided the conveyance toward the house. Dr. Arthur LeBeau?

What was he doing here? She wiped her hands on her smudged canvas apron, but there was little remedy for her dirt-caked nails. She frowned. What if something had happened to Ben? Her shoulders tensed. Would the doctor be the one to bring the news?

She bit her lip and headed down the row between bean and squash plants. A gopher darted into a tangle of vines. Maybe the doctor had come to check on his patient. After all, he probably wouldn't be aware that Ben was away on the trail. She rolled her sleeves down to her wrist, covering her bare, tanned arms.

Dr. LeBeau donned a black frock coat over his white shirt and hopped down from the cushioned seat.

Dare she attempt to slip in the back door? It'd give her a chance to wash up and comb her hair. Her step faltered at the path that led around back.

Dr. LeBeau waved. "Good day, Miss Scott."

Jack charged around the corner yelping. Their brave guard dog must have been sleeping on duty.

She tugged her apron off and shifted her steps toward her guest. She'd greet him as she was. "Good afternoon, Dr. LeBeau. I pray there hasn't been any trouble."

"Trouble?" He gave Jack a quick pet and looped his Morgan's lead rope around the hitching post.

She frowned. "I mean, like someone getting hurt." The apron dangled from her hand. "Mr. McKenzie is out on the trail."

"I can see why you'd worry." His mustache twitched. A

slight smile spread across his face. "I heard McKenzie's trying to round up your mavericks. But as far as I know, he hasn't managed to hurt himself yet."

She blinked at him. No emergency. And he was aware of Ben's absence. Even reciprocated the same twinge of disrespect Ben evidenced toward him. So why had he come? A red cravat offset the bright white of his collar and the black of his frock coat, waistcoat, and trousers. The man was dressed more for a social call than a ride across the prairie. Only a thin layer of dust coated his garments. Had he stopped somewhere shy of here and dusted himself off?

His smile broadened beneath her perusal.

She glanced away. "I'm sure Mr. McKenzie will do well with the cattle. He's a fine horseman. He served in the cavalry during the war."

"If you say so, Miss Scott." Murky blue eyes drank her in beneath the shade of his finely woven topper. "I'm no expert rancher. Spent too much time studying medicine and helping my father manage his cotton plantation, but I've heard cattle can be ornery at times."

"True, but he has an experienced cowhand with him." Did the doctor feel himself superior to Ben? "Mr. McKenzie is an educated man like yourself. He was in the newspaper business before the war. An editor, I think." Why did she feel the incessant need to defend Ben to this man? And how, after seven weeks in Texas, had Ben managed to not tell her exactly what he did at the paper?

"So he's a working man?"

"Don't all men work?"

"Some of them have to work just to scrub by. Others work for the betterment of their community and beyond."

"Mr. McKenzie's father is a part owner of the paper."

"That accounts for it, then."

"Accounts for what?"

"Him rising to the position of editor."

She jabbed a hand to her hip. "Dr. LeBeau—"

"I'm teasing you, Miss Scott. Testing your willingness to defend the man." His smile returned. "And you have done me a grave disservice—"

"I have not."

"On the contrary, you have denied me the pleasure of properly greeting you." He held out his gloved hand.

The man was flirting. She rolled her eyes. Whether or not he deserved a greeting, he was the one who'd sat beside her when her father lay dying and the one who'd helped Ben get on his feet. She rubbed her hand on her wadded apron and extended her ungloved fingers.

The epitome of a Southern gentleman, he bent at the waist and brushed his thin, smooth lips to her knuckles. His well-trimmed goatee and mustache tickled her skin. A tingle ran up her arm. With a wiggle, she slipped her hand free.

He straightened. "I brought you a present."

"Sir, I'm not in the habit of accepting gifts."

A shadow of a frown flickered across his fine features. "From whom?" He pivoted to the gig. "From your doctor? From a friend? Surely, you are not so endeared to your house guest that you would decline an offer of friendship from a gentleman who has been in your acquaintance for months."

What was he suggesting about her and Ben? She jutted her chin. "I'm not endeared to anyone."

"Glad to hear it." He retrieved a rectangular package, about the size of a book, wrapped in brown paper and string. "Though to be honest, I hope to remedy that."

She blinked wide. Was the man talking about himself?

He motioned to the cane-back chairs on the porch. "May we sit? I don't wish to keep you out in the sun, and I've had a long ride."

Ten miles. To call on her? Her legs wobbled as if they'd

turned to sponges. "Certainly. Forgive my manners." She climbed the two steps to the wide oak planks. "Have a seat, and I'll fetch us a couple of glasses of water."

"Much obliged." He tipped his hat and glanced around the yard. "Where's the boy, Charlie? I figured he'd be about the place."

Too bad he wasn't. "He's out hunting. He should be back anytime." The sooner the better, to make this visit more proper.

"Hopefully, he'll bring you supper." His voice flattened. He turned to his bay Morgan at the hitching post. "If you don't mind, I'll tend to my horse, draw her a bucket from your well, while you fetch our water."

She agreed and headed inside. In the privacy of her kitchen, Cora closed the door behind her and the shutters, as well. No telling where this man might drift. This wasn't quite the Dr. LeBeau she'd come to know. While he'd always been gentlemanly and amicable, he was usually more distant and guarded. But he had held her hand when she'd come to seek help for Ben, and then previously at her father's death. However, those had been attempts to comfort, hadn't they? She tossed off her hat and unbuttoned her dress one notch below her collarbone, the back and collar dampened with sweat.

But here he was calling on her. Her stomach swayed, not in the pleasant flutter Ben set off every time his eyes lingered on her. No, this was more of a clench.

She poured water from the pitcher into the washbasin and dampened a cloth, washing her face and neck. In the back yard, Jack barked. Maybe he wasn't quite sure of the doctor's intentions either.

She should welcome Dr. LeBeau's interest. Frank Taylor was her last beau, and that had been over five years ago. Dr. LeBeau was handsome in a slender, angular sort of way, well-educated, a man of means, and well-respected. A man who'd ride through the night to help a patient.

What better defense against her stupid heart's rebellious inclinations toward a certain hazel-eyed, dark-haired Yankee who had invaded her life and showed little inclination to depart from it? If only she could be so sensible.

Collar rebuttoned and stray strands secured into her braid once more, she proceeded down the wide hall with a small pecan-wood tray, balancing two glasses and two saucers heaped with buttered cornbread.

"Smells heavenly." Dr. LeBeau accepted a saucer and a glass.

She scooted a small wicker table between them and sat.

The mystery gift lay across his lap as he spoke of his weeks in Dallas, between bites. During her time in the kitchen, he'd removed his hat. His dark hair looped in a wave away from his forehead instead of mirroring the flattened pattern of the hat brim. Did the man have a comb up his sleeve?

Dabbing his mouth, he handed her the package.

Setting her empty saucer aside, she loosened the string and unfolded the wrapping to reveal a tea brick. Stars decorated the top of a black rectangle of leaves pressed solid as wood, an engraving of a garden gate flanked by trees covered the middle, and Chinese letters lined the bottom.

"All the way from China by way of England." He studied her reaction. "I have it on good report that it's the finest available in the port of Galveston."

"Thank you." She trailed her fingers over the embossed design. "I love tea, and it's been years since I've had any as fine as this. Before the war. Before the frontier."

He settled back in his chair and hooked his thumb in his waistcoat pocket. "You're welcome. I'm pleased to give you something you can enjoy. And I'm thankful to have been able to acquire it before the Yanks snatched it up."

"In Galveston?"

"Yes, I had business there. Not a place I'd recommend traveling to any time soon. It's crawling with bluecoats wanting to assert their authority over Texans. Not the same sort as the Federal soldiers I saw on the battlefield. The occupiers are more like the bottom of the barrel, not much more than a drunken mob when they're off duty. Thankfully, they keep mostly to the coastal cities for now."

"Surely, they cannot all be that bad."

"In my opinion, the ladies of Galveston cannot walk the street safely. The town leaders have asked that the soldiers be unarmed when off duty—not that the officers will listen." He sipped his water. "But I do not mean to disparage all Yankees. I'm sure your brother was a fine man. And no doubt, Mr. McKenzie has good intentions in wanting to keep his commitment to his friend. It's regrettable that the man's time in Andersonville weakened his health and will."

She lifted her chin. "Mr. McKenzie has recovered quite nicely thanks to the quinine you provided. He's worked hard to fix up the outbuildings around the ranch. He's the reason the gate is secure once again and the corral is no longer falling down in sections."

"That's excellent." He smoothed his fingers over his mustache. "Most opium eaters don't get past the initial two or three weeks of abstaining."

"Opium eater? Ben…Mr. McKenzie is no such thing." She bristled.

"I apologize. From what you've told me, he's managed to stick with the milder version. Laudanum. And now that he's made it beyond the first couple of months, the odds are, he'll soldier through many more weeks, even months, or a year before a setback."

"Ben is not…" She stood. "I'd rather not discuss this anymore."

"Certainly." He rose to his feet. "Please forgive me for overstepping, Miss Scott. I wouldn't mention it if I didn't feel that you've taken him under your wing like that pup in the back yard. You have a generous heart, and you loved your brother. You want to do right by his good friend." He tugged on his lapels. "I...I don't want to see you hurt. From the little I know of your life, I understand you've suffered much loss." His voice dipped to a gentle rumble, like a creek flowing over rocks.

She gripped her hands together. Sweat stuck her chemise to her armpits. "But isn't it possible Ben...Mr. McKenzie is cured? Haven't there been cases where a man has given up laudanum for the rest of his life?"

Air leaked out of his lungs. "Yes. There have been such cases. Though rare, it's possible. But are you willing to take that risk?"

"What risk?" She jabbed a hand to her hip. "The man is helping me get my ranch in order. Nothing more." She snatched up the empty saucers and the tea. "If you'll excuse me." She marched into the house. If the man had come here to run down Ben, he could go home. And what did he know of her feelings toward Ben? She didn't even have a clue herself.

She clanked the plates onto the work table. Arthur LeBeau was no friend of Ben's. But he was right about one thing. Ben wasn't cured. Not if he was whispering about laudanum in his sleep. Nausea rolled through her. She'd promised herself she wouldn't become attached. And what had she done?

Footsteps halted at the threshold. She stiffened.

"Forgive me, Miss Scott. I didn't intend to upset you."

"I'm fine." She turned and folded her hands in front of her, fighting the urge to cross her arms. "It's just that Mr. McKenzie was Jeb's friend. My brother loved him like a brother. I want him to succeed in his battle. If you truly want to help, perhaps you can tell me if there's any remedy that would bolster his recovery."

He stood with one hand behind his back, the other resting against the jamb. "If I knew of any such cure, my bank account would be full, for many would need it. But I'll offer some advice. Of the cases I've known, the cravings win out when the patient hits a rough spot. The strong can endure it when life is going well, but when setbacks or calamity come, old habits rear their head with a vengeance." He cocked his eyebrows. "My other advice? Your will cannot conquer it for him. Victory or defeat rests with him. But I reckon you already know that. From...past family experience."

She flinched. She knew it all too well. Her mind, her heart, and her youth bore the scars.

He cleared his throat and glanced down at his boots. "My father is no angel either. Only, instead of the bottle, his vice is his obsession with controlling the lives of his family members. If he and I got along, I'd have opened up my medical practice in Columbus near his plantation instead of Dallas."

She gnawed the inside of her cheek. "I...I'm sorry about your father."

He shrugged. "He's a small part of my life." His gaze fixed upon her. "But you are the one I'm concerned about. That is why I've expressed myself so pointedly."

"I thank you for your concern, but there is no need—"

"I've thought of you much since our last meeting." He drew his hand from behind his back. In his fingers, he held a thin book with an embossed red cover. "I brought this as a token of my affection. Proof that you have taken possession of my thoughts, even when I am far away."

Her throat tightened. "Dr. LeBeau—"

"Arthur. Please. It would give me great pleasure if you'd consent to call me by my given name out of friendship. That's all I ask for now. That and the right to call on you." He stepped a few feet into the room and held the book out to her. "I saw this copy of Shakespeare's sonnets in a Dallas mercantile. I was walking along thinking of you, and there it was in the window.

I've had my own copy of years. I'd like to share the beauty of poetry with you."

Romantic. But did she want a peek into the interior of this man's heart? Her brow furrowed. Not a door she wanted to open. At least not yet. "I appreciate the gesture, Dr. LeBeau."

"Arthur." His eyes glistened as he extended his hand to her, without coming closer.

She stared at the book. "You said friendship." She picked up the tea brick from the table and hugged it to her chest as if it might ward off further intrusion.

"Friendship." He smiled, as smooth as honey dripping from a spoon. "I'll leave the sonnets in your parlor on my way out. A gift in waiting, so to speak." He withdrew his hand. "And if I could humbly beg an open invitation to come calling? Perhaps next time, I could bring my chess set. Do you play chess, Miss Scott? May I call you Cora?"

She tightened her hold on the tea. Next time, she was going to have Charlie at the house with them. "I play chess." It sounded innocent enough, but this was the man who adorned his desk with a statue of a gladiator wrestling the lion. Which one was he?

Either way, he was nothing like her father.

CHAPTER 20

The wind ripped Ben's newly boiled and rinsed shirt from Cora's hand and slung it toward the dirt. She snatched it in midair and pinned it to the clothesline. If the breeze picked up anymore, she'd have to hang the clothes inside the hallway to save them from a coating of sand.

Charlie ran around the corner from the garden with Jack at his heels. "Ben's home. He's coming through the gate." The boy charged past.

Ben. Home. Her pulse strummed. Thank God, he'd made it back safely. How many cattle had he been able to round up? He'd be at dinner, telling stories of his trip...if he wasn't too busy reading his newly arrived perfumed letter from Pennsylvania. She'd had Charlie take it to the stables before she threw it in the woodpile.

She glowered as she flipped strands of hair from her face. The chignon at the back of her neck hung loose. She should have braided her hair this morning. Puffing her cheeks out, she yanked the ribbon off. A couple of hairpins tumbled to the ground. She'd bother with them later. Smoothing a hand over her wayward hair, she left it to fall free over her shoulders.

Throwing her shoulders back, she strolled to the front of the house. Ben McKenzie should have a chance to see what he was missing.

Dressed in a walnut-colored shirt and leather chaps, Ben dismounted at the hitching post.

Charlie wrapped his arms around the dust-covered man. "You made it back."

"Missed you too." Ben squeezed Charlie's shoulders as Jack yelped at their heels. "No one to ask me any questions."

Cora's steps faltered to a halt. They looked so much like a father and son—the type of father she couldn't even remember. The kind of father Charlie needed. Her heart swelled.

Ben lifted his gaze to hers. Deep hazel irises drank her in. A thin covering of dark beard shadowed his usually clean-shaven cheeks. His lean muscles filled out the shirt more fully now than a month ago when he'd emerged from his sickbed.

Her belly fluttered all the way to her chest.

Ignoring Charlie's questions, he smiled at her. "I got you eighty-seven cattle. Your family's brand and their mavericks. Hired a couple of locals to help drive them to Goodnight's herd."

"That's wonderful." She beamed and clasped her hands to her mouth.

"That's a whole big bunch." Charlie scooped Jack up and wiggled as the dog licked his face. "Did you have to lasso any?"

"Thank goodness, no." Ben held out his fingers to Jack's eager tongue. "I probably need to practice on a fencepost before I try it on a longhorn."

"You probably just gave them orders, and they fell in line like your cavalry troopers," Cora teased as she drifted closer.

Ben nudged his slouch hat off his forehead. "I know it's nothing compared to the herd your family used to have."

"You did better than I dared imagine. After all these years, and too many stray cowhands helping themselves, I'm thankful to have any. I'm sure Mr. Goodnight will look after them well and get *us* a good price at market."

His nose twitched, not quite a flinch, but still enough to destabilize his smile for a second. A reaction to her use of the word *us*? More likely to the mention of Goodnight. How would he react if or when he learned Arthur had come calling?

She should have told Charlie not to mention it. At least not right away. She could still do it. Tell him to keep secrets from Ben? What kind of example would she be setting? Besides, Ben had that perfumed letter waiting for him up in his room. What right did he have to get his back all arched up over her having a gentleman caller?

"Did you see any buffalo?" Charlie set the squirming dog down.

"No, but Juan, the cowhand who helped me, told me about how he'd seen miles of them last spring, west of here in Young Territory. Hundreds of thousands. Watched them from a mesa." Ben unwrapped his canteen strap from his saddle and took a swig. "Maybe we'll see something like that someday."

"On a cattle drive." The boy bubbled. "I have to stay around the ranch and help Cora this summer, but next summer, I could come with you."

Ben's gaze jerked to Cora. His smile dimmed.

Her swallow stuck in her throat. Ben wouldn't be here next year. He had a life to get back to. Did he want her to say it? Correct Charlie before he built his hopes further? But his lips didn't move, and neither did hers. Charlie's voice faded into the background.

Ben broke eye contact and reached into his saddlebag. "I brought you something."

Who was he talking to?

"What is it?" Charlie tried to peak around Ben's back.

"Close your eyes," Ben commanded and placed a length of greenish-tan scales into the boy's outstretched hand.

Charlie's eyes flew open. "A rattlesnake skin." He smoothed a finger over it as if it were silk. Silver-like fragments shimmered in the sunlight. "Did you shoot it?"

"You better believe it. The thing tried to crawl into my bedroll one night. Thankfully, I saw it before I stuck my feet in."

Cora shivered.

Ben pulled a grayish stick-like object out of his pocket and shook it. The hiss-like rattle jarred against her nerves.

"Is that for Cora or me?" Charlie eyed it.

"Definitely not for me." Cora waved it away.

Ben tossed it into the boy's hands. "For you. I brought Cora something else."

"If it's a tarantula, I'm running for the house." Cora placed a hand on her hip.

"I might have to chase you, then." Ben chuckled.

Her lips curved upward. "I'd beat you inside and bolt the doors."

"We'll see about that."

Charlie shook his rattle. "You two could race. Cora's pretty fast, but I bet you could beat her."

"Another day." Ben turned back to his saddlebag. "Sadly, I didn't find any tarantulas this trip, but I did find…"

A small object wrapped in an almost-white handkerchief lay in the palm of his callused hand. Her throat tightened. Whatever lay beneath the cloth, even if it was simple as a thimble, would likely outshine anything Arthur had given her. If she had any sense, she'd yank the book off the parlor table and hide it before Ben set foot in the house.

He unfolded the hankie.

Cora's breath caught. A wooden hair comb, engraved with Indian blanket flowers across the top. The one she'd been eyeing in the glass case at Miller's for months. How did Ben know? Of course, he'd spent too much. He was already going to have to buy supplies on credit. "We…the money…we can't afford…" She should shush before she spoiled the moment. The man deserved a hug, not a scolding. "Thank you." A smile broke across her face.

He toed the dirt. "I figured one little impractical trinket wouldn't break the ranch."

"Trinket?" She caressed the fine craftsmanship. "It's a beautiful treasure. And you know it."

He cocked a glance her way. "I know a treasure when I see it." His eyes twinkled. As if he were talking about more than the comb.

～

Ben stood in the cool overhang of the stable roof, weaving the curry comb in circles along Penny's neck. He'd had enough of the scorching sun for the day. Flecks of embedded dirt loosened from the sorrel's copper-colored hide.

The way Cora's face lit up at the sight of the hair comb had sent his head sailing in the clouds. She glowed as she caressed the engraved flowers—Indian blankets, she'd called them. Giving her anything personal was stepping over a line. He'd planned on waiting to give it to her—a day, a week, maybe even a month—but before he knew it, he'd whipped the present out of his saddlebag. She needed to know how special she was.

He'd momentarily lost track of every word in his head when she came around the corner to greet him with her hair cascading over her shoulders and down her back, like spun honey. Was it possible she'd worn it loose with him in mind? Not likely. She'd probably just been in a hurry to get to the laundry this morning and hadn't bothered to braid it. Still… He smiled to himself.

The back door of the stable swung open, and Charlie plodded out with a bucket of water. The boy had already asked him a couple of dozen questions about his two-week adventure of scouring the county and beyond for the VS cattle brand. "I finished filling up your tub in the back stall. Are you sure you don't want to ask Cora to heat the water over the fire first?"

"I have no intention of troubling your sister. What's the full bucket for?"

"I figured Penny might want another drink."

"I'm sure she does." Ben swiped his forearm across his sweated brow. "What's Cora making for supper tonight?"

Charlie set the bucket in front of the mare. "Venison, turnip greens, and sweet potato pie."

The other two horses at the end of the corral lifted their heads and moseyed toward the water.

"I love sweet potato pie." Ben worked the comb toward Penny's shoulders.

"Me too." Charlie unrolled the snake skin from his pocket. "She didn't make it for Dr. LeBeau when he was here."

The curry comb paused in mid-motion. "The doctor was here while I was away?"

"Yep." Charlie stretched the snake skin along the top rail of the corral.

The bulge in his throat wrenched up, then down. "Was somebody sick?"

"No." Charlie ran his finger along the scales. "He just came to visit. Twice."

"Twice? In two weeks?" Ben pivoted to face the boy.

Charlie shrugged and scuffed his shoe against the short grass. "I got home from hunting right before he left the first time. I had me a squirrel." The boy brightened. "Cora cooked it for supper."

Ben ground the comb against Penny's hide. "Did Dr. LeBeau stay for the meal?"

"No." Charlie lumbered over to the tack shelf attached to the back of the stable. "But he did the second time. We had to eat early so he could head back. I thought he ought to take it in a sack with him and eat along the way. And before that, Cora made me stay around the yard while they played chess on the porch."

"Chess?"

"Took a long time too. Cora wanted me to watch and learn, but I could tell he didn't want me to."

Ben clenched his jaw. "Sounds like the man needs more work to do." In another county. Away from here.

"Gave her a book too."

"What kind of book?"

Penny flicked flies away from her tail.

Charlie fingered a hanging bridle. "Poetry by some guy named Shakespeare. A bunch of flowery, romantic stuff. The man doesn't even know how to talk right. But Cora has it on the parlor table."

Love poetry. Ben spit a wad of saliva on the ground. LeBeau didn't waste any time. Cupid needed to have his arrow bent. Ben clamped his mouth shut. He wouldn't ask more questions. Shouldn't stoop to using the boy as a spy.

Flakes of dirt flew beneath the scouring rake of the comb. He might have known that weasel doctor would set his eye on Cora—the way he'd driven her out in the buggy that day when she could have just ridden her horse home. The whole house call was likely nothing more than a charade on LeBeau's part, an attempt to impress Cora.

Charlie picked up a second curry comb and came along the other side of the mare. "I don't like him."

"Your sister is free to keep company with whom she pleases." His voice ground like pestle to mortar.

Before dinner, Ben took a bath, cold water and all, then donned a clean set of clothes. No frock coat. He wasn't a guest. This was partly his home, for now. But he wore his white cotton shirt and royal-blue waistcoat. After shaving, he would have slapped on a sprinkle or two of bay rum, but he hadn't seen the need to bring along such frivolity when he'd embarked on his mission to rescue Jeb's family.

He had no right to be jealous. No right to object to LeBeau calling on Cora. After all, he was the one with a girl back in Pennsylvania, an unannounced fiancée. But his heart and his temper had thrown logic out the window.

Ben stuck his watch into his waistcoat pocket and straightened his collar. He glared at Olivia's letter, lying on the bunk right where he'd found it when he'd walked in. Fit to be tied after his conversation with Charlie, he'd torn open the envelope and quickly perused the contents. Parties. Eager beaus hanging around the piano as Olivia played. Charity visits. A severe scolding for him even thinking of spending months in a dried-out wilderness chasing cows. A warning that these people might be trying to leech off his good heart. An insistence that he turn the matter over to an attorney, leave enough funds for the sister and brother to move into town where they belonged, and get himself on a stagecoach headed east. She was already looking at houses where he and she might live as husband and wife, a cozy neighborhood between his and her family's well-endowed homes. He'd given his word to her. She wouldn't wait forever. Her final words. Except for a p.s. of whispered allusions to their once-heated kisses.

He expelled a breath and tossed the letter toward the bed. It skidded across and fell to the floor. Olivia's world was a lifetime away.

CHAPTER 21

Ben lumbered in through the wide-open front door. Now that the heat of early summer was upon them, Cora made it a habit to leave every door and window in the house open during the day for maximum airflow and cooling.

"Dinner's ready," Cora called from the kitchen.

But he paused at the parlor entrance before heading down the hall. He'd never set foot in the room before. Had LeBeau?

The breeze ruffled the curtains. Thank goodness, the blistering wind had settled down to a whisper, or the forest-green sofa and high-back chair would be coated in dust. A bookshelf, a couple of oil lamps, and a rocking chair filled out the sparsely populated room. The walnut side table stood empty with nothing more than a doily gracing its surface. No book, but that didn't mean it hadn't been there. He stepped into the room and perused the titles on the shelf, works by Jane Austin, James Fennimore Cooper, and a copy of *The American Frugal House-wife*. He wagered the family Bible was in her room. Had Cora taken the poetry book there, too, or hidden it away from his view?

He turned back into the wide-planked hall.

Cora stood in the kitchen doorway, arms crossed. Her hair hung over her shoulder in a loose braid, no trace of the comb he'd given her. "Can I help you with something?"

"Nothing in particular." Hands in his pockets, he ambled to the kitchen past the barrels and the two cane rockers which lined the hall. "Just checking to make sure there weren't any tumbleweeds blowing in."

She snorted. "If you see any, let me know."

"You can bet on it." He tugged on his waistcoat and slipped between her and the doorjamb.

She glanced back at the parlor and then at him. Her look said she knew exactly what he was up to. If she wanted to bring the subject up, she was welcome to do so. For his part, he wasn't going to say a word.

Charlie dried his hands at the washbasin and hopped into his chair, Jack at his heels. "Can you tell me more about the roundup over dinner? I was hoping you'd bring the cattle by here."

"Maybe next time. I had to hurry them off to Mr. Goodnight."

Charlie pointed to the floor, and Jack sat. "Were there any bulls in the herd? How did you get them to not fight?"

Ben poured himself a cup of coffee and took his seat. "Yep, there were a couple in the herd. Best way to keep them from fighting is to keep them out of each other's territory." He flicked a glare Cora's way as she set a venison roast on the table.

Charlie shot out another string of questions.

Picking over the meal he'd looked forward to for two weeks, Ben answered the boy and responded to Cora's inquiries about the cattle transaction with sparse words. Beneath the table, his knee jerked up and down faster than a horse trot. It was all he could do to not drum his fingers on the table.

Halfway through the meal, Cora's eating picked up speed.

Chomping her food, she finished before Charlie and sat there, hands clasped, lips pursed.

As Charlie scooped his last bite of pie into his mouth, Cora nodded to the skillet on the grill. "Why don't you take Jack outside and feed him the scraps?"

"He'll love that." The boy jumped up. "Then maybe you can read to me and Ben."

"Not tonight. I'm sure Ben's tired." She placed her palms on the table. "After you finish with Jack, I want you to take the horses into the stable. I'll read you a quick Bible story before bed."

Ben swallowed the rest of his coffee. If she wanted to talk, he was ready.

Jack, who'd been napping under the table, scurried to his feet and followed Charlie into the hall and out the back.

Cora fiddled with her napkin. "You might as well say it."

"Say what?"

"Whatever is bothering you."

"What makes you think something is bothering me?"

She held her hands wide. "A couple hours ago, you were all excited about your success, and now smoke is practically coming out of your ears."

He blew out a breath. "You exaggerate, Miss Scott."

"'Miss Scott'?" She crossed her arms. "Charlie told you about the doctor coming to visit, didn't he?"

He leaned forward and pushed his plate out of the way. "Yes. Was it supposed to be a secret?"

"Of course not. It's none of your concern. The doctor merely—"

"Don't you mean Arthur?"

She blew out a breath. "Charlie told you that as well?"

He shrugged.

She narrowed her eyes. "Well, I'm not the one receiving

perfumed letters with the cursive scribbled so poorly that a body can hardly read who it's addressed to."

"You read it?"

She swatted a fly. "Only the envelope. To make sure of who it was addressed to. I could care less what it had inside."

He cocked his eyebrows. "Is that why you sat around on the porch all afternoon drinking tea with the overly friendly neighborhood doctor?"

"My keeping company with Arthur has nothing to do with you."

"For your information, I threw the letter behind my bunk."

She jutted out her chin. "That sounds about like what you'd do with a letter from a woman pouring out her affection on you."

He pushed up from the table. This woman! Back turned to her, he flexed his hands at his sides, fighting the urge to clench them. Fighting the urge to turn around, take her in his arms, and kiss her. He had no right. "Send Charlie out with my breakfast in the morning." He shoved his fingers through his hair. "I'll leave day after tomorrow for the widow's in Palo Pinto."

He slammed the door behind him.

~

Cora clanked her silverware against her plate. Let him storm off in a fuss. She'd spoken the truth. Hadn't she? As much as one could string together a clump of facts and yet not have them convey the real story. She clomped her arms down on the table and dropped her forehead to her wrists.

How had the conversation gotten so far off track? What business of hers was it what he did with his letters or who wrote to him? He wasn't her beau. As a matter of fact, she should encourage his entanglement with the perfume princess. Build another wall between Ben and herself. Right. Any such suggestion would die on her tongue. The best she could hope for was to keep her mouth shut, but tonight, she'd failed miserably even at that.

She pushed up from her chair and slung her napkin across the room. How in the world had Ben ended up proposing to some upper class flirt? Influence from his family? Maybe it was the laudanum, and now that he was free of its influence...

The looks he gave her sometimes jellified her knees and filled her stomach with butterflies. It couldn't all be just her imagination. There had to be something to it, especially the way he'd fumed all evening over LeBeau's visits.

She leaned over the dry sink by the window and slid back the curtain. Ben wasn't in sight, but the chop of an ax boomed through the air. Surely, he wasn't chopping wood. That was Charlie's chore, and they already had a pile big enough to last two or three days.

She should find him and make amends. Tell him it'd be fine with her if he never spoke to Olivia again. Tell him that Arthur wasn't the man she wanted to come calling. What if something happened while Ben was away? Rounding up cattle across country he didn't know? And who could be certain when the Comanche or Kiowa might strike? She shuddered. There were no guarantees.

Rubbing her hands up and down her arms, she slipped across the hall to her bedroom for a better view, the room which had once been her parents'. Kneeling on her bed, she peeked out.

In the half dark, Ben stood at the woodpile, swinging away at a log on the chopping block. *Smack.* The blade came down with a vengeance. Split in half, two sections toppled off the block. He swiped his wrist across his brow and raked his fingers through his dark hair. He'd unbuttoned his shirt at the neck, and his waistcoat lay atop the rain barrel. A fine-looking man. And the most stubborn one she'd ever met. What would it be like to have those strong, muscular arms wrapped around her?

Goodness. She shoved the curtains aside and yanked the shutters closed, blocking out sound and light and encasing the room in heat. What had gotten into her? Spring? Not to mention, she was twenty-four years old, on her way to becoming a spinster.

That's why she'd allowed Arthur to come calling. To bolster her heart's resistance to a man with invisible chains.

CHAPTER 22

*B*en awoke with a start into pitch black. Why?

Ruff-ruff. Jack barked in the yard. The dog was supposed to be in the house.

Ben swung his legs over the side of the bunk. He grabbed his trousers and stumbled to the window, banging his knee on a chair.

Ruff-Ruff.

Charlie's voice drifted upward. "C'mon, Jack."

What was the boy doing outside? Worried about raiders, Cora forbade Charlie to leave the house in the middle of the night. She had him use the chamber pot instead.

Ben shoved the window up. Cool air whisked inward. Moonlight lit the yard.

Dressed in trousers but no shirt, Charlie grabbed Jack's collar and dragged him toward the porch. The pup stiffened his legs and clawed the dirt like some mule destined for a bath, forcing the boy to pick him up.

A dead stillness pervaded the night. The air hung heavy.

Ben glanced toward the palisade walls. The gate...it almost looked as if it were ajar. Not wide open, but not closed either.

Couldn't be. He'd checked it tonight as he always did when he was home. *Home.* But it looked… A chill shivered through him.

Ruff-ruff. Jack squirmed out of Charlie's arms and ran in a circle around his feet.

Ben bolted for his holster at the bedside. Had the Colt in his hands by the time he made it back to the window.

A shadow by the pecan tree moved.

"Get in the house," Ben yelled to Charlie down below. "Now."

The boy stooped to scoop up the dog.

The shadow became a man, bow raised and arrow nocked.

Ben squeezed the Colt's trigger. The man dropped.

A war whoop rang out. A man jumped from behind the oak. An arrow zinged by Ben's cheek and plunked behind him. Ben fired. The front cabin door slammed open, and Cora bolted onto the porch, dressed in nothing but her chemise.

Ben unloaded his gun in the direction of the oak, providing cover.

An Indian on horseback charged from the other side of the house. Cora lunged and hauled Charlie onto the porch.

Ben lifted his Colt, one bullet left, and set the sight on the Indian's bare, painted chest.

"*Kee! Kee!*" The Indian yelled and held his hand toward the oak. Two eagle feathers dangled from a scalp lock affixed to the crown of his head. A rifle lay across his lap. "No fight." He lifted his chin toward Ben's window.

Ben's finger twitched on the trigger. One bullet. Not enough. His rifle stood in the corner on the other side of the bed, loaded. But what could happen in the time it took him to retrieve it? The front door hadn't slammed shut yet.

A scuffle on the porch. More words from the rider.

Another Indian yanked Cora and Charlie into the yard, his grip locked onto one of their arms each. Stumbling beside her captor, Cora shook her head at Ben. *Don't provoke them?*

Trailing behind, Jack growled and nipped at the intruder's foot. The Indian kicked the pup. Jack yelped.

"Don't." Charlie tried to jerk free.

"Good puppy. We're all right." Cora crooned a soothing note toward the pet.

The Indian on horseback, dressed in nothing but a breech-clout and buckskin leggings, glanced from them to Ben. Two more Indians emerged from the shadows of the outbuildings, knives drawn. From behind the oak, the shooter stepped out, arrow nocked and bow drawn.

The leader rested his hand on his rifle. "Come down."

Ben lowered his Colt. "Take me. Leave them."

"Down." The man pointed at the ground.

Heart pounding, Ben backed away from the window. *Dear God, protect them. Please.* He snatched his gun belt from the peg on the bunk post. Hands shaking, he spun out the chamber on his Colt and fished out five cartridges from his cartridge box. He shoved them in one at a time before grabbing his cap box and affixing a cap to each nipple on the gun. Load secured, he spun the chamber back. Half a minute at most. On the battlefield, speed could make a difference between life and death.

Colt in one hand and his rifle in the other, he clamored down the steps to the ground floor of the stables. His eyes clawed at the darkness, lest the enemy already be inside. But no, the door was secure, the bolt still in place. The horses stirred in their stalls. Voices sounded in the yard, in a language he didn't understand.

Praying he wasn't making a mistake that would cost all of their lives, he set his rifle to the side of the door behind a pitchfork and stuck his revolver beneath a clump of straw. Going out there unarmed might be the most foolish thing he'd ever done. But all they'd have to do is hold a knife to Cora or Charlie, and he'd drop his gun in a matter of seconds. Best leave it here where he might have a chance to grab it if needed and where they wouldn't readily find it.

Tossing the bolt on the ground, he stepped into the yard.

An Indian with two long braids and a face smeared with red paint latched onto him from behind and shoved him toward the mounted leader.

Pale in the moonlight, Cora met his gaze. The wind whipped her hair and the hem of her thin cotton chemise. Her eyes flared with warning. If only he could read their full message.

He ground his molars. If these men touched her... His hands clenched.

The leader dismounted. "I Wolf Heart. Comanche. You"—he jutted his finger at Ben—"killed my warrior."

The man behind jerked Ben against him and slid a knife blade a hair's breadth from Ben's Adam's apple.

"Your man"—Ben's swallow stuck in his throat—"was about to kill a defenseless boy."

"Not boy." Wolf Heart waved his rifle toward Ben. "You. Had orders not to shoot boy."

"I saw him ready to shoot." Sweat dampened Ben's back and underarms. "So I shot."

Wolf Heart uttered Comanche words.

The knife came away from Ben's throat as a fist struck him upside the head. Ben staggered.

Cora gasped. "Don't hurt him."

A second warrior grabbed Charlie while the other tightened his hold on Cora.

Ben threw back his shoulders. "I shot your man. Do what you want with me. Let them go. Warriors don't stoop to bullying women and children." Arms bent at his elbows, he held his clenched hands close to his body, ready to defend or strike.

Wolf Heart's eyes narrowed. "You protect Little Wolf?"

"Little Wolf?" Ben glanced at Charlie. Did this Indian know the boy? "If that's what you call him, yes. I am his protector."

Wolf Heart nodded to the Indian beside Ben.

The brute cast his knife away and slammed a fist into Ben's jaw. Pain seared upward to his ear. Ben stumbled back but dodged a left hook. Would fighting back save their lives or endanger them? Red-face's foot struck Ben's side, and another fist followed.

A flash of memory. Andersonville. The robber gang trying to steal Jeb's boots. Ben spun out and whammed his shoulder into the Indian's chest. The man's fists slammed into Ben's gut. Ben drove his knuckles into the man's throat. Red-face gasped. The blows ceased. Ben kneed the man's gut and dodged a foot. They fell on the ground in a mess of fists and blows.

Not Red-face anymore, but Duggar, the leader of the robber gang. Grimy, scarred, a killer, willing to take man's life for a thimble full of peas. Ben head-butted the man and rolled on top of him. Pinning him to the ground, he rammed his hand against the enemy's throat and halted. The man's eyes bugged, and his free hand slammed into Ben's arm. Chest-heaving, blood dripping from his mouth, Ben held firm, blinking as blood or sweat marred his vision. Red-face. Not Dugger. Cora and Charlie would pay if he harmed this man further.

Ben's grip loosened a fraction. Red-face jabbed deep into Ben's armpit, throwing him off. Both men scrambled to their feet.

"Kee. No more." Wolf Heart stepped forward. He waved his hand at the warrior, and Red-face limped off to the porch muttering under his breath.

Limbs shaking, Ben swiped his mouth. "Now you let the girl and the boy go?"

"Never planned to take. Wanted see you fight. See if you able protect Little Wolf. See if you good enough to show him how to be a man. "

"A man? So you attacked us? What if the boy had been killed?" Ben scowled and wrapped an arm around his aching gut.

"My men might have shot you. Not him."

An acid taste soured his mouth. "He's like a son to me."

"Hmmph." Wolf Heart folded his arms. "And how long you stay? One moon, two moons, summer and a winter? Making man takes many seasons."

Ben spit. What kind of a commitment was this man looking for?

"Boy needs to learn. Needs father. Or I take him to his people. I his uncle. I watch. You not do good enough, I take him."

Cora sputtered behind them where a warrior held her fast. "You...can't take him. His mother, your sister, brought him here for us to raise. For me to raise."

"Woman not enough for boy. Need father."

"He'll have a father. Sooner or later. When I marry."

Wolf Heart shrugged. "Marry this man."

Ben's stomach dropped.

"He..." Cora pulled free of the warrior holding her and stepped forward, hands clasped. "This man came here as a friend of my brother to help us. His home is far away toward the rising sun. He has—"

"His home here with Little Wolf. Or I take the boy. Here and now." The crow's feet at the corners of his eyes deepened. A scar cut across his cheek. The man stood tall, feet planted firm, and rifle in hand. He meant what he said.

"I recognize you." Cora pleaded. "You spared my life once. The day your men—"

"I remember. If your heart were not good, I take the boy now. I give you chance keep him for a few more winters."

Ben's tongue scratched his mouth like sandpaper. He shuddered a glance at Cora and then Wolf Heart. "I will be the boy's father."

"You take woman as wife. Make family."

Ben's knees wobbled down to his toes. "In my own time. A man decides for himself when to take the woman. Wins her affection first." They had to at least make a show of complying.

"You don't have to do this." Cora's voice scraped his heart.

Wolf Heart jutted his chin. "I watch. My men watch. Not do you harm. You do good. You make family. You keep boy more winters. But one moon when older, I come for him, show him way of his people."

Ben straightened. "I'm taking my family inside our home. You and your men leave. And next time you want to visit your nephew, knock at the gate."

Wolf Heart chuckled. "You talk big." He waved toward the house. "Woman, take care your warrior. Bleeding."

Cora blinked at him.

Before she could react, Ben took her by the arm and motioned Charlie to his side as he limped toward the house. "We'll figure it out later," he whispered as he led his family onto the porch.

Marry Cora? Be a father to Charlie. His mind reeled. Stay in Texas? Break his engagement. Give up the newspaper? The back of his lower ribs throbbed. And bile from the punches to his gut burned his throat. Not to mention the cacophony of aches that pulsated throughout his face and head.

But as Cora lowered the bar across the now-shut door and clicked the lock, he pivoted and pulled her into his arms with no intention of letting go. He could have lost her and Charlie.

ora sank against Ben's chest like parched earth soaking up rain, her body trembling almost as much as Ben's battered one. He could have been killed. A chill swept over her body. Her hands dug into the back of Ben's rumpled undershirt and held on tight. Thank God, Ben was alive, standing, and breathing. Thank God, they hadn't taken Charlie. That they were all still here safe.

Charlie came alongside and hugged them both.

Ben slipped one hand from Cora and wrapped his arm around the boy's shoulders.

Jack scurried around their feet, panting.

Safe. Cora bit her lip and squeezed her eyes shut. She choked back a sob. She wouldn't cry. Strong and steady beneath the hard wall of his chest, Ben's heart pounded against her cheek. His warmth permeated the dirty linen of his shirt and the thin cotton of her chemise, drawing her like a humming-bird to nectar.

Moisture dropped onto the back of her head. A metallic smell. Blood.

Her breath caught. What was she thinking? Releasing her hold, she pulled back a few inches, her hands still lingering on his sides as if they belonged there. "You're bleeding." Every inch of her wobbled.

"I'll be all right." His words slurred across his swollen lip, an open wound. Another cut marred his cheek just below his puffed-up eye.

Her fingers trembled to brush the hair from his brow, but would such a touch cross a line? "You need looking after." She tugged him toward the parlor.

He hesitated in the doorway. "The kitchen. I'm too dirty for your fancy furniture."

"It's the parlor or my bed. I'm not sitting you down in any hardback kitchen chair." She led him to the sofa, navigating by the hallway light, which filtered into the dark room. "Charlie, fetch me a pan of water and some rags."

Ben groaned as he eased down onto the cushion and settled back, resting his head against the wall.

She grabbed her shawl from the stuffed chair where she'd left it. Draping it over her shoulders, she tied it in a knot across her chest before lighting a lamp and turning back to him.

How badly had he been hurt? Her gaze trailed over his dirt-smeared undershirt and trousers to his bare feet. "You didn't even put your shoes on."

He swiped his sleeve across a trickle of blood on his chin. "Can't take time for shoes when a boy's life is at stake."

If this man didn't hush, she was going to have to kiss him. Instead, she grabbed a doily and gently touched it to his cut mouth.

A crevice formed across his brow. "The doily will never be the same."

Neither would she. "I don't care about the doily." She sat beside him. The fold of her chemise brushed against his trouser leg.

"In the morning, you might."

"Taking care of you is more important than a scrap of crochet or linen."

His good eye widened. "I'm still the same man I was at dinner, Cora."

"I didn't quite know what I was talking about at dinner."

His eyebrows shot up, along with a corner of his mouth.

Charlie pattered in. "Here you go." Water threatened to slush over the sides of the basin. A towel dangled from his arm.

Cora hopped up and relieved him of his load.

Charlie knelt on the other side and patted Ben's arm. "I'm sorry they hurt you."

Ben lifted the boy's chin and bore into him with a hard gaze that matched his tone. "They could have hurt you too. Don't you ever go out there alone at night again."

Charlie blinked back tears. "Jack wanted to go out."

"We don't care what Jack wants." Cora dipped a clean cloth in the cool water. "You need to do as you're told."

Charlie swiped his eyes. "I will, but they're not going to bother us anymore. Wolf Heart said so."

"We're not going to take his word for it." Cora dabbed the cloth to Ben's lip, her elbow grazing his chest.

Ben winced. "We'll see if our horses are still in the stable tomorrow morning. That would be the first sign that maybe Wolf Heart meant what he said." His words came out thick. "My body's not feeling their goodwill." He coughed. A grimace curled his lips. "Fetch a bucket, Charlie."

The boy scurried to the kitchen.

Ben coughed again and bent forward, elbows on his knees.

"You all right?" Cora scooted out of the way.

"My stomach." He choked.

Charlie clamored across the threshold.

Ben grabbed the bucket, hung his head down, and retched.

When he finished, Cora gave him a wet cloth to wipe his mouth, then handed the bucket to Charlie. "Cover it and put it by the back door. No one's setting foot outside till morning. Then, bring Ben a cup of water and me the vinegar jug."

Would there be a dead body waiting for them in the yard in the morning, or would the Comanche take their own with them? Her throat tightened.

Hand to Ben's shoulder, she eased him back until he reclined against the wall once more. "Enough talking for now. You rest while I tend to your wounds."

He nodded and laid his hands across his waist as she dabbed the cloth to his facial wounds, tinting the basin water red.

Charlie brought the glass of water and watched as Ben's Adam's apple bobbed with each swallow. "Ben's going to be all right, Cora." Brow in a deep furrow, the boy knelt and placed both palms on Ben's thigh. "You don't have to worry."

Eyes barely open, Ben handed her the glass and ruffled Charlie's hair. "Remember what your sister read to us about Daniel in the lion's den and David in the caves hiding from Saul? God protected them."

Charlie laid his cheek on his hand and gazed up at Ben. "God will protect us?"

Ben laid his head against the wall. "Yes, He will."

Would He? What about Jeb? What about her uncle who had died at the hands of the Comanche? And her dear mother who hadn't lived to see the death of the husband who'd brought both pain and love? Would her mother have been relieved or broken with more grief? Cora bit back her doubt and poured vinegar on a rag. Her hand hovered over his chest.

Ben squinted his good eye at her and whispered, "What's wrong?"

Fear. The past. The future. God help her. She'd fallen for the man before her. She shivered.

"You cold?" Concern filled his voice. The purplish hue beneath his left eye and over the lid continued to deepen.

A slight snore broke the silence. They glanced at Charlie. He'd fallen asleep, head still on Ben's leg.

"The boy can stay in the parlor with me tonight if it's all right with you," Ben whispered. "He's probably still shaken up."

"So am I." The words slipped out.

Their gazes met. "What do you propose?"

Best not say it. Better to wipe the possibility from her mind. "I need to finish cleaning you up." She touched the vinegar to the cut on his cheek.

He flinched. "I could carry him to your room for you."

"You'll do no such thing. Not in your condition." She wrinkled her nose at the smell of the liquid and continued to dab away.

More vinegar and more winces until she finished with his face.

The shutters rattled. The wind. Nothing but the wind. Still, her heart pattered. *Dear Lord, please look after us...*

She wrung out the rag. Ben didn't stir. Surely, he hadn't gone to sleep too. She touched his undershirt's torn collar, close to where his pulse throbbed. His eye opened.

She bit her lip. "The warrior hit your chest pretty hard, and your stomach. I should check—"

"Never mind." He latched onto her hand. "I can take care of the rest."

"Of course." Her cheeks heated. "I can go into the other room and leave you with the basin."

"It can wait until tomorrow. I'm sure it's nothing but bruises."

"Bruises can be serious."

"Nothing water's going to help. I'll heal." His gaze caressed her face as he slowly released her hand. "You never said if you were cold."

"Shaken. That's all." Trembling. Hungry for the comfort of his arms. On the verge of throwing good sense out the window. "I'll go get blankets and pillows."

"For Charlie and me?"

The wind rattled the shutters again. Thunder rumbled in the distance.

"All of us."

All of us. Had she really said that? Ben gaped at her. In a flurry, she scurried across the threshold, scolding herself as she shuffled down the hall. No doubt she'd temporarily lost her mind. But she had no intention of sleeping in the back room by herself, jumping at every creak of the house.

In her room, she stripped her bed of its quilt, then dug in the cedar chest for a couple of blankets. Arms loaded and a trail of bedclothes dragging around her feet, she trudged back to the parlor.

By the time she returned, Ben had scooted Charlie onto the

sofa and moved the end table with the cleaning and doctoring supplies off to the side.

He stood when she entered. "I'll help with that."

"No, you sit." She dropped the blankets and pillows onto the center rug, heat crawling up her neck to her scalp. What in the world was she doing? "I'll fix a bed for me and Charlie on the far side of the carpet, and one for you closer to the sofa. Just like when we camped out, except no stars, rocks, or critters." She knelt and worked to create order out of the jumble.

He lowered himself down to the edge of the sofa. "You never can tell when there might be a critter around."

Was he trying to make fun of her, or merely teasing her? His leg jiggled up and down. Obviously, ill at ease with her impropriety. If she had any sense, she'd snatch up a blanket for herself and go hide in her room.

"You probably think I'm ridiculous." She smoothed her grandmother's quilt across the top layer for her and Charlie, then stretched out her thickest bedcover as padding for where Ben would sleep.

He studied her for a moment. "I think you're rattled like the rest of us. And no one needs to be alone tonight."

"Thank you." She extinguished the lamp as Ben moved Charlie to the side of her bedding closest to the middle of the carpet.

The soft glow of the hall lamp she'd lowered to half wick cast long shadows and saved them from inky darkness.

As Ben slipped his hands from beneath Charlie, the boy's eyes flickered open, his pupils huge. "I want to stay with Ben." He latched onto Ben's ankle.

"Don't worry." Cora knelt on the other side of him. "We're camping out in the parlor. Ben will be here."

The boy's eyelids slipped closed as his head sank into the pillow. Cora tucked the blanket up to his chin, her gaze lingering on Ben's swollen eye, lip, and bruised face. "I'm sorry they hurt you." Her voice was barely more than a breath.

Ben's gaze locked onto her. "I would do anything to protect you and Charlie." His voice had thickened.

Goosebumps spread across her limbs. She'd been horrible to him for weeks. Too long. And he treated her like this? A wellspring of gratitude burst forth from her heart. Before she could think better of it, she reached across, grabbed Ben by the shoulders, and kissed him on the cheek.

He startled.

Warmth cascaded through her.

She jerked away from him before she did something even more wanton, like kiss him on the mouth. Tumbling backward, she landed on her bottom. Would her legs even work anymore?

Ben gaped at her, his one good eye opened wide and his lips parted, one corner of his mouth still swollen and puffy.

What had she done?

Turning from him, she dove under her blankets, curled into a ball, and pulled the pillow over her head. Suggesting they sleep in the same room, then laying her hands on him and kissing him? He'd be convinced she belonged in a saloon or worse. How could she ever show her face to him again?

CHAPTER 23

ora! Ben couldn't even swallow. He rocked from his heels and dropped his knees to the carpet. *Cora.* Every thought in his head scattered to kingdom come. Sparks exploded within, obliterating the cacophony of aches and pains. He scrubbed his hand over his face, but nothing could wipe away his smile. She'd kissed him. Probably out of gratitude. He'd best get his head straight, not read too much into it. But his heart was practically doing somersaults.

Charlie mumbled and rolled over. Ben placed his hand on the boy's chest. *Don't wake up, please.*

"Cora?" His voice dipped.

Her silken hair flayed behind her, she squeezed the pillow tighter to her head as if to block out even a hint of sound.

"Cora..." Did she really expect him to lie down and go to sleep after that without a word? He reached across the divide, his hand dangling in the air. A touch might spook her. He curled his fingers inward and withdrew.

Best keep his hands and his thoughts to himself before he scared Cora into the next county. He retreated to his side of the carpet and edged beneath his blankets one limb at a time, gritting out a couple of groans.

His heart beat like a drum as he pressed his cheek against the borrowed pillow. Cora's pillow from her bed, scented with soap and rosewater. One deep inhale, and it was as if she, not the covered goose-feather fluff, was in his arms.

Across the carpet and on the other side of Charlie, she shifted around. Facing the wall, she burrowed deeper beneath the covers.

Regretting her action? Afraid of his reaction?

His breath roared in his ears. Just as well she had the pillow over her head. Otherwise, she might think he was having a heart attack. Where was a clear thought when he needed one? He'd never sleep if he didn't say something.

Maybe it'd best if he acted as if the kiss hadn't happened. He could address the real reason Cora wasn't herself tonight. She was afraid. That's why she was in here on the floor with him and Charlie. She needed to be comforted.

Thunder boomed. Lightning shown through tiny gaps in the chinking in the logs. The wind had blown up a storm.

Movement on the porch. His ears perked up. A rhythmic *thump-thump*. The rocking chair.

Cora squirmed within her burrow.

He projected his whisper. "It's just the wind."

She loosened her stranglehold on the pillow. Maybe she was awake.

"God will keep us safe. We don't have to be afraid."

She blew out a breath and rolled onto her back. "I'm not bothered by the storm."

"The Comanche?"

Silence followed within the parlor except for Charlie's breathing.

Cora clung onto her quilt with both hands. "It's not always

like David and Daniel. Sometimes...God allows people to get hurt or die." Her voice sounded small in the dark.

How many men and friends had he lost in the war, Jeb the best among them? Men who'd never see home again. But that wasn't what Cora needed to hear tonight. He raised up on his forearm. "You're right. But I don't believe he brought me to Texas to have one of us die. We have to trust He will protect us and work everything out for the best. That you...that we're done with grieving." If only he could engrave such faith onto his heart and never waver.

Cradling an arm beneath her head, she rolled to face him across the distance. "I don't trust easily."

I've noticed. "I understand."

She whispered, "I admire your faith."

He sniffed back a snort. His faith was riddled with holes. He'd prayed for the Lord's healing. From his battlefield and Andersonville memories, from the nightmares, from the cravings for laudanum. Would he ever be the man he'd once been? Even now, the thirst for the medicine throbbed in the back of his mind. A half dose, even a few drops, would take the edge off the pain and settle his stomach.

And forever lose him the respect he'd fought so hard to gain.

"My faith is patched together." He rubbed his thumb across the soft linen of the pillow. His eye throbbed, and so did his lip. His whole body ached, but none of that mattered. Cora had kissed him. "Your courage and determination are two qualities I admire about you. Your love for Charlie, and the way you came back out here to make a life for you and him."

She sniffed. "Most of the folks in town would call me foolhardy."

"No. It's just that it's a huge undertaking for two." Dare he venture such a prospect? "You need a...partner."

She pushed up on an elbow. "Temporarily. Until you get us on our feet. You...have a life back in Philadelphia."

He blew out his cheeks. Entanglements, not a life. "Is that where you want me to go?" He fought to temper the words into an honest question, not an accusation. "Back to Pennsylvania?"

She bunched the quilt in her hand. "I don't know."

He should shut his mouth. But more words spilled forth. "Because that's not what I want. I'm going to write the letter I should have written weeks ago. I'm going to break my betrothal to Olivia." As if that were his only tie there, and not his promise to his father.

Her breath caught.

Rain pattered on the roof.

The quilt slipped from her shoulders. "I won't allow you to sacrifice yourself for me and Charlie. If you're saying this because of Wolf Heart, we'll find another way. Charlie and I can look after ourselves after you help us get the ranch up and running. We'll move into town if we have to."

Give up on her dream? Was she afraid of burdening him, or just afraid of him, period? Maybe the kiss had been all gratitude, and she couldn't wait for him to depart. But he couldn't accept that. "It wouldn't be a sacrifice. I have no intention of marrying a woman I don't love."

She bit her lip. "You're talking about Olivia?"

"I was wrong to propose to her."

She rubbed the quilt edge between her thumb and forefinger. "Why did you?"

Why did he? He ran his hand over his hair and exhaled. How had he gotten himself into talking about this? He could tell her it was none of her business. But that wasn't true, not if he hoped to win her affection. "I thought I was in love with Olivia when we first courted. And I probably was." That sure made him sound steadfast and faithful. His stomach clenched.

"But when I returned from war in 1865, I wasn't the same man. I acted as if everything was as it had been, in hopes that it would be again. I sought to fulfill expectations, but I was only going through the motions." That and too many hours spent in each other's arms. Too much laudanum soaking his brain and dulling his heart. "On the eve of our betrothal announcement, I realized I couldn't do it. I had a promise to keep to Jeb, and if I failed at that, I wouldn't forgive myself. Coming to Texas to keep that promise felt like the first real thing in my life since I was taken prisoner."

Her brow furrowed. Tracing a line on the carpet with her finger, she cast her gaze to the floor. "Love is risky."

"Yes."

"And scary."

His swallow stuck in his throat. "In what way?"

"My mother married for love."

He ground his molars. A mistake. A pain shot from his injured jaw deep in his skull. He'd had enough of being compared to her father. He strove for a neutral tone, but his words came out with a bite. "Did you ever ask your mother if she had it to do over again what she would have done?"

She flinched.

He should shut his mouth, but he pushed up to his feet. "Are you going to give up on love? The real question isn't what your mother did or didn't do. It's what you are going to do. Are you going to allow your father to rule your life beyond the grave?"

Her hand clenched in her lap. "How dare you?"

"Because I care about you. Because I want to court you." *Because I love you.* He spread his hands wide, then let them drop to his sides.

She gaped at him.

His stomach knotted again. He needed air.

Pivoting, he strode into the hallway, slipped the front door key from the doorjamb, and inserted it in the lock.

Coming up from behind him, she grabbed his arm. "What are you doing?"

"Getting some air."

"You can't. It's not safe."

"They're gone. No one's out in the storm." The lock clicked, and he opened the door to a bluster of wind. Rain smacked him in the face and pelted his shirt. The branches of the oak waved like a madman. Lightning struck the ground beyond the palisade.

Cora tugged him from the threshold and shut the door. "I don't want you going."

"I was only looking out. Not leaving."

Strands of damp hair clung to her face. Droplets dripped from her chin to her chemise and shawl. Beautiful, wounded doe eyes stared up at him. "You're the most stubborn, hardheaded man I know." She shivered.

"I'm sorry I lost my temper." His voice dipped. "It's been a rough night. Not a time for confrontation."

Rubbing her hands over her arms, she stepped closer, her toes within inches of his. "Jeb meant the world to me. He and I were close. Best friends."

Was that loss another layer further encasing her heart? "I know his leaving hurt you a lot," he whispered across his swollen lip. "He regretted—"

She held up her hand. "Jeb gave me many things and did so much for me over the years." She swallowed. "But you...are the best thing Jeb ever did for me."

His eyebrows shot up.

Tears filled her eyes. "I don't want you to go."

The long, drawn-out last word resonated down to his knees and made his legs wobble. He touched a fingertip to the fringe on her shawl, then nudged a strand of hair from her eyes with his knuckle.

He wrapped his arms around her and nestled her to his chest. Soft curves pressed against him. It was all he could do to keep his hands still and his lips to himself. "There's no other place on this earth I want to be. No other girl I want to court."

He could not fail her. He would not fail her.

CHAPTER 24

Cora kicked a hickory limb out of her path as she led her bay sorrel to the corral. Mud oozed around her hard leather shoes. Robins warbled from the nearby hickory trees.

Wolf Heart had left their horses alone, thankfully. And the man Ben shot was nowhere in sight. Was he dead or wounded? Thankfully, the Comanche had taken him with them when they left, and the rain had washed away all traces, except for a red tint coloring the sparse grass around the spot where he had fallen.

How did Ben feel about the possibility of potentially having killed someone? No doubt he'd killed many during the war.

The way he'd held her last night in the foyer had set her whole body atremble. She'd turned into a pool of warmth, incapable of speech. She'd nestled her head against his breast and clung to the back of his undershirt, unable to let go. They'd stood like that for immeasurable heartbeats. Until her legs felt as if they'd give out, and reason at last reigned.

Love. How had it crept in past the wall of her heart? If she had any sense, she'd shove it right back out again.

Sandy nickered, and Cora rubbed the mare's neck. "Morning, girl." Horse hooves sank into the moist earth as they walked.

Cora unlatched the corral gate. An oak limb lay across the top rail of a section on the far side. But other than a teetering post, the corral had survived the storm intact. She'd tiptoed out of the parlor, stepping over Charlie, careful not to wake him or Ben. She needed time to think, not be bombarded by the boy's questions. Plus, Ben needed to rest. His poor right eye had swollen shut, and the right side of his mouth wasn't much better. The way that warrior had pummeled him, Ben might very well have a cracked rib or two, as well.

He'd kissed her hair as she slipped from his arms in the foyer last night. A sweet, gentle kiss that almost buckled her knees. She'd scurried away, almost tripping over Charlie, and dropped into the sweetest sleep she could recall, dreaming of being in his arms.

My goodness, she had to get ahold of herself while she had any sense left. The best thing she could do would be to act as if nothing had happened between them. Like trying to contain the banks of a river after a hard spring rain.

~

*B*en sipped his soup. Cora had butchered a chicken in his honor. The steaming broth soothed his unsettled stomach and fortified his battered body. Chunks of carrot, rutabaga, noodles, and chicken bobbed in his bowl.

A fresh breeze wafted in the open kitchen window, offering relief from the heat of the day and the cook fire that simmered in the hearth.

Cora swiped a thin line of sweat from her brow as she settled down in the chair across from him. "Would you like some cider?" She raised a pitcher.

"Yes, please." He held up his porcelain cup.

She'd avoided eye contact and kept him at a pole distance all day long. Any trace of a smile had been so muted that one might almost need a magnifying glass to detect the upturn of her lips. Yet she'd sent Charlie to him with wet cloths, and poultices and salves for his facial wounds and the bruises along his ribs. She'd even sliced a slab of smoked venison for him to lay across his eye. In addition, she'd cooked a delicious meal and served it in a porcelain bowl instead of tin.

As she poured the cool tan liquid into his cup, the sweet apple scent mixed with the savory aroma of the soup. His stomach rumbled for more.

Her gaze flickered away from his as she plunged her spoon into her soup. Did she regret their unguarded moments of comfort and cuddling in the hallway last night, or was she merely shy and embarrassed? The woman was a myriad of palisade walls more impenetrable than oak, but she'd gifted him a step inside the gate last night. He would find his way in again.

"The soup is delicious." He swallowed another bite. "Thank you. It's just what I needed."

"You're welcome." She nudged a strand of hair from her forehead. The silky knot at the back of her head had loosened over the course of the day. A couple ribbons of chestnut tresses framed her face. Where was the comb he'd given her?

Charlie's spoon clunked against his bowl. "She wants to feed you well and get you strong because you're our protector."

Cora squirmed in her chair. "That's not exactly what I said."

A smile tickled the left corner of Ben's mouth. "What did she say, Charlie?"

"Never you mind." She narrowed her eyes at Ben, but nothing could hide the rosy pink that blossomed across her cheeks. "And Charlie, you need to finish your dinner so you can go take care of the horses."

Charlie swallowed a bite. "And I'll lock the stable. Ben's going to sleep inside with us tonight, isn't he?"

Ben tipped his spoon toward the boy. "I'm double-checking the locks on everything before I turn in. I'll be fine in my loft tonight."

Charlie's countenance sank. "Please sleep in the house. I don't want you hurt."

Ben glanced at Cora. "I'll just be across the yard."

"But what if we need you here?" Charlie's voice faltered.

Cora stirred her soup. "You're welcome to sleep in the parlor again tonight. I'll be in my room, and Charlie in his. I know the sofa or the floor isn't as comfortable—"

"He can have my bed, and I'll take the floor." Charlie beamed.

"I'm not taking anyone's bed." Ben fingered the edge of the table. They were shaken from last night. He couldn't blame them, but how in the world was he supposed to leave on a cattle drive in a few days?

"I'd be fine on the floor." Charlie stood. "I want you to get better."

"Sit." Cora pointed to the boy, then turned to Ben. "It won't hurt Charlie to sleep on the floor one more night. Your poor ribs could use a mattress beneath them."

His living in the loft was one thing, but staying in the house was far from proper. There were probably already rumors going around town. He scrubbed his hand over his jaw.

Cora gnawed her lip, her doe eyes speaking what her tongue would not.

A man had been shot in their yard last night. It could have been one of them. They were his family to protect. "Who am I to argue with the two of you and my ribs?"

"Wise man." She smiled.

The best medicine she'd given him all day. If only his thumping heart could take it as it was likely meant, relief to have a protector in the house, not as *how can we arrange an accidental meeting in the foyer after Charlie's asleep?*

The way Cora had melted against him last night as he'd drawn her into his arms, surely, even for her, their embrace had been about more than fear and protection.

~

Cora stood in front of the beveled dresser mirror in her room. Her hair was a mess. She quickly plucked out the pins and ran a brush through it. This morning, she'd been too focused on tiptoeing out of the parlor to do it up proper. Then, with the housework on top of her wrestling with the chicken and all of that preparation, she'd hardly taken a moment to check her appearance.

Steps on the front porch. Ben and Charlie would be in soon from locking up the stables and checking the gate. She slipped her hand inside her apron pocket and fingered the fine teeth on the wooden comb Ben had given her yesterday. How could it only be yesterday that he'd returned from rounding up her cattle to give to Goodnight?

The way she'd clung to him last night in the hallway... And here she was practically insisting he spend another night in the house. His embrace had very little to do with it. It was just that after the attack, she didn't feel quite safe without his presence now that darkness was falling around them. But would he understand that, or would he read more into it?

She grimaced at her reflection in the mirror—a mirror that had traveled from Tennessee with her mother and should have been sold a year or two ago for supplies. But better to savor her mother's memory than to put cash in her father's hands.

Her throat tightened. No. She would not, could not define Ben by her father's actions. Ben McKenzie had more strength of character than her father could even fathom. If only she could scrub the last few years with her father from her brain.

The front door opened.

Charlie's voice carried down the hall. "I should start wearing moccasins. They're quieter. I could sneak up on prey more easily. Maybe shoot me a big buck. Plus, they wouldn't hurt my feet as much."

Cora lowered her brush to the dresser.

Part of Ben's reply drifted her way. "We'll talk to your sister. You need a hide to make moccasins..."

Charlie needed to learn ranching, not raiding and fighting. Ben was clear on that, wasn't he? Otherwise, the boy would be asking to wear a breechclout and painting his face before she knew it. Charlie was the only family she had left. She had no intention of losing him to the Comanche or anyone else.

Ben had given his word to Wolf Heart that he'd raise the boy. Exactly what did that mean for her and Ben? Would Ben someday sleep in the bed beside her as her husband? Her cheeks flushed. My goodness, she was getting ahead of herself. She'd go back to clerking or take on a position at the new schoolhouse in Weatherford before she'd allow any man to marry her out of obligation.

But what if it was out of...love? *There's no other place I'd rather be. No other girl I'd rather court.* Even now, Ben's words made her legs wobble. But did he mean them? He might have whispered the same thing once upon a time to the lady awaiting him back in Philadelphia.

～

ora strode into the parlor with Ben's comb still in her pocket and her sewing basket on her arm. Best keep her hands busy and her eyes on her thread. Time and distance to think straight, that's what she needed.

Ben's face lit up as he stood, his injured eye half open now in its circle of purplish-blue. "You look mighty fine."

She flipped a few strands and the end of the black velvet ribbon over her shoulder, where her hair cascaded down her back. "It was too hot to leave my hair up."

He cocked his eyebrows.

She stuttered to a halt. Had she really just said that? Too hot to leave it up? My goodness. The man would think she was daft. "I meant, it was too hot to go to the trouble of styling it." The lie didn't sound any better.

The left side of his mouth curved upward in a crooked smile. "That's why I think we should step out on the porch a bit and enjoy the cool air."

She tensed. "Outside?"

"It's not dark yet. And I've got my Colt just in case." He tapped his fingers to the holster that swung from his gun belt.

"I want to come too." Charlie hopped off the stool by the hearth, knife and a slender piece of wood in hand. His dark bangs fell across his forehead.

"No, you stay put, young man." Ben pointed at him. "Your sister and I need to have some grownup time. You can work on whittling your stick."

Her insides jiggled. What if she wasn't ready for grownup time, or whatever that entailed?

Charlie puffed out his chest. "It's an arrow, not a stick."

"Very good. I'll inspect it when we get back."

"You're not going far, are you? It's almost dark."

"We'll be close by." Ben snagged his slouch hat from the parlor table. "Just around the porch."

Charlie nudged a suspender back over his shoulder. "I'll come find you when I finish my arrow."

"No, I'll look at it when I get back in. If you finish early, you can pick a book off the shelf."

"But I need you or Cora to read it to me."

"You sound out the words the best you can till we get back." The firm tone cut off the barrage of objections.

Cora shivered as she stepped onto the porch. An orchestra of cricket chirps filled the air beneath the misty blue dusk. An orange glow hovered on the western horizon. What a beautiful evening. She should relish the chance to escape the stuffy confines of the parlor. Still, she rubbed her arms and scanned the distant bluffs.

"Would you like me to fetch your shawl?" Ben stepped alongside her.

"No, thank you. It's just me being ridiculous. Seeing shadows where there's nothing." The hickory wood plank creaked beneath her footfall.

He hooked his thumb over his gun belt. "You have every right to be concerned. But we're on a rise here. We can see everything for miles. And they can't harm us unless they get inside the gate."

She gnawed her lip. "They got over last night." The warrior's sinew-tough hands had dug into her arm and jerked her off this very porch. Charlie, Ben, any of them could have died.

"I'm sorry they got anywhere near you or Charlie." He flexed his hands at his sides. "One climbed over and unlocked the gate for the rest. I aim to do something about that. They could have killed us or taken us captive if they chose to."

"As I mentioned last night, I recognized Wolf Heart. He's the warrior I told you about, the one who spared my life eight years ago when my uncle and I were attacked." She clasped her hands across her middle. "Saved me. Let my uncle die. Maybe even killed him. He spared us all last night, but..." He'd practically told Ben to take her as his wife. As if it was Wolf Heart's decision to make. "I'm not ready to put my life in his hands."

"Me neither. That's why I'm heading into town tomorrow." He drifted to the end of the porch.

She followed him. "Tomorrow? You need to give your body a chance to heal before you ride off anywhere."

"I'm delaying my trip to see the Widow Jackson's herd until the beginning of next week for that very reason."

"Town could wait too."

His gaze drifted down the lane. "No, we need an iron chain and lock for the palisade gate, something no one's going to get undone without a key."

"The Comanche could still climb over."

"But they'll have to leave their horses behind."

"You don't think they'll return anytime soon, do you?"

Ben rubbed the back of his neck. "I think not. Wolf Heart gave his word. But as you said, I'm not going to let down my guard. I'm not going to leave you and Charlie here alone when I head off to the widow's for the cattle. I either want to hire a hand, someone respectable, older, who can be trusted, or have you and Charlie stay in town while I'm away."

"In town? What about the garden?"

"There are things more important than the garden."

She skirted around the heart-fluttering, personal implications and steered the conversation to the practical. "We can't afford to hire someone."

He held up his hand. "Why don't we hold off on discussing this until after I have a chance to speak to Miller? He might know someone trustworthy, or offer you and Charlie a room. Or if you know of someone else you have a stronger connection with and who you can count on, I could speak with them."

She and Charlie didn't need a room, but she pressed her lips shut. All these years in Parker County, and there was no one who hadn't left the frontier or died in the war whom she'd count as a close friend. "There's no one else." Her family had never been one to ask for help, even when they needed it, especially after her father's behavior became the talk of the town.

"Miller will be fine." She shuddered. "But after my nerves

have a chance to settle down for a couple of days, I'll be all right here with just me and Charlie."

"I admire your spunk." He tilted his head as if to see her from a different angle. "But I plan to hire someone all the same."

"The day you rode up, I had my shotgun at the end of the garden row. I know how to take care of myself." Then why was she so uneasy about stepping outside after dark?

He leaned against the post and studied her. "Is that how you want to live?"

"What do you mean? Are we still talking about you hiring someone for a few weeks?"

"No. I mean alone with just you and Charlie."

Alone. Heart baking as hard as the soil beneath the July sun, parched for love and companionship. Her life before Ben showed up.

Ben tipped his hat. "I have another reason for going to town." He touched his hand to his pocket. "I have a letter to mail."

"To Olivia?"

"Yes."

He was going to follow through on his decision to break his betrothal. Because she was the girl he wanted to court, or because he felt she needed his protection? "You don't have to. You're under no obligation to me." She grimaced. Why couldn't she just shut her mouth and accept his attentions?

"I don't have to?" He took her by the elbow and turned her toward him. "It'd take a bullet or an arrow to stop me from mailing that letter." His gaze dove into hers, penetrating layers deep.

Her pulse drummed at the base of her neck. "You sound pretty determined."

"In case I haven't made myself clear here..." His voice dipped. "I'm in love with you."

Goosebumps spread across her limbs. Her gaze fell to his scuffed boots. If she had any sense, she'd crawl back behind the shield of indifference. Wasn't that why she'd allowed LeBeau to come calling, to bolster her resistance to Ben's charms? She should ride into town herself tomorrow and propose to the doctor. A safe marriage. Without heart. Sealing herself into an ill-fitting life that protected her against the potential of repeating her mother's mistakes.

No. Her fingers curled inward. She was done with hovering inside her walls. She was finished with not living. Words trembled on her lips. "Be gentle with my heart," she whispered. "It is yours."

His breath caught. He trailed his fingers from her elbow to her hand, snagging her pinky with his, gently swinging her hand. "Your heart will be my most precious treasure, Cora."

CHAPTER 25

*D*awn. Traces of pink lined the eastern horizon. Patches of hickory, mesquite, and oak dotted the prairie between the ranch and Spring Creek. But Ben's direction lay south across the Brazos River and into Palo Pinto County. He scraped his sandpaper tongue over his lips as he tugged on the cinch strap. He should be staying here to protect Charlie and Cora, not riding off.

Penny snorted and tossed her midnight-hued mane.

Cora stood at his side, wrapped in her red shawl. The comb he'd given her rested snug in her flowing hair. Her eyes were still puffy from sleep.

He laid the reins across the saddle horn and turned to her. *Lord, watch over her and Charlie.* "Mr. Franklin should be here around suppertime every evening. He understands he'll take his meals in the loft."

"That's good. I wouldn't want another cowhand to get the idea he can run the ranch because he gets invited to the supper table a few times."

He blinked at her.

The corners of her mouth quirked upward.

He chuckled. "For your information, Cora-girl, I'm more of a partner than cowhand."

"See what a few dinners did for you?" She edged the toe of her unlaced shoe against his boot. Dew and bits of grass dampened the leather. "But you're more of a knight."

He took her cool hand in his. "Only for my princess."

She blushed and fidgeted as if not quite accustomed to the endearment. When he returned, he'd shower her with attention and court her proper.

But when was he going to tell her about his obligation to his father? One that a letter wouldn't get him out of, not if he wanted to maintain his family's respect. Until their embrace in the foyer five nights ago, Cora knowing or not knowing hadn't mattered, but now he was creating heart-deep expectations. He'd told himself he'd tell her before he left for Palo Pinto County and the widow's, but how could he do that minutes before riding off for weeks?

Cora fingered the tooled leather of the saddle's pommel. She'd insisted upon loaning— more like giving—him the finest of her family's three remaining saddles. "You should take Mr. Franklin with you instead of leaving him with us. You need all the help you can get with the cattle. Charlie and I will make out fine. We promise to stay locked in the house from sunset to sunrise, and you know the double cabin is impenetrable. Plus, no one's getting the gate open with that chain on there, without a key."

Ben stretched his forearm over the saddle seat, just shy of Cora's hand. "It's not open for discussion. If anything happened to you or Charlie, I'd never forgive myself. Franklin will just be here for the nights. Getting paid to sleep. Can't ask for any easier position than that. He may be past his prime, but I have it on good account from Miller that Franklin is a very able shot and one who can be trusted."

She jutted her chin. "Franklin is an experienced cowhand, and he knows his way around the frontier and cattle—"

"If I need more hired hands in addition to Goodnight's two men, I'll stop by Major Ramsey's place in Palo Pinto, hire a couple of his men on commission."

"Working with cattle on the range can be dangerous, Ben."

He cupped his hands around her upper arms, massaging her tense shoulders with his thumbs. "You and Charlie can pray for me while I'm away."

Air swooshed from her lungs. "I suppose you don't know how time works on this ranch. For every day you spend out on the range or in some far-off county, three days pass here..." She fingered a button on his red cotton shirt just below his collarbone.

"I know I'm going to miss my girl." His swallow worked its way down his throat. "And we'd best express our private good-byes before Charlie finishes tending the horses and hurries over here." His voice dipped.

"Private goodbyes?" She crossed her arms as if she didn't know what he was talking about.

"Got to say see you later to my girl in the proper way." He drew her against him.

She slid her palms over his chest and around the back of his neck, igniting fire in his belly. Golden flecks lit her hazel eyes as they delved into his gaze. "You stay out of trouble and come back soon as you can, you hear?" A small crevice formed over the bridge of her nose.

Was it only the dangers of the trail she was concerned about, or was it the draw of the laudanum too? He brushed his fingertips across her silken hair. "I'm serious about you praying for me. And if LeBeau shows up, tell him his calling days are done."

"I will." Her voice firmed.

"You take care of yourself." His gaze dropped.

Her unkissed lips...inviting as a ripe peach...parted.

His heart pounded. Who knew how long he'd be gone. Surely, it'd be understandable if he gave her one kiss. The letter to Olivia would reach Philadelphia. His betrothal would be over. Surely, one kiss based upon the promise of all of that would be understandable. What if something happened while he was away? What if he didn't make it back? The war and Andersonville had taught him not to take tomorrow for granted.

Lowering his head, he slipped his hand beneath her hair and drew her mouth to his. "You're the girl I want to spend the rest of my life with."

Their lips met...sunrise and sunset intertwining and bursting forth in a single moment.

His breath came short and hard as he withdrew his mouth and dipped his forehead to hers. Her chest rose and fell against his. He needed to marry this girl. *Dear Lord, let it be.* The rest of his life with Cora. He'd said it, and he meant it. He squeezed his eyes shut.

And what of his promise to his father?

～

Shakespeare sonnets and a half a tea brick in hand, Cora crossed the threshold of the wide open hall to the porch, bracing herself for a barrage of objections.

Arms folded, Charlie stood at the end of the porch. His knife hung from a sheath secured around his waist with a strip of rawhide, as was his custom since the Comanches' night visit. The boy wasn't going to make this any easier.

"Good afternoon, Cora, Charlie." Sporting a fine black frock coat and trousers, Arthur LeBeau crested the top of the steps. His roan American saddlebred waited at the hitching post.

"Afternoon." She rolled her shoulders, working out the tension.

Arthur's gaze dropped to her hands. His smile dimmed as he removed his hat. "Either you're eager to read poetry or—"

"Ben's courting my sister." Charlie gripped the porch post and leaned outward, swinging back and forth. "She don't need your presents—"

"Charlie." Cora jabbed a hand to her hip. "This conversation is for grownups. Get yourself out to the barn and muck out the stalls. Then give Sandy a good brushing."

The boy's lips vibrated beneath his hard exhale. "I'll brush her in the yard." He scuffed his boot against the porch board.

"Right outside the stable, no closer. Then you'll muck the stalls." Not a bad idea to have the boy in sight, but out of hearing distance.

Bracing herself, she turned to Arthur as Charlie stomped off the porch. "I apologize for the boy's manners."

A smirk slipped across his lips. "I see Mr. McKenzie has made significant headway in the last few weeks." He raised an eyebrow. "I was under the impression we had a pleasant afternoon last time I called."

"We did. It's just that...we...I..." She held out the gifts to him. "My connection with Mr. McKenzie goes back to my brother Jeb, and my friendship with Ben...Mr. McKenzie...has grown into more." Did she really need to explain all of this?

"You're free to keep the gifts." His voice had stiffened.

"It wouldn't be proper." She shoved them his way.

"McKenzie isn't sophisticated enough to appreciate Shakespeare's sonnets?" He slipped the book from her fingers.

"Mr. McKenzie is every bit as educated as you."

Arthur snorted and tapped the book against his leg. "He looks more like a second-rate cowhand to me. And didn't you tell me his father helped him get the job at the newspaper?"

"I'll not stand here and listen to you denigrate him." She pushed the tea into Arthur's hand.

He laid the gifts on the table. "I'd think a young woman of your standing would appreciate a second opinion when it comes to making the most important decision of her life. You'd ask for as much if you were purchasing horses, or cattle, or a piece of land."

"If I need a second opinion, I'll ask the minister." Couldn't the man just leave?

"The circuit rider who shows up once a month?" He scoffed. "Personally, I'm surprised McKenzie has time to court. How long does he plan on staying in Texas? Doesn't he have an editing job to get back to in Pennsylvania?" His eyes glistened like steel.

She gnawed her lip. "I can't see that it's any of your concern." She clasped her hands to her middle. "I'm sorry you had to ride all the way out here for disappointing news. I've appreciated your professional help with my family, and I—"

"I have very much enjoyed your company, Cora." Arthur settled into one of the cane rockers. "I'd graciously take my leave if it weren't for the fact I rode eight miles under the expectations I'd be a welcome guest." He tossed the tea onto the opposite rocker and set his hat atop the book. "If I might be so bold as to impose upon your hospitality, I'd appreciate a few minutes in the shade of your porch and a glass of cider."

She blew out a breath. "If you want cider, you need to pick another topic of conversation."

"As you wish." He drummed his fingers on the chair arm.

She'd give the man a half hour. If he still dilly-dallied, she'd call Charlie over to the porch to sit on the steps and snap beans. "Wait here." She gritted her teeth and headed inside. She wouldn't allow Arthur to rattle her. He was a genius at disrupting her calm with pinpricks aimed at every potential wound she possessed. How had she ever thought she should consider a life with him?

Gray clouds rolled overhead as she passed out the back door and down the hill to the springhouse to fetch the cider jug. Pin pricks of moisture dotted her skin. Arthur needed to finish his visit and be on his way before he had the excuse of rain to keep him here.

What were Ben's future plans? Since his arrival, he'd stubbornly insisted he'd stay until she no longer needed his help. But that was before the kiss two weeks ago and his words—*you're the girl I want to spend the rest of my life with*. Surely, he knew the rest of their lives meant the Texas frontier.

My goodness, she was getting so far ahead of herself that she'd left the train station in the dust without the train. There was no guarantee Ben would propose. She pushed the thoughts aside as she ducked her head and entered the cool dark of the springhouse.

Upon her return to the porch, Arthur rose. "Thank you, Cora." His gloved fingers brushed against her pinky as she handed him the glass. "None for yourself?"

"I'm not thirsty." She smoothed her hands against her skirt. "I thought I'd—"

"Surely, you'll grant me the pleasure of your company for a few minutes." He motioned toward the second rocker. "For the sake of our friendship."

Didn't she have dusting to do? But what kind of hostess would she be if she ignored her guest? He'd traveled here based on her open invitation. He'd sat with her as her father died. She could at least be civil.

He settled into his chair once more, and she perched on the edge of the other rocker. Charlie glared across the yard, where he positioned himself and the mare at the very edge of the stable. Plumes of dust flew from Sandy's hide as he worked the curry comb back and forth.

As Arthur sipped his cider, he talked about his patients in Dallas, then about the land his father had given him, north of Weatherford, land that had once belonged to his cousins, where he hoped to start his own ranch.

She drew her silk fan out of her pocket and waved it back and forth in front of her face as she listened and commented, now and then. If this conversation lasted much longer, her chemise would be plastered to her back with sweat.

Charlie tromped up to the end of the porch. "I'm finished." Smudges of dirt marred his cheeks and his once-white shirt.

Arthur reached into his trouser pocket. "I'll give you a dime if you feed and water my gelding."

Charlie tipped his head to the side as if weighing the size of the dime. "I got work to do."

Arthur laid the coin beside his hat on the table. "As soon as my horse is taken care of, I can be on my way."

Charlie's glance flickered between the money, the man, and Cora. "I'll do it." He huffed and headed for the roan.

She stared after him, half tempted to jump off the porch and go help.

Arthur leaned back in his chair. "I'm sure Mr. McKenzie is a fine fellow in many respects."

"I thought we weren't going to talk about him." Cora swatted a fly.

"It's my duty as your physician and friend to advise you." Arthur puffed out his chest.

"My decision to accept Mr. McKenzie's courtship isn't a medical issue."

"If you end up with your dreams and heart crushed...like your mother's...it's every bit the concern of your doctor and true friend."

Her eyebrows edged upward. True? "I'm not my mother. And Mr. McKenzie, despite a supposed similarity, is not my father."

"So is that what he's convinced you of?"

"He hasn't convinced me of anything." She stood. "Have you finished your cider yet?"

He held up his half-empty glass, the contents of which he seemed to be consuming at tortoise speed. "I'm sure he doesn't mean to deceive you. He's likely deceiving himself."

She jutted her hand to her hip. Couldn't this man get out of her head? "I know it must be difficult for you to understand, Dr. LeBeau—"

"Arthur. We're still friends, I presume."

She had so few friends. But was this man really one? "I've determined to give Mr. McKenzie the opportunity to prove himself. I decided to show him grace."

He studied her a moment and exhaled a sober sigh. "You're willing to risk your security and happiness on McKenzie's ability to abstain?"

Flashes of memory stole her breath. Her father with head down on the table, too drunk to sit up. Or worse, sprawled on the floor passed out, or using their hound dog as a pillow. Her stomach clenched. That was not Ben. She shoved the images aside. "I'm sorry, but it's time for you to go." She snatched his hat from the table and handed it to him. The dime toppled to the floor.

"I'm sorry if I upset you." He cleared his throat and picked up the coin.

She pressed her nails into her palms. "It's getting late. And I'm sure you want to get home before it storms."

He stood. The upward twitch of his lips did little to soften the flint sparks in his eyes. "I'll go see the boy at the stables and give him his money."

She lifted her chin. "I'm sure he'll appreciate it."

He tapped his hat to his head. "If you ever need anything, don't hesitate to ask. Even if I'm in Dallas, send a note by the stage driver, and I'll be at your service as soon as I can."

"I'll keep that in mind." That day would never come.

He shifted toward the steps, then pivoted, his gaze as sharp as a scalpel. "I also plan to speak with Mr. Keely, the druggist."

She frowned. "Why?"

"To ask him to let me know if Mr. McKenzie purchases any laudanum."

"I have no intention of spying on Ben." Her voice wobbled. "Besides, he...Mr. McKenzie...no longer has need of the medicine."

Arthur hooked his thumb in his watch pocket. "Are you afraid of what we might find?"

"No." She rubbed her arms. "I trust Ben." She picked up the book and the tea and shoved them toward him. "Good day, Dr. LeBeau."

She was done letting that man prick her heart. But what if he was right...and laudanum had not lost its grip on Ben?

CHAPTER 26

*E*scaping the blaze of the late-afternoon sun, Ben squinted as he stepped inside the dimly lit tavern—little more than a glorified shed with a shingle. He had no business darkening the threshold of such an establishment, but Charlie Goodnight's seasoned trail hand had left word to meet him here. And goodness knows, after two weeks of rounding up the widow's stock, Ben needed an experienced guide if he hoped to get his newly acquired cattle to market.

Pecan hulls lay scattered about on the rice-sack-covered floor. Probably nothing but hard-packed dirt lay beneath the poor man's carpet. Scarce sunlight filtered in through an open square of a window. The furnishings consisted of three shoddy tables and hardtack crates in place of chairs. An unshaven man with a wide-brimmed hat sat in the far corner. His fingers curled around a shot glass next to a half-empty bottle of whiskey. He nodded toward Ben.

Ben tipped his slouch hat in acknowledgement and headed for the bar, a wagon bed laid across short posts. He needed something in his hand. He'd never been a whiskey man, just an occasional touch of brandy on cold nights during the war and a few sips at social gatherings prior to that. But that was before Andersonville and before his first taste of laudanum. He placed a coin on the worn bar and ordered coffee. Only a fool would purposefully slice open the yawning cavern of craving.

Cup in hand, he crossed the room to the corner. "Mr. Cornet?"

"Eagle Ed. That's what they call me. They say I can see clean across the prairie." He rubbed his palms on his trousers. "You must be McKenzie. I heard you were looking for me."

"Yes, sir. I'm here to talk cattle."

"You came to the right place. Pull up a crate."

Ben shoved the makeshift seat toward the table with his boot and took a seat. "I heard you're one of Goodnight's best men and that you might be interested in hiring on for a cattle drive."

Eagle Ed glanced at the tin cup. "What's that?"

"Coffee." Ben took a swallow.

"Coffee?" The man's lip curled. "If you dump that out, I'll give you a drink of something that'll put hair on your chest." He clinked his forefinger against the whiskey bottle.

"Coffee suits me fine." Ben placed his hand over the top of his cup. "Any man hires on with me will drink coffee on the trail."

Eagle Ed smirked. "I get the work done. After Goodnight and Loving, and maybe Chisholm, I'm the next top man."

Maybe. Probably not. "I'm curious as to why you stayed behind and didn't head out on the trail with Goodnight a couple weeks back."

"Sick. Had a fit of fever. But I've been on my feet for a week now, tired of sitting around this hole." Eagle Ed finished off his shot of whiskey.

Ben had heard as much. Was there more to the story? "I purchased the Widow Jenkins's cattle. Goodnight loaned me a couple of hands—"

"I heard. How many head did you manage to round up? I reckon some of them are scrawny."

"Three hundred and fifty. Most are fit. They'd been lollying by streams, filling themselves on the grass nearby, and I'm looking to get them to market. Goodnight told me he had an idea for a new trail headed to Colorado by way of New Mexico Territory. A way to avoid Comanche raiders—"

"I know the territory he's riding through." Eagle Ed dug in his trouser pocket and pulled out a plug of tobacco. "A camel would have to carry a canteen on that route, and even then, they'd reach their destination minus a hump."

Ben frowned. "You know of a better route?"

Eagle Ed bit off a chaw. "Not unless you're willing to risk losing your scalp. I can lead the way to New Mexico for the right price." He rubbed his grimy thumb and forefinger together. "We'll have to drive the cattle hard, and the men and horses even harder. Maybe we'll catch up with Goodnight at Fort Sumner. Or maybe the U.S. Army at the fort will buy our beeves."

"My beeves." Ben set his cup down.

"Pay me in money or beeves. No difference to me. Just as long as you pay me. We're liable to leave a dozen or two of the creatures hooves up, bones drying in the sun." Eagle Ed leaned toward a spittoon in the corner and shot a stream of brown liquid through his teeth. "But it's either that or wait for Goodnight. He might make another run for Colorado before fall. But I wouldn't count on it if I were you."

Ben scrubbed his hand over his jaw. The New Mexico trail was a risk, and so was trusting this man. But what if Goodnight didn't make another run? Ben needed to get the cattle to market for Cora and secure the ranch on solid financial footing. They'd receive some money from the remainder of Cora's family's herd he'd sent with Goodnight three weeks ago, but that wouldn't last but a few months, and they were already in debt to Miller's store. Cora needed income to buy more cattle, not struggle by for months.

Ben puffed out his cheeks and exhaled. "I'll pay you a percentage of what makes it to market."

He glanced at the brown liquid in the bottle. Just a little lighter amber color than laudanum. His finger twitched. Time to get out of this place.

～

*B*oots and stirrups damp from fording the Brazos River, Ben led his gelding through waves of prairie grass the next day. Three covered wagons stood in the shaded perimeter of a strand of cottonwoods along a creek. Not far from there, men worked on an almost completed double cabin. Although one cabin appeared to be finished, except for missing a chimney and window frames, the walls of the second stood beneath bare rafters. Horses grazed in a roped-off area. South of the creek, seedling plants populated a large stretch of over-turned brown soil. A garden, and a good size one at that.

The Ramseys and the Reynolds had made significant progress on their homestead in the five weeks since he'd met them in Weatherford. But they still had plenty to do. What if they couldn't spare him the help he needed?

"Welcome." Hammer in hand, Devon Reynolds waved from the top of a ladder pitched against a rafter.

A fellow holding the other end of a shingle looked up.

At the corner of the unfinished cabin, Garret Ramsey rose, dropping a spatula into a bucket of mud-colored chinking. "McKenzie, you're just in time to help."

"I'd be happy to for a day." Ben dismounted a few yards from the house. No hitching post in sight, he tethered his horse to a stake.

"My husband would ask no such thing. You're a visitor."

Mrs. Sky Ramsey stepped through the door, Baby Katie on her hip. Strands of wavy dark hair hung loose from the mother's braid and cascaded in ringlets around her face.

"I was only teasing the man." Shirt sleeves rolled to his elbows, Garret smiled as he walked over, his left foot not quite matching the cadence of the right.

"Afternoon, ma'am." Ben tipped his hat to the handsome woman and turned to Garret. "I'd be more than happy to give you a day's worth of work. It'd make me feel a whole lot better about what I've come to ask."

"We're your neighbors." Garret wiped his hands on a rag and stood tall, surpassing Ben's height by an inch or more. "Ask away."

"Neighbors with a good thirty miles in between."

Garret extended his hand for a shake, his grip firm. "We're Yanks in Reb territory. A hundred miles in between would still make us neighbors."

"Where's the boy?" The small voice perked Ben's ears. Little Star, holding tight to her mother's brightly colored calico skirt, poked her head out from behind Mrs. Ramsey.

Garret chuckled. "I'm afraid Little Star is quite struck by your Charlie."

"Am not." The girl moved from behind her mother. "I just want to race him on a horse."

Ben grinned. "I bet Charlie would be happy to race you. He'd give you a run for your money."

"Don't want no money. Just to beat the boy."

Her mother touched the girl's head. "He might beat you."

"I don't think so. I've been practicing." Little Star twirled her braid.

They all laughed.

The baby began to rub her eyes and nuzzled her mother's arm. Mrs. Ramsey bounced the chubby-cheeked, brown-eyed cherub and pivoted toward the door. "Little Star, come help me fix the men a treat while they talk. Maybe you can write a letter to Charlie and send it by way of Mr. McKenzie."

The girl hopped up and down. "Can I, Mr. McKenzie? I know all of my ABC's and how to make words. Can the boy read?"

"You better believe he can." Ben bent down, hands on knees. "I'll take your letter to him. Only, it might be a while before I get back that way."

"Why?" She looked up at him big-eyed.

"Enough questions." Juggling the squirming baby, Mrs. Ramsey tugged the child into the cabin with her. "We need to get busy before your little brother wakes from his nap."

Ben turned back to Garret. "Now, about that chinking..."

Four hours later, the two men, joined by Devon, sat in the shade of a cottonwood. Its towering branches stretched over them like a giant hand.

Over lemonade and gingersnaps, Ben laid out his plans to drive his cattle to Colorado via New Mexico with Eagle Ed as guide.

Garret rolled his shoulders. "I'd be happy to let you talk to my men. There's the three from my old regiment that came along to try their hand at ranching, and then there's Kuruk, an Apache friend of mine from my days at Camp Cooper before the war. If you give us a few days to make headway on the cabins, I'd be willing to spare one or two men if any of them want to hire on with you temporarily. It'd give them good practice for when we have our own drive next year."

"As long as it wouldn't cause you too much hardship, I'd be much obliged. According to Eagle Ed, we need at least two or three more hands, in addition to the two Charles Goodnight loaned me, if we hope to keep the cattle in line." Ben's lips puckered as he sipped his lemonade.

"I'm interested in signing on, McKenzie." Devon scrubbed his hand over his stubble-covered jaw. "If Garret doesn't mind holding down the fort without me for a couple of months. But I'll have to talk with my wife first."

A whole month or two. Yes, it'd take at least that long. Mid-August probably, before he could get back to Cora. Ben's insides squirmed. How could he consider leaving Cora alone for that long? Yet it was the surest way to provide for her and Charlie. If he wanted any hope of catching Goodnight at Fort Sumner and avoiding traveling the rest of the way to Colorado, he wouldn't have time to see Cora first. "I'd welcome your help, but I hate to ask you to leave off working on your cabin."

Devon leaned forward, elbows on knees. "I know the territory better than any man here. I'm Texas born and bred. All the rest are Northern city boys."

"City boys?" Garret shoved his boot against his brother-in-law's. He narrowed his eyes, but he couldn't quell the upturn of the corners of his mouth. "I could keep pace with you on a scout any day if I didn't have to lead this operation here."

Ben leaned back against the ridged bark of the tree. "The war took the city out of all of us."

If only that was all it'd taken from him.

CHAPTER 27

Camped at the edge of the headwaters of the Middle Concho River, Ben sat atop his bedroll and scooped beans from his tin plate to his mouth. A week in the saddle and nights spent beneath the open sky on hard ground. Almost like being in the cavalry again. He'd have a few hours of rest before Eagle Ed would wake him for his turn at watch.

Smoke trickled up from the campfire, illuminating the scrub brush, mesquite, and juniper along the muddy river-banks. On down the shore, where the land was flatter, the cattle stood in patches of prairie grass near the water.

Ben's shoulders ached from lifting filled water barrels onto their wagon. According to Ed, they needed to fill every barrel, canteen, and jug to the brim. They'd allow the cattle to drink to their hearts' content here before heading out tomorrow in the heat of the afternoon.

Plate in hand, Devon ambled over and sat down on a log across the fire. "I hope Ed knows what he's doing. Eighty miles till the next watering hole?"

"If it was only Ed, I'd have more worries. But Goodnight is

the one who scouted the trail and mapped it out." Ben poked a piece of fatback on his plate.

"Goodnight's a fine man." Devon chomped on a biscuit. "I brushed elbows with him a time or two in the early days of the war when he was with the Frontier Regiment and I was a scout. But from what you say, even Goodnight's not completed a drive on this trail before."

"He's up ahead of us, I reckon. So he must have made it through." Ben swallowed another bite.

"If Goodnight can handle it, we can too. I'm just concerned about the cattle." Devon glanced at the dark horizon toward limestone bluffs.

Ben finished off his beans. "I'm thankful to have yours and Mrs. Reynolds's help. And your man Philip's too."

"Once Morning Fawn heard I was considering the adventure, she had no intention of being left behind."

"She and Cora would get along mighty fine."

Devon studied him a moment. "You and Miss Scott? More than a sister or friend? If you don't mind me asking?"

Ben blew out a breath. His chest felt as if it'd explode if he didn't say something to someone. "I have many hopes in that direction."

Devon nodded. "I thought as much. Maybe that's why God sent you to Texas."

Had God sent him to Texas? Most likely. But how did his love for Cora fit with his promise to his father? Would the Lord make a way for him to fulfill both commitments, or would he be forced to choose? His throat constricted. And who knew if Cora would even have him. Maybe her affection the last few days between the Comanche attack and his leaving to buy the widow's cattle was nothing more than romanticized gratitude.

Devon cleared his throat.

Ben shook himself. Time to shift the topic of conversation.

"It's mighty fine you and your extended family were able to return to Texas and start a ranch."

"Texas is in our hearts and our dreams." Devon threw back his shoulders. "Garret did more than his share in making the dream come true. That's one of the reasons I'm helping with this drive. My brother-in-law is very generous, but I want to raise more capital of my own. I want to contribute to our joint funds, with cash, not just experience. When the Lord blesses me and Morning Fawn with children, I want to provide for them properly." His voice dipped on the word *children*. The crinkles around his eyes deepened.

"I can understand that." Ben dropped his gaze to the fire. How long had they been married? Two years, and no little one on the way? But they had years ahead of them.

Tree frogs trilled in the distance in between the grunting of the cattle. What was Cora doing this evening? Had his letter reached her yet? Hopefully, Mr. Franklin was doing his job and watching over the place at night.

Footsteps crunched on the gravel. Morning Fawn strode up, a gallon-size coffeepot in hand. "Want a refill? This is all that's left for the night." Buckskin leggings showed beneath her skirt hem which she'd shortened a couple inches above her ankles. More of her Comanche past seemed to come out every day they were on the trail.

Ben extended his cup. "Thank you, kindly."

The three of them sat and talked, finishing their meal.

Morning Fawn lifted her gaze to the sky and blew out a long, slow breath. "*Tatsinuupi.*"

"Excuse me?" Ben's brow furrowed.

"Stars." Her gaze drifted back to the earth, her voice wistful. "It's the Comanche word for *star.*"

Ben fingered the rim of his cup. "If you don't mind me asking, Mrs. Reynolds, how did you come to leave the Comanche?"

"My uncle paid my now-husband to kidnap me." She elbowed Devon in the ribs.

"Ooww." He dramatized a wince. "How else was I supposed to get me a wife?"

"You're lucky I didn't scalp you."

"I figured I was safe. You wanted a husband with a full head of hair." He bumped his shoulder to hers. But his smile faded. "Seriously, though, Ben, we tease each other now, but after I turned her over to LeBeau—"

"LeBeau?" Ben's eyebrows quirked upward.

"My uncle, Mr. Robert LeBeau, is determined to rule every relative all the way out to his tenth cousins with an iron fist." Morning Fawn scuffed her booted foot against the gravel. "Thankfully, Mister Tall, Dark, and Handsome here realized the error of his ways, and came on a secret mission to rescue me. Thought he'd try rescuing the whole of Texas too."

Ben scrubbed his hand over his jaw. "Yeah, Garret told me about that. Mighty fine work."

"Not as fine as it could have been."

She scolded him. "Fine enough to get you thrown in jail with a noose waiting for you down the road."

"But my angel, here, rescued me."

"Not all by myself. I did have a little help from the Federal cavalry and the resistance group. But most of all from the Lord." Her voice wobbled.

Devon exhaled. His eyes glowed with more than the campfire. "The Lord made a way where there was no way. He worked through Morning Fawn's courage and love to make it happen." He beamed and wrapped his arm around her shoulders.

Ben drank in the sight before him. That's the kind of relationship he wanted with Cora. Head over heels in love, able to laugh and kid and be at ease with each other and stand by each other no matter what. And most of all, a relationship with the Lord at the center, their love for Him coming first.

He dropped his gaze to his boots. "I admire the two of you. You've made good work of your marriage."

Devon gazed at him. "We'll pray for you and Miss Scott."

"Miss Scott?" Morning Fawn's eyes widened. "The older sister of the boy Little Star is smitten with? I thought something would come of you working hard to help her with her brother's ranch."

Devon nudged her with his shoulder. "You're embarrassing the man."

"No. I must hear this." She leaned forward. "So you two are courting?"

"Yes." Ben shrugged, but he couldn't contain his grin.

"I knew something had changed with you from the time we met you in Weatherford to when you showed up at our place."

Ben half chuckled. "Well, I got walloped by a Comanche a few weeks ago, and my face still tells the tale. Thankfully, I still have my scalp."

"But that's not the difference I'm talking about."

"What is it, then?"

"Your whole demeanor has changed." She fingered the end of her hair. "I wager you're in love and have reason to believe it's reciprocated."

Was it reciprocated? If only Cora was sitting beside him tonight by the fire, beneath the stars. A hollowness enveloped his chest. He should have found a way to bring Cora and Charlie with him.

Devon placed a finger to her lips. "Give the man his privacy."

Morning Fawn grabbed his finger and kissed it. "No more questions, just a statement." Her voice lilted. "I'd love to plan a wedding."

His and Cora's wedding? Ben's brain stuttered. He chuckled. "There's a little matter of courting first. And a mountain-size bit of convincing that I need to do on my part."

"I'm sure she'll come to see your charms in no time at all."

He could only wish. "Before we go too far down that road, I wanted to ask about LeBeau. I recognize the name. There's a Dr. Arthur LeBeau—"

"Arthur LeBeau?" Morning Fawn straightened. Her eyes widened. "That's my cousin. Where did you run across him at?"

"Weatherford." Ben brushed off his hands. "He's headquartered in Dallas, but he comes to Parker County one week a month to fill in until the town finds a new doctor. But more importantly, the man"—the words slipped around the boulder in his throat—"has taken a keen interest in Miss Scott."

Morning Fawn lifted her chin. "I haven't seen him since childhood, but I've heard enough about his actions to know he's not a man of honor, at least not in my definition of the word. I had a friend, a slave at my uncle's place. Arthur kept asking his father to send her to him in the army as his cook. But it wasn't her cooking he was interested in, if you get my meaning."

A chill swept over Ben. "I get your meaning."

"I had no idea my cousin was anywhere near here."

"From what I've heard, he has some land in Parker County that he hopes to turn into a ranch."

"Land?" Morning Fawn leapt off the log. "I bet that's my family's land." She turned to Devon. "Land that I almost traded my freedom for."

Devon took her hand and tugged her down to sit. "You were never really going to go along with your uncle's scheme." He intertwined his fingers with hers and turned to Ben. "Morning Fawn and Mrs. Ramsey's parents acquired a large plot of land in the northern part of the county, near the Trinity River, back in the 1850s before they were killed in the Comanche raid. Mr. Robert LeBeau tried to bribe my wife with it."

"It was my parents' land." Morning Fawn's voice firmed like oak. "My sister and I have a right to it."

Devon stretched back and ran his fingers through his thick waves of hair. "That may be, but until we get Federal troops in this area of Texas, the local courts aren't going to side in favor of a woman married to an ex-Yankee cavalry officer, especially one originally from Texas who acted as a spy and saboteur against the Confederacy. If anything, your cousin's presence could pose a potential threat."

Ben frowned. "What kind of threat?"

Morning Fawn puffed her cheeks. "We don't expect a warm welcome from any devoted Rebs who recognize us."

"We figured the frontier is fairly safe. That we're not likely to run into any who recognize my face, and I don't advertise my name around Weatherford. Garret signs the accounts and handles any business transactions." He interlaced his fingers with Morning Fawn's. "I made the front page of the papers back in January 1864. Branded as a wanted man and a traitor to the cause."

"And yet you came back to Texas?" Ben cocked his eyebrows.

"We're not going to allow anyone to keep us out of Texas." Devon threw back his shoulders. "This is our home."

"The East is entirely too citified." Morning Fawn turned up her nose. "Besides, we wanted to partner with my sister and Mr. Ramsey."

Ben lifted his head. "I won't make any mention of you to LeBeau. But when I return to Weatherford, I'm going to rid that man of any notion he has of courting Miss Scott." His hand curled into a fist. "And if you ever need any help defending yourselves against him or anyone else, you just let me know. Your whole family has been more than kind to me."

Driving the cattle to market would take weeks more. Time for that weasel of a doctor to make inroads with Cora. *Dear Lord, don't let it be so. Please guard her heart till I return.*

CHAPTER 28

The simmering sun slipped behind the western canyon walls, leaving the expanse of cacti, sage, and scrub brush in shadows. Sunset at last, but there'd be no rest. Ben's tongue felt like cotton, and his cracked lips stung with every twitch. His eyes burned. A night and three days without water for the cattle, and even with rationing, the riders and the horses had drained every barrel and canteen to the dregs earlier this afternoon. They'd driven the cattle through the night. No sense in trying to stop. The night before, the animals had walked and stomped about, requiring everyone to be in the saddle in order to prevent a stampede.

Riding at the left point, Ben gripped his reins and coaxed his gelding onward. The mass of cattle groaned behind him, their eyes sunken, skin tight across their ribs, and tongues hanging. Goodnight's man, Juan, rode point on the right, while two hired hands, Dan and Henry, kept to the sides of the middle. Fighting to keep the stragglers moving, Devon and Morning Fawn brought up the drags. They'd already had to put a bullet in almost a dozen head who'd either wobbled to the ground or turned to fight, crazed with thirst.

In the distance, dust flew as Eagle Ed rode toward them.

Ben loped his horse to meet him. "You find the Pecos?"

Ed removed his hat. Ten days' worth of grime coated the trail guide's face. His sweat-soaked hair lay plastered to his head. "No, but I caught sight of Castle Canyon. That means we're close. I'm betting we'll reach the river before sunrise."

"We'd better." A sigh rattled through Ben. He could only pray that this man's wealth of knowledge was at least half of what he claimed it to be. "The cattle won't stand much more of this."

"We'll get there. At least most of them will." Ed unscrewed the cap on his canteen.

Ben's eyebrows shot up. "You still have water?"

Ed worked his jaw and recapped the lid. "No. Just dreaming of a drop."

Ben narrowed his gaze but pressed his lips shut. No use starting a confrontation with the man who knew the most. "Why'd you come back? Don't we need someone out looking?"

Ed swiped his mouth. "Wanted to give you a choice. When these cattle catch the scent of water, and they can do that from miles away, there's liable to be a stampede." He rubbed his nose. "Either you can take our canteens and ride ahead scouting, or you can stay here and keep them from going wild."

Ben scrubbed a hand over his jaw. "I don't know anything about the area."

Ed puffed his chest out. "You know less about cattle. I figure you can follow the stars. Plus, on your return, you'll be able to hear us from miles off."

Ben glared at the man. Ed was under his hire. He could order this seasoned cowhand to ride out for water, but if he did that, and the cattle stampeded? "What about Juan or Dan? They've ridden with Goodnight. They could help me keep the cattle in line."

"Whatever you say, boss man." Ed tapped his hat back to his head. "But I'm the best cowhand of the lot."

Ben ground his teeth. Juan was hardly more than a kid, and Dan wasn't much better. Devon was an excellent rider, and so was Morning Fawn, but they weren't cattle experts, and neither was Phillips. "All right. Bring me the canteens."

Canteens swinging from his saddle, Ben rode ahead, praying for direction and grace.

Close to midnight, he jaunted his gelding down the side of a slope into the moonlit limestone walls of Castle Canyon. A cool breeze rippled across his parched skin. Water. Pebbles and sand flew as he skidded the gelding down to the canyon floor. The horse sensed the water, too, and picked up speed.

Less than an hour later, Ben dropped his knees into the mud flats of the snake-like Pecos. *Thank God.* Water at last. He dipped his hand in and tasted. Tolerable under better circumstances. Tonight, it tasted almost like molasses. While his horse quenched its thirst, Ben swallowed his fill, careful not to overindulge, and filled the canteens. He looped the strings around every point of his saddle possible. An owl hooted from a lone scrub oak.

Ben scanned the landscape. The way he'd come down would be treacherous for the cattle, but north of that spot, the slope was more gradual. He'd warn Ed to drive them that way.

Less than two hours later, cowbells, worn by the lead cattle, clanged in the distance as Ben loped his horse toward the herd. They'd made amazing progress in the few hours he'd been gone.

When he was within sight of Ed and Juan, he held up the canteens and waved. He might not be an expert, but even he knew enough to not yell or make loud noises around cattle who were already rattled. A cool breeze ruffled his shirt sleeves.

Horse hooves pounding the pebbled sand, Ed rode out to

meet him, barely keeping ahead of the trotting longhorns. Had they started moving faster?

Grunts and moos echoed through the mass.

"Two hours from here." Ben handed the man a canteen as they nudged their mounts to move alongside the lead cattle. "Enough sweet water to fill them all. But we should direct them to the northeast a couple of notches. The descent is more manageable there."

Ed upended his canteen to his lips until moisture dripped off his chin. He swallowed and swiped his mouth. "Sounds good. Ride around to the others and hand out canteens. Don't make a lot of racket—"

A gust of wind tugged at Ben's hat and toppled Ed's from his head. A sweet smell tickled Ben's nose.

Moos cascaded. The lead longhorn picked up speed, the front runners outpacing Ben and Ed.

"What the..." Ed rode for the head, the rest of his sentence lost in the rumble of hooves, the hard *thud, thud, thud* of over a thousand hooves. Running. "Turn 'em right. Turn 'em right," Ed hollered.

Dust plumes billowed. Ben rode hard to catch up with Ed. *Drive the animals right. Turn them until they're circling. Mill them up. Tighten the circle.* Ed had drilled the instructions into his, Devon's, and Morning Fawn's heads during the first couple days of the drive.

On the right, Juan fell back to encourage the turn and avoid spooking the animals.

Ben's gelding snorted and skidded away from the wild thrash of a longhorn. Ben gripped the reins and pressed his thighs to the horse's flanks. Choking dust and sand bit his eyes and clogged his throat.

Dan yelled behind him.

Bent over the neck of his horse, Ed charged in close. "Turn 'em."

Ben moved in, heart pounding. So many horns. The herd at his side shifted. He squinted, searching for Ed in the haze. The gelding's flanks rippled beneath him. Keep driving right. It didn't matter if he could see.

Wind whipped at him. From the cattle or the canyons?

Moos. Up ahead, the curving trajectory of beeves cut left. A horse on the right reared. The rider teetered and toppled. Ed or Juan?

Ben jerked his horse to the left. Let them go straight for now. Save the rider. Ben hovered on the side. The gelding whinnied. The mass of bovines pounded past them. Should he go after the cattle or help the man? Across the mass, another rider waved his hat at him and thrust his hand toward Ben and then the cattle, then repeated the gesture.

Ben signaled with his own hat and goaded the gelding forward, waving for Dan to follow behind. Take care of the cattle, slow them, turn them from the precipice. The rider would look after the fallen man.

Canteens tumbled from their hooks as Ben charged into the night. Let the beasts get clear of the fallen rider, then work them to the north, as best he could. He had an hour, less. Surely, chunky, water-deprived animals couldn't run for that long. They'd probably drop and need water hauled to them if they were to survive.

The gelding's hooves pounded beneath him. Sand plastered him. Coated his throat and his lashes. Coughs rattled through him. Tingles ran through his half-numb fingers from his strangling the reins, and his thighs clung to the animal with all his might.

To the right, to the right, not a circle. They'd given up on a circle. Other riders helped. Dan behind him, and Morning Fawn trailing farther back, on the far right. Devon's voice rang out from the back. No sign of Juan or Ed.

Castle Canyon loomed in the distance. They were going to

make it. The trajectory had shifted from the steep embankment. Grunts, snorts. A few animals had dropped, but the mass picked up speed. Water was near. Just keep them like this. The river. The Pecos. Salvation from thirst. Almost within reach.

The herd pulled farther right.

"Shift 'em back. Keep 'em straight." Ben's voice scraped as he beat his hat against the air.

Across the way, Perkins drove in, pushing. Down the line, Devon swooped close. Ben eased off, giving the animals room to drift left.

But cattle burst through the gap in front of Dan like water ripping through a hole in a dam. The stream exploded into a flood. Dan's horse reared, but the cowboy held tight and galloped from the path of the charging mass.

Stupid cattle. They were going to miss the river. Couldn't they smell the water? Unless the river curved south. Decimating sage, grass, scrub brush beneath their onslaught, the longhorns tore across the ground, crazed for moisture. A rise, then a drop up ahead—not the canyon, a stubble of a mesa.

Ben drove his gelding. He needed to get on point.

Bovines charged over the edge, skidding down helter-skelter. The ones in the lead slid toward a murky pond bathed in moonlight. Rows of longhorns slammed into the front runners, until the latter mass butted head to end, sending some of the cattle into a tumble. Helpless, Ben and Dan swung to the side. Devon and Morning Fawn worked to turn the stragglers, remaining at the top.

Cattle in the pond and others shoving their way in bullied the leaders clear to the other side. Water. Others struggled to their hooves, some bellowing, injured. Every creature who could manage a stumble fought its way into the soupy mixture and guzzled.

Dan scrubbed his hand down his face. "This can't be the river."

"No." Ben worked to catch his breath. "They turned too sharp. The Pecos is a little farther north."

"Just a large pond?" Dan swung down from his horse, his voice rising. His gaze scoured the ground. Dodging the back end of a couple of heifers, he dropped to his knees and scooped his hand into a puddle.

A chill swept over Ben. Pond. Standing water. No flow.

Dan spit out the sip. "Poison. Alkaline. We got to move them." His voice crescendoed.

Ben charged into the mass, followed by the other riders, reining in their pawing horses who fought against their bridles in desperation to moisten their tongues.

The herd leaders plodded to the muddy flats, followed by others. The mass of those who'd had a taste slowly submitted to the riders. The first animal made it a couple hundred feet before it dropped.

CHAPTER 29

Cora clicked the reins. Her finely woven straw hat shaded her face from the late-afternoon sun. "Giddy up." Couldn't these two horses move any faster?

Nestled in the front corner of the buckboard behind her seat, Charlie groaned. "Can't we slow down? Please." Resting against the pillows, he cradled his arm against his chest.

She pressed her lips together and inhaled slowly. *Be calm.* She had dealt with much worse than a broken arm. "I'll slow them up a bit, but we need to get to Weatherford before the end of the day." Pointed skyward, her rifle lay against the side of the seat. This road wasn't a safe place to be after dark.

"I don't want to see Dr. LeBeau."

"You should have thought about that before you decided to hang off the side of your horse while riding."

"But that's how Comanche ride." He grunted as the wagon wheels rumbled over a bump. "Makes it hard for enemies to shoot them."

"How do you know that's how they ride?"

"Wolf Heart."

Her voice rose. "You've seen him since the attack?"

"Once."

Her swallow worked its way down her throat. "And you said nothing to me about it?"

"I thought you'd be mad. He showed me riding tricks. Helped me practice archery."

"And he came into our yard?"

"No. It happened when I went to pick blackberries."

"He shows up again, you come tell me." Her jaw clenched. "Tell him I want to talk to him." She was done cowering. If that man wanted to harm her or worse, he could have already done so. "You don't keep secrets from me, young man."

Charlie grunted.

Beneath her blouse, her chemise clung to her back and her underarms. Ben needed to get back here. Five weeks he'd been gone. According to the letter he'd sent by way of Mrs. Ramsey, it would be at least another month before he returned to Weatherford. He'd written of missing her, but couldn't he have at least sent word for her to meet him in Weatherford or even farther west? Surely, he could have spared a day or two from his journey? Still, he'd closed with *To the girl who has captured my heart...*

Keeping one hand on the reins, she swiped a strand of hair from her brow.

Mrs. Ramsey, the first female visitor to the ranch in ages, had hand delivered the letter with her daughters while her husband and young son were in Weatherford for supplies. Sky, a fine-looking woman, carried herself like royalty atop her stallion. But her smile was warm and her words kind. She'd offered an open invitation to visit the R & R Ranch. Maybe she could be a friend one day. With Cora's father's behavior and her mother's illness, there'd been little time for friends over the years.

Baby Katie had been a delight, crawling across the porch to Cora's skirt and wanting to play peekaboo. And Little Star?

That girl had spunk. Charlie had alternated between making himself scarce and showing off.

Cora sucked in a breath. "You were practicing to show off for Little Star, weren't you? That's why you were trying to ride like a Comanche." She glanced over her shoulder.

Teeth gritted, he lay against the pillows. His lower arm had swollen against the two sticks and strips of cloth she'd used to brace it. A black-and-blue mark radiated from the center of the red patch.

"She can't beat me." He scooted farther against the stack of pillows, sinking into them. "I'm going to show her I'm a warrior." His voice faltered. "My arm's got to get better."

"There'll be no racing until it's completely healed. And if you try to hang out of the saddle again with nothing but your foot atop it, there won't be any race."

"But Cora—"

"But nothing. And I'm sure Ben will have something to say about it when he gets back."

"I want him to come home."

Home. "I do too." Sweep her into his strong arms and hold her close. "He's taking the cattle to market to secure our ranch, our future." Did Ben include himself in that *our*? When it came down to it, would he really turn his back on everything in Pennsylvania and count the ranch as his home? Would their love take root and weather the storms to come? *Dear Lord, please let it be so. Please bring him back safe and sound.*

An hour later, she drove up to the livery stable, gently helped Charlie out of the back, and left the wagon. She wrapped her arm around the boy's shoulders as she directed him toward the doctor's office. Her free hand twitched to straighten her hair. But no. She wasn't going to tidy herself up for that man. "We'll try Dr. LeBeau's office first. If he's not in town this week, we'll head to the bonesetter."

"The barber?" Charlie grumbled and dragged his feet.

"He's trained in setting breaks, but the doctor is the expert." A breath shuddered through her. It'd been three weeks since she'd returned LeBeau's gifts and ended his calling privileges. Maybe it'd be better if this wasn't his week in Weatherford. By all rights, it shouldn't be. But Charlie needed the best care.

A few blocks later, she led the boy down the walk and up the steps.

Mrs. Ruddy answered the knock. "Miss Scott? It's been ages." Her gaze scoured her, then landed on the boy. "What's happened, child?"

Cora laid her hand on Charlie's shoulders. "Fell off his horse. I believe his arm's broken. Would Dr. LeBeau happen to be in town?"

"You're in luck." The lady smiled. "He arrived a week early. Rode in this morning. Come in." She stepped out of the way and motioned toward the small waiting room. "Have a seat. The doctor is down at the café having his supper, but I'll fetch him myself."

"I'd hate to interrupt—"

"For you, I'm sure it'd be no trouble." Mrs. Ruddy grabbed her shawl from a hook and tucked it beneath the loose chignon of faded auburn hair. "We wouldn't want the boy to suffer any longer than necessary." She tipped her chin. "I reckon some people have discovered they need the doctor more than they thought they did."

Cora blinked. Was the lady addressing her?

Mrs. Ruddy swooped out the door with one last grumble. "Yankees think they can waltz into Texas and steal whatever they want." The door clicked behind her.

Charlie frowned. "What did she mean?"

"Never you mind." Cora drew him toward a chair and sat. Either Arthur had confided in his housekeeper, or the woman was an observant snoop. The way that lady gossiped, half the town probably had some fool notion of a love triangle between her, Ben, and LeBeau.

The mantel clock ticked for fifteen minutes before the door opened. Arthur stepped in, dressed in his usual black frock coat and top hat. His thin mustache twitched as his stormy blue eyes lingered on her. "Afternoon, Cora." Cora still, not Miss Scott. But his voice was stiff. "I hear the boy took a fall." He hung his hat on the coat tree in the foyer.

"I was charging on my horse." Charlie raised his head from her shoulder and cradled his injured arm. "But I'm all right now. We can go." Sweat beaded on his forehead.

"Well, young man, I'm going to take a look just to be sure." Down to his shirt sleeves and waistcoat, Arthur tossed his coat over the back of one of the waiting room chairs.

"I'm afraid it's broken." Cora perched on the front of her seat.

Arthur knelt in front of Charlie and extended his hand. "Let me see."

The boy slowly lowered the arm to his waist, keeping it close to his body. The swollen red skin puffed against the ties and sticks.

Arthur frowned. "We'll have to ice it overnight to get the swelling down. I'll check it again tomorrow afternoon."

"Ice?" Charlie's brow crinkled. "I've never seen ice. Will that hurt?"

Cora bit her lip. "Where would we get it?"

"Gruder's ice house on the other side of town. He has it shipped all the way from New England, packed in straw and sawdust."

"Sounds expensive."

Arthur tipped his angular face toward her. "Not for you to worry about. I'm the doctor. I'm prescribing. I'll send for a small slab for this evening and then again early in the morning."

She fingered her reticule. "We need to find a room in town."

"You're welcome to stay in the infirmary. Free of charge." Arthur's lips ticked upward. "There's a bed in there, and I could provide a cot."

With his bedroom just up the stairs? "No."

He snorted. "I've had patients in there from just born to ninety years old. Mrs. Ruddy sleeps on the premise, as well. Built-in chaperone."

Still, it'd leave him free to come talk to her at any hour he pleased. There'd be little escape from his attentions. Besides, it was the room her father had died in. She shuddered. "I have money."

"Hmmm. I'm sure there are other things you could use it on. Especially with your Don Quixote off for weeks at a time."

"Who's Don Quotie?" Charlie perked up. "Ben looks after us. I bet he's got a thousand cattle."

"I'm sure he does." Arthur smirked.

Cora lifted her chin. There were so many other necessities she needed the money for, but there were things more impor-tant than money. "I thank you for your generosity, Dr. LeBeau, but we'll find a room at Mamie Sykes." Or maybe even the Millers. If she dared ask. "Mr. McKenzie entrusted our—my cattle to Mr. Goodnight, and the latter stopped by a couple days ago with a tidy sum from the sale."

Arthur puffed out his cheeks and stretched to a stand. "Mr. Goodnight came calling?"

Men and their jealousies. "Mr. Goodnight came to pay his bill. Never stepped foot in the house. He was in a hurry to visit neighboring ranches and round up more cattle for another drive to New Mexico." If only Ben had waited and sent the newly acquired herd with him. She stood. "Do you need to look at Charlie further, or should we go find a room and await the ice?"

Arthur smoothed his hand over his goatee. "Why don't you locate a room for the night, and I'll keep Charlie here for now.

I'll make him a new looser split to tide him over until tomorrow. You can return for him and have dinner before you two go."

"Dinner?" She gripped her reticule.

"You don't plan to starve, do you?"

"I brought a pouch of dried venison and biscuits for the road."

"Very good. You can eat it when you drive home tomorrow afternoon. Meanwhile, I had Mrs. Ruddy order a meal for the two of you from the café, and she should show up here any minute with it. I'll have her keep yours warm."

"Dr. LeBeau—"

"Arthur."

She blew out a breath. "Arthur, I can't accept your generous offer."

"It's a meal, Cora. I even ordered a slice of chocolate cake for the boy."

Charlie's eyes widened. "Chocolate?"

The man should be a hawker. "We can't—"

"It's too late." A fox grin twinkled his eyes. "The cook has prepared the food by now. Mrs. Ruddy and I have already eaten. It'd be a shame to see it go to waste. Besides, what's a meal between friends? You did say we could still be friends?"

How was she to refuse without appearing to be inconsiderate, unappreciative, and wasteful? The man had her boxed in. She acquiesced.

That night, Cora fell in and out of a restless sleep, her arm across Charlie in the small bed. His arm lay atop a folded rubberized blanket with towels around the edges absorbing the run-off from the melting ice. Now and then, a moan escaped his chocolate-tinged lips. Arthur had offered a bit of laudanum for the boy's pain, but she had absolutely refused to allow it.

Their bellies full from pot roast, potatoes, and carrots, they'd headed over to the boarding house shortly after eating.

Charlie's drowsiness had saved her from Arthur's insistence on a game of chess. *Between friends.* The man wielded the statement like a legal document. But it'd been Charlie's pale face and feverish eyes that had led her to accept Arthur's offer to drive them to the boardinghouse in his buggy. It was all she could do to keep him from carrying Charlie inside.

Mrs. Sykes had already asked about the Yankee, the one who'd only stayed one night in the boardinghouse before moving out to Cora's ranch. Cora had commented on Ben's loft over the stable and told the woman how her brother's friend was away often on cattle drives. The answer had hardly satisfied the lady, and now the doctor was giving her and Charlie personal attention. Mrs. Sykes would take note of that.

Ben needed to come home. It felt like a year since he'd taken her in his arms and said goodbye. And that kiss... Even now her cheeks heated and her pulse quickened. If only he were here. He could sit across the room or even sleep in different quarters as far as she was concerned. The steady reassurance of his presence would penetrate the floorboards and walls, leaving her safe and secure.

But what if...

There were no what-ifs. Ben was done with laudanum. He was not like her father. And whatever ties he had in Pennsylvania... Surely, the Lord would not have brought this man into her life and allowed her to fall for him if it was to end in their parting.

*C*ora held Charlie's shoulder and his good arm. "It'll be over in less than a minute."

"Please don't." Charlie's voice faltered.

Arthur grasped the boy's wounded arm at the elbow and

the wrist. "As soon as you get your cast on, we'll go to the café. See what kind of dessert they have today."

"I want to go home." Charlie stuck his lip out.

"You're a warrior, remember?" Cora fought to transform her grimace to a smile. Two days in the boardinghouse, waiting for the swelling to go down and declining Arthur's offers of hospitality as best she could. And Charlie thought he was the one who wanted to go home the most? "Warriors are brave."

Arthur pulled. *Snap.*

"Oww." Charlie's holler echoed through the room. He sank against her shoulder. "It's over?"

"It's over." Arthur maneuvered a sock with the foot cut out over the boy's hand and onto his injured arm.

Cora kissed Charlie's head and brushed her hand over his dark hair. "You'll sleep in your own bed tonight."

The boy breathed heavily and watched as Arthur dipped strips of coarse cotton cloth in a bucket mixture of water and plaster of Paris and carefully molded them around his sock-covered arm. By the time he'd finished the cast and Charlie's arm was in a sling, he was ready to wiggle and bolt out the door.

Arthur handed the boy a dime. "A reward for bravery."

"I didn't do nothing." Nevertheless, Charlie took the dime.

"You lived through the setting of the bone without a whimper. That's bravery in my book." Arthur tweaked his mustache. "With your sister's permission, why don't you go spend it at the general store?"

"Can I?" He shifted his gaze to Cora. "Maybe I can buy me a knife or something for Ben."

Arthur's plastered smile faltered.

"You already have a knife." Besides, a dime wouldn't buy a knife, but she wasn't about to point that out and have Arthur dish out more. "You can go to the store while I walk over to the livery stable for our wagon and horses."

Arthur reached for his coat. "On second thought, the boy could meet us at the café after he's finished at the store."

"Us?" Her eyebrows edged upward. "After I settle our bill with you, Charlie and I are heading home. I want to arrive in plenty of time before dark. We have the dried venison to eat on the way."

Arthur pinned her with his gaze. "Having one last meal with me would settle your bill."

"Can I go?" Charlie squirmed.

"I'll settle my bill proper like. I have no intention of taking advantage of our friendship further." She lifted her chin.

Charlie looked from one to the other. "I'm all right with venison. But maybe we could take the slice of cake with us."

She waved her hand toward him. "Go on and wait at the store for me." No use dragging him into the conversation. She needed to go there and pay a portion of the bill, anyway. Not the whole thing, in case Ben had another use for the money. She shifted toward the door as Charlie left.

Arthur drew his silver watch from his waistcoat pocket. "Two o'clock. Plenty of time to eat and then be on your way to safely arrive back at the ranch before sunset."

Couldn't the man take no for an answer? "I can't be beholden to you any further."

"You refused to eat with me yesterday after I checked on Charlie's arm."

"He needed to rest. Besides, you still had food sent to us."

"As any friend would do." He leaned a manicured hand against the doorjamb. "Have I offended you in some way, that you can't share a meal with me in a public café in broad daylight?"

She blew out a breath.

He pinned her with his devouring gaze. "Was I not a perfect gentleman when I called at your house? Were you tortured by our time spent playing chess and conversing?"

She folded her arms. "You were, and I wasn't. But Ben and I have an understanding now."

"What kind of understanding?"

"That we're going to start courting."

An *aha* victory smile lit his face. "Don't you have to wait for his return?"

"I'm sorry, but I can't have dinner with—"

"One last meal together. That's all I ask. Once he returns and your courtship has officially started, I promise to not even glance your way unless you call upon me. You owe me nothing either way for the bill. I'll instruct Mrs. Ruddy to not accept your money. I never charged you for my care for your father either. I won't start now."

"Why didn't you ever charge us?" She blinked up into the eyes of...what? A snake-oil salesman, a flatterer, or a man who actually cared?

His smile turned sad as he reached for his hat. "Because, my dear lady, you have captivated me from the moment I first saw you. And I could tell that life had treated you unfairly."

She stared at him. How was she supposed to reply to that?

He donned his hat and opened the door. "Shall we go?" He held out his arm.

An hour in a café or the finest love sonnets Shakespeare had ever written wouldn't make a difference. Arthur had lost his suit the night Ben had taken her into his arms.

CHAPTER 30

*B*en gripped the worn railing of the Weatherford stockyard fence and hung his head. Forty-five longhorns out of three hundred and fifty. That's all he had left to call his own. The realization had dropped him to his knees in the mire of the mud flats as he'd gazed in horror at the gut-wrenching scene eight days ago.

If only he could stuff cotton in his ears and block out the moos. That might work here for the cattle in front of him, but nothing could suppress the moans that haunted him from the night at the pond and the day after. Dead cattle. Bellies bloated. Not all of the casualties had been from the water. There were also the ones who'd severely injured a leg or two in the mad dash down the slope and lay lame, unable to walk. Ben and his crew had dealt bullets of mercy as the only option.

They'd been left with more meat than a cowboy could carry or preserve. A waste. Wasted effort, wasted funds, wasted hopes and dreams.

He'd sent a pack mule loaded with meat along with Juan who trailed Eagle Ed behind his horse on a travois—payment to the trader five miles down the Pecos who agreed to take Ed in. Perhaps the trader's Kiowa wife would be able to nurse Ed back to health. Legs crushed by stampeding hooves, Ed would likely never walk again.

Ben scrubbed his hand down his face. He'd given Dan charge of ten cattle for Ed and a longhorn each for him and Juan. He'd paid Devon and Morning Fawn five and given one to the man from Ramsey's place. A man paid with what he had when his pockets were empty.

Ben's shoulders sank. He should have never started on the drive with only Ed to guide him. He should have waited for Goodnight to return, taken a gamble that the rancher would make a drive before fall. He should have...

Laudanum. The whisper sent a shiver through him. His mouth watered. He'd been fighting it for ten days, the itch under his skin that crawled up his spine and pulsed in his brain. If he could only have a taste, just a taste, it'd ease the misery, pull him out of the pit, for just an hour or two, but that would be enough.

No. He curled his hands into fists. The rail wobbled as he pushed away from the corral. Plumes of dust rose as a wagon rattled by on the nearby road. One way led past the tannery and out of town, the other into the center of Weatherford.

When the livery stable owner and the stockyard manager had inquired about what happened on the trail, Ben shook his head. "Don't ask." If he were smart, he'd slip out of town, ride out to the ranch, and face Cora. How was he even going to begin to tell her how miserably he'd failed?

Money jingled in his pocket, payment for the cow he'd sold to the stockyard manager. Funds for living on. He needed to see Miller and reassure the man he'd be paid, before the rumors started to spread. His tongue stuck to the roof of his mouth. He'd need to save enough cash to pay his way back East. How else could he hope to provide for Cora and Charlie, and keep his word to Jeb? He wasn't a rancher. The remnant of forty-five longhorns he'd brought back to the stockyard for Cora would only go so far.

The mid-July sun beat down on his grime-covered clothes. If he had money to spare, he'd pay for a bath and a shave, clean himself up so he'd look halfway respectable when he showed up at Cora's to deliver the news. When he got to the ranch, he wouldn't even go into the house. He'd tell Cora outside, then drag himself to the stable loft. He'd not sit through a meal with her beneath the weight of her disappointment in him.

Hands in his pockets, he trudged down the main street past a scattering of log and frame structures. He'd find a water pump, wash up there, and maybe take a meal at the café to bolster his strength. For two weeks, his rations had tasted like sawdust, and his stomach had cinched up tighter than a prune. He hung his head, barely tipping his hat to the passersby. The town square lay up ahead a few blocks with its two-story brick courthouse in the center.

Ben halted at the intersection by the clothiers. A buggy rumbled past on the side street, and a cargo wagon loaded with crates headed onto the main road. His gaze drifted to the slender green building. Every hair on his arms stood on end. The druggist. He couldn't swallow. Just one little taste. A spoonful. Would it really do that much harm?

Sweat broke out on the back of his neck and his forehead. His feet turned down the side street. He'd stroll past. He wouldn't stop. Passing a barbershop, a two-story wooden structure with no sign, and more, Ben walked on toward the well at the end of the street.

Hat off and hands trembling, he cranked the bucket up and doused his head. Water ran onto his shirt, streaking through the embedded dirt and grime. Rinsing his neckerchief in another bucket, he washed his face, neck, and hands, then ran his fingers through his hair, before donning his hat.

Finished, he gripped the stone wall of the well. *God help me.*

The tremble had spread from his insides to his core. He *needed* laudanum. His skull throbbed. He should go through the alley, cut over to the next side street and get back to Main that way. With a shudder, he started that direction, walked past a trash heap and a stray cat. Waste water ran through a ditch, headed for the town run.

His feet halted. He couldn't do it. He couldn't make it back to Pennsylvania without it. How many times had he prayed and asked the Lord to take away the hunger, the cravings? He'd prayed until his knees were stiff and his fingers numb. And still, it persisted. No answers. No healing. And why had the Lord allowed him to lose the cattle, all that he had left of his early inheritance money?

He scrubbed his hands over his jaw. No. He wouldn't lay the cattle at the Lord's feet. That had been his haste and gamble, his doing. But still... if only the Lord would scrub his heart, make it clean. Hadn't He done as much for David?

Ben kicked a tin can back into the heap.

"You lost, mister?"

He turned. He hadn't heard the woman approach.

Her gown hung off her shoulder. A smudge of dirt here and there marred the green silk. Rouge covered her cheeks, matching her bright red lips. "You just ride into town? I saw you washing by the well. I got a bath at my place if you want to get cleaned up." She smiled and touched a finger to his sleeve.

"No, thank you, ma'am." He pushed her hand away and pivoted toward the street, double-quick.

"I ain't no ma'am," she called after him.

He didn't turn around.

The green building loomed large as he neared the corner. His stomach clenched like a claw striving for its last morsel of sustenance...

What if he bought the smallest bottle they offered? Just in case he needed it for his travels. He wouldn't touch a drop until he got on the stagecoach. *If* he got on the stagecoach. How could he not if he had any hope of earning real money? He paced in front of the establishment for a full fifteen minutes before he went in.

~

The small glass bottle pressed against Ben's thigh through his thin trouser pocket, burning his conscience like a red-hot poker. His feet dragged along as he strode past the Weatherford town square and beyond. What in the world was he thinking? He should go back to the druggist, throw it on the counter, and ask for his money back.

He sniffed. Fresh-baked bread. Chicken. Probably baked. The scents drifting from the café rumbled his empty belly. He should eat something, bolster his strength, and then see if he could bring himself to go back by the druggist before he headed out to the ranch. A bowl of soup would end this rawness in his stomach.

But what of the rawness in his soul? Cora might in time regain respect for him if he worked hard in Pennsylvania and proved himself an able provider, despite the horrendous loss of the cattle. But if he followed through on what was in his pocket, he might as well say goodbye to her forever.

Voices buzzed beneath the canvas-topped outdoor seating. One sounded familiar. A railing separated the diners from the street. A waitress emerged from the log cabin kitchen with a tray of steaming dishes. She worked her way between the small tables.

Ben's heart constricted.

Cora sat with Arthur LeBeau, chatting away. Her braid hung down her back, but loose strands framed her face beneath her finest straw hat. LeBeau smiled and played with his fork, oblivious to anything but the lady before him.

Ben clenched his jaw. Cora had promised to end any notion LeBeau had of courting her. And here she was enjoying the man's company. How many times had she seen the doctor in the six weeks Ben had been gone? Had she allowed the man to call at the house and sit in the parlor visiting as if she and Ben had never spoken words of affection to each other? Ben had declared his love, and she'd hinted at her own for him. Their kiss had stirred him from the crown of his head to his toes. And here she was, sparking with this puffed-up toad, as if she didn't have a care in the world.

Heart thumping like a locomotive in his ears, Ben strode into the café, shoved a chair out of his way, and marched to their table.

Cora startled. "Ben? What...when? I thought you were—"

"Away? In New Mexico? Colorado?" He shifted his gaze from her to the scoundrel.

LeBeau pursed his lips, but he wasn't man enough to tame the weasel smile that broke through. "Afternoon, McKenzie." His eyes gleamed as if Robert E. Lee had been elected president.

Cora bumped her water glass as she withdrew her hands from the table. Water splashed over the rim before she saved it from a full tumble. "Your letter said you'd be—"

"So you thought you'd have plenty of time before I returned?"

"It's not like that at all."

Ben clenched his hands. "What are you doing here, then?"

She blinked.

LeBeau threw his napkin down. "It's none of your concern."

"Charlie broke his arm." She scooted back her chair. Her brow furrowed. "I had to bring him to Arth—Dr. LeBeau to have it set."

Ben snorted. "Well, this isn't the doctor's office. And I don't see Charlie."

LeBeau narrowed his eyes. "Are you questioning the lady's word? Or does she need to show you the cast? It's not Cora's fault the arm was swollen and they had to spend a couple of days in town."

"A couple of days?" Ben's voice rose.

"I figured the least I could do was ensure they were properly fed." LeBeau snickered. "Somebody had to."

"They had plenty of food." Ben gritted his teeth. "I was driving cattle to market..." He flinched. The cattle. He had failed.

"Ben left us plenty of everything." Cora stood and pivoted to Ben, lowering her voice. "I agreed to share a meal with Dr. LeBeau as friends. He has been my family's doctor for years. Charlie's at Miller's buying something. Probably something for you." She glanced around at the staring patrons. "We can finish discussing this at the ranch."

LeBeau drummed his fingers on the table. "The lady doesn't owe you any explanation, McKenzie. And if you were a gentleman, you wouldn't cause a scene in public."

Ben glared at him. "You don't know the first thing about being a gentleman, you weasel."

"Ben." Cora reached out as if she might touch his coat sleeve. "We need to go."

"Excellent idea." LeBeau stood. "Obviously, the man lost all of his manners while he was off chasing windmills."

~

"Arthur." Cora gaped at her supposed friend. Couldn't he be done throwing oil on the fire? "You're the one without manners now."

"It's fine." Ben's voice steeled. He jerked his arm away from her would-be touch. "LeBeau, I'll see you on the street." He dug a fifty-cent piece out of his pocket and plunked it down on the table. "I'm paying for Cora's meal."

Arthur puffed out his chest and headed for the door, a few steps behind Ben. Chairs scraped the floor around them. Everyone in the restaurant was coming.

If only she could get these two men alone in a room and talk this out. Not all together, one at a time. Even better, just her and Ben. Arthur was acting obnoxiously. She needed to convince Ben to head home with her and Charlie, where she could explain everything and find out what he was doing back here a month early. Something must have gone wrong.

Arthur filled the exit. Lifting her skirts, she nudged past. Sweat plastered her chemise and camisole to her upper back and chest. She almost tripped over the café placard.

In the street, Ben pivoted, tossed his dust-covered hat aside and removed his gun belt. The look he'd given Wolf Heart the night of the attack paled in comparison to the glare that hardened his features now, eyes narrowed and jaw clenched.

Arthur sauntered up beside her.

She jutted a hand to her hip. "You should apologize."

His mustache twitched. "It's that manure-shoveling Yankee who needs to apologize. To you."

"I don't need an apology."

Voices rang out. "There's going to be a fight." Men crossed the street. Even ladies quickened their pace. A buggy drew to a halt.

She blew out a breath so hard that it lifted the hair wisps from her forehead. "Ben." She turned toward the street. "Please, don't do this. We need to talk."

"Stay out of it, Cora." He yanked off his dirt-streaked sack coat.

Arthur stepped beyond the shelter of the crowd. "You'll have to excuse him. A man in need of his medicine can't always control his temper."

"Arthur." She grabbed him by the arm and spun him toward her. "You're despicable."

Ben closed the distance.

Arthur shook free. "Cora, I'm not going to allow you to throw yourself away on a man with a wounded soul. A man like your fa—"

Smack. Ben's fist collided with the doctor's face.

Cora jumped back. So did the crowd. Arthur was really going to say *like her father*? Here in front of everyone?

Arthur reeled, regained his footing, and swung at Ben.

Ben dodged and drove another punch into Arthur's left jaw. "I'll show you wounded." He struck a blow to Arthur's gut.

Arthur groaned, doubled over, and rammed his shoulder into Ben's stomach. They tumbled. The two rolled, a flurry of jabs and knees and grunts. Ben regained his feet and swiped his sleeve across the trickle of blood from his lip. Breathing heavily, Arthur pushed up, crouching, hands ready, his eye swollen, and his nose bleeding.

"Enough," Cora called out.

"No, they're not finished yet. Let 'em go at it some more," a farmer yelled.

Charlie squeezed through the crowd on the side and ran to her. "What's happened?"

"Ben and Dr. LeBeau—"

Arthur charged. Ben jerked away and slammed a hard right into Arthur's ribs. The doctor stumbled but swept his feet beneath Ben's, taking them both down. Punches and jabs. They wrestled. The smack of flesh to flesh.

Arthur jerked free, his white shirt smeared with dirt and blood. He rammed a boot into Ben's gut.

"Uhhn." Ben flinched.

Arthur drew back for a second kick. Ben grabbed his booted foot and yanked him down. He pounced on top of him, pinning him to the ground, knees on the doctor's thighs, grinding his hands into the dirt with his own. "You finished shooting off your mouth, scum?"

Cora shoved Charlie behind her and edged forward. Drops of blood and sweat dampened the ground near the two men. This needed to stop. "No more. You're done." She gritted out the words.

Hair poking out in every direction and face swollen, Arthur sliced a glare up at Ben. His lip curled. "I bet even now if you smelled laudanum, if someone had a bottle and took the lid off..." His voice became barely more than a hiss. "You'd drop to your knees and beg for a taste."

Ben's left hand clamped down on the man's throat. Arthur gasped and clawed at the vice-like grip. Ben drew his right arm back, fist clenched, ready to drive a powerful blow into LeBeau's face.

"No." Cora latched onto Ben's shoulder and lowered her voice to a whisper. "You're better than that."

His upper arm trembled beneath her hand, like a steam engine held back by a loose brake, ready to burst forth.

"You're better than that." She repeated the reminder and curled her fingers around his muscle.

He puffed out breaths.

"No, he's not..." Arthur huffed, struggling for air. A vein bulged across his left temple.

"Only for you." Ben grunted, shook free of her hold, and struck the ground with his fist inches from Arthur's head.

LeBeau flinched.

Ben loosened his grip and stood.

LeBeau rolled to the side and coughed.

"Way to go." Some of the crowd cheered.

"What are you talking about? That's our doctor," others rebutted.

"Snooty nose doctor."

"Snooty doctor's better than a Yank," another hollered.

Cora stiffened her wobbly limbs. "My brother, Jeb sent him." Swiping her nose, she turned in a circle, meeting their eyes. "Anyone dishonors him, they dishonor the Scott family."

Ben swung his gaze to her.

Surprise? Pain? What else? The unfathomable hazel eyes held hers for a breath, then he retrieved his gun belt and strode off. The crowd parted in his wake.

Arthur pushed up onto his hands and knees.

She wasn't waiting for him to regain his feet. Charlie threw her a glance and took off running after Ben. She lifted her skirts and followed. Ben was already a block ahead, storming toward the livery stable, as if he would smash through anything in his path. She picked up her pace. They needed to go home together.

Charlie caught up to him, calling out and tugging on his loose shirt. Ben's hat and coat? He'd left them. Should she go back?

Ben halted his headlong charge and turned to the boy. He dropped down to one knee. They spoke, and Charlie threw his good arm around the man. But then, Ben ruffled the boy's hair and pointed toward her. Charlie back-stepped while Ben tromped ahead double-quick.

Not good. Cora halted and placed her hand to her chest.

Charlie plodded up to her. "He said I had to wait and come home with you."

If Ben had waited, they could have all traveled home together. "That's fine. We'll fetch his hat and coat and meet him at home." Why did her stupid voice have to tremble?

"I can go get it."

"Hold on." She placed a hand on his shoulder, adjusting the loop of the sling away from his neck. "What else did Ben say?"

The boy lifted his chin. "Not much. That he'd missed me and that he was glad I didn't get too hurt from the fall. I told him I didn't like the doctor. And I understood Dr. LeBeau said something mean to him. And that I think the doctor is trying to steal you."

"Me?" Cora winced. That's the last thing Ben needed to hear. She pressed her lips together. She wouldn't scold the boy.

Charlie wiggled a finger against the opening of his cast. "The doctor's sneaky with his money. I took his nickels and dimes, but I know what he's up to."

She tapped her fingers to his back. "Go fetch Ben's coat and hat. Then meet me at the livery stables. We need to get home."

Dear Lord, help that man listen to reason.

CHAPTER 31

ora's stomach wobbled as she drove the wagon through the ranch's open palisade gate. According to Mr. Dawson at the livery stables, Ben had returned to Weatherford with forty or fifty head of cattle. Where were the other three hundred he'd written about? She pulled the horses to a halt in front of the open stable. Maybe Ben had run into some of Goodnight's men on the trail and sold them the cattle? But if that was the case, why the glum look, and why had he been so quick-tempered at the café? Something was wrong. She set the brake.

Charlie scrambled out of the wagon back. "I'm going to see Ben."

"No." Her voice cut sharp. "I need to talk to Ben, and you need to rest after everything you've been through with your arm."

"I'm not tired." He groaned. "It's not even close to dinner time yet. I haven't seen Ben in a long time." He edged toward the door.

"I said no."

He made a face, then brightened. "I could unharness the

horses and feed them while you talk." So he could be right there in the stable overhearing what was said. He ran over to Sandy, his hand already on the bridle.

Cora hopped out of the wagon. "Charlie, listen to me." She walked over and slid her hand under his chin, drawing his gaze upward. "Ben and I have things to discuss. Grownup things. If you want to help, you can unharness the horses here and now with my assistance. Then you take them to the well, give them a drink, and walk them to the far field to graze. And you stay put. If I see you any nearer to the stables than the well, you'll go to bed without supper, and you won't see Ben until the morning. You hear me?"

"The well is all the way across the yard."

Not nearly far enough. "I asked if you heard me."

He squirmed and frowned. "I hear you."

"Then do as I say." She released his chin and started loosening the harness.

"Everything is going to be all right, isn't it?" He gazed up at her.

"Of course." It sure wasn't all right at the moment. Ben had been quick-tempered, thought the worst, refused to listen, and Arthur had been an incendiary, fueling the fire until it exploded in his face. Worst of all, he'd besmirched all of their reputations, himself included, with his breach of patient confidentiality. She'd ride to the next county before she went to see that man again.

Horses unharnessed and Charlie headed for the well, Cora climbed the stairs to the loft and knocked.

Rustling and movement whispered through the hardwood, but no voice. The odors of manure and hay wafted up from the horse stalls below.

"Ben." She knocked again. "We need to talk."

No answer. She banged. "You're not being fair. I did nothing wrong."

The door swung open. "Never said you did." He stalked across the room, pulling his suspenders over the shoulders of his silkaline undershirt.

A pile of dirty clothes lay on the floor by the chair. Trousers, underclothes, stockings...it looked as if he'd stripped off every filthy garment he'd worn on the trail. A dirty washcloth dripped from a hook by the basin. Murky water filled the porcelain bowl.

She exhaled. How should she even begin? "You had no right to storm into the café and yell at me. You gave me no chance to explain—"

"I've never yelled at you." A deep red streak stretched across his cheekbone just beneath his eyes, but no black and blue yet.

"Your look did."

He snorted. "I was supposed to be pleased that you were keeping company with the man who's been chasing after you? You told me you'd end things with him."

"I did end them. The first and only time he called while you were away, I gave his gifts back and told him not to call anymore."

"But there you were having the noon meal with him."

"Charlie broke his arm. He needed a doctor—"

"That didn't explain the smile." His lower lip puckered around a gash.

"What smile?"

"The one on your face when you were chatting away with him at the café." He grabbed a clean cotton shirt from a pile on his bed and stuffed his arms into the sleeves. It was about time he covered up his snug undershirt that clung to his muscles and scattered her thoughts.

"I...we... He probably said something about Charlie. I don't remember. It was probably the only time I smiled in his presence the whole two days I was in town."

"Two days."

"Charlie's arm was too swollen for the cast. We had to wait. We ate in the café once—"

"The man is a snake in the grass, Cora. I've heard it from others. It's not just me." He spread his arms wide. "But you're free to do as you see fit."

"What's that supposed to mean?"

He knelt and dragged his carpetbag from under the bed.

"You're not being fair." She rubbed her hands over her arms. "I agreed to one last meal as a friend after he refused to accept payment for Charlie's care."

"You don't need his charity." He plunked the royal-blue carpetbag with a black-and-gold diamond pattern on top of his quilt and opened the trunk at the foot of the bed. "I'll leave payment at his office when I'm in town."

"You need to stay away from him and his office."

"I'm paying him." He shoved a handful of drawers and undershirts into the bag. "I won't have you beholden to him for a single penny."

"What are you doing?" She crossed the room to the bunk.

He jerked the bag open wider and tossed his socks in.

Packing. He was packing. Her stomach dropped to her feet.

He layered the shirts in next.

Acid rose up in her throat. He couldn't just up and leave. "Ben." She touched his arm.

He glared at her and shrugged off her hand.

She grabbed one side of the heavy cloth bag. "Why are you packing?" Her voice faltered. "Because I went to dinner with Arthur? You have or had a betrothed. How dare you? You're the most hard-headed, quick-tempered man—"

"It's nothing to do with you and Arthur." He yanked the bag from her grip.

"There is no *me and Arthur*. You're the one I want to keep company with. You're the one who has stolen my heart. The one—" *I want to spend the rest of my life with.*

His gaze locked onto hers for the first time since she'd entered the room. A bruise had deepened along his jawline. "I'm going back to Pennsylvania."

"What?" She stumbled back a step.

"I made the decision before I ran across you and that scum. I don't regret whipping him. He deserved it. But I'm thankful you saved me from that last blow, when I already had him down. Goodness knows I wanted to break his nose after..." His jaw clenched. "But for your sake, I'm sorry I fought in front of the town."

For her sake? Her reputation was tarnished. The whole town now probably thought she and Ben were out here carrying on. But that wasn't what mattered most. "You can't leave."

He rolled up his extra pair of clean trousers and stuck them in the yawning mouth of his luggage.

What if he'd decided he still had feelings for his betrothed? Her heart contracted. "Is it Olivia?"

He jerked to a halt. "It'd suit me fine if I never saw her again." He drove his fingers through damp hair, revealing the shadow of a bruise on his temple. "I gave my word to Jeb that I'd look after you and provide for you, and that's what I aim to do." He retrieved his toiletry pouch from the table and stuffed his comb in, followed by his toothbrush. "I'm going to accept the editor position at my father's paper and earn real money."

"Why?" She yanked the carpetbag from his grasp and sat on it as he reached for it. "You promised you'd stay and provide for us. Protect us. And now you're leaving? What about Wolf Heart? LeBeau? What about your big talk about ranching?"

He flinched as if she'd slapped him.

Forty to fifty cattle, not three hundred and fifty. She bit her lip. "What happened? Mr. Cleary at the livery stable said—"

"What did he say, Cora?" He tossed his toiletry case toward

the bed, but it bumped against the post and bounced off. "Did he tell you how I failed?"

Air seeped from her lungs. "No, he didn't say any such thing."

"Well, I did. I failed." He paced. His bare feet struck the worn boards like the slap of a clothes paddle against wet clothes. "I'm no rancher. I was only fooling myself. I know how to live rough. I did well enough as an army officer. I survived the hell of Andersonville. But I don't know cattle. I know words and news and business. I'm an editor. I'm going back to Pennsylvania where I can earn a good living. I'll send you money."

He was giving up? "It's you I care about, not your money." She sprang off the case. "I want you here."

He jerked to a halt in front of her. Deep crevices formed across his brow and at the corners of his eyes. "I lost everything, Cora." He cupped his hands around her shoulders as if to steady himself. "I lost it all." His voice trailed off.

"What do you mean?" Her eyebrows shot upward.

His hands dropped away. "I lost the cattle." He scrubbed his hand down the length of his face and sank onto the hardback chair.

"How?" Her voice faltered. "Were...you attacked? Comanche? Bandits?"

He shrugged and threw one arm wide. "I wish it were the Comanche or bandits. Instead of..." He shoved his fingers through his hair with such force that it tugged on his scalp. "Instead of over two hundred and fifty of them lying hooves up a mile from the Pecos."

She dropped to her knees in front of him. "H...how?" Their hopes and plans for the ranch? All of Ben's money? Gone?

～

*B*en's tongue clung to the roof of his mouth. The longhorns died because of his stupidity and impatience. If he'd waited for Goodnight. If he'd stuck with what he knew best. If he hadn't wanted to impress Cora... "Alkaline water. Most of them. The rest shot because they'd injured a leg in a mad rush down a plateau."

He buried his face in his hands—anything to block out Cora's upturned, pale face and wide, disappointed eyes. The rest of the story leaked across his lips.

Silence fell after he finished. His horse whinnied from the stable beneath them. He needed to finish this and head to town by nightfall. Before Cora's disappointment and loss of respect for him cut him to the core.

She touched his knee. "But you couldn't have known about the pond, Ben. It was dark. You'd never been to the area. You didn't even—"

"I should have known or put someone in charge who did. It was my operation, my responsibility. I'm the one who made the decision to drive the cattle to market without waiting on Goodnight."

"You were only trying to do what was best for us."

He raised his head. "I'll make this right. I'll be on the stage at the end of the week. It might take two months before I have a good sum of money back here, but you can sell off a few of the cattle at the stockyard, or use the money Goodnight—"

"I don't want you to go." Moisture dampened her eyes. Her slender fingers wrapped around his weathered ones, her gaze so bright it took his breath away. "We'll get through this somehow. Here. Together."

"Together." He sank back against the wall. His eyes stung. She would stand by him? Despite everything? He squeezed his eyes shut and sucked in a quick breath, fighting against the surge of hope threatening to explode within him. "You don't understand. I'm broke. Except for what I got for the sale of a heifer to the stockyard owner. And most of that is owed to Miller, except for what I'm saving for traveling back East. I came to Texas with my early inheritance determined to set you up fine...and I've blown it all."

"You own half a ranch. Good land with lots of potential."

"I'm not claiming your ranch, Cora. And it takes money and cattle to run a ranch. I'm not going to have you and Charlie just scraping by. I'm going to provide for you the best way I know how. As an ed—"

"I'm not letting you go." She released his hands and pressed her palms to his thighs, raising her gaze to his. "Families stick together. Mine never fully did." Her eyes glistened with the most beautiful gift anyone had ever given him. Her trust. And her love.

He slid his hand along her jawline. "I don't deserve such grace."

Her voice turned silken. "And I don't deserve the overwhelming generosity you've shown me since the day you first set foot on the ranch."

He leaned forward, skimming his hands over her hair and down her back, drawing her closer. He dipped his forehead to hers. Warmth flooded through him. Hope. Love. "You're not going to allow me to give up, are you?" His voice more of a breath than a whisper.

"Absolutely not." She slid her hands over his chest and shoulders in a caress that sent his heart skipping like a stone across water. Her fingers curled around the back of his neck.

"I'm sorry I assumed the worst and lost my temper at the café, Cora."

Her lashes fluttered against his nose. "You're the one and only man who has my heart." She lifted her gaze, cornflower blue calling to him.

His lips found hers in a kiss that obliterated the disappointment and doom, and any thought of a stagecoach and the road east. He pulled her onto his lap and wrapped her in his embrace, moving his hands up and down her sides and across her back, losing himself in kisses...

A knock. Ben raised his head. Cora stirred from her cuddled position on his lap. Shadows had fallen across the room, but he'd been in no mood to release his girl from his hold. Had they sat like that for an hour or more?

"Charlie's probably wondering what happened to us." Cora touched her hair, which now cascaded down her back.

Should they act as if they'd only been talking?

Cora edged off his lap, and he rose beside her, his legs numb from her weight, and his other muscles aching from LeBeau's blows. "Come in." He wrapped his arm around her shoulders and drew her to his side. The boy might as well see the truth.

Shirt untucked and his arm in the sling close to his body, Charlie halted on the threshold and studied them. "Are you two going to get married?"

Ben half laughed. "We're thinking on it."

Cora blushed.

"Good." Charlie skipped over. "I want to show you the whistle I bought." He dug the wooden object out of his pocket. "And I'm wondering when we're going to eat."

Cora smiled. "I'm going to get right on dinner. You stay here and visit with Ben."

Marry Cora. It was what he wanted more than anything in the world. But what was he to do about his promise to his father?

He had no answers to that, but he knew what he would do with the small medicine bottle in the pocket of his dirty trousers on the floor.

An hour later, with Charlie in the house washing up and preparing to eat, Ben quickstepped to the outhouse. As the door clunked shut behind him, he dug the bottle out of his pocket, opened the lid, and poured the contents into the hole, careful not to allow a single drop to touch his skin. The odor was bad enough. Made his head swim. But he would not disrespect Cora's gift of trust and respect. With the force of David slinging the rock toward Goliath, Ben hurtled the bottle and lid into the mire of waste. *Lord, I give this craving to You. You can do what I cannot do alone. Let me be worthy of her love.*

CHAPTER 32

The cool evening air whispered against Cora's skin as she walked onto the front porch and settled onto the room-for-two wooden swing. Ben had spent his entire first day back on the ranch working on the project—not the most practical use of his time, but one dear to her heart. Although Charlie had hovered around him, helping the best he could one-handed, Ben hadn't allowed her out front until just before supper.

They'd hardly spoken a word about the cattle. After the hurricane of emotions yesterday with the confrontation at the café, Ben's fight with Arthur, the threat of Ben leaving, and the sweetest reconciliation imaginable in Ben's arms...a day of ordinary had definitely been in order.

Ben stepped onto the porch and leaned against the post. "Everything's locked up for the night."

"And Mr. Franklin?" They could ill afford to keep the watchman, but Ben had agreed to continue employing the man for night duty for propriety's sake. Now that the whole town was well aware of Ben's romantic intentions toward her.

"He'll likely sit out in front of the stables and have a smoke."

Ben smiled. "I did my best to politely discourage his coming to the porch to join us."

She smoothed her skirt with her palms. "I tucked Charlie in. He wasn't quite acquiescent to the principle that children need more sleep than their elders."

"Tomorrow evening, I'll help you put him to bed and read a story." He ambled over to the swing. He'd washed up from his day of work. Clean dark-blue shirt, buckskin-colored trousers, and suspenders. A couple of bruises discolored his cheekbone and jaw. If there were injuries to his body from Arthur's blows and kicks, he seemed to have no intention of letting on.

The swing creaked as he sat beside her. Her pulse quickened. Would he hold her hand or wrap his arm around her shoulders? Would he talk for a while before he kissed her? He would kiss her, wouldn't he? She'd waited all day for it.

"The swing is a beautiful gift." She lowered her gaze to her lap and fiddled with a fold of her skirt. "I love it."

"Perfect for courting my girl." He stretched his arm behind her, drawing her closer, thigh to thigh. The scents of bay rum and soap emanated from his presence. "Couldn't very well cuddle like this in two rockers, even if they're side by side."

He seemed back to his usual self, even more so. Had her encouragement yesterday meant that much to him? Not on her own doing. Perhaps the Lord had answered her prayers.

Ben pushed with his legs, and the swing moved back and forth. The supporting chains creaked with each movement. Across the western horizon, the sunset blushed pink. The traces of light slowly faded as pricks of brightness popped into the twilight sky one by one. Katydids chirped from the swishing grasses.

She laid her head against his shoulder, and he pressed his cheek to her hair, taking her hand in his and drawing it to his thigh as they watched the fading blue of the sky give way to night.

Twilight fully reigned by the time he spoke again, his voice low and gentle but sprinkled with an edge of matter-of-fact. "We need to talk, Cora."

"I'd be perfectly fine if we didn't." Surely, any serious discussion could wait until morning. She snuggled closer.

A light chuckle lifted his chest. He kissed her hair. "You are the girl who has captured my heart, and I'd like nothing better than to kiss you all night long, but I need to let you know about an obstacle."

"If it's about the cattle, we'll find a way to make the finances work." She raised her head and scooted away a couple of inches, putting just enough distance between them so she could see his face. "I didn't mention it yesterday, but Goodnight came by a few days ago."

"He's already back from the trail drive? How?" Ben's arm slipped away.

"He only had to go halfway. Ended up selling the herd to the army in New Mexico. The troops forced the Navajo onto a huge reservation there but had no way to feed them. The army officials bought all of the steers, and Mr. Loving took the cows and yearlings on to Colorado. Goodnight gave me the profit from the sale of my cattle you'd rounded up. We have cash for now. Enough to last until fall and beyond because of you."

He rubbed his hand over his hair. "If I'd waited, I could have persuaded him to take the longhorns I purchased from the widow with him if he made another run..." A groan vibrated from his throat.

"You did what you thought best for us. You took one of Goodnight's seasoned hands as a guide." She curled her fingers around his biceps. "And I have a sack of coins hidden under my mattress because of your quick thinking and hard work with my family's herd. This is the frontier. Losses—great losses sometimes—are part of survival here." And didn't she know it, heart and soul. Her whole family, save Charlie. Gone. Was it worth it? She shuddered. "But Goodnight is going again. He was headed to Weatherford for supplies, and he's roaming the range looking for more cattle—"

"He could take our forty-five head." Ben sat taller.

"Yes." She brightened.

"A handful compared to what might have been." He inhaled. His voice firmed. "I should leave tomorrow. Ask around town. Find out which direction he headed. If I ride hard, I should be able to catch him—"

"Tomorrow? You just got back."

"I have to catch him before he hits the trail. As is, I might need to hire a cowhand to help drive the cattle to Palo Pinto to meet up with him."

She slid her hands down to his. "But you won't go with him, right? Not all the way to New Mexico?" *Please say no. You've been gone enough.* "Goodnight said he might winter there."

Ben studied her for a moment. "If he invited me, it wouldn't be a bad idea. I'd likely learn a lot. But I have other matters to consider." His voice trailed off. He brushed his fingertips down the length of her hair as if he'd discovered a great treasure. "The last thing I want to do is be away from you for months."

The last thing she wanted either. "The ranch doesn't feel quite like home anymore when you're gone."

His eyes widened. "It's the only place that feels like home to me." His voice dipped.

She touched her hand to his chest.

He tipped her chin upward. "I haven't even told you how beautiful you are tonight. With your hair down...and the way the moonlight glistens in your eyes..." His gaze fell to her mouth.

Her lips parted. He dipped his head and brushed his lips to hers, like butterfly wings, before deepening the kiss and scattering all thoughts of the world beyond his arms. Melting in his embrace, she lost herself in love.

"Ahem." Someone cleared their throat.

Cora startled and slipped halfway out of Ben's arms.

A pinprick of light emanated from Mr. Franklin's cigarette as he ambled toward the porch steps.

Ben shifted and withdrew his hand to his lap, blowing out a sharp exhale. "Can I do something for you, Mr. Franklin?"

"Just wondering if the miss might have any coffee left." Franklin drew up to the bottom step and hooked a thumb around his suspender. "I'm hankerin' for a cup before I turn in for the night."

She could almost hear Ben's teeth grinding. "There should be at least half a cup in the pot in the kitchen." She fought the temptation to roll her eyes.

"You're welcome to it." Ben straightened and wrapped his hand around hers as if he were afraid she might volunteer to play hostess. "Only, be careful not to bang around in the kitchen. Charlie's a light sleeper."

"Obliged, Mr. Mckenzie. Ma'am." He tipped his hat and ambled up the steps and through the open door into the hall.

"He wants to remind us he's here," she whispered.

"I don't need any reminders." Ben caressed her hair, then handed her the comb which had fallen to her lap in the midst of their kissing.

She lowered her gaze to her skirt and strummed her fingertips across the folds. "You know, there is a way to remove the need for a chaperone." As soon as the words left her tongue, she winced. Had she really just said that?

Ben cocked his eyebrows.

Her face heated. "Please ignore that remark." Someone should paste her mouth shut. It wasn't her place to hint at marriage. She'd definitely been on the frontier too long.

"I'd greatly relish the lack of need for a chaperone, Miss Scott." He captured her wayward fingers and drew her hand to his lips. "I can think of nothing I'd like better than to settle matters between me and my girl." He brushed his lips to her knuckles.

But the way the words trailed off... His tender touch couldn't hide the slight trace of...what? Doubt?

He raised his gaze to hers. "However, there is the obstacle about which I spoke."

So it was more than finances and the loss of the cattle? She braced herself. "What is it?"

"My father."

Not what she'd expected. "You think he'll disapprove of me?" Why wouldn't he, when the previous fiancée had been a polished, high-society lady?

"No. That's not it." He took both of her hands now and held them in the juncture between his lap and hers. "And I'm not asking his opinion on that. But..."

"But?"

Air leaked from his lungs. "I promised him, years ago, that I'd take over his share of the newspaper. The editorship was just the first step to eventually owning a controlling share. To carrying on his work."

Her swallow worked its way down her throat like quicksand. Of course, a father would want his son to carry on his work, his legacy that he'd poured himself into. Her stomach flopped. "Don't you have any brothers?" She bit her lip. Couldn't she hush? What did it matter if he had brothers? He likely wanted to manage the paper. Had she ever asked him if he wanted to be a rancher? Did she think she was the only one with dreams and commitments?

He half chuckled, but the laugh ran dry. "I have a younger brother who has defied our father since his youth. He joined the Navy during the war. Afterwards, he signed on with a British shipping company as first mate. Sails the world. He has no head for words and has never shown interest in the paper. For all practical purposes, my father has disowned him." He shifted and sighed. "My father laid all of his future aspirations on me."

"Heavy load." She rolled her lips inward.

Ben shifted his gaze to the horizon. "Leaves a man with only a narrow trough in which to find his way."

She squeezed his hands and steeled herself. "What will you do?"

"I don't know. I don't have any answers. I can't leave you, yet I can't commit to making a life here long term."

"Are you asking me..." Surely, he wouldn't ask her to leave Texas. "You wouldn't... I couldn't... This is my home..."

"I would never ask you to give up the ranch."

"What, then?"

"Pray about it." He squeezed her hands. "I'm sure I have until winter. I could probably put my father off a year, even."

A year, but not forever. "You knew this weeks ago when you declared your desire to court me." She drew her hands close to her body and shifted toward the yard. "You should have told me." *Before my heart threw away its shield and opened its dungeon doors to welcome your love.*

"I am sorry." He stood and rubbed the back of his neck. "Before the Comanche attack, I believed I had no hope with you. Afterwards, I was afraid to risk dampening the spark between us. It was on my mind to tell you before I left to round up the widow's cattle. But it wasn't the kind of news I wanted to give you before I hopped into the saddle and rode off for weeks or months."

"You could have told me yesterday too."

"Yesterday, I was lost in the mud and mire, and you pulled me out and showed me the sunrise."

She fiddled with her cuff. "I don't understand why you broke your engagement to Olivia...if you had thoughts of returning to Philadelphia."

"Cora." He nudged her shoulder with his knuckle, but she

refused to face him. Blowing out a breath, he knelt on one knee in front of her. "I don't love her. I love you. "

"Men don't always marry the girl they love."

"You're the one I want to marry."

A proposal. Almost. Not quite. *Want* was not *will you.* Was there a hidden *can't* in there, or would there sooner or later be a *could you come with me*? She was the one who'd started the whole discussion. If she'd waited a month or two and let him bring it up, maybe he'd be asking her a direct question.

She glanced toward the horizon. Her family had invested their lives in this land. Her parents' dreams would live or die with her. "Maybe you can change your father's mind...or start a paper in Weatherford or Dallas." But what if it was his intention to head back to Pennsylvania as soon as he got her ranch up and going, to the life he wanted?

Footsteps.

She stood, and so did Ben.

Mr. Franklin ambled out the door, cup in hand. "Thank you kindly. I'll be sitting in front of the stables enjoying the night air."

Watching from a distance. Well, the chaperone could rest assured. She and Ben were no longer in danger of getting carried away.

Franklin's footsteps faded into the dark.

Standing beside her at the post, Ben nudged his pinky to hers. She folded her arms, feeling as bristly as a prickly pear.

Ben swept his hair back from his forehead. "We've talked enough about this tonight. We need to both pray on it. If I have my way, Cora, you, Charlie, and I will one day be a family." He turned and met her gaze across the divide of rattled hopes. "Meanwhile, I plan to ride out tomorrow morning to find Goodnight. We need to get most of the cattle we have left to market." His voice wavered, but he lifted his chin. "I'll save out a bull and a few heifers. And I'll get back here as soon as I can because I don't want to be away from you a day longer than I have to."

He was shouldering the huge loss and moving forward. Exactly what she'd encouraged him to do and what she'd vowed to support him in doing.

Ben extended his open hand toward her, waiting for hers.

Leaving again. Tomorrow. Hopefully, he'd be back in a few days. But it could be a week or two. Even longer. They didn't need her stubbornness dividing them while they were apart. She unlocked her arms and let her hand drift to her side.

He stepped closer and moved his hand to within a finger's length of hers, calling to every fiber of her being, as if she were a compass needle and he was due north. Forgoing his hand, she slipped into his arms, laid her head against his shoulder, and snuggled close.

Dear Lord, please make a way. If it be Your will for Ben and me to marry, for us to live here, and Ben, me, and Charlie to be a family. I've lost everyone else. Please, if it be Your will...

Your will. Dangerous words. What if it wasn't the Lord's will? But how could it not be?

Ben whispered, "We'll find a way."

She lifted her gaze to his. His lips found hers, melting her to the core.

It was well past midnight before they left the porch.

CHAPTER 33

Two days after Ben left, a messenger rode into the yard. Cora had seen the youth around town before, doing errands. While Charlie went to fill the young man's canteen at the well, the fellow dug an envelope out of his saddlebag.

"From Dr. LeBeau."

She stared at the proffered item with its fancy script. "Did he say what it was about?"

"No, ma'am." The youth scratched his head. The beginning of manly fuzz dotted his chin. "Just said it was important. And he paid me a handsome sum to deliver it."

She should refuse it. But that could create more problems. Arthur might decide to deliver it himself. He'd surely heard that Ben had left again. The whole town had probably been tongue-wagging since the fight. She pulled it into her hand as Charlie rounded the corner. "Thank you for your service. I'll get a coin—"

"Doc says I'm not to accept money from you." The messenger tipped his hat.

A paper cut nicked her finger as she slid the envelope into her apron pocket. Would the words also slice?

She dismissed Charlie's questions and went about her day. Evening found her pacing the kitchen, the unopened envelope on the work table. Arthur would have nothing good to say. She'd be better off burning it. But what if he was threatening action against Ben for the fight? With a shudder, she picked it up and sat down on the back stoop to read in the growing dusk.

Two pieces of paper fell out, one in Arthur's hand. An embossed engraving headed the other—*Keely's Apothecary*. Her stomach tumbled. No. It would not say what she feared. It'd be conjecture only. With a trembling hand, she read Arthur's note first.

For your own sake, Cora, I pray that you will heed Mr. Keely's words. I have included them with this missive so you might read them yourself in his own handwriting. If you have any doubts, you may question the man yourself. He sent this to me the day after the fight.

You might want to ask yourself if this could be the reason that Mr. McKenzie was so quickly overcome with jealousy and rage at the café. He would have likely broken my nose and worse with further blows if it were not for your intervention. My words to him about the medicine were truthfully spoken. He'd beg for it if he had to. In the end, laudanum rules him. His feelings for you will always be secondary.

Write to me when the blinding scales of infatuation fall from your eyes and you're ready to listen to reason.

Yours,

Arthur

Her breath caught in her throat. She threw the poisoned letter on the ground and stood. It was a lie. Whatever Keely's letter said, Arthur must have twisted it. Arthur was jealous and bitter, set on revenge. Ben hadn't partaken of laudanum for over four months. He or the Lord had broken its hold on him...

Ill to her stomach, she paced. Keely's note lay on the stoop, beneath the open envelope flap. It didn't matter what it said. Did it? Knees wobbly, she crept to the step and sank down, whispering a prayer before she unfolded the letter.

Doctor LeBeau,

You asked that I inform you if your patient, Mr. Benjamin McKenzie, stopped into purchase any laudanum. Two days ago, on Thursday, about half an hour before the fight, Mr. McKenzie entered my establishment, looking sickly and used up. He asked to purchase a small bottle of laudanum. I sold him four ounces. His hand trembled as he paid. In my estimation, he was a man in desperate need of his medicine.

At your service,

Mr. Howard Keeley

The paper slipped from her fingers. Nausea rolled through her. She ran for the outhouse, stumbling over a root in the twilight. The door banged against the wooden side as she entered the hovel and emptied the contents of her stomach.

The letter didn't make it true. Arthur could have paid the druggist to lie. Would Mr. Keeley really do that? She wiped her mouth on a handkerchief as she drifted back to the house. Laudanum had lost its hold on Ben months ago. Then why had he purchased it?

He'd been desperate on Thursday. He'd lost the cattle and blamed himself for it. Hadn't Arthur warned her weeks ago that hard times could lead a man to succumb to the cravings? Although Arthur's word wasn't one to be trusted regarding Ben, hadn't she seen the same with her own father? He'd abstain for a week or two or even a month or two, but then a disappointment or a hardship would come, and the alcohol would call him back like a siren. The alcohol always won.

A slight moan slipped through her lips. She clapped her hand over her mouth. Ben was not her father. She repeated it to herself. Ben was not her father. A shiver rattled through her. No. She would not believe it, not without further proof. She gripped the wall of the well to steady herself.

When she'd confronted Ben in the loft after the fight, he'd claimed he'd failed her. He'd been ready to pack up and head to town to await the stagecoach with plans to return East to earn money for her. What if he had failed in a much worse way than losing the cattle? What if he'd broken his word and used the medicine? Back slidden off the edge of a cliff?

～

Three days later, Cora sent Charlie to the other side of the ranch with Jack to collect raspberries. Her doubts had gotten the best of her. She trudged up the steps to the stable loft with an armload of Ben's newly laundered clothes. Her lungs deflated as she opened the door and stood on the threshold.

He'd left the place in order. Bed made, chairs pushed in, dirty clothes picked up and given to her. A corner of the empty carpetbag poked out beneath the bunk. His two books, Dickens's *Great Expectations* and James Fenimore Cooper's *Last of the Mohicans*, stood on the short shelf, no Bible in sight. He'd likely taken that with him.

She had no right to search the room. But the contents of the letters had gnawed away at her peace and her trust. So here she stood, ready to cross the line.

Chickens clucked in the yard. Just as long as Charlie stayed away until she was done.

Slowly, she ambled into the room and laid the folded

clothes on the end of the bunk. If Ben had purchased the medicine, he'd likely taken the bottle with him. However, if he left it, and she found it, she could see if he'd opened it and taken any. Maybe he'd bought it but thought better of it afterwards. If she found the bottle, she'd have evidence, either reassurance or devastation.

Her gaze fell to the worn floorboards by the rag rug. The spot where the other bottle had fallen and spilled the day he'd knocked the spoon from her hand. She'd never witnessed such desperation before. It was as if the very scent of it would poison him. On his hands and knees, he'd worked to scour every droplet from the floor. She cringed and hugged herself. He'd fought to stay away from it. Why would he purchase it again?

She sank down to sit on the bunk. Did she really believe he could have it in his possession and not partake of it? And who knew if there might not be other bottles hidden in his room from other missteps.

Had love blinded her to the truth? Alcohol won every time with her father. How could she think it was any different with Ben, only with a smaller bottle and a different label? Except Ben was trustworthy, dependable, generous, strong, determined, committed to his word... He was all of this and more. And yet, if the bottle gained the upper hand, its poison would taint every drop of his soul.

Cora dropped to her knees and dragged the carpetbag out. The trunk at the foot of the bed was next. He didn't have a lot of possessions. Her search took less than half an hour and included the windowsill, loose floorboards, and beneath his bedding. No trace of a bottle. There was only one surprise, a slender leather briefcase tucked beneath the horsehair mattress.

A millstone weighted her shoulders and chest as she sat cross-legged on the floor and examined the case. She pressed against the exterior, feeling every side. No odd-shaped objects or bottles as far as she could tell. It felt more like books, but could the width of the books hide a smaller object?

The latch was unlocked, but whatever was in here was private, not meant for her eyes. Otherwise, why would he have hidden it under his mattress?

She should put it back where she'd found it and get out of there. But wouldn't this be the perfect place to conceal a small bottle if he had one on the premises? Instead of snooping, she should confront Ben when he returned. But could she risk her future on the chance he'd not be honest? She buried her face in her hands.

Feeling lower than the dirt on the sole of her shoe, she opened the flap and slid the contents onto her lap. Two notebooks slipped out, their hard covers battered. Age or weather had yellowed and bowed the edges of the pages. Someone had written *Andersonville* across the front of one and *Andersonville II* across the second. Her breath hitched. Ben's journals or possibly even Jeb's? No, Ben would have given them to her if they were Jeb's. Still, they could contain information about her brother.

More importantly, they likely contained Ben's soul. Not hers to open without an invitation.

She felt around in the case, fingered the edges of the notebooks, then slipped them back into their hiding place.

Ben had spoken little about the prison camp, and he had likely only skimmed the surface of the horrors he and Jeb had suffered. Was it any wonder he'd come back scarred within?

CHAPTER 34

Clean-shaven and hair still damp from his visit to the barbershop, Ben quickstepped past the thin green building near the corner of Main Street in Weatherford. He had no intention of giving temptation a moment to take root. If he hurried, he could make it home in plenty of time to share the good news with Cora before supper. Goodnight had taken forty of the cattle on the trail with him and, in light of the recent catastrophe, agreed to charge a smaller fee than the first time. The experienced rancher and cattleman said that he had even lost a few cattle near that very spot on the Pecos his first time through.

At the corner, he turned right toward the livery stable, the opposite direction of LeBeau's office. No use looking for trouble. Fielding the barber's questions about the fight had been enough. Obviously, the whole town had nothing better to do for entertainment than spread gossip about the battle for Miss Cora Scott's hand.

Ben slowed his stride. There was no battle for Cora's hand. Cora was his girl. But was that a question to leave open in everyone's mind for another year or even until winter? He needed to find a way to keep his word to his father and yet be free to court Cora with the full intention of proposing.

"Mr. McKenzie." A voice rang out behind him.

Ben stiffened. His hand fell to his holster flap as he turned. On the frontier, one never knew how far another man might go for revenge.

But it was only Mr. Miller waving a piece of paper at him and hurrying along on the other side of the street. Tension ebbed from Ben's shoulders. He waited for a mule-driven wagon to pass and then crossed the street in front of a buggy.

Miller caught up to him. "I heard you were in town." He removed his slouch hat and dabbed his damp forehead with his handkerchief.

"Passing through on my way to the ranch." Ben tugged on the lapels of his too-warm frock coat. "If I'd known you wanted to see me, I would have stopped by the store. You did receive the payment I left with your clerk before I rode out of town last week, didn't you?"

"The payment was fine." Miller smiled. "And I would have understood if you'd taken another month to send it. No hurry." He held up the paper. "But I wanted to get this to you. The telegram clerk left it with me yesterday. Figured you'd likely stop by the store when you got back to Weatherford."

Ben frowned at the envelope. Anything that had to be sent in that much of a hurry probably wasn't good news. "Thank you kindly." He took the telegram and shook the man's hand. "I'm just sorry you had to run out of your store to catch me."

"No trouble." Miller hooked his thumbs around his suspenders beneath his open coat. "I heard you were at the barber's, and I fancied it was about time I got myself a shave, only before I got there, I saw you headed up the street here."

Ben blinked. Did this town keep a running tab on where he was at any given moment when he was in Weatherford? His throat tightened, but he managed an uptick in his lips.

"Thank you for all of your help. I won't keep you from your shave."

Miller tipped his hat. "I'd better hurry off so I can get back before Mrs. Miller has to abandon the storefront to cook supper. I hope your telegram brings good news."

"Good day, Miller." Ben pivoted.

"McKenzie?" Miller called behind him.

Ben turned.

"Good luck with the girl. I'm voting for you." Miller grinned.

Ben half snorted. How did one reply to such a remark? "I'm working on it." He stuck his tongue in his cheek and hurried off before the man could ask the particulars.

But it was the telegram that worried him. He tapped the paper to his leg as he strode along. He wasn't about to open it in front of prying eyes. Who knew how many people in this town were aware he'd received a telegram? The booming size of Philadelphia definitely had its advantages when it came to privacy.

Standing against a wall in the back of the livery stable, Ben opened the envelope. Best to read it while he was in town in case he needed to send a reply.

Your father is seriously ill with pneumonia. We do not know if he will survive. Come home immediately. Love, Mother

Air leaked from his lungs as he sank back against the planed wood. His father had always enjoyed good health, except for a couple of bouts with fever. Ben scrubbed his hand over his jaw. He would have to catch the next stage east. Get to Galveston, book a berth on a steamer...

He removed his hat, closed his eyes, and bowed his head.

Lord, please watch over my father, strengthen him, and heal him. Please let me make it there in time. If it be Your will. Be with my mother and Evelyn. And Lord, watch over Cora and Charlie. Help her to understand. Open the doors, make a way for us to marry. Please, she's the woman I want to spend the rest of my life with.

With wobbly hopes, he found his horse and headed home to the ranch.

~

As soon as Ben rode through the palisade gate, Charlie ran out to greet him, with Jack yelping at his heels.

Ben halted his gelding halfway across the yard and climbed out of the saddle.

"You're back." Charlie beamed and threw his arm around Ben's waist. The arm in the sling bumped against Ben's gun belt. "You're gone too much."

"I've missed you, partner." Ben squeezed the boy close. How would Charlie handle the announcement that Ben had to head east and be gone for who knows how long?

One ear bent, Jack pawed at Ben's leg.

Charlie scooped the dog up and held him out to Ben. "Jack wants to say hello too."

"Howdy, Jack." Ben scuffed his hand across the pup's head, then brought him up to his shoulder and gave him a good pet.

"Did you save us a bull?" Charlie scanned the road beyond the gate. "Cora said you might bring some longhorns back. I'm ready to help. I've got to practice for the next trail ride, you know." He puffed out his chest.

"The bull's at the stockyard, along with five heifers. Tomorrow morning, you and I will ride into town to fetch them." One of the last duties he'd have time to perform before he caught the next east-bound stage, two days from now.

"I get to wrangle cattle." Charlie jumped up and down. "I can't wait. I've got a rope. I'll go tell Cora."

Ben laid a hand on Charlie's shoulder and scanned the porch and yard. "Where is your sister?" He'd expected her to come running, or maybe at least quickstep off the porch with a big smile aimed his way. The scene had played in his imagination for the last two days. The hug, a kiss, with the promise of more tender ones to follow after Charlie's bedtime. And the way her eyes would light up in welcome before she even reached him—

"She's not been feeling the best." Charlie wiggled. "But I bet she'll be all better now that you're home. I'll go tell her."

"Wait," Ben called after him. If Cora was anywhere near the house, she'd heard the commotion. She knew he was home. Maybe she was feeling poorly, or maybe she wanted a private welcome. "You can help me out by taking care of Cooper." Ben patted the gelding's neck. "He needs a good brushing and a rubdown. He worked hard on the trail helping me get the rest of the cattle to Mr. Goodnight. I'll check on your sister."

Charlie blew out a breath. "All right." He perked up. "I'll give my horse a good brushing too. Get her ready for the trail tomorrow."

"Sounds good, partner." Ben patted the boy's back, then retrieved his saddlebags before heading toward the house. How was he supposed to leave these two? He'd have to see if Mr. Franklin would be willing to hire on full-time for a couple of months. A couple of months? Only the Lord knew how long he'd be gone. And if his father died? Ben shuddered and stuck one hand in his pocket while the other steadied the bags over his shoulder. His father and he had talked so little since his return from war. Sure, they'd spoken every night at the dinner table or in passing. But Ben couldn't recall the last time they'd really talked.

He'd have to work at least a little while at the paper to earn money to pay Mr. Franklin. But he couldn't allow himself to get trapped there. He had Cora and Charlie to look after, and they needed a husband and a father, not a bank note or a bag of coins.

Heart heavy, he stepped onto the back stoop. With the late-

July heat, the entrance door to the hallway stood wide open. A fly buzzed past as Ben entered.

Hands stuffed in her apron pockets, Cora met him at the threshold of the kitchen, lips tight and hair coiled in a braid at the back of her head. Not a speck of welcome in her demeanor. Maybe she'd been worried about him.

His heart thumped. "Good news. Goodnight took all of our cattle, except for the four and the bull." He slid his saddlebags to the floor. "He's going to charge us less commission too." He drew her into his arms. That would bring a smile to her face. He needed to hold her close, visit with her, enjoy a good meal, before he broke the news about his father.

Her arms came around him slowly, halfheartedly, but when he sought to draw back a step to look into her eyes, she buried her face in his shoulder and held on as if a flood might sweep her away.

"I've missed you too." He brushed his lips against her hair. That was the problem, wasn't it? That she'd missed him? And she had no idea he had to leave again, and for much longer. He tightened his hold on her, and they swayed there in the hallway for several minutes. *Lord, give me the strength and wisdom to know what to do.* "I love you, Cora," he whispered. "You are the girl of my heart."

A jolt seemed to ripple through her. She pulled away, eyes moist.

His knees jellified. "What's wrong?"

"Nothing." She swiped her cheek.

"It's not nothing." He touched her shoulder. What if she'd reconsidered his loss of the cattle? Or maybe LeBeau had bothered her? "I want to know what's wrong."

"I was going to try to wait until after dinner. I know you're hungry."

"My appetite is quickly evaporating." He reached for her hand. "Why don't we sit down at the table, and we'll—"

She stuffed her hand back in her pocket. "I think we'd best go outside to the garden, away from little ears. I've got some cucumbers to pick." Without meeting his eyes, she grabbed a pail from the floor and her straw hat from a hook.

He exhaled and followed. Trouble.

She strode ahead with purpose, too much like her stride the day he first laid eyes on her. On that day, she'd marched out of Mr. Coffin's office with her head held high, determined to hold onto her land at all costs. Was she preparing for a battle of some sort now?

He trailed behind her past the peppers, beans, and squash until they were deep on the other side of the garden by the cucumbers. She pivoted to face him. The hard, sunbaked clay cracked beneath the heels of her shoes.

"What's wrong?" He braced himself.

She closed her eyes and flexed her hands. A hot breeze rippled her hat brim, tossing its red checkered ribbon aside.

"Talk to me, Cora." His shoulders tensed.

She scuffed her shoe against something hard. Bending down, she picked up a piece of broken pottery and handed it to him.

"What's this?" He turned it over in his fingers.

Her voice trembled. "It was my father's from one of his jugs. After he died, and we came back here, I'd run across one of his hidden stashes, and I'd smash the jugs. I found this piece here today while I was weeding."

His eyes narrowed. "And what does this have to do with me?"

She flicked a strand of loose hair from her face.

He repeated himself, his voice taking on an edge. "What does your father's whiskey have to do with me?"

Her face scrunched up as if she might throw up. Reaching into her pocket, she withdrew a piece of paper and shoved it toward him.

The shard slipped from his fingers. Defenses on full alert, he unfolded the letter from Mr. Keeley, the druggist. His stomach dropped to his knees as he read. The man might as well have paraded him naked up and down the street...*sickly and used up...hands trembling...in bad need of his medicine.* Cora might as well have run over him with a horse. "You spied on me? You had so little trust in me...that you spied on me?" Spit flew with his words.

"Not me. I didn't ask for it. I didn't want it. Arthur—"

"Oh, yes, the good doctor. Muttering his diagnosis in the middle of the street in broad daylight for all to hear. A real man of honor, let me tell you." He crumpled the letter in his fist. "And now he's got Keeley in league with him? And you?" He turned his back on her and kicked a clod so hard that it flew into the air and toppled a beanpole.

"I told Arthur not to spy on you, not to talk to the druggist."

"And when did you do that?" He pivoted back toward her. "At the café? Or have you seen him since? Has he been out here?"

"How can you even ask if he's been here since the fight? Of course not. You and I are...courting. I don't want anything to do with that man. But he came up with the idea about the druggist weeks ago on his last visit when I told him he wasn't welcome to come calling anymore. I told him I wanted no part of his plan, and that's the last I heard of it. Until he sent a messenger five days ago with this letter." Tears trickled down her cheeks.

Ben clenched and unclenched his hands at his sides. "Are we?"

"Are we what?"

"Still courting?"

She sucked in a breath and another, as if struggling for control. She pointed to the crumpled letter. "Did you?"

"Did I buy laudanum?" His throat tightened.

"Yes." She hugged herself, her brow furrowed deeper than a garden row.

"Does it matter what I say?" He snorted. "It looks like you've already judged me."

"I'm asking for the truth." Her voice shivered.

He jabbed his fingers through his hair and paced down the row. Why had he ever set foot in the druggist's? He'd been stupid.

After the fight, he'd been concerned LeBeau might retaliate by challenging him to a gunfight. But he'd inadvertently handed LeBeau a much more potent weapon.

Stomach nothing more than a pit, he marched back to where Cora stood. "I'll tell you the truth." He jutted out his chin. "I bought a small bottle of laudanum right before I saw you at the café with that weasel. I planned on saving it until after I left Weatherford and headed back East." His tongue scraped his mouth like sandpaper.

Her gaze scoured his face. "And where is the bottle now?"

His eyes narrowed. "I have to give you proof? You can't take my word for it?"

She hung her head. "I don't know."

Might as well have rammed a spear through his chest. "The bottle and every drop of the poison is in the pile of waste beneath the latrine."

Her head jerked up.

"Nine days' worth of waste, to be exact." Acid rose in the back of his throat. "I poured it out, without touching a single drop, after that beautiful speech you made up in the loft about how you would stick by me, and how we were in this together. But I guess I misunderstood the context. It just applied to cattle, not life. And only as long as you could have evidence."

She flinched as if he'd struck her.

He squeezed his eyes closed. Maybe if he'd shut his mouth and cool his temper, she'd find a way to trust him. The pottery shard crunched beneath his boot. He picked up what was left of it, hauled his arm back, and hurled it away from them as far as he could. If only he could do the same with her doubts.

"Cora." He struggled to contain the torrent raging through him and keep his voice quiet and steady. "I thought about taking the medicine. For an hour, the cravings almost got the better of me. I was feeling lower than mud after what happened with the cattle. I bought the poison, but the lid stayed on until I poured it down the outhouse hole. I never touched a drop. I swear to you. After the love and trust you showed me in the loft, I knew I didn't want anything to do with the medicine. I threw it away, but I have no evidence. Only my word."

Her gaze shifted to the horizon. Bees buzzed around them. She took off her hat and crunched it in her grip. "I want to believe you." Her voice quivered.

"But you don't know if you can. After all this time, you don't know if you can trust me." With a heavy sigh, he met her gaze. His heart clenched. In her eyes lurked what he'd thought he'd see there the day he told her about the loss of the cattle, but he'd been spared, until now. The loss of respect... Shoulders sagging, he lifted his chin and walked off, his chest hollow.

CHAPTER 35

That evening, Ben ate his dinner off a tin plate in the loft, sitting with his legs draped over the side of the bunk.

Charlie sat beside him on a stool. "You're not feeling well? Just like Cora?" The boy frowned, his gray eyes only slightly lighter than the brewing clouds outside. His father's eyes, a father who had hardly acknowledged him, according to Cora.

"No, I'm not feeling good." Maybe he'd never feel well again. He picked over his food. The argument with Cora, the disappointment in her face when she looked at him, had shriveled his appetite to the size of a prune. "But don't worry. Tomorrow morning, we'll still head into Weatherford and get our cattle. On the way there, I'll tell you what you need to do in order to help handle them. As long as you promise you'll be careful with your arm. That cast doesn't mean you're ready to go lassoing and wrangling yet."

"I know." Charlie rolled his palm-sized ball around in his hand. "But I can hold the reins in my teeth. I tried it once."

"That's something I don't want to see anytime soon."

"But maybe I should practice lassoing one-handed."

"Not tonight. I need to rest." Ben ate a bite of chicken. Cora had killed a chicken for him again, but no amount of hospitality could erase the words said in the garden. "Why don't you grab my saddlebags off the table there? I have something for you."

Charlie hopped up and pulled his worn suspender over his shoulder. The boy needed a new set of clothes.

Ben couldn't spare the money now, but he'd send some with a portion specifically marked for Charlie to have a new outfit. He set his plate down as Charlie lugged the heavy leather pouch over.

"I found it on the trail in Palo Pinto." Ben dug the foot-long object, wrapped in a dirty shirt, out from amongst his extra set of trousers and drawers.

Charlie cast the cloth aside and gasped. "A buffalo horn." He held the bone-hard object and grinned, running his fingers over the dark-brown curve, all the way to the pointy tip. "Did you kill the buffalo?"

"The animal was long dead. I bought the horn from a trader. But I figured this could tide you over until you get to hunt one someday."

"Maybe you and me can go hunting next spring." He picked up the dirty shirt and began polishing the dull, nail-like material.

Ben's chest tightened. He had to tell Charlie the news. "We need to talk."

"We are talking." Charlie spit on the cloth and rubbed the horn. "What's the knob here? Is that where it connected to the bone?"

"We'll talk about the horn later." Ben exhaled. "I have something serious to tell you."

Charlie blinked.

"My father is ill. I have to go see him."

"What's wrong with him? How sick is he?"

Elbows on his knees, Ben laced his fingers together. "He has pneumonia. I don't know all the details, but it's serious. And I need to go be with him for a while."

Charlie frowned. "Is he going to die?"

"I hope not." Ben dropped his gaze to his hands. What would it be like to never see his father again? So much left unsaid. "But only the Lord knows such things. We can pray and do what we can for the person, get them the best doctor, give them good care."

"I pray at night before I go to bed. I can pray for your pa."

"Thank you." A weak smile ticked the corners of Ben's mouth upward.

"When will you be back?" Charlie stopped fiddling with the horn and allowed it to lie in his lap.

Ben winced. "I can't say for sure. Philadelphia is far away. And how long I stay once I get there depends on my father's recovery." Duty loomed like a dungeon door, ready to slam shut behind him. And who knew if Cora would want him back here? From her actions in the garden today, she'd likely be relieved to be shed of him.

Charlie drooped. "I don't want you to be gone a long time, Ben. I need you to help me learn to be a cowboy and a warrior. Cora needs you too." He wiggled a finger beneath the edge of his cast just past the hole for his thumb.

"I don't have all of the answers, Charlie." Ben scooted over and patted the side of the bunk beside him. "Why don't you come here?"

Horn clasped in his good hand, Charlie trudged over and plopped down next to Ben. "Maybe Cora and I could come with you."

As if Cora would ever agree to that. "That wouldn't work, partner. Not for this visit. Maybe someday. For now, you two need to stay and take care of the ranch. I'll get Mr. Franklin to help more while I'm away."

"But he's not you."

Ben wrapped his arm around the boy's shoulders. "I'll be back as soon as I can. Sometimes a man has to do hard things. He has responsibilities. His word has to mean something. I have duties here, but I have them at home...in Pennsylvania, as well. I don't know when I'll be back. But don't ever doubt that I love you. And even while I'm away, I'll see that you and Cora are taken care of."

"What about Wolf Heart? You told him you'd be my father."

Ben stared at the worn rag rug at his feet. How was he going to answer that without discussing the rift with Cora? "If Wolf Heart shows up, tell him I'm still your pa. That I had to travel far away to take care of my sick father, and that you're learning to be a man by taking care of the ranch and protecting your sister while I am gone."

Charlie scuffed his shoe against the floor.

Ben hugged the boy close. "Shouldering your duty is as much part of learning to be a man as learning to lasso a calf or shoot a gun. When your sister writes me about you, I want to hear a good report."

"You can count on me." Charlie swiped a tear. "You'll be back to teach me more."

Thank goodness his last sentence wasn't a question. The answer was as unfathomable as the distance to the stars.

~

Hair down her back, not yet done up for the day, Cora wrapped the hot biscuits in a checkered cloth and stuffed them in the empty haversack. Ben had sent Charlie with the message that they'd eat their breakfast on the road to town. The man hadn't spoken with her since their confrontation in the garden yesterday. He'd left it to Charlie to deliver the news that his father was seriously ill and that he was leaving. Had Ben really received a telegram, or was it a story made up to spare further hurt?

What if he never came back? It'd be for the best, wouldn't it? No more worry about her emotions overcoming her common sense and logic. No more fear of following in her mother's footsteps. But what a hole it would leave in her heart, in her soul.

With a shudder, she added a pouch of fatback to the haversack. What if she was wrong about him? What if she was sending away the only man she'd ever really love? But she wasn't exactly sending him away. He had an obligation to his father. Who was she fooling? Her words to him yesterday cut the tie between them more surely than any telegram ever could.

Specks of flour clung to the fringe of her shawl. She should change out of her chemise and put on her day dress before Ben showed up at the door to collect the food. Instead, she shuffled over to the floor by the cupboard and retrieved a couple of cucumbers from the basket. Ben had seen her night clothes before, the time she'd spied him pacing by the corral after midnight, and the coyote howls had kept her awake. Had he been thinking about riding into town for laudanum that night? What if the day Mr. Keeley had written about wasn't the first time Ben had given in to the craving?

Her chest tightened. Maybe Keeley's report and Ben's decision to leave, whether his father was ill or not, was all part of God's way of saying no. His way of stopping her before she made a terrible mistake. She'd been naïve to believe Ben had shaken the need forever. And yet her stupid heart went on hurting and yearning. Too stubborn to listen to reason.

She tucked the cucumbers into the haversack and turned to head to her bedroom. The back door creaked. She tugged her shawl closed across her chest as Ben stepped into the kitchen.

Dressed in a gray frock coat and blue cotton shirt, Ben

drank her in, eyes wide. A lock of dark hair dipped across his forehead, and stubble darkened his jaws. As handsome as she'd ever seen him, except there was no light in this gaze. His frown twitched upward for a moment before hardening into a straight line.

She had his attention, but that's all she had. "I'm almost finished packing your breakfast." Her voice wavered.

He reached into his coat pocket and withdrew an envelope. "In case you need proof of my father's illness." He tossed it onto the work table. "I wanted to save you the trouble of having to search my room for it."

The envelope fluttered onto the flour-dusted surface.

She flinched. "I...I believed—" But she hadn't.

He cocked his eyebrows. "You didn't put the leather case back the right way under my mattress." His voice hardened like granite. "Did you read my journals?"

"No, I swear to you. I didn't. I figured they were private."

He crossed his arms. "Private. I'm not sure you even know what that word means. But in a way, it's probably too bad you didn't take a peek. Maybe it would have taught you a new word. Mercy."

She hugged herself and closed her eyes. "I am sorry. I—"

He cleared his throat. "I've already spoken with Mr. Franklin. He's agreed to stay here full-time and help out at least through the fall."

The fall? Of course, he'd be gone that long. "Thank you. But I...we can't afford—"

"I'll send the money."

Her lips moved. "I wouldn't want—"

"I said I'm paying him." He hooked his thumbs in his gun belt. "When Goodnight returns, he'll send or bring you the money for however many of our longhorns make it to New Mexico. But that might not be until spring. I'll send extra funds before then in case." His eyes narrowed as if daring her to object.

Spring? The length of his absence had gone from fall to spring in a matter of sentences. Was she daft? He didn't plan to return.

She picked up the envelope and held it to her chest without reading it. "I'm so sorry about your father."

"I'll send you word of what happens." His expression said her sympathies meant about as much to him as Jeff Davis apologizing for the rebellion.

"I'll...be seeing you before you go?" Why wouldn't her voice cooperate? It made her sound like she was Charlie's age or younger.

"Not likely." He jutted his chin. "I'll have to pack up tonight after we return. Probably take my meal in the loft. Then I'm heading out before sunup. I want to be there in plenty of time for the stage."

She glared at him, half tempted to throw the envelope at him. "You're not even going to say a proper goodbye? After everything between us?"

He snorted. "I figure a woman who doesn't trust me would be relieved by my absence. That way, she wouldn't have to spend her life second-guessing me, forever wondering when I was going to slip up and transform into her father." But his voice wavered, too, as if it were a flag flipped about by a strong wind.

She stomped over to him, her shawl falling off her shoulders and slipping to the floor. "Regardless of what you think, I love you. I want to see you succeed..."

"But?" He glared at her.

But I don't know if I can marry you.

The parlor clock chimed six times.

The slight crinkles around his eyes aged him a decade in a minute. "Your silence says more than enough, Cora." He pushed past her and grabbed the haversack. "A man can't marry a woman who doesn't respect or trust him."

"I trust you."

He smirked. "To be an errand boy? Or a trail hand?"

"The ranch is half yours." What kind of stupid reply was that, totally missing his point?

He shouldered the haversack. "Speaking of the ranch, I plan to stop by the land office and sign over any claim I have to you. It'll be yours to do with as you please."

Another part of their connection severed.

She sucked in a breath. She would not cry. "I don't care what the deed says. Half is yours. It'll be here when you want it."

He strode right up to her bare toes. "I'll want it when I see the doubt gone from your eyes. Replaced by respect and trust. Until then, you'll have my provision as often as I can send it."

He marched out of the room. The back door slammed.

She knelt to pick up her shawl and cradled it close to her chest. But instead of rising, her knees dropped to the floor. What if Ben was asking for something she couldn't do?

∾

Fading starlight still graced the pre-dawn sky. Orange shimmered over the horizon. A lone robin filled the air with its song as Ben tightened the ties on his saddlebags. Was he really going to ride out without saying goodbye to Cora? He'd managed to avoid any private conversation with her yesterday when he and Charlie had returned with the five heifers and the bull.

She'd loaded praise on Charlie as they'd led the animals into the corral for the time being. But she'd only given Ben a scant thank you, with a smile that failed to reach her eyes, and a gaze that traveled every which way to avoid his.

He'd been harsh on her yesterday morning when he'd collected the haversack, but he'd meant what he'd said. He wouldn't marry a woman who didn't trust and respect him.

Still, the hurt in her eyes had wrecked him. And what in the devil was she doing in the kitchen still dressed in her night clothes when she knew he might come inside? The thin cotton chemise, with its lacy hem just past her knees...it was more than enough to make a man long for a wedding night. And the red shawl hanging off her shoulders and her chestnut locks cascading down her back had only added to the flame...all at the same time she'd looked at him with those eyes of doubt, throwing an unbreachable wall between them.

He clenched his hand. It was high time he left this place, before he got himself twisted into such a tangled knot of hurt there'd be no hope of unraveling it.

Obviously, his father's illness had come at a providential time.

With a glance toward the still-dark cabin, he jabbed his boot toe into the stirrup and swung into the saddle. It was better this way.

A door clicked. He held his breath. Cora ran around the side of the house, a sack in her hand.

Chest tight, he dismounted.

She slowed. This morning, she wore her violet dress, the one she'd been wearing the first time he'd laid eyes on her at Coffin's office. Except today, her hair flowed behind her, barely brushed, and her feet were bare.

"We'll be praying for your father." She shoved the sack toward him. "Food for your journey. Ham, potatoes, dried apples, and more."

His fingers curled around the rough cloth. Unspoken words clogged his throat.

Her eyes gleamed in the not-quite dark. Moisture? She held out her hand, as if he might shake it. He scowled instead.

Lip quivering, she threw her arms around him. His breath stalled in his chest. He stiffened, but she didn't let go. Slowly, he slipped his arms around her.

"God be with you," she whispered.

He inhaled. Rosewater with a sprinkle of citrus. She'd put on perfume. He squeezed his eyes shut. "Why do you push me away with one hand and hold onto me with the other?"

Her hold tightened, and she buried her face against his shoulder. "My heart is torn."

He pressed his mouth to her ear. "Cora, I swear to you, I emptied every drop of that bottle into the outhouse hole. I haven't tasted a drop since I left Pennsylvania."

Silence, except for Cora's sniffle, and the pounding of his heart in his ears.

The robin's song erupted as a faint trace of orange burst across the horizon.

Ben slipped from her hold and stepped back.

Her tear-filled eyes gutted him.

"I have to go." His voice barely scraped above a whisper.

Riding away was like ripping off skin.

CHAPTER 36

The hot mid-August wind rippled across Cora's dress and skin, tossing her straw hat from her head and down onto her back where it swung at the end of a string. Prairie spread out in front of her. Indian grass, flopping over with its flowery yellow plumes shooting straight up, brushed against her knees as she loped Sandy through the field.

Summer's heat had long ago withered the bluebonnets and Indian paintbrush, but purple cornflowers and orange Indian blanket blossoms with their yellow tips populated patches not dominated by the grasses. Rolling hills extended south toward the Brazos River, but the line of scrub oak along the creek up ahead was the end of Scott land.

Her land. And Charlie's. And Ben's if he ever came back. Why couldn't she have opened her stupid mouth the morning he rode off? Her silence had guillotined any hope for a future with him.

Everything he'd done for her and Charlie evidenced dedication and commitment. He'd shown he could be counted on and trusted. Couldn't she have at least taken his word about the bottle?

She slowed the mare to a walk and fanned herself with her hat. Sweat dampened her underarms and back. Sleeves rolled to her elbows, her bare forearms soaked in the sun. What did it matter that her skin wasn't pearly white? She had no hope of competing with a city girl like Olivia Edmondson, especially after she'd practically slammed the door in Ben's face.

The day he'd left, she'd discovered one of his two journals lying atop the quilt she'd loaned him. Had he left it to share a deeply personal part of himself with her, or was it merely because she was Jeb's sister, and it contained a portion of Jeb's story as well? She could only hope he'd come back to retrieve it someday.

In the four weeks since his departure, she'd started sleeping with the journal beneath her pillow, praying every night for the man who had endured so much. The small script, written so as to conserve paper, utilized every white space on the page, a challenge to decipher, but it was the descriptions of the hardships and deprivations Ben and Jeb had suffered that tore her heart.

If Ben were here now, she'd wrap her arms around him and never let go.

If he could see her eyes now, he'd know she was sorry, and that her love would win out over all misgivings. She didn't need to behold the bottle to believe him.

Her horse snorted.

An eagle circled overhead, sailing on the wind. Suddenly, it dove. Grass parted a hundred yards ahead. A hare bounded through the thick tassels. Talons extended, the eagle swooped in and snatched the rabbit from the ground. A squeal pierced the quiet. Cora followed the bird with her gaze as it pumped its wings and retook the sky with its prey dangling beneath.

As her gaze returned to earth, she startled. A rider sat atop the nearest hill. An Indian. Chest bare and wearing nothing but a breechclout, he held his lance upward, resting the base on the ground.

Her stomach dropped. Two weeks prior in Jack County, a Comanche raiding party had struck two farms, stealing horses from the corral and killing the cattle. A farmer who'd tried to stop them ended up with arrows in his gut and his scalp missing.

She gripped the reins in one hand and slowly drew her Enfield rifle out of its scabbard with her other hand. Was the warrior alone, or was there a raiding party on the other side of the bluff? Her heart pounded. If she turned and fled right now, she might have time to get away, but Comanches could outride anyone on the plains, and the Kiowa weren't far behind. Even if she made it to the palisade, no guarantee she'd have time to lock it. And who knew if Charlie would be inside or out? She wouldn't risk drawing the one Indian or many to the boy.

Back stiff and a prayer on her lips, she held the loaded Enfield across her lap, ready to snatch the butt to her shoulder in a blink.

The warrior nudged his horse forward at a trot. "Haa." His voice boomed across the prairie.

The Comanche equivalent of *hello*. Still, her fingers twitched to raise the rifle. A greeting meant nothing. She might only get one shot, or she might accidentally start a fight that could have been avoided.

Down the hill and across the creek, he rode. His face unpainted, his long braids flapped against his muscular chest. Wolf Heart?

Her finger eased off the trigger.

Driving his black mustang to a lope, the man closed the distance between them, coming to a stop twenty or thirty feet from her. Three eagle feathers hung from his scalp lock. Creases spread out from the corners of his eyes, and a scar marred his right cheek.

He nodded toward the Enfield. She loosened her grip on the weapon.

"Where is one called Ben?" He lifted his cleft chin. A bow string lay across his chest, and a quiver hung from his shoulder. Another scar marred his breast.

"He had to travel far away toward the sunrise to a place called Pennsylvania. His father is greatly ill. Might die."

His hooded, dark eyes studied her from head to toe. "Not winter yet. And he is gone."

"He will be back as soon as he can." She leaned forward on her horse. The threat was more subtle than the spear, but it was there. Charlie's future rested on her words. "Charlie is helping me on the ranch. He is my protector. The man of the family for now."

"Tsssk. The boy needs a father to teach him."

"Ben will be back. His father is ill. The duty must go both ways. He has responsibility to Charlie and to his father."

"Hmmpf." Wolf Heart nudged his mount to the right and walked the mustang in a full circle around her.

Her tongue felt like sandpaper, but she sat tall. She had a knife strapped to her thigh if he attempted to misuse her.

"What about Cora? What responsibility to Cora?" His circle complete, he aimed his gaze into hers.

There was only one safe answer. "Ben will return to make me his wife."

"Has not done it?" A glow lit his eyes. "Cowboy is slow. Too slow?"

"He wisely chose to wait until he's finished caring for his father." Until he could find a woman who would trust him.

Wolf Heart puffed out his chest. "Will see. If he come back. If he too slow."

Before she could think of a retort, he wheeled his mustang about and struck out at a gallop toward the hills and the horizon.

Exactly what did all that mean? Had the warrior happened to run across her, or had he been watching? Following her? Maybe he'd come out to see Charlie again. For all she knew, Wolf Heart could have been part of the raid that killed the farmer. He'd been with the party that killed her uncle.

She could tell the men in Weatherford about the Indian that kept showing up on her land. A posse would be more than pleased to stake out the area and wait in ambush. But she wouldn't do that. She would not break the verbal treaty Ben had brokered between them. But what if Ben never came back?

~

Collar undone and shirt sleeves rolled to his elbows, Ben settled into the high-back chair by his father's bedside. Ink and newsprint darkened his fingertips. The smell of carbolic acid stung his nose, overpowering the earthy aroma of steaming mullein tea on the table by his father's bed.

"What is the news of the day?" His father scooted his shoulders farther up on the pillows. Dark circles underscored his eyes. The lung fever had broken earlier in the week, but it'd left him weak as a baby. Yesterday was the first time he could manage a full sentence without it leaving him breathless.

"The Texans finally figured out they lost the war." Ben chuckled. "Some of them will probably still refuse to accept the fact ten years from now."

"See, I told you." His father raised his chin. "You're better off away from that place."

Ben pressed his lips together. He'd not argue with a sick man. "There are some fine people there, in amongst the hard-headed Rebs." His chest hollowed at the mere thought of Cora. "But the fact of the matter is that eighteen months after Appomattox, the Texans finally elected a state government and ratified a new state Constitution acceptable to President Johnson…"

His father listened as Ben moved on to the rest of the headlines. In ten days, he'd receive his first month's pay. He'd send Cora half of it. Had LeBeau set up camp on her porch once more? He shifted in his seat and crossed his ankle over his leg. If only Cora could see him in the newspaper office, where he was proficient, respected, and more than capable.

Somewhere in the cacophony of odors surrounding the sick bed, the sweet, sickly smell of laudanum invaded his nostrils and turned his stomach. The bottle wasn't in sight today, but the doctor had prescribed it for his father along with a litany of cathartics, cupping, and bloodletting. Ben's mouth didn't water, nor did his hand tremble in response. Had the Lord loosened the brown liquid's grip on him? He wouldn't test the possibility.

Upon his arrival, he'd insisted he be allowed to stay in the guest room, not his old bedroom, where the memories of being under the influence of the poison were too strong. And he'd let it be known that he didn't want a laudanum bottle in his presence. His mother had looked at him as if he were out of his head, but she had complied and ordered the servant girl to do so as well.

A cough wracked through his father, shaking his body. Mother rushed over with a handkerchief. Together, Ben and she held him up from the pillows. Reddening in the face, his father held the handkerchief to his lips as his chest crackled.

When he had quieted, Ben lowered him down. "You'll better rest now."

"I'll rest." His father settled against the pillows. "Knowing my boy…is here to take charge…of the paper."

"Randolph Thorson is in charge. I'm working alongside him." Ben wiped his palms on his trousers.

"You'll be at the helm." His father sipped the water offered by Mother. "When I'm better. We'll work out…a plan."

"When you're better, we'll talk." Ben exhaled.

Mother shot him a frown.

"I'm going to check on Evelyn. She's in the kitchen attempting to bake cookies. Baking is not her forte." Ben turned toward the door. Best get out of the room and join his sister before his father insisted on promises.

"What of Olivia?" His father's voice rasped. "You've seen her? Apologized?"

Ben stiffened. "I sent her a note. Last week, I called at her house, as you asked, but wasn't admitted. No apology will make up for a broken courtship."

"Broken betrothal." His father aimed a finger at Ben. "Only one way to fix it." His father coughed. "Keep your word to her. Marry her. You've got to—"

"James, we need to talk about this another day." Mother patted the sick man's shoulder while shooting daggers at her son. "You've got to give Ben time."

"Too much time already. Never should have gone to Texas." His father waved her hand away. "Edmondson's throwing his weight to Thorson. Not going to stand for the jilting of his daughter." He sucked in, struggling for breath. "Only way to gain...control of the paper...is for Ben...to do his duty." A powerful cough propelled him forward.

Ben hurried to his father's side and helped support him.

Mother placed a firm hand on her husband's back, then waved Ben away. "You'll only aggravate him. Go find your sister."

Ben stuck his hands in his pockets and tromped out of the room. Better to be single the rest of his life than marry a woman he didn't love.

And since every thought of the woman he *did* love felt like scraping an open wound, bachelorhood loomed large on the horizon.

Cora thanked Mr. Miller for the letter and exited the mercantile. Thankfully, the man waited to give it to her until Charlie headed for the wagon with an armload of supplies. She rubbed her finger over the script, Ben's writing, addressed from Pennsylvania. She'd best read the contents before showing them to Charlie.

It'd been almost seven weeks since Ben's departure. Felt more like a year. She stuffed the letter in her skirt pocket and slowed her step as she passed the clothiers. Arthur LeBeau strolled toward her, his face covered in a thin beard instead of his usual goatee. Maybe he was trying to look more rugged.

Her chest tightened. Their gazes met, no smile. She dropped hers to her feet and walked on. If only he would pass without a word. But two shiny boot toes crossed into her path. With a slow inhale, she halted and looked up into ice blue.

"Good day, Miss Scott." He tipped his top hat. "I hear Mr. McKenzie headed back east."

"His father fell seriously ill. Mr. McKenzie had to leave immediately."

The corners of his lips tugged upward. "Is that so?"

She squeezed the knuckles of her clasped hands and waited for a farmer's wife to pass. "That *is* so. Do you need to see a copy of the telegram?" My goodness. To her shame, she almost sounded like him. "Not that it's any of your concern." She gritted out her response barely above a whisper.

There might as well be a limelight shining on them given the way heads turned from even across the street. She had no intention of providing the town with entertainment.

"I take it that you didn't appreciate my note from the druggist." Arthur's voice sharpened. "If I have to suffer the loss of your friendship and affection, or even the temporary loss of some of my patients for saving you from a terrible mistake, so be it."

"If you've suffered the loss of clients, it's probably due to you disrespecting one of yours and announcing his diagnosis in the street." She bristled. "Good day, sir." She moved to the side and quickstepped toward Charlie, who hurried toward them with a scowl.

Arthur called out behind her. "If you need me to take the cast off—"

"I already cut it off myself." She lifted her chin and marched on.

In the privacy of her bedroom that evening, she opened Ben's letter dated August twenty-third. She scanned the paragraph about his family. His father's recovery was slow, but the doctor believed him to be out of danger. Thank God. However, it might take months for him to regain his full strength. Months that Ben would have to be there. He would send her funds from his first month's wages.

Of course, due to his generous nature and determination to keep his word to Jeb, he'd send her more than necessary. Cut himself short. Of that she was certain. He'd be faithful to his commitment to her and Charlie, despite her obstinacy.

He wrote two paragraphs about his work, polishing others' writings, deciding what was news and what wasn't, shaping the finished product that would roll off the presses. A role of influence. Excitement rang in his words.

His love for his work echoed between the lines. Realization twinged through her. She'd almost kept him from that. Her belly felt like lead. How could she have ever thought he'd be satisfied with ranching?

Tears welled in her eyes, blurring the final words of his inquiries about her and Charlie and how he missed them. He sent his love to Charlie. What about her? Or did he reserve those words for people who trusted him?

Her eyes halted on the final lines. *I continue to abstain from the medicine, as I have done since last March. And by God's grace and strength, I pray that I may continue to do so.*

"Yes, Lord, yes. Let it be so," she spoke aloud as she closed her eyes and clasped her hands.

Her gaze lingered on the salutation. *Yours, Ben.* Her foolish heart hitched. *Yours.* A grain of hope, despite everything. *P.S. Did you read my journal?*

She slipped her hand under the pillow and pulled out the yellow-paged notebook...

*B*en stomped his boots on the foyer rug and handed his dripping overcoat and hat to the Edmondson butler. This was his third visit to Olivia's house, and the first time he'd been allowed in the door. Just when he'd been ready to convey his message in writing, the butler had stepped out of the way and invited him in.

He hesitated at the parlor threshold. Blue-and-green images of peacocks decorated the papered walls, complementing the forest-green chairs and matching horsehair sofa. A sofa on which he'd spent too many hours sitting with Olivia in his arms. His cheeks heated. She had every right to be angry with him. She'd been a very willing participant in their kissing and cuddling, and she'd hinted time and time again for a proposal, but he'd been the one to ask.

He ran his hand over his combed-back hair and stepped across the scarlet carpet to the mantel. Too many promises to too many people. He could not keep them all, nor did he want to.

Heels clicked across the marble-floored hall. He braced

himself. *Lord, give me wisdom.* The parlor doors closed. He waited a beat, then turned.

Olivia stood there in violet silk, trimmed in black lace. A black snood loosely held her honey-blond hair. Very much a woman who would turn men's heads, and with enough family money to keep their gaze.

She looked down her slender nose at him and lifted her chin. "I thought it appropriate to dress in half mourning." She brushed her gloved hand against her skirt and sashayed to the piano.

Dare he ask? "Did someone pass away?"

"Not a physical death." She seated herself on the stool. "The death of a man's word." She glared at him.

He should have known. "I'm here to apologize—"

"For what? For proposing without meaning it? For breaking your word? Or for your lapse in self-control and sanity when you allowed yourself to become infatuated by some Texas charwoman and broke your engagement to me?" She plinked a few notes in a minor key on the piano, the beginnings of a dirge.

Best avoid an argument, as well as he could. There was no sense in extoling Cora's virtues to a woman who would denigrate her all the more. Better to simply lay the blame on himself and leave it there. He wiggled a finger into his too-tight cravat and sat down on the high-back chair.

She plinked a few more notes. "Cat got your tongue?"

He edged forward on the seat. "I apologize for any hurt and embarrassment I've caused you. For that, I'm truly sorry."

She huffed and rolled her eyes. "The only reason I'm able to leave my house is because your dissolution of the betrothal is only known within our family circles."

"We never announced our engagement. No one beyond our closest family members should be aware of the fact."

"But everyone expected it." She strummed her fingers across two octaves and stood. "Anyone with eyes and ears knew which way our relationship was headed. All of our friends and acquaintances, our fathers' business associates… How else was I to keep gentleman callers at arms' length than to hint at the deep connection between you and me?"

He ran his hand over his hair and settled hard against the back of the chair. How could he have ever fallen for this woman? "Well, if they were only arm's length away, I'm sure they'll be easy to retrieve. They hover around you at the piano, like moths to a flame. You'll have your pick. Tell them that you are the one who broke the betrothal. Tell them I have a fault in my character."

"I'm sure you have many faults in your character." Her glare sliced like a knife. "But do you think my reputation is all I care about?" She grabbed a handkerchief. "You…" She wadded the linen in her hand and pointed at the end of the sofa where they used to sit. "There. There. There." She punctuated each word with a jab of her finger. "There is where you sat countless times, partaking of my lips and my affections, and promising me your undying devotion."

He covered his eyes and slowly slid his hand down his face. He'd never promised his undying devotion, but the rest was too true. *Don't argue with her*. He deserved the berating. "Olivia, I have no excuse. It isn't your fault. I am not the same young man who sat in your parlor the spring of '63. Andersonville changed me. Wounded me in ways I still do not fully fathom."

She snorted and held her arms wide. "There was plenty of sofa time in the year after your return from war. Plenty of picnics and moonlight walks. If you faltered while in Texas, if that charwoman—"

"She's a ranch owner, not a washwoman."

"Then she doesn't need your help, does she?"

He stood. "Olivia—"

"If she lured you into her arms some evening, tell me. I'll

give you a public lashing, and we'll be done with it and continue our engagement. You think I never allowed anyone to sneak a kiss while you were gone?"

"I hope that's all you let them sneak."

She marched across the room. *Smack.* Her slap stung his face.

He rubbed his cheek. "Forgive me. I should not have said that. I didn't mean—"

"You're horrible." She burst into tears and sank down on the sofa. "You know I'd never do anything like that. You and me... we never...."

"I know." He sat on the sofa edge, a full three feet from her. "You're not that kind of girl. But neither is Cora."

"I don't want to hear her name." She slammed her fists into her lap. Tears dripped from her lashes and her chin.

"You're a fine lady, Olivia. I'm the problem. Andersonville changed me, hardened me. I went through the motions of love and romance. I wanted everything between us to be as it had been when we first courted. I even proposed in hopes of making it so." He pressed his palms to his knees. "But my heart is not what it was, and all the acting on my part, and all of your admirable qualities, will not fix it. I didn't fully understand this until I went to Texas."

"And met that woman."

"It would be true whether or not I ever met her."

She wiped her nose with the handkerchief and leveled her gaze on him. "So reinstate our betrothal. Together, we'll work on mending you." She slid across the distance between them and clutched at his hands, wet hankie and all. "I will be your wife. I will heal your heart and warm your bed until the war is nothing but a distant memory."

"Olivia..." He pulled one hand free.

Wet hazel eyes begged. He should have stuck to the chair.

His stomach knotted. "We can't—"

"I don't accept that." She leaned in, thrust her hands around the back of his head, and pressed her lips to his.

He jerked his head away and broke her hold. "I'm sorry." He jumped off the sofa.

Her glare sliced sharper than a guillotine. "You ingrate." She slapped his arm and leaped to her feet. "You'll pay for this. Your father will pay for this. There will be ice inside Mount Vesuvius before you take charge of the newspaper. You'll be hawking penny copies on the street corner by the time my father is done with you."

He snorted. "Thank goodness my future isn't dependent upon your father." But what about his father's future? He back stepped toward the door. No telling if she was done attacking. "I pray that when you do marry, it won't be for the sake of the paper." His father was going to kill him. But he wouldn't commit the rest of his life to a woman he could no longer tolerate. His boots beat against the marble hallway floor as he headed for the front door.

Olivia's voice struck him from behind. "I heard you stopped taking your medicine. Maybe that's your problem."

He clinched his hands and pivoted. "The problem is that I finally came to my senses."

～

That evening, Ben stepped into his family's parlor. Evelyn sat curled up in a chair reading while his mother sat at the desk going over the family accounts, a snood holding her hair at the base of her bent neck. They looked up, faces expectant.

"How did it go?" Mother asked.

Ben loosened his collar. "If anyone calls at our door from

the Edmondson household for the next couple of days, tell them Father isn't well enough for visitors. As a matter of fact, you'd best say that to anyone who calls from the paper."

His mother clunked her pencil down. "So you didn't make amends with her?"

Evelyn's gaze percolated with questions.

"There will be no reconciliation." He stuffed his hands into his pockets and ambled over to the sofa.

His mother pinched the bridge of her nose and lowered her head.

"Olivia is too much of a high-society person for Benjie." Evelyn snapped Elizabeth Gaskill's *North and South* shut. "A frontier girl is much more his style."

"I haven't been Benjie for a couple of decades, Evie." He scolded and nudged her feet from the second cushion.

"Neither of you has any business sense." His mother lifted her head and pressed her palms flat against the desktop. "The *Sentinel* means the world to your father. His sweat and brains built the paper, along with Edmondson's and Thorson's money. And if you don't handle matters, Benjamin, he'll fight for control of the paper with his last breath. And the way he's going, that might just happen."

"Mother, he doesn't need to fight for anything at the moment." Provided Mr. Edmondson had more business sense than to cater to his daughter's whims. "I'm working with Thorson for now. When Father is well, he can step back in and take the lead from Thorson."

"That is only temporary, Benjamin. It'll take months for your father to fully regain his strength. And even then..." She leaned forward, elbows on the desk, pinning him with her gaze. "He has pains in his chest and back. He doesn't have the strength of a forty-year-old anymore."

"He *is* fifty-eight." Evelyn curled her arms around her book.

"This conversation is between me and your brother." His mother pointed a finger her way before turning back to Ben. "I'm worried about your father. The doctors are guessing rheumatism. But I'm not convinced."

Ben's frown traveled all the way down to his heart. "Would it be so terrible if he worked out a compromise where he shared the management with Thorson?"

"Young Thorson?" His mother's eyebrows rose to her hairline. "A man twenty-five years his junior? Share the editorship with someone who criticized Lincoln? Your father would be out of his sick bed tomorrow at such a thought."

"You'd have me marry a woman I can no longer even tolerate?"

"You are the one who courted her. Your father and I never asked you to."

"But you were delighted when I did."

"Yes, of course. Olivia is a charming young woman, an accomplished pianist, with a caring heart. She visits the soldiers' hospitals—"

"She also thinks quite a bit of herself and likes to be doted on by every bachelor under forty." Evelyn twirled a wave of her hair around her finger.

"The point, young lady and young man"—Mother's chair scraped against the floor as she stood—"is that you, Benjamin, started the trouble, and you're refusing to keep your commitment. You've offended the Edmondsons, and now you must shoulder the responsibility. You must fight for the managing editorship of the paper. You owe it to your father." She drew herself up to full height and crossed her arms. "If you care anything for your father or have any gratitude for everything we have done for you over the years, you'll give up any foolish notion you have of going back to Texas."

He dipped his gaze to the floor as the crushing weight of her words landed on his shoulders.

Evelyn nudged her toe beneath his knee, a show of support from their childhood days. "I could help with the paper, Mother. I love to write. And I can edit and organize—"

"You are a girl." Mother slammed the ledger down like a gavel. "And the day is coming for your brother to be the man of the family."

Ben pinched his chin as his mother marched out of the room.

Evie tipped her head to his shoulder.

Silence, save for the tick of the mantel clock and the crackle of the fire in the hearth.

He cleared his throat. "No one can stop you from writing, Evie. Write something, turn it in anonymously, and I'll see that it gets in the paper."

"You really care about this frontier girl?"

Air leaked from his lungs. "Yes." His voice scraped. "But even if I can manage to get back there, chances of her agreeing to be my wife are about as slim as having a Fourth of July blizzard."

"She'd have to be blind not to see all of your good qualities." She bumped her knee against his.

"I'm afraid you must be thinking of the brother you used to have before the war."

"I'm certain I am not."

"Well, even if you're not, Cora has had a hard life and endured many losses. She's afraid that despite the qualities you mention, life wouldn't be any better at my side."

"Then she is either blind or doesn't love you quite enough yet, because if she did, her love would overcome all."

He chuckled. "You've been reading too many romance books."

"Look at me." She sat up straight and tugged his chin until his gaze met hers. "Do not give up on this woman. I see it in your eyes. You love her. And I'm glad you've stopped taking the medicine. Your eyes were never clear when you were."

He smiled, despite his chain-weighted heart. "Thank you."

"You could ask her to come here."

"She's fighting to hold on to her family's ranch. It's all she has left of her family, except for a nine-year-old half brother. It would be like tearing her heart out to ask her to leave it. I went to Texas to save her ranch and provide for her, not steal her away from the land her family lived and died for."

Evie studied him for a moment. "If she loves you, she'll come if you ask her."

"Too many novels, Evie." He squeezed her hand and stood. Best get out of there before she inflated his hopes. "But if you find a way for me to return to Texas in the future and plead my case with my fair maiden, without forsaking Father and causing mayhem, you let me know."

"I will." She hopped up and stood on tiptoe to kiss his cheek.

Should he write Cora a different type of letter from his last two? Declare his love as he had back in Texas? But that would require hope. Hope that Cora might have a change of heart. Hope he could somehow fulfill his obligation to his father without binding himself to permanent residence in Pennsylvania. More hope than he could scrape together tonight.

The Lord had delivered him through harrowing battles and from the hell of Andersonville. Then led him to Texas, to Charlie and Cora. But why had the Lord put such an amazing woman in his life and left every door to their future shut? So that he could save their ranch?

Ben ran his hand over his hair. Cora and Charlie's need and love for him and his wanting to be his best for them had helped loosen laudanum's hold. The Lord had worked in the situation to break the chains, although the shadow of the fetter remained. The cravings had dulled significantly, not vanished.

But God had fortified his stomach and will. Maybe that was another purpose for his time with Cora.

What did the Lord have to say about a future with Cora in light of his promise to his father? The Bible said that all things were possible through the Lord. But Scripture didn't look lightly on a man not keeping his word.

CHAPTER 38

ora found the first gift, a gutted deer, in late September, on the far side of the garden, a few feet from her largest pumpkin. An arrow lay beside the animal, like a calling card. Mr. Franklin had said nothing of an intruder, had probably not noticed the giver who must have climbed over the palisade wall, probably from horseback. As soon as Charlie saw the arrow, he confirmed her suspicions. It was Wolf Heart's arrow.

No use starting trouble. They were safer if they kept Wolf Heart on friendly terms. She said nothing to Mr. Franklin who still came every evening, and occasionally stayed for the day to help out. With only the five longhorns and the garden to care for, she and Charlie could manage the daily workload. Her heart ached every time she looked at the stable loft where Franklin slept now instead of Ben. A hollowness akin to homesickness plagued her day and night.

A second gift, a dressed-out buffalo loin, appeared in mid-October. In between, Charlie reported a couple of visits from Wolf Heart while the boy was on the far side of the ranch. The third gift came the first week of November—a pair of buckskin moccasins, lined with fur. Too big for Charlie. She'd taken them into her house, set them by the coat rack in the hallway, but hadn't put her feet in them.

"Tell him I can accept no more gifts," she said to Charlie. She didn't want to think about what the gifts meant.

"He only wants to help us."

What if he aimed to fill Ben's place in more ways than one? "Ben wouldn't want me to take the moccasins."

Charlie studied her for a moment. "Maybe Wolf Heart and Ben could be friends."

"I don't think so."

"When is Ben coming back?"

She rubbed her arms. "I don't know." *Never*? "His father is still recovering. Ben has to take care of his father's newspaper. His mother and sister are temporarily dependent on him." Temporarily? More like a permanent entrenchment, encasing his feet in cement. He was probably too kind to come out and tell her that his heart had cooled toward her. His second letter had contained more money than she'd dared expect, but it was Ben McKenzie she wanted, not bank notes. "You tell Wolf Heart we appreciate the meat, but Ben sends provisions from afar. He's still looking after us."

Charlie frowned and scuffed his own moccasin. If she didn't take action, Wolf Heart would have him wearing a breechclout next.

"You tell him that." She placed her hand under his chin and lifted it.

"All right."

That evening, after she'd put Charlie to bed, she stood on the porch, hugging herself and staring at the swing. She hadn't sat in it since Ben's departure more than three-and-a-half months before. He poured himself into making it for her as a gift. Yet they'd only had one evening on it before LeBeau's letter had destroyed everything. Correction. Before she'd allowed the letter to destroy everything.

A stiff wind blew across the yard, creaking the swing. She shivered and went inside.

The parlor sofa wasn't much better, treasured memories of the few evenings between the Comanche attack and Ben's leaving for the widow's when they cuddled close. Arms folded, she drifted through the house. He'd only been here four months, but it wasn't home without him.

Her heart as lifeless as an empty sack, she slipped Ben's journal from beneath her pillow and returned to the parlor. Feet curled beneath her on the sofa, she opened the notebook to the last entry she'd read. She'd halted at the night before Ben and Jeb's escape attempt. It had not succeeded. She knew that much.

The parchment bookmark, made of much cleaner paper, obviously added after the war, contained a scribbled note in Ben's hand. *Read no further unless you want to know the truth.* Had he written the note specifically for her? It had stopped her in August, but now she needed to know. She turned the page.

....I tripped on a log. My leg twisted. I could go no farther. The dogs were coming. I begged Jeb to continue without me, but he wouldn't. We used sticks to defend ourselves. Jeb was bitten, keeping them off me. The guards called the dogs off and hauled us back. By the time we were punished and thrown into the stockade again, Jeb's leg was infected. God forgive me. It was my fault. My fault. I should never have agreed to be part of the escape party. I should have insisted he go without me.

Then came several brief entries dated over several weeks.

Jeb continues to weaken. He's out of his head with fever. His leg is puffed up. I can hardly do more than crawl. My legs are bent with scurvy. I pay everything Jeb and I have left—a coat, our makeshift washboard, both Jeb's and my threadbare trousers that stopped reaching below our knees months ago, and more—for any scrap of sustenance I can buy for him. Only a couple of men in our mess are well enough to fetch water, and they bring it for all of us...

My heart breaks as I watch the life wane from Jeb. He won't reach home again. He'll never see the mother and sister he loves so dearly, or the father he wishes to make amends with. I have vowed to go in his stead, and I pray that the Lord will make it so. I will look after his family. I can do nothing less for my best friend. Dear Lord God in heaven, forgive me. Please let me survive to fulfill my pledge.

Tears slid down her cheeks. Her poor, suffering brother died because he'd stood by a friend. It wasn't Ben's fault. Her generous-hearted brother would not have gone on without him no matter what he did.

She hugged the journal to her chest. Why had the Lord not healed Jeb and allowed him to return home? When Jeb had left all those years ago, none of them knew he'd never see home again. She shivered. The future wasn't guaranteed. Her mother had always encouraged her to say "I love you" freely to those who mattered most. For only the Lord knows what tomorrow holds.

What if she never saw Ben again? Was she going to allow fear and mistrust to rob her of every hope of happiness? Rob her of the possibility for a lifetime of love?

~

A week later, beneath a sky filled with white puffs and an occasional hawk, Cora rode back from church with Charlie. She didn't make it into town every time the circuit rider held Sunday service. Often, she and Charlie would have devotions at their kitchen table, but today, she'd wanted to hear the preacher's words. His sermon had been on Abraham about how long he'd had to wait after God's promise of a son and many descendants before Isaac was born. Twenty-five years. What must that have been like? She was only twenty-four years old herself. Years of waiting and uncertainty, doubt as well, for Abraham and Sarah, and them trying to take things into their own hands and make the promise happen their own misguided way. They made a mess that carried across generations. But God was faithful. God fulfilled his promise in the fullness of time. Would the Lord eventually answer her prayers about Ben? But what if His answer was no?

A rider walked his horse out from a patch of scrub oak and hickory down by the creek.

Cora stiffened and drew rein.

"Wolf Heart." Charlie shot Cora a quick glance and rode off to meet the warrior.

She touched the small revolver tucked in her skirt pocket that she carried as a precaution while on the road, then nudged her horse forward.

There had been another raid two weeks before on three homesteads. Horses stolen, two men shot, and a child taken captive. But there were thousands of Comanche. No reason to lay the deed at Wolf Heart's feet.

"Haaa, Cora Scott." Wolf Heart nodded to her as she approached.

Today his dark hair hung loose against his buckskin hunting shirt, well past his shoulders. His eyes simmered.

"Look at the arrow he gave me." Charlie grinned as he ran his finger along the thin wood.

"Cora walk with me." Wolf Heart swung out of the saddle without waiting for her agreement. "Little Wolf watch horses."

Walk beside him? She'd prefer to stay atop her mare, more distance between him and her, less intimate.

"I'll let them drink from the creek." Charlie dismounted.

Nerves on edge, Cora followed suit. She stuffed her hands in her pockets as she walked alongside the warrior whose fringed hunting shirt flopped against his breechclout and bare muscular legs. He was older than her, maybe by about ten years. With his sun-weathered skin, it was difficult to tell, but he was still very much a man.

She kept her eyes straight ahead and inhaled the scents of bear grease and horse.

The creek bubbled beside them, having recently sprung to life again after a parched summer.

She should thank him for the gifts, but her lips remained silent. This man needed no encouragement.

Wolf Heart's moccasins crunched against the grass. "The boy needs a father to teach him." That topic again. Direct and to the point.

She braced herself. "Ben will be back. His father is ill, as I said."

Up ahead, a blue-winged teal landed in the creek with a splash. Another teal paddled from around the bend.

"Birds know it best not to be alone." Wolf Heart pointed at the pair.

Her swallow worked its way down to the pit of her tumbled stomach. "Even birds have their time alone."

They walked on in silence.

She needed to get out of here. "I should head home soon. I have chores."

He flexed his hands at his sides. "Not good for woman and child to be on own. Could come with me. To live. Life on horizon instead of stuck to dirt patch."

Her breath caught. Be Wolf Heart's woman? Her head swam. What if she said no? Would he take her, anyway?

She stopped walking, and so did he. He turned. Their gazes locked.

His dark eyes sized her up. "My first wife died. Childbirth."

She glanced at Charlie downstream by the horses. Sweat dampened her palms. "My heart is still with Ben." She placed her hand on her chest. "The miles, the forests, rivers, and mountains in between don't change that."

"Then why you not with him?"

"The land." But that was only part of the reason.

He frowned and crossed his arms. "If the land holds you from him, then your roots too deep."

"More than the land." She fiddled with her sleeves. Would it be wrong to tell this man the truth? Much safer than telling Arthur. "Ben...the whites...have something that they call medicine, but it's like firewater. Once a man tastes it, it's hard for him to not take a second taste and another. I'm concerned that for Ben, now that he has tasted, the hunger will not go away."

"Have seen too many warriors like that. I never tasted. Do not plan to." He jutted his chin. "But how you expect Ben not think of firewater, with his woman and son here, and him far away?"

She swallowed. "He says he hasn't drunk of it since he set foot on the ranch. Even though he's now far away, he writes on paper to me."

Wolf Heart studied her. "Go to him or become my wife in the spring. It is simple. Decide. Show him your trust. Bring him back. If you stay, too much sun, your heart will wither like the flower, without rain."

He turned, called to Charlie, and headed for his horse.

Leave Texas? Show up on Ben's doorstep with no certainty as to whether he even wanted her there? His family surely wouldn't.

She rubbed her hands over her arms and stared after the warrior.

∼

*C*losing the bedroom door behind him, Ben wiggled the noose of a cravat free from his neck and tossed it on his bed. With hesitant fingers, he opened the envelope. Cora's letters were too few and far between, and each one had the potential to repair or rend.

He skimmed the parts about the ranch and Charlie's adventures. His eyes ground to a halt and edged forward with caution at the sentence *I have been reluctant to write to you these past few months on matters of the heart.*

He slipped down on the guest bed he'd made his own.

I know you are where you need to be, with your family helping to take care of your father and filling in for him at the newspaper. I understand your family obligations. And I know that though you do not say so to me, your work at the paper means a lot to you. And your father expects you to take over his position there.

But you are missed by both Charlie and me. The house, the yard, they are filled with you. And my heart cinches every time the wind creaks the swing you made for me. I haven't sat in it since you left. It was our swing.

Ben lay back against the pillow and rubbed his thumb over the words. She missed him. Could it be possible she ached for him as he did for her? What he wouldn't give to be sitting with her on the porch swing, losing himself in those lake-blue eyes, then pulling her close, lavishing her with his love…

Within three days of when you left, I realized I was wrong. I don't need to see the bottle. You are a man of integrity. You have my respect and my trust.

Hope surged through him. Did she truly mean it?

I also want you to know that I finished your journal. I deeply appreciate you sharing this part of yourself with me. You're not to blame for Jeb's death. As your close friend, he would have willingly done everything in his power to help you survive and protect you. Just as you did for him. Any debt you owe him is paid. You're free of any obligation to me and Charlie.

The last thing in this world he wanted was to be free of his connection to her and Charlie. A crooked smile spread across his face. She didn't blame him. Her words soaked in like a balm.

Finally, I should let you know that we've seen Wolf Heart on several occasions. He has shown concern for Charlie and me. Yesterday, in his own warrior way, he proposed to me. I have until spring to give my answer.

Ben's eyebrows shot up to his hairline. She couldn't be serious. He leaped to his feet. Wolf Heart had proposed? Had there been a courtship? And what did she mean by *warrior way*? How did a Comanche court or propose? Did he sit in the parlor? Or maybe he'd invite her to go riding or hunting? Or maybe he'd give her a buffalo skin to clean?

Wolf Heart was just as liable to throw her on the back of his saddle and haul her off to Indian Territory as wait for an answer. The warrior had asked her? And she hadn't said no immediately? Maybe she was afraid of his reaction.

But she didn't sound frightened. Cora didn't scare easily. She wouldn't actually consider the offer, would she? What if she thought it was the only way to keep Charlie from being taken?

Ben tromped back and forth across the carpet. The letter fluttered from his grasp. He snapped it up from the floor.

November tenth. Eighteen days ago. A lot could happen in eighteen days.

He needed to get back there, but even if he could somehow bolt out of here tomorrow, drop everything at the paper and break his commitment to his father, it'd take two-and-a-half weeks for him to get to Weatherford. Not quick enough.

He headed downstairs, taking two steps at a time, and grabbed his coat from the coat tree. He had a telegram to send. No guarantee Cora would listen to a few lines scribbled from him. He needed someone who could talk to Cora in person, get her away from the ranch if needed.

~

Three evenings later, Ben stood in front of his father's desk in the library. His tongue felt like sandpaper. Father looked up from reading the *Philadelphia Inquirer*. A stack of competitors' papers lay next to his inkwell.

"Have a seat." Father motioned to the padded chair in front of the mahogany desk. "We need to talk strategy now that everyone has stopped coddling me and hiding the news from me." His face remained pale, but not as colorless as when he'd been at his worst. His paunch no longer protruded over his trouser waist, and his waistcoat wasn't snug, but he was dressed and at his desk for a few hours every day.

Ben glanced at the seat but remained standing. "Father, I know you're not going to understand this. I want to reassure you that I'm not abandoning the paper, but I need to travel to Texas for a few weeks."

His father expelled a swoosh of air. "Are you out of your head? You just returned from there."

"Almost four months ago. And this would only be a brief trip." So he said, but was that realistic? He couldn't ask Cora to come here, and he couldn't stay in Texas. Did he really intend to propose under such conditions?

"Out of the question. I saw how brief the last trip was. If I hadn't fallen ill, you'd still be there." Father snatched his reading spectacles from the bridge of his nose. "You have a responsibility to your family. And to the paper. You gave your word. The *Philadelphia Sentinel* isn't a hobby to pick up and leave off when something else gains your interest."

Ben straightened to his full height. "I worked hard at the paper before and after the war. And when I received the telegram informing me of your illness, I caught the first stagecoach east. But Miss Scott is in great need of immediate assistance."

"You've done enough to help that family."

"If it hadn't been for Jeb Scott, I wouldn't be standing before you today. I owe him my life, and I'm paying that debt to his sister and little brother."

His father jabbed his finger against the newsprint. "Your first responsibility is to your family. Do you think I slaved at the paper, starting it from the ground up, to have it die with me? I wanted a legacy, not just for me, but for you, your sons, and their sons. The *Sentinel* is a paper to be proud of, and it's in a fight for its place in the Philadelphia market. We need you at the helm. I'm sorry about your friend Jeb." A cough wracked through him. "He has our eternal gratitude. But you've paid your debt to him. You threw everything aside and traveled to Texas. Not to mention, you spent every penny of your early inheritance from your grandfather." His face reddened as the cough erupted again.

Ben winced. Maybe he should postpone this discussion to another day after his father had more fully recovered. But time was of the essence. Garret would ride to Cora's and invite her and Charlie to his ranch as Ben had asked. But who could guarantee her response? And Wolf Heart was anything but predictable. He gathered his nerve. "I'm in love with Miss Scott."

His father cocked his eyebrows. "You were in love with Miss Edmondson eight months ago."

Ben narrowed his eyes. "I was in love with Olivia three years ago. When I returned from the war and Andersonville, I merely did what was expected of me."

His father wiped his mouth with a handkerchief. Puffy bags underscored his eyes. "Then why don't you keep on doing that? A man carries on. Keeps his commitments. Masters his emotions."

Ben glared at him. "I'm a man of my word. I'll find a way to help the paper thrive. But that may or may not be with me at the helm."

His father sputtered. "I might have known this was coming. You cause an uproar with the board by forsaking Miss Edmondson, and now you want to run off to Texas again to marry a farmer's daughter. I thought you were the son I could count on. The son who knew how to keep his promises."

Gravel filled his throat. "I'm the son who has worked since childhood to be the person you could count on. But I'm also the son who has made too many promises, and I'm caught in the tug of war between them."

"Impetuous. That's what you are. Wait a year. If you're still all google-eyed over Miss Scott, send for her to come visit."

Ben lowered himself down to the edge of the seat. "If I don't act now, I might lose my chance with her forever."

His father snorted. "If that happens, she wasn't the lady for you. Problem solved."

"I'm sure you were not so laissez-faire about it when you pursued mother."

"Don't you get uppity with me, Benjamin."

The door clicked.

"Who's there?" his father called out.

Evie peeked around the door's edge.

"What are you doing, daughter?"

"You two are speaking so loudly, I couldn't help but hear."

Despite his knotted gut, Ben's lips threatened to erupt in a smile. She'd probably had her ear pressed to the door panel.

"Well, get on down the hall with you, then." Father dismissed her.

She clasped her hands behind her back and wiggled into the room, closing the door with her foot. Dark waves of hair cascaded across her shoulders and down her back. "But I could help."

Father's eyebrows bunched together. "What are you talking about?"

"I'm a good writer, and I could learn to be a decent editor." Her complexion glowed.

"You're a girl." Father's voice rose.

"A girl you sent to college at Oberlin." She crossed the room to the desk. "Let Ben go to Texas and rescue his maiden from the Comanche. I'll help while he's away—"

"The Comanche?" Father's eyes popped wide.

"She's not under literal attack at this moment." Ben rolled his eyes toward his sister. Just like her to dramatize and romanticize the facts he'd shared with her privately. "But the danger is real. A war chief is the one who proposed to her. If she declines, he could take her captive."

"If she's entertaining a war chief, she deserves what she gets. I can't believe you'd keep company with such a woman."

Ben clenched his jaw. "She lives on the frontier alone with her nine-year-old brother. If a war chief comes calling, she has little choice but to feign interest to buy time." She *was* feigning, wasn't she?

"Send her a telegram. Tell her to either move into town or call troops to protect her."

Ben narrowed his eyes. "You don't understand what it's like there."

"Let me help with Ben's work." Evie swung her arms wide. "There's no law that says a newspaper reporter has to be a man. Women can write. Look at Harriet Beecher Stowe. Lincoln said her book helped start the war."

"See what trouble writing got her into?" Father glowered. "Your place is in the home, young lady."

"You sent me to college."

"So you can be a helpmeet to your husband and teach your children. If you go poking your head into a man's world, you'll ruin your chances of marrying a decent gentleman."

Ben scoffed. "Any man should count himself blessed to have a chance at winning Evie's heart. She's a gem, and in addition to her feminine charms, she can write as well as I can. I'm sure she could polish her editing skills in no time and be an asset to the paper."

"I'm not throwing my daughter into the world of men." Father slammed his fist on the desk.

"I can look after myself, Father." Evie flipped her hand against her skirt.

"You have no idea." Father snorted. "Thorson, Edmondson, all of the rest would have no respect for you. They'd have a good laugh, escort you out of the room, and then proceed to write me out of any real authority in the paper, make me a partner in name only." A hacking cough rattled through him.

She threw herself down on the sofa, her lips in a pout. "Too bad they can't look at my writing and keep their eyes off my sex." She huffed out a breath.

Father drank from his water glass. "The newsroom is too coarse for anyone of the gentler—"

"I could work from home." She brightened. "Ben could give me a quick course in editing. Then he could have an errand boy bring the assignments or articles to me. We could pretend that it's you doing the work, or that Ben can't come to the office for some reason."

"Brilliant," Ben cheered.

"You expect them to believe that Ben's too unwell to come to the office for two months? They'd demote him to errand boy. I might as well be doing the work." His father threw himself back in his chair. "Might as well go into the office and take on the whole load again."

"No." Ben sat forward, elbows on knees. "Your doctor laid down the law. You're to stay home for now. Evie can do it. I know she can. If we but give her the chance. She's been waiting for such an opportunity. She could even travel into the city each morning to pick up work for you. Tell them I've been called away on an emergency. She could handle the lion's share of the work, and you can do a portion."

"A portion?" His father sputtered. "You two think you can tell me what to do? That'll be the day. I'd have to be not just on but under my deathbed before I'd stoop to being ordered about by my children. If I can't count on my son to live up to his duties, I'll—"

"You can count on your son to delegate appropriate responsibilities to your very capable daughter." Ben stood and hooked his thumbs beneath his suspenders, hope rising in his heart. "You appointed me to be your representative at the paper. It's my decision."

"You'll not regret it." Evie hopped off the couch and bounded over to him.

"I haven't agreed to it, young lady." Father sank against the padded back of his chair. "I won't pave the way for my son to toss his duties aside while—"

"He's not tossing, Father." She leaned halfway across the desk. "He's rescuing his maiden. You taught him to be a knight."

His father gawked at her as if he didn't know whether to

laugh, scold, or banish them both to the dungeon until further notice.

"You wear me out, daughter." He returned his spectacles to the bridge of his nose. "But no amount of your bubbling enthusiasm is going to set things right at the paper. Your brother has offended Edmondson to the core."

Ben huffed. "Tell him I'm deranged if you have to. But if Edmonson has any business sense, he'll put the good of the paper before his daughter's temper. And if it'll satisfy his wrath, let him appoint Thorson editor for now."

Father's lip curled.

Evie tossed her hair over her shoulder. "Don't tell him any such thing about Ben. The whole controversy will be forgotten once another beau catches Olivia's eye. I can't imagine that it'll take too much longer."

"Evie." Father shook his head. "You see rainbows where others see clouds. The trouble is that the clouds are the reality."

"But, Father..." She swung on Ben's arm. "The clouds are just in the way. Once they shift or a strong wind comes, we can see the blue that was there all along."

Ben's heart lifted. He squeezed his sister's hand. Maybe the Lord would open the door to Cora, one step at a time. If he could get her and Charlie to winter at Garret's, maybe he could convince them to stay longer. A year or more if needed, until Ben could work out something with the paper...

A winter without Cora? A year without her? His heart clenched. But he would not give up. He was going to Texas, and he would propose, no matter how long the wait for her hand.

CHAPTER 39

 ate-November rain pinged against the porch roof and
the side windows as Cora lifted the curtain. A rider
dismounted by the hitching post beneath the gray
afternoon sky. The rubberized poncho and wide-brimmed hat
with a low crown hid the identity of the man, but it wasn't
Arthur. He'd get his fancy clothes drenched before he'd don
such practical wear. And the visitor was too tall to be Mr.
Franklin.

Charlie squeezed in beside her. "Who is it?"

"I don't know. But fetch me my rifle just in case. Then get up
to your loft and stay put."

"I'll get mine too. And hide in the kitchen."

"You'll do as you're told. It's probably just someone passing
through or someone from town come to check on us."

"I'll get both rifles and take mine to the loft."

She exhaled and peeked out once more as the boy scurried
off.

The stranger knocked. By the third time, she had the rifle
behind the door, and Charlie's feet pitter-pattered on the
stairs.

Rivers of water ran off the stranger's hat. "Miss Scott? I'm Major Garret Ramsey. Perhaps Mr. McKenzie mentioned me?"

"Yes." She opened the door wide. "Come in." Her swallow stuck in her throat. Had something happened to Ben?

He stomped his boots on the rug, then removed his hat and shook it on the porch. Charlie crept back down the stairs and up to her side as Major Ramsey disposed of his poncho on the floor by the door.

"I'll put some coffee on, Major, and I have some stew simmering. But first, I have to know if you've heard from Ben. Is he all right?"

The major ran a hand over his damp hair. "Ben didn't mention anything about himself, but I'm sure he's as well as can be expected considering he's missing the ones dear to him in Texas." His hazel eyes twinkled.

"Us. He means us." Charlie beamed. "When's he coming back?"

Ramsey directed his gaze at her. "I'd greatly appreciate a cup of coffee. Perhaps Charlie could fetch it for me?"

"Grownup talk again?" Charlie groaned.

Ramsey chuckled.

"Go fetch him a cupful and walk back carefully so you don't spill a drop." Cora scooted him down the hall, then turned to the major. "What's wrong?"

"Ben's worried about the two of you here on your own. He asked me to check on you."

A full day's ride each way, and it couldn't wait for the rain to end? "Did he say what the concern was?"

"Not specifically." He avoided her gaze. "Said something about the potential for Indian trouble."

Indian trouble? She blinked wide. Wolf Heart? Was that what this was about? She'd gotten Ben's attention, all right. She swallowed back a smile. "I don't suppose there's any hope Mr. McKenzie will be able to return by spring to help us out with that, is there?" Stupid question. Of course not, but she could hope.

Ramsey stomped his boots again. "I couldn't say, but he expressed interest in seeing you move to safety for the winter. And as soon as I read his telegram—"

"He sent a telegram? Not a letter?"

"I'm sure a letter will follow, but he felt the case needed immediate attention. And as soon as I read it, I had an idea. My wife, Sky, could use help with the children. We'd love to have you stay with us at least until spring. Not much ranching to be done before then. Mr. Reynolds and I could drive our wagon here, haul a load of whatever you wanted to take with you, and lock the rest up tight. And we could bring your few farm animals along."

She gnawed her lip. Pack up and leave? With no assurance that Ben would return. Surely, this couldn't be the Lord's answer to her prayers. But the Lord didn't always answer prayers the way one might imagine.

Leave the ranch behind for the whole winter and more than likely for the spring, as well, if Ben had anything to do with it. Trade her independence for safety and company. A guest in someone else's home. Either that or risk Wolf Heart not being able to take no for an answer. And even if he accepted it in her case, there was Charlie to be worried about.

Her chest tightened. "Not a matter to be settled in an hour, Major."

"I understand."

"Here's the coffee." Charlie came down the hall carrying the porcelain cup with both hands.

"Thank you, young man." Ramsey tugged off his gauntlets and wrapped his hands around the steaming brew.

"Pardon my manners, Major. Please have a seat in the parlor." She motioned toward the room.

Ramsey reached inside his coat pocket. "One more item for

you to consider. As I passed through Weatherford, Mr. Miller heard I was headed this way and asked me to deliver this."

He pulled out a damp envelope, but *McKenzie* and *Philadelphia* were still plainly evident.

She clutched it. "Charlie, please take the major into the parlor. If you ask nicely, he might tell you a story." Without waiting for a reply, she hurried to her room. Maybe this letter would show her what to do.

Her hands trembled as she opened the envelope.

Miss Scott,

We're not acquainted, but I feel as if I know you from the way my brother talks about you all the time. I look forward to meeting you someday. I know it's not my place to say anything, but my brother needs to see you. My mother and father are treating him horridly, expecting him to carry on generations of legacy at a paper our father helped start only twenty-five years ago. Ben completely cut all ties to his former fiancée, but that has only landed him in more trouble with our parents and my father's business partners. The hope of you is his only bright spot. He is homesick for you but cannot travel to you right now. If there was a way that you could see clear to come...

His only bright spot. Wolf Heart wasn't the only one who thought she should go to Ben. Evelyn McKenzie was asking her to leave Texas, at least for a visit. Brow furrowed, Cora sank onto her bed. From the sound of it, Ben was deeply entangled in obligations. She'd be foolish to think he'd be free by spring or even a year from now.

After the way she'd treated him in the garden, picking up the shard from her father's whiskey jug and accusing Ben of having a similar character, could she really expect Ben to fight his way back to her? Unless she gave him a reason to?

And what of her dream? At this point, the surest way to

hold onto the ranch would be to ride into town and tell Arthur she'd reconsidered. Live in misery for the sake of cattle and acres?

She glanced around at her mother's wallpaper, the frilly curtains, the carved walnut bedframe, and the cedar chest. Hollow without someone to share them with. All of the furnishings were from Nashville. Her mother had brought them along when she'd forsaken everything familiar to go with her husband to the unknown.

But she was not her mother.

~

Saddlebags over one shoulder and a carpetbag in the other, Ben strode down the gangplank of the *Mary Belle* as he disembarked in New Orleans. The Mississippi lapped against the bow. A fleet's worth of frigates, schooners, steamboats, and ocean-going steamers flanked the wharf. Hopefully, one of them would head out tomorrow for Galveston. Coal smoke and damp stung his nose. Better that than the odor of the liquid sludge which flowed through the city's drainage ditches.

It was a city full of sights, but the only sight he cared about was across the Gulf and half of Texas. Blue eyes, uburn-tinged chestnut hair, and maybe, just maybe, a smile for him.

He shifted the weight of the saddlebags as his boots struck the worn boards of the dock. The ticket office was farther down on the wharf, if he recalled correctly. "Excuse me." He nodded and stepped around a lady dressed in a wide hoop skirt.

"Mr. McKenzie? Mr. Benjamin McKenzie?" A young man wearing a black wool wheel cap and a brown sack coat quick-stepped down the dock, calling out like a newspaper boy hawking the morning edition. He scanned the crowd coming down the gangplank. "Benjamin McKenzie?"

Ben waved at him and strode over. "I'm Mr. McKenzie."

"Benjamin McKenzie of Philadelphia?"

"I am he. What do you need of me?"

"Telegram, sir." The youth whipped an envelope from his coat and held out his hand.

Ben dug in his pocket for a coin and exchanged it for the message.

"Much obliged." The boy tipped his hat and hurried off.

Ben grimaced as he opened the envelope. If his father or mother were trying to drag him back already... Surely, no new crisis could have arisen in the ten days since his departure. He paused. Maybe he shouldn't read the message. Just act as if he never received it, at least until he set foot in Texas.

A groan rumbled in his throat. He couldn't not read it. But nothing short of a life or death emergency, verified by a telegram from Evie, would turn him eastward before he saw Cora.

He uttered a prayer and pulled out the message.

Received wire from Ramsey. Cora on way to Philadelphia. Can catch her in New Orleans. Arriving on the steamer Harlan. *Evie.*

On her way to Philadelphia? Cora was coming to him? Mouth agape, he stumbled against a post. A smile crescendoed through his whole being. His girl was coming to see him —not really his girl, the way they'd left things, but if she was on her way to New Orleans, maybe all was right in the world, and she would be again. More than he'd dared even pray for. It didn't mean she was coming to stay or that he'd ask her to. But she was willing to travel across the country to visit him. He swiped his hand over his face, but nothing could wipe away the smile.

His hand dropped to his side. What if he'd already missed her? The *Harlan* could have already landed as far as he knew, and if he didn't catch her when she disembarked, he might never find her in this city. He took off at a fast walk.

"Hey, mister. Forget something?"

Ben pivoted toward the voice.

An unshaven dockworker pointed at the carpetbag Ben had left by the post.

Ben hurried back and grabbed it. "Much obliged. Can you tell me how I can find the schedule for when the *Harlan's* due in port?"

~

The next day, Ben stood on the wharf. Since yesterday, he'd soaked in a bath, washed his clothes, and even stopped by the barber's for a shave and a haircut. He clutched a half dozen roses wrapped in paper in his sweaty palm. Cora's ship was due any hour. Thank God, he hadn't missed her.

Would Charlie be with her? The telegram hadn't said anything about him.

Ben scanned the rows of steamers moored along a stretch of docks a mile long. Laborers hustled around him, working their way between piles of sacks and crates and towers of cotton bales. Down along another stretch of wharf, passengers disembarked from a steamboat. An egret croaked from a nearby piling.

Last night, he got down on his knees and prayed, and he did so again this morning. His hope for a future with Cora would likely be decided in the next few days. His girl was coming to see him. How much dare he ask of her? He squeezed his eyes shut for a moment. He was here to rescue her, not ask her to leave Texas. Even if he had to glue his mouth shut.

He had to be patient. On the way to wharf this morning, he'd booked them separate rooms in the St. Charles Hotel. He'd visit with her a few days here in New Orleans. Gauge her feelings. Then, if he believed he stood a chance, he'd propose. It was a lot to ask that she'd agree to be his wife under the stipulation that it could very well be six months, a year, or even longer before he could return to Texas and claim her as his bride.

He paced. Whether her answer was yes or no—*Dear Lord, please don't let it be no*—he'd need to convince her to stay with the Ramseys and Reynolds, until either he could return to Texas someday to make her his wife and work their own ranch, or they could find another safe alternative. Dare he ask so much of her? Either way, he'd need to travel to Texas to make sure she got settled in with them.

A petal on one open bud fluttered. He slowed his pace. Flowers weren't the most practical gift, and Cora was a very practical lady, but he had to show her that she was a treasure.

He strode to the edge of the wharf and gazed down the murky flow of the Mississippi. A steamer churned toward him, its smokestacks puffing black fumes. Passengers gathered along the white railing, taking in the sights, probably eager to disembark. Was Cora amongst them? Holding onto a piling, he stretched forward. The name on the side of the ship... He squinted. The last two letters were -*an*. He stretched farther. The bow sliced through the water, moving closer to a dock. *Harlan*. His chest expanded. Hope was in sight.

CHAPTER 40

Cora gripped the white rail as New Orleans came into view. A myriad of clippers, barges, steamers, and steamboats lined the wharfs and docks along both sides of the Mississippi River. Great cranes loaded bales and crates onto the decks and into the holds of vessels. Beyond the docks stood an infinite labyrinth of buildings. So many people. Enough to make her want to head for the river instead of the city, if it wasn't for the way the waves had turned her stomach topsy-turvy for the last two days. Besides, she was on a mission to earn Ben's forgiveness and regain his affection. Adventure, the unknown, and discomfort were to be expected.

Once she reached land, she needed to find the ticket office and book passage for a lady's cabin on a steamboat heading for St. Louis. From there, Major Ramsey had instructed her to take a boat across to the Illinois side of the Mississippi and catch a train for Philadelphia.

What if Ben wasn't overjoyed to see her? It was his sister's idea for her to come. But Ben hadn't asked her to do so. Hadn't even mentioned love in his letters. Is that how his letters to Olivia had gone?

She was getting herself too worked up. The divide between her and Ben was her doing, not his. If he didn't speak of love, it was her mistrust that had led to it.

A salted breeze whipped against her skin and tossed her hair. Streams of coal smoke snaked upward from the smokestacks of steamers and other boats in port. The *Harlan's* whistle blasted a shrill toot. Unease filled her belly. She closed her eyes and prayed. She'd trust the Lord to see her through the journey ahead to Philadelphia, Ben's heart, and beyond.

Seagulls cawed overhead as the pilot maneuvered the *Harlan* between two other steamers. Sailors threw the mooring lines to their counterparts along the dock. Cora picked up her carpetbag and filed in behind other passengers waiting for their turn to exit. The line edged forward. She reached the top of the gangplank and headed down.

A man stood off to the side at the bottom, clutching a bouquet of red roses. As if he were waiting for his sweetheart. A slouch hat shadowed his face, but the way he stood, tall with his shoulders thrown back, coat open, and his head tilted... Black sack coat and trousers, royal-blue waistcoat, and a white shirt. Exactly what Ben had worn the day he came to tell her he'd saved her ranch from Mr. Coffin.

Her knees wobbled. No. It couldn't be. She picked up her pace and squeezed by the gentleman in front of her. She was halfway down when the man with the roses glanced up. She gasped. Ben. Her bulging carpetbag dropped to the weathered boards beneath her. People stared and shuffled past her.

Ben grinned up at her, the biggest grin she'd ever seen on a man. Her noodle legs started moving, and so did he, pushing against the flow of people.

She stumbled into him. "What..." She couldn't even breathe for smiling. "What are you doing here?" The world spun.

Ben's firm hands curved around her upper arms, steadying her and pressing the newsprint-covered stems against her cloak. "Did you imagine I was going to allow my girl to wander around New Orleans all by herself?"

"You...you and Major Ramsey planned this?" She could hardly speak. Could hardly stand. Her brain had obviously ceased working.

"Nothing that clever." Hazel eyes drank her in, searching her gaze, with their gold-speckled pools. "I was on my way to Weatherford to protect you from Comanches. But when I disembarked from my steamboat, I received a telegram that my girl was on her way to me." His grin wavered. "Forgive me if I overstep by referring to you as *my girl*." He raised an eyebrow in question.

"You do not overstep." She lightly touched his coat lapels and gnawed her lip, attempting to squelch her smile. Words bubbled forth. "But you know those Comanche can be quite formidable suitors when they take a mind to court." What in the world was she doing?

"And what is that supposed to mean?" His hands slipped to her waist.

She spread her palms against the black wool of his coat. Was that his heartbeat or hers? "I mean, I was on my way to having all of the meat I could eat for winter, and then there were the moccasins—"

"What moccasins?" A growl rumbled in his throat.

"The ones Wolf Heart left by the corral for me."

"You accepted a personal present like that from him?"

"I didn't wear them, but it would have been bad manners to return them."

He narrowed his eyes. "I'll show you good manners. I'll throw them in the trash heap if I find them."

She batted her lashes. "There's only one man I want to come calling. And I had to hop on a stagecoach, take a train, and book passage on a steamer to come find him."

His whole face lit up. "Only to discover he was on his way to find you." His voice dipped.

She leaned into him, her skirt lapping against his trousers. His strong arms tightened around her, turning her legs to jelly. Bay rum and soap filled her nostrils.

"I'm so sorry...about what I said in the garden. I was wrong," she whispered.

"What matters is now." He lowered his lips to hers, a soft velvety touch, awakening hunger for more.

Tingles exploded within her. His muscles flexed beneath her palms. She latched onto his lapels and pulled him closer as she lost herself in the kiss.

~

Ben's heart soared. Cora loved him. He pressed his hand to the back of her head, weaving his fingers through her silken hair as he deepened the kiss. Four-and-a-half months without his girl. Much too long. Liquid fire flowed through him by the time he broke the kiss and dipped his forehead to hers.

People jostled past them. Some with giggles, others with grumbles. It didn't matter.

This wasn't going as planned. Now that he had her in his arms, he didn't want to let go. How was he supposed to leave her at her rented room for the night, let alone escort her to Texas in a few days with the intent of parting with her? It was all he could do to not propose here and now and suggest they find a minister before nightfall. "When I received the telegram saying you were on your way here, it was like Fourth of July, sunrise, and sunset all rolled into one." He brushed his thumbs back and forth across her shoulders.

"That's exactly how I felt. When I saw you waiting on the

dock, I almost fainted." Her voice was barely more than a breath.

He inhaled soap and river. "We should have talked before we got around to the kissing. Now I can't think of anything else." He trailed his lips down to hers once more.

"Me either."

"Well, I never." A lady grumbled as she stalked past them.

Someone clunked a carpetbag at their feet. "Excuse me, sir, ma'am." A male voice interrupted further.

Ben lifted his head.

A blue-coated employee of the *Harlan* stood a couple feet from Cora's elbow. "Have to ask you two to move. We have unloading to do."

Cora blushed.

"Excuse us, sir." Ben, hat askew, nodded to the fellow and picked up Cora's carpetbag. The roses wobbled in his other hand. A petal fluttered to the ground. "For you."

"They're beautiful." She beamed and pressed the bouquet of drooping buds to her nose, inhaling deeply.

Dock workers hustled around them.

"We'd best go. Did Charlie come too?" He scanned the crowd.

"The Ramseys volunteered to let him stay at their ranch while I'm away."

"They'll take good care of him. But what did he think of that?"

"Reluctant to stay in the same house as the little girl who is sweet on him. But Major Ramsey promised him lots of adventure and time outdoors."

"Little Star will probably follow him outside." He chuckled and held out his arm to her. Time with Cora alone? He owed Garret big for this.

CHAPTER 41

$\mathcal{B}$en savored his oyster stew and listened to Cora tell of Charlie's recent adventures. Quiet conversations from the café's other customers hummed around them, but Cora was his focus. Light from the short-trimmed oil lamp on their small table flickered across her features, deepening the blue of her eyes and highlighting the height of her cheekbones. She'd coiffed her hair, framing her face with loose tendrils of waves and weaving the rest into a masterful sculpture at the back of her head, safely secured with pins and the engraved comb he'd given her. In addition, she'd fastened one of the rosebuds to the bosom of her glimmering green dress. Beautiful from head to toe, inside and out.

His knee jigged up and down beneath the table. How would Cora respond to his proposal? Her letter had said she didn't need proof that he could be trusted and that he was done with laudanum. And she'd traveled here, prepared and willing to go all the way to Philadelphia to see him, but that didn't mean she was ready to join her life with his until death do us part.

If she said yes, the nuptials would have to wait until he settled his commitments in Philadelphia. How would he be able to concentrate on his work at the paper—or anything else, for that matter—knowing Cora and Charlie were two thousand miles away waiting for him?

Across the table, Cora nudged a tendril from her face. "And then Charlie shot a buffalo."

"What?" His eyebrows spiked.

Her smile widened. "I was teasing, seeing if you were listening."

"If I've missed anything you've said, it's because I'm mesmerized by your presence."

She blushed. "It's time for you to talk. I want to hear about your work and your family. I already know a little about your sister, Evelyn."

"And what do you know about her?"

"She sent me a letter. Arrived the same day as Major Ramsey."

He blinked wide. He might have known Evie would see fit to play matchmaker in one fashion or the other. "What did it say?" He laid his open hand across the table.

"And what is that for?"

"The letter. I'd like to read it."

She folded her arms. "I don't have it with me. Besides, it was written to me, not you." Her eyes sparkled with mischief.

"Don't torture me, Cora. I want to know what my sister said."

She tapped a finger to her chin. "The gist was that your parents are holding you prisoner, and that she felt a visit from me would cheer you up."

"That sounds about like how she would put it, but her comment about you cheering me up is the understatement of the year. Having you come see me is more than I'd dared hope for or imagine."

She touched the rose at her bosom. "I think you've almost turned into a poet since you left Texas."

"If I have, it's love that makes me so."

She traced the swirled pattern stitched into the linen tablecloth. "Either love, or because this is your world." She waved her fingers in the air and glanced around the café with its china, crystal, and elegant black-and-red color scheme.

"I've been in New Orleans for less than a week my entire life."

"Not New Orleans." Eyes downcast, she toyed with her spoon. "But the fancy café, the people, city life." Her smile had evaporated.

In other words, not the frontier, ranching, and Texas. "My world is any place where you and I and Charlie are together."

She inhaled. Her brow twitched.

Goodness. He was getting too close to a version of his proposal that he couldn't make.

She bit her lip. "Where—"

"Excuse me, monsieur and mademoiselle." The waitress delivered two plates of blackened red fish, buttered rice, and green beans.

Not ready for the *where* yet, Ben said grace, then said, "Tell me about your travels. You caught the stage and then—"

"I'll tell you more after I hear all about the *Philadelphia Sentinel* and your family."

He cut a slice of the seasoned fish. "I love my parents, but talking about them this evening might spoil my appetite. However, I'll tell you about the *Sentinel*, Evelyn, my grandfather, anything else you like."

"Fine by me." She poked a couple of green beans.

In between bites, he described his duties at the paper and the excitement of the newsroom, sidestepping the management conflict. He moved on to a brief introduction to Evie, the whole description deserving a couple meals' worth of discussion, and ended with an abbreviated version of his summer days at his grandpa's.

"You loved your grandfather greatly." Her tender tone bathed him in warmth. "I'm sorry I missed getting to know him."

"He's the one who taught me how to dream. And to love the outdoors."

Cora raked her fork through her remaining pieces of rice. "But you also love your work at the paper."

"Maybe I just want you to see that I'm actually competent at something. I still have nightmares about all of those cattle lying there—"

She leaned forward. "Goodnight himself barely avoided the same mistake, and he has lived on the frontier since boyhood."

He slipped his hand over hers. "In the newsroom, I'm confident. I know how to succeed. I enjoy writing..."

Her smile drooped.

He squeezed her limp fingers. "But I hate the office politics and the confinement of four walls surrounded by miles of buildings. I lived outside for four years of war and prison."

"That might be enough to make you never want to set foot outside again."

He chuckled, then sobered. "Those years burned images in my mind and heart that will never fade away, and that continue to haunt my dreams. But they also taught me about honor, friendship, endurance, and courage."

"I'm sorry about everything you went through." She brushed her thumb against his knuckles.

He gentled his voice. "I know your past has left scars on your heart, as well."

She glanced away. Uncomfortable with the focus on herself? He would avoid it for now. If all went well, there would time be enough in the future to ease her down that path.

He drew her hand to his lips. "I wasn't happy in Philadelphia after the war. I was a walking shadow. Coming to Texas was one of the best decisions I've ever made."

Her eyes glistened. "I should have latched onto you the first time you walked into my kitchen and not let go."

Warmth simmered within him. Words spilled out. "No one says the newspaper room has to be in Philadelphia."

Her brow furrowed. "Your father does."

"But a wise ranch woman told me differently."

His gaze met hers.

"What are you saying?" Her eyes sparkled in the lamplight.

His collar scratched his throat. He needed to get his head on straight. Even if she accepted his proposal, working or starting a paper in Texas wasn't something that could happen in a month or two. He was too deeply entangled in his family's affairs in Philadelphia for such a project to move at anything more than tortoise speed. Dabbing his mouth with his napkin, he pushed his plate back. "Shall we take a stroll?"

A few minutes later, she curled her fingers around the crook of his arm as they headed down the wooden plank sidewalk toward the French Quarter.

Gas streetlights glowed along Canal Street. He led her across the streetcar tracks. She snuggled close and stared wide-eyed at the buildings they passed. This was not her world. He had no right asking her to leave her home. But it was only a matter of time before his proposal worked its way up his throat. He flexed his hand at his side. He wouldn't be able to sleep, get on a boat, or be anything but brain-addled until he asked.

The five-story Saint Louis Hotel with its huge dome loomed ahead. He'd heard of its marble floors and eighty-foot-high rotunda with towering columns. A beautiful place once, but not an ideal setting for a proposal, considering its use as a slave market before the war and a Union hospital during the conflict.

He led them down another street until they reached a garden accessible from a side street.

"Is this a public park?" she asked as he led her through the wrought-iron arch.

"No. But I walked for miles yesterday looking for a quiet outdoor place to bring you for…a chat. The owners are a sweet elderly couple who live in the brick house on the other side of that giant oak at the end of the walkway."

She halted and turned to him. "You went to all that trouble just to find a place for our walk?"

Most important walk of his life. "I couldn't find a porch swing, and I know you love the outdoors."

She beamed. "It's beautiful. Thank you." She wrapped both hands around his arm as she glanced at the neatly clipped rows, vine-covered trellises, and arches shadowed in moonlight and the gaslight from the streets. He drew her to a wrought-iron bench beneath the branches of a magnolia, still clinging to its covering of leaves in December.

Instead of snuggling next to her, he sat at an angle, his knees resting against the folds of her skirt and cloak. With a silent prayer, he took her hands in his. His pulse throbbed in his head. "I love you, Cora. I started falling for you the moment I saw you march out of Mr. Coffin's office, ready to take on the world. I admire your strength, determination, courage…your love for Charlie, your heart for the Lord, your beauty inside and out…"

She squeezed his hands, her own sweat mixing with his. "I greatly admire you, too, Ben McKenzie. You're a man of honor, strong character, courage, perseverance, willing to sacrifice for those he loves, a man of faith who can be counted on—"

"The war and prison battered my faith pretty badly. But you and Charlie turned all of that around. I wanted to be my best for you, and I knew I couldn't do that without the Lord's help. I don't ever want to go back to the way I was before Texas."

She didn't flinch at the subtle reference to laudanum. Thank God.

Instead, she smiled. "You're a mighty handsome man too."

She leaned forward and kissed his cheek, igniting a spark within him.

He slipped his hand beneath her jaw and drew her mouth to his. His lips closed over hers in a kiss that left him breathless and Cora clinging to him by the time he lifted his head.

His gaze settled into the fathomless sea of blue eyes. "Do you know what I see in your eyes?"

"What?" She breathed.

"The western horizon, and waves upon waves of grasses and prairie flowers..." His swallow stuck in his throat.

"How in the world did all of that get in there?" She teased.

"Because it's part of you. And I cannot take you away from that." His heart pounded. "I'm asking you to marry me." He choked back the words ready to burst forth, *tomorrow, this week, here in New Orleans*, and forced out others. "With the intention that we'll marry after I'm able to settle my affairs in Philadelphia and move to Texas."

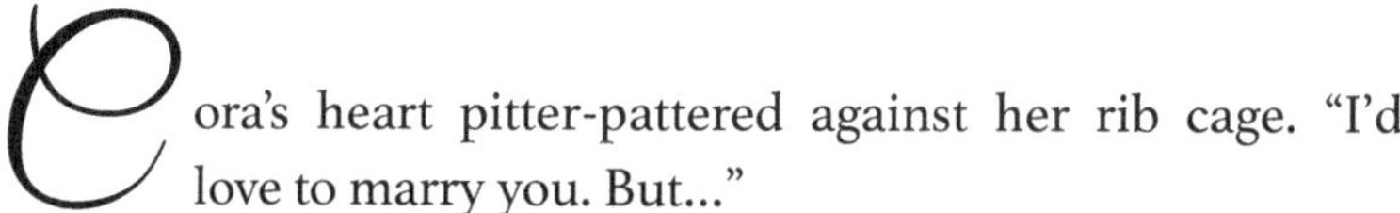

Cora's heart pitter-pattered against her rib cage. "I'd love to marry you. But..."

"But?" He leaned back a few inches and straightened as if bracing himself. His chest deflated.

Was she really going to say this? Her voice barely scraped above a whisper. "What good is the horizon if I don't have you to share it with?"

"Excuse me?" He quirked his eyebrows. His lips twitched.

"Settling your affairs in Philadelphia could take a while. What if I don't want to be without you that long?"

He eyed her as if she'd just proposed a new Texas Reconstruction plan. "I couldn't... I can't ask you to give up your Texas for me. I came to save your ranch, not to see you leave it."

"But we would come back to Texas, wouldn't we? The

ranch? I mean, eventually?" She squelched the child-like fear that threatened to arise in her chest.

"Yes." He nodded. "We'd come back." His voice surged like a wave. "I'd find a way to keep the paper strong even without me at the helm. It would take a while. It probably wouldn't happen by spring. It might even be longer than the following spring. But I wouldn't give up, and God willing, you, Charlie, and I would return to reclaim the ranch." He inhaled deeply and loosened his hold. "I'll understand if you'd rather wait in Texas for me. The Ramseys would gladly open their home to you. You could merge your starter herd with theirs for now. Grow the herd and have a good-size one ready for me to drive back to your...our ranch when I return."

His hands slipped away from her, unmooring her from his hold. "I love you enough to wait. I want to do what is best for you and Charlie." He cleared his throat. "You waiting for me in Texas would be the more reasonable action to take. Then we could marry when we're ready to start life in the home we treasure. In the meantime, Charlie would have good men around to teach him."

"But not you." *Charlie needs you. I need you.* Was he saying all of this out of pure concern for her and Charlie, or did he want the space and time before taking on a wife and child? "Charlie wrote you."

"He did?"

She unclasped her reticule and pulled out the envelope.

He took it, stood, and walked down the path to a gaslight. She didn't need to follow. Charlie had allowed her to read the message before he sealed it.

Ben, I miss you. Wolf Heart has been teaching me about hunting, but he's not you. I'd be all right coming to your home for a while if you can't come see us yet. Love, Charlie

Above her, a mockingbird fluttered from one magnolia branch to the other, whistling a tune.

What if they married and Ben couldn't find a way for them to return to Texas? What if she were giving up her dream?

But the dream had changed. It now included Ben and would never be whole without him. The Lord would work it out in the end. She had to trust and have faith. Ben understood how important the ranch was to her and Charlie. However long it took, waiting would be much better at Ben's side.

He turned and walked back, open letter in hand. "Did you put him up to this?" His eyes glistened.

"No. It was his idea to write, and the words are his own." Her heart pounded. She stood. "I've reached a decision."

"What is it?" He clutched the letter.

She bit her lip. "I don't want to be reasonable."

A smile twitched at the corners of his mouth. "You and Charlie would be giving up a lot."

"Just temporarily." She touched his sleeve. "Mine and Charlie's home is with you."

His grin sparkled all the way to his eyes. He took her in his arms. "I could see us in a cottage just outside of the city."

"Nowhere near your parents."

"Agreed. And we'd have a little land. And horses. I need to stay in practice for the frontier."

She slipped her hands up over his chest and around the back of his neck. "I'd train the horses." Her smile matched his. "And maybe I'll drop by the paper now and then. I figure if your sister can, I can too."

He chortled. "We'll see about that, Miss Scott."

"Well, you know that's the thing." She wove her fingers through the back of thick hair. "Maybe Miss Scott couldn't do it, but surely, Mrs. Benjamin McKenzie could."

"As long as you don't treat the management like Mr. Coffin."

"You'd have to rescue me again."

"I'd only be returning the favor." His mouth enveloped hers in a kiss that sent her to the stars and back.

They swayed there in each other's arms as the mockingbird serenaded. Ben's heartbeat pounded against her chest. The Lord had blessed her abundantly in this man. She prayed one day, Jeb would know what a gift he'd given her in sending Ben McKenzie to her door.

Ben brushed his lips to her ear. "So, Miss Scott, should we get married in New Orleans or wait until Texas? We'll need to travel there to pick up Charlie."

"New Orleans. That way, Texas will be our wedding trip."

He nuzzled his cheek against her hair. "My thoughts exactly. And we'll find us a steamer that takes a long way around."

Did you enjoy this book? We hope so!
Would you take a quick minute to leave a review where you purchased the book?
It doesn't have to be long. Just a sentence or two telling what you liked about the story!

Love Christian Historical Romance?
Looking for your next favorite book?
Become a Wild Heart Books insider and receive a FREE ebook and get exclusive updates on new releases before anyone else.
Sign up for our newsletter now.
https://wildheartbooks.org/newsletter

I first heard of laudanum when I watched the movie *Amazing Grace* about William Wilberforce's eighteen-year battle to end the slave trade in Great Britain. Wilberforce played a pivotal role in ending the slave trade and eventually slavery itself in Britain by speaking, campaigning, and introducing bills into the British parliament. However, Wilberforce was also addicted to laudanum, a tincture of opium. It wasn't his intention to become dependent upon a drug. A doctor prescribed it to him when he was twenty-nine years old for ulcerative colitis and other health ailments. Laudanum was used to treat a number of health issues and ailments in the eighteenth and nineteenth centuries, and no one, including doctors, had much understanding about addiction and dependency. The word *addiction* didn't even exist as we use it today. But the soul-deep struggle was very real for too many people, even a man of faith like Wilberforce.

Addiction is pernicious, and laudanum took its toll on Wilberforce. He suffered physically, mentally, and spiritually from its poisonous effects.

Years later, I learned that even some of the nineteenth-century authors I admire, such as Louisa May Alcott and Elizabeth Barrett Browning, struggled with laudanum dependency.

During that era, doctors and the public viewed opium, in its various forms, as an essential medical tool. Hundreds of thousands of soldiers were wounded in the American Civil War, and many more suffered from debilitating and potentially life-threatening illnesses. According to Dr. Jonathan Jones author of *Opium Slavery: Civil War Veterans and America's First Opioid Crisis,* "Thousands of ailing soldiers became addicted, or "enslaved," as nineteenth-century Americans phrased it. Veterans, their families, and communities struggled to cope with addiction's health and social consequences, which included much victim-blaming that compounded suffering unnecessarily.

My heart went out to Wilberforce, Browning, Alcott, and others enslaved to laudanum or other substances through no fault of their own. Many, once ensnared, can suffer a lifelong battle, one many do not win on their own. But there are victories.

As a college professor at a Christian college, I have had students who have overcome addiction through the Lord and/or with the help of rehab, treatment, and programs like Celebrate Recovery, AAA, etc. I've also had a relative who struggled with addiction. I thank the Lord for these victories.

I asked a former student and friend of mine, Rev. Mark Little Elk, about his deliverance from addiction. He had this to say: "It was a lifetime ago. My addiction was strong, but my pain was stronger. I've lost so much in my life, but then I found that God's love was deep, and He was even bigger to forgive. Out of His mercy, He set me free, and through His grace, He healed me from my past."

That is my prayer for all of those who struggle.

In researching *Texas Reclaimed*, I utilized several primary documents, including *Opium Eating an Autobiographical Sketch* written in 1876 by an anonymous author. He, like Ben McKenzie in my story, became addicted when he was being treated in a hospital for life-threatening health issues after his imprisonment in Andersonville. John Ransom's *Andersonville Diary* was also an excellent source about the horror of life inside the prison.

But *Texas Reclaimed* is also the story of Texas after the Civil War and the beginnings of the era of the cattle drives. My research included *Charles Goodnight: Cowman and Plainsman*, the biography of Charles Goodnight, one of the most famous ranchers in the Old West. The breaking of the blue roan horse in *Texas Reclaimed* is based upon a real event, and Ben's failed cattle drive is inspired by Goodnight's drive that almost ended in disaster but didn't.

Lori Morton, a reference librarian at the Weatherford Public Library, helped connect me with excellent sources on Parker County and Weatherford, such as *The History of Parker County and the Double Log Cabin* by G.A. Harland and *Weatherford: The Early Years* by Jonelle Ryan Bartoli.

I'd also like to express my deep appreciation to my husband for his enduring and faithful support for my writing and to my mother, posthumously, for encouraging me in the pursuit of my dreams.

I want to thank my editor, Denise (Weimer) Farnsworth, for her belief in my writing. I also deeply appreciate my writing critique partners, Erma Ullrey, Patti Shene, Becky Van Vleet, Jack Cunningham, Sarah Hanks, and Kathy McKinsey, for their weekly encouragement, support, and input.

And finally, dear reader, I want to thank you! I greatly appreciate you reading my story. It is for you and the Lord that I write. If you have a chance, please leave an online review. If you're part of a book club, check out my website for extra resources for book clubs.

I'd love to connect with all of you!

ABOUT THE AUTHOR

Originally from Tennessee and the Shenandoah Valley, **Sherry Shindelar** is a romantic at heart and loves to take her readers into the past. She is an avid student of the Civil War and the Old West. Her latest novel is set in 1860 Texas. When she is not busy writing, she is an English professor working to pass on her love of writing to her students. Sherry is an award winning writer: 2020 ACFW First Impressions winner, 2021 Maggie finalist, 2022 Crown finalist and 2023 Genesis finalist. She currently resides in Minnesota with her husband of forty years. She has three grown children and three grandchildren. Visit her website and subscribe to her monthly newsletter at sher ryshindelar.com

If you love historical romance, check out the other Wild Heart books!

Sophie Edwards has survived two years in the Texas wilderness with four daughters and her wits. When a stranger falls injured near her hidden cabin during a thunderstorm, she discovers he's the spitting image of her late husband—because Clay McClellen is her husband's twin brother, a man who never knew his brother existed.

Clay came to Texas seeking justice for his brother's murder. What he finds instead is a ready-made family, a rundown ranch, and a fiercely independent woman who doesn't need rescuing—even when danger comes calling. Sophie may have pulled him from a flooded creek, but Clay is determined to be the protector she deserves, whether she wants one or not.

As vigilantes close in and old enemies resurface, Clay and Sophie must learn to trust each other and God's plan. But can a mountain man used to solitude embrace life with four talkative daughters? And can Sophie open her guarded heart to love again—especially when the man looks exactly like the husband who broke it?

A heartwarming tale of second chances, faith, and finding love in the untamed West.

~

The Maiden and the Mountie by Denise Farnsworth

A marriage of protection. A past full of pain. In Georgia's wild gold country, love might strike when it's least expected.

Genevieve Gillbard knows she's no longer safe in the rough-and-tumble gold rush town when she overhears her controlling guardian's plot to steal gold from a local mine owner. It takes every ounce of her courage to escape, and now she'll do anything to keep herself safe, even accept a temporary marriage of convenience from a man who clearly wants nothing more than his independence.

After losing his first wife, surveyor Jesse Holden swore never to let anyone close enough to need him again. But when he discovers the woman he knows as the Songbird of Auraria injured and unconscious in the woods, he can't abandon her, not with the memory of his failure to protect his wife hanging over him. He'll keep this woman safe until she's out of harm's way, even if it means doing the one thing he swore he'd never do again.

As Genny recovers under Jesse's care, she discovers he's nothing like the manipulative men of her past. But can she trust him with her heart—knowing he plans to leave as soon as her guardian is brought to justice? And even then, she fears the sham marriage might not be enough to keep her safe from her guardian's long reach.

The Bandit's Redemption

A holdup gone wrong, a reluctant outlaw, and the captive she's sworn to guard.

Life in the American West hasn't been easy for French refugee Lorraine Durand. She has precious few connections and longs to return to her native land. So when the man who rescued her from a Parisian uprising following the Franco-Prussian War persuades her to help him with a deadly holdup, she reluctantly agrees. Despite his promises otherwise, the gang kidnaps a man, forcing Lorraine to grapple with the fallout of her choices even as she is drawn to the captive she's meant to guard.

Jesse Alexander must survive. If not for himself, then for the troubled sister he left behind in Los Angeles. At the mercy of his captors, he carefully works to earn Lorraine's trust, hoping he can easily subdue her when the time comes. But as they navigate the treacherous wilderness and he searches for his opportunity to escape, he realizes there may be more to her than he first believed.